A million-dollar idea. A city girl in the country. And a man who brings out her wild side...

Anna Delaney is thrilled to leave Boston for Austin, Texas, when her small tech company is bought out by a conglomerate. Born into a family of over-protective brothers, this is her chance at true independence—and a name-making professional breakthrough.

Even when gorgeous billionaire rancher King Sanders forms a one-man welcoming committee, Anna insists that she doesn't need a tour guide—or another bodyguard. But after she narrowly escapes a kidnapping attempt, she can't say no to King spiriting her away to someplace safe...and very private.

Someone wants the valuable software Anna's developing, and King is determined to keep her safe until the culprit is caught. The hunky cowboy lights her up brighter than the Lone Star sky at night, but neither one of them is prepared for just how wild Texas can get—and just how hard they're willing to fight to stay together...

I0677319

Also by Gerry Bartlett

Texas Pride
Texas Fire
Texas Heat

TEXAS LIGHTNING

A Lone Star Suspense

Gerry Bartlett

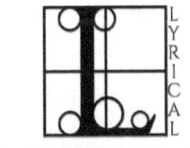

LYRICAL PRESS
Kensington Publishing Corp.
www.kensingtonbooks.com

Lyrical Press books are published by
Kensington Publishing Corp. 119 West 40th Street New York, NY 10018

Copyright © 2018 by Gerry Bartlett

All rights reserved. No part of this book may be reproduced in any form or by any means without the prior written consent of the Publisher, excepting brief quotes used in reviews.

All Kensington titles, imprints, and distributed lines are available at special quantity discounts for bulk purchases for sales promotion, premiums, fund-raising, and educational or institutional use.

To the extent that the image or images on the cover of this book depict a person or persons, such person or persons are merely models, and are not intended to portray any character or characters featured in the book.

Special book excerpts or customized printings can also be created to fit specific needs. For details, write or phone the office of the Kensington Special Sales Manager:
Kensington Publishing Corp.
119 West 40th Street
New York, NY 10018
Attn. Special Sales Department. Phone: 1-800-221-2647.

Kensington and the K logo Reg. U.S. Pat. & TM Off.
LYRICAL PRESS Reg. U.S. Pat. & TM Off.
Lyrical Press and the L logo are trademarks of Kensington Publishing Corp.

First Electronic Edition: October 2018
eISBN-13: 978-1-5161-0715-5
eISBN-10: 1-5161-0715-2

First Print Edition: October 2018
ISBN-13: 978-1-5161-0718-6
ISBN-10: 1-5161-0718-7

Printed in the United States of America

For Pattie and David Spradley, who survived a lightning strike in their own truck and have proved that love can last for over fifty years. I love you guys.

Acknowledgments:

Thanks to my awesome editor, Esi Sogah, for steering this ship, my incredible agent, Kim Whalen, for still believing in me after all these years, and my critique group. Nina Bangs and Donna Maloy, you are the epitome of patience. Your help through a hurricane and every other meltdown possible means the world to me.

Chapter One

Someone was watching her. She could feel it. Had since she'd moved to Texas, the so-called land of opportunity. *Paranoid much?* Maybe, maybe not. She knew what she'd created was valuable. And today she'd finished it. Almost. Just a few more tweaks and... Anyway, it had seemed like a cause for celebration. So she'd come out of her cave to finally explore her new city.

Anna Delaney scanned the vast room around her but couldn't concentrate. Black dots danced in front of her eyes. Her favorite pink sweater had become her enemy, itchy and so hot she wanted to rip it off and let the world see her in the last clean bra in her underwear drawer. Sweat gathered between her breasts and under her arms. Hello, Austin, didn't you get the memo? It's winter!

Swaying where she stood, she dragged in a breath and almost passed out. Would anyone care if she just dropped to the cool marble floor? She'd lay her burning cheeks against it and... Someone grabbed her arm.

"Move aside, make way. Sorry, ma'am." The deep voice had that Texas twang she was trying to get used to. His grip was firm as he dragged her through the crowd.

What the hell? Anna opened her mouth to scream for help, but nothing came out. Her efforts to jerk loose were feeble. Through a blur she saw a tall man in a suit, boots, and a cowboy hat. Where was he taking her? Why didn't anyone stop him? He shoved her onto a hard bench, his hand firm on the back of her head as he pushed it between her knees.

"Breathe." He pulled at her backpack and Anna finally came alive.

"Get your freaking hands off of that!" She sat up and slapped at him, not about to lose the only thing that mattered to her.

"Whoa, whoa, whoa." He let go and held out his hands in surrender. "I wasn't trying to steal your stuff, lady. Just trying to keep you from fainting."

Too late. She blinked, determined not to give in as the room dipped and swayed. When her vision finally cleared, she looked him over. For a kidnapper, the man wasn't exactly trying to blend into the tourist crowd. This big guy with broad shoulders would turn heads anywhere. He wore boots of some kind of exotic skin and flashed a gold watch worth more than her fancy computer system. His suit alone cost thousands. Her brother Chance had taught her to recognize expensive threads.

All right, so she believed him—he didn't need to steal her stuff. She shrugged off her backpack and dropped it into her lap. When the heat got to her again, she swallowed nausea and leaned over, resting her forehead on the leather pack.

"You all right?" He hadn't left, just sat beside her on the stone bench.

"No." She took shallow breaths. She hated Texas. Hated the unpredictable weather and interfering strangers who wouldn't let her die in peace.

"Stay here, sugar." He patted her shoulder before he took off.

No problem. Anna was pretty sure if she stood she'd fall flat on her face. She was so damned stupid. This morning she could have sworn those looked like snow clouds when she'd left her apartment. It was January, cold outside. This sweater, warm and cozy, had been perfect back home. Here in Austin? It was about as useful as ice skates in hell. From now on she was checking the weather app on her phone before she went anywhere. Hindsight. Always twenty/twenty.

She didn't know how long she'd sat there, leaning on that backpack, when she sensed he had returned.

"Feeling any better?"

Anna put a shaky hand to her face. "Um, sure. Thanks. I'll be fine." Big lie.

"No wonder you were about to hit the floor. You're overheated." He slapped a bottle of cold water in her hand. "Drink first."

"What?" Anna swayed right into his red striped tie and hard chest. Bossy men. She'd sworn off them. But cold water... He obviously wasn't letting go so she sipped until she steadied. She'd needed that. He took back the bottle and dropped something else into her hand before she had time to say another word. He pulled her to her feet and looked into her eyes. She tried to sit again before she fell over.

"Oh, no you don't. I got you something." He kept his hand under her elbow. "Ladies' room is right across here. Take off that wool sweater and put this on, sugar. T-shirt. You're a little thing and I had to guess at the size, but I think it'll fit." He smiled down at her with straight white teeth, obviously pleased as punch that he'd come to her aid.

"I, uh, you didn't have to…" Anna studied the neon-green tee and tried to look grateful. Did he really think that would fit her? Maybe when she'd been twelve. But short sleeves and cotton! The very idea of shedding her wool had her almost dropping her pack in her eagerness to clutch the ugly shirt to her breasts. "Thanks!" She shoved away from him and wobbled.

"Easy now. Just a few steps and you can go in a stall and change. You'll feel much better when you're dressed right for this crazy weather." He kept his hand under her elbow, supporting her as he guided her across the floor toward the restroom.

"It *is* crazy! And wrong. Where did winter go?" Anna heard the whine in her voice but couldn't stop herself.

He just laughed and kept steering her across the vast lobby. "Don't worry, it'll be back. There's probably a blue norther already headed this way." He stopped in front of the door to the women's restroom. "Can you make it from here?" He looked around. "Ma'am? Would you mind giving her a hand? My friend here is suffering from the heat."

Anna stared up at him when he pulled off his hat. Dark eyes, black hair, and deeply tanned, this man was a stranger, not a friend. Where she came from you had to earn that label. Not that she would mind knowing this guy, who would have looked at home in the pages of *GQ*, the cowboy edition. The woman striding toward them in high heels, a red power suit, and carrying a leather briefcase stopped in her tracks. She sized him up with a smile and nodded. Clearly she'd be happy to do whatever this hunk wanted.

"Of course." She took Anna's arm. "What on earth were you thinking, girl? Wool? In this heat? You must not be from around here." She threw a flirtatious look over her shoulder. "How could you let her leave the house like this?"

He shrugged and winked, silently saying that he'd never understand women.

"Well, we'll get her squared away. Where are you from, honey?" The woman pulled Anna inside when the Good Samaritan pushed open the bathroom door.

"Boston," Anna murmured as the door swished closed behind them. Why did everyone around here think they could call you "sugar" and "honey" like they knew you?

"No wonder! Is this your first Texas winter?" She ran water over a paper towel and handed it to Anna, who fell into the first stall and sat on the toilet seat. She hoped like hell it wasn't wet. "Press this against your face before you try to change tops. Your face is as red as a beet."

Anna nodded, having nothing else to say. She just used the towel to wipe her face and leaned over again. Still had her backpack, that was something. After a few moments to cool down while the other woman obviously used the facilities, she sat up and pulled off her sweater. Sitting there in just her bra was a pure pleasure.

"Feeling better?" The woman handed her the green tee. "I tore off the price tag. Men! He bought a size small. Guess he wanted you to show off your figure." She glanced at Anna's bra. "You sure will with that flimsy thing under it."

"Yeah. This one has seen better days. Laundry isn't on the top of my to-do list." Okay, so she was being defensive. The stretched-out bra was a decade old but comfortable. Anna jerked the shirt over her head and struggled to get it down over her boobs. Of course it clung. A sudden whoosh of cool air came as a welcome relief but made her nipples put on a show. How could she go out there now? The man was probably waiting for her and she should offer to pay for the shirt. She held her pack against her chest and stood.

"Now they turn on the air conditioning. Guess they have to hit a magic number or something on the thermostat. I swear it's over eighty outside. Even for Austin I bet it's a record." The woman freshened her lipstick in front of the mirror. "Blew your mind, didn't it? Being from Boston and all. January probably means snow up there."

"Yes!" Anna thought about dumping her sweater in the trash but figured she'd get to visit home again someday so it went into her backpack. Home. Snow, family... Oh, she'd better quit thinking about it or she'd burst into tears. She'd committed to Texas for the time being and she had to learn to love it, crazy weather and all. "Thanks for helping me."

The woman closed her purse with a snap. "That guy your boyfriend?"

"I don't know him. He caught me as I was about to fall over when the heat got to be too much. Nice guy." Anna took her own look in the mirror above the sink and winced. "I'm sure he'll take off as soon as he sees me come out of here, if he hasn't already."

"A gentleman, to take care of a stranger like that. Handsome too. No wedding ring, though that's no guarantee he's not married. I know that from experience." She turned and stuck out her hand. "Pamela Allred, State Railroad Commission." She pulled a card out of her jacket pocket. "Welcome to Texas, Boston."

"Anna Delaney, Zenon Technologies." Anna shook her hand, then leaned against the sink. "Seriously, I appreciate your help, Pamela. You like the guy out there, go for it. I'll thank him and be on my way."

"Zenon's a big deal computer firm. I heard they brought some Yankees down here when they bought a new company." Pamela smiled. "You must be a techie."

"Yes, I'm a computer geek and proud of it. Several of us came with the buyout." Anna washed and dried her hands and face. "It's an adventure. That's what I hoped for, anyway."

"I'm sure it will be. You feeling all right now?" Pamela looked her over. "You can't hide in here forever, you know."

"Better, thanks. I'm going. In a minute." Anna dug in her pack and produced her own card. She didn't have many friends in Austin and could always use another one. Pamela seemed nice. "Here. If you're ever out by Zenon and want to do lunch, give me a call. I don't know a thing about railroads, but maybe we could find something to talk about."

Pamela laughed. "The Railroad Commission deals with the state's natural resources and the environment—energy, oil and gas, things like that. It has an old timey name we're stuck with, but that's Texas for you." Pamela studied Anna's card. "My job lately has been all about bringing our old system of keeping track of oil well production into the high-tech world. I'm one of the few women they've brought on board. Lunch sounds good, I'll call you. We may have more to discuss than you realize. Now, you hide for another minute or two and catch your breath while I make a run at the handsome stranger. You okay with that?"

"Sure. Go for it. I'm more into the nerd type. This guy's way too big, and with those boots?" Anna laughed. "I'm pretty sure we have about as much in common as filet mignon and hamburger." She shook her head. "Obviously I'm hungry. Must be lunchtime. Anyway, we just happened to be in the capitol on the same day at the same time." Pamela was blond and pretty, with a perfect figure and a competent air about her. The cowboy would probably put her number in his phone in a heartbeat.

Pamela raised an eyebrow. "I don't know. He did buy you that tiny tee. That says interested to me. He could be into dark hair and blue eyes; a lot of men are." She gave her hair a final fluff. "They say blondes have more fun but I certainly have my dry spells. Can't hurt to take a shot though. Did you *smell* him? Positively yummy." She sighed. "Anyway, give me five minutes, then come on out. You have lipstick and a comb in there?" She gestured to the backpack Anna had set on the counter next to the sink.

"Never leave home without it. My mother's rule. I carry the pack instead of a purse but all the necessities are in there." Though it would take more than lipstick to make her look presentable. Her hair, always unruly, had gone wild thanks to wet paper towels and sweat.

"My mama too. Guess Yankee mamas aren't so different from Texas mamas." Pamela grinned. "So use 'em, Anna. At least one of us should get a date out of you having a fainting fit at the feet of one good-looking guy." She let loose the top button on the white silk blouse under her suit jacket so a little cleavage showed, then picked up her briefcase before she eased out the door.

Anna studied herself in the mirror, then rooted around for lipstick and a brush. Pamela was right. Self-respect was something her mother had drilled into her from an early age. And then there was that man's delicious smell. She might have been a little woozy but she'd have to have been unconscious to miss that subtle hint of something he wore that made her want to see him without all those layers, lose the tie and…

So far, her life in Texas had been spent mostly chained to her computer. Once she'd arrived in Austin, it had been drilled into her that it was *her* program that had made Zenon's owner spend an obscene amount of money to buy her old company. She'd been under pressure ever since. But coming to Texas had given her an opportunity for a change, an adventure, like she'd told Pamela. She'd worked hard since she got here. Zenon had certainly got its money's worth. So it was time for her to look up from her keyboard and give Texas a chance.

Maybe almost fainting in the rotunda of the Texas capitol building was a sign. Okay, so she might not see a future with Mr. Tall, Dark, and Too Cute for His Boots, but she wasn't about to go out there looking like she'd been dragged across that beautiful marble lobby face first either.

* * * *

King waited outside the ladies' room and wondered what the hell he was thinking. His sister would laugh her ass off at the idea that he'd swooped in and helped a stranger like that. Of course, much as he loved Karen, he knew she'd have stepped over the body and kept walking. Not his style. But, damn it, this had made him late for a meeting. He hated to be late for anything. When his phone chimed he knew exactly what the text was about. Yeah, State Senator Derek Cutler was pissed. There'd be no arm twisting about that agricultural bill over steaks and drinks today. He'd have to let the man cool off before he tried to smooth his ruffled feathers. Now he might as well see how the little gal he'd helped was coming along.

He knew the signs when a woman was about to faint. His twin sister had gone through a spell of fainting fits when they'd been growing up. White face, flop sweat, and boom! she'd hit the deck. This woman had been steps away from him as he was striding across the vast lobby. She'd wobbled and damn if he was going to let her fall and maybe split her head open on that hard marble floor. When the bathroom door swung open, he stuck his phone in his pocket and smiled. It was the little blonde.

"She'll be out in a minute. She's fine. Just taking a breather. Believe it or not, she's from Boston. Our winter warm spell was a shock to her system. She'd obviously dressed for a Yankee winter." She laughed and pressed a card into his hand. "Pamela Allred, Railroad Commission."

"Hey, thanks for your help, Ms. Allred." King took the card and held out his hand. "King Sanders. I have some dealings with your commission from time to time because of the oil wells on my ranch southwest of San Antonio. Maybe I'll see you in the office while I'm in town."

"Oh, I hope so." She smiled and shook his hand, holding on when he would have let go. "And it's Pam." She frowned when her phone chimed. "Well, shoot. Duty calls. Nice to meet you. And that was sweet what you did for Anna, buying her a T-shirt and all. She said you're strangers."

"Right. I didn't even know her name until you told me just now." King tucked Pam's card into his pocket. "I'll be seeing you, Pam." He watched her stride off but his mind was on the woman still behind the restroom door. Anna from Boston. She was different. Interesting. Pam was cute but so much like a dozen other women he knew he could imagine a factory, churning them out. They worked for the state, or maybe they didn't work at all but lived off Daddy's money. Nothing at all wrong with them. Nothing quite right about them either. Of course, he'd had his heart bruised recently, so maybe he was just being an asshole about women. Was entirely possible.

The door to the restroom creaked open and Anna peered out. Was she hoping he'd be gone? Probably embarrassed since she'd almost fallen in front of him. He strode forward, determined to make her feel at ease.

"You look better." He saw she still clutched that backpack like it was a lifeline. It was an expensive leather so he doubted she was down and out and it held all her earthly possessions. Her jeans were faded but he knew that was a style statement, not necessarily a sign of wear. Her tennis shoes were top-of-the-line. He bought that brand himself for when he went running. "T-shirt looks good on you. Bright color. Reminds me of new peas."

"Um, yes. I want to pay you for the shirt. I'm much cooler now. Thank you for coming to my rescue." She smiled. "It says 'Keep Austin Weird.' Is that really a slogan around here?"

"People around here are proud that Austin is known for strange happenings. Where else would you have an annual bat festival? And I'm not talking about baseball bats." King liked that she smiled at that nonsense. He reached for her elbow and steered her away from the bathroom entrance when a herd of women came toward them. "We need to move out of the way."

"Oh, yes." She flushed. "About the shirt."

"Have lunch with me. That's how you can pay for the shirt." He moved her toward the door to the outside. She wasn't exactly digging in her heels, but she wasn't making it easy for him either, trying to put space between them.

"I don't think so." She stopped dead and he obviously wasn't going to move her without dragging her or picking her up. She shrugged into her backpack.

"Let me start over. King Sanders." He held out his hand, trying not to stare at how the shirt molded to her breasts. Oh, boy. To his relief, she shook hands but was quick to pull free.

"Anna Delaney. Thank you for saving me. Really." She dug a twenty-dollar bill out of her jeans pocket and thrust it at him. "Here. For the shirt. Now I'd better be going."

He wasn't about to take her money. "Look at the time. It's after noon, and I bet you're hungry. Hot and hungry. No wonder you were about to faint." He ignored the bill she waved at him and stayed with her as she headed for the exit at a pretty fast clip for a gal who'd been down for the count just minutes ago.

"I'm okay now. That cold water helped a lot." She spared him a smile but just kept going.

"Let me at least walk you to your car." He should give it up. She wasn't interested. He'd been shot down before. No big deal. So why wasn't he giving up?

"I don't have a car. I'm going to catch a bus." She stopped next to the guard station where tourists had caused a temporary roadblock. Security guards had a protocol, running backpacks and purses through scanners similar to those at an airport before anyone could be allowed inside. They didn't scan people who were leaving but there was still a logjam near the exits.

"You're kidding me. A bus? Where do you live? Let me give you a ride. My truck's just outside." King followed her when she took advantage of a break in the crowd and scooted through. Outside, the unseasonal heat hit him in the face. He saw Anna stop and take a breath.

"Look, it's hot. Even in that new shirt you're going to feel it. Where's the nearest bus stop?" He looked around. There was no way a city bus would be allowed anywhere near the building. Security was tight.

"Three blocks away." She said it quietly, as if gathering her nerve. Her shoulders drooped but she started walking. "I'll be all right. This shirt makes it easier. Thanks again, Mr. Sanders."

"King. Seriously, I swear I'm not a serial killer, or desperate to abduct you for nefarious purposes. I'd just like to make your life easier. A ride. Lunch. Whatever you're willing to agree to." He waved over a nearby policeman who'd been stationed next to the circular drive. "Mike, can you vouch for me to this pretty lady?" And she was pretty—wild black hair, white skin that probably never saw the sun, and blue eyes the color of the sky. He'd be damned if he was going to let her get away without a fight.

"Well, I don't know, King. What do you want me to say? I wouldn't call you harmless, pal. You do like the ladies." The guard grinned when King gave him a look that said "Knock it off." "Ma'am, King's well-known here. The lawmakers run when they see him coming because he usually wants something for that ranch of his out west and the people of the town near there. Gets it too, because he's damned persistent. And I know for a fact that he raised a bit of hell at the University of Texas when he was there. Of course, that was a few years back. Rumor has it he's settled down some since then."

King laughed, then elbowed the cop with a bit of force. "Thanks a heap, Mike. You were one of the guys who raised hell with me, if I remember right."

"Those were the days. My wife broke me of that." Mike grinned. "Truthfully? He's okay. I'd trust my daughter with him. Of course, she's only five."

Anna examined King like he was a rattlesnake who'd crawled out from under a rock. Then she smiled and he knew he'd made some progress. "I, uh, don't know what to say about that. I wasted my college years studying instead of raising hell." She shook her head and aimed her smile at his friend in uniform. "You'd really trust your child with him?"

"Sure would. He's a good guy. He gives you a problem, let me know. Give me your phone." Mike held out his hand. When Anna dug hers out of her backpack and unlocked it, he punched in his number. "There you go. Backup. I'm a Texas Ranger, a member of the Texas Department of

Public Safety, at your service." He tipped his cowboy hat as he gave her back the phone.

"Well, thanks." Anna's smile turned into a grin. "I guess I'll take you up on the ride then, King. You can't know how much I dreaded getting back on the bus. I had to change three times. It would take forever to get back to my apartment."

"Nice to know I beat out that torture." King laughed when Anna flushed. "Hey, I'll take it." He knocked fists with his buddy. "I owe you, Mike."

"You bet you do. You two taking off now?" Mike nodded toward the truck parked at the curb. "Because if you don't, King, I'm going to have your vehicle towed."

"Fixin' to move it now, Mike. Sorry it took longer than I expected. Thanks for watching it for me." King slapped him on the back. "Come fall, you've got tickets to the Longhorn game of your choice. Text me."

"I will. Never doubt it." He waved them off and turned to talk to a man in a business suit.

"Here we go." King eased Anna toward his truck illegally parked at the curb. It paid to have old friends in convenient places. He was lucky that way, always had been. "I was just running inside to pick up a man for lunch. That got canceled, so I'm free to take you home or to lunch then home. How about it, sugar? Will you have lunch with me?" He held his hat over his heart.

She appeared to think it over for a beat, then nodded. "Why not? I told you how bad the ride here was. Obviously I got so overheated I couldn't even enjoy my sightseeing once I got here. And I am hungry." Anna looked over his truck. "This is a fancy one." Then she looked him over. "Nice suit too. So I suspect you can afford to buy me lunch."

"I do all right." He opened the passenger door and put out his hand, waiting while she took off that pack she guarded so carefully. "Let me help you up and in. It's a pretty high step."

"I can manage." She grabbed the bar to pull herself up into the cab, obviously determined to prove something.

It was a tall order for a little woman. Not that Anna was so short, about five feet five if he was any judge. But his truck was high enough to make it tough. He got a nice view of her rounded bottom while she climbed in. He could give her a boost but figured she wouldn't appreciate it.

He took off his suit coat and tie and tossed them, along with his hat, into the back seat before he settled behind the wheel. "If you haven't explored Austin much, let me treat you to one of our famous downtown restaurants.

Nothing fancy, just good eating." He started the engine and hit the AC so it would blast cold air on both of them.

"What's a Texan's idea of good eating? In Boston it's clam chowder or a lobster roll." Anna still held on to that pack, clutching it to her chest. "Maybe you should just take me home."

"Now, that wouldn't be right. I heard your stomach growling. You admitted you're hungry." He grinned. He couldn't hear it over the roar of the air conditioner but he just bet it did it again because her pale cheeks really lit up. He bet she never got out in the sun. His own skin was dark to begin with, thanks to his Mexican mama, and he was in the sun almost every day. Anna would probably burn if she spent any time next to his pool. He pictured her in a bikini and had to clear his throat.

"Not going to chicken out on me, are you? We don't eat weird things. That's not part of the 'Keep Austin Weird' slogan."

"Okay, okay. I'm starving and sick to death of eating what I can get close to my place or delivered. So why not? I'd love to see more of Austin. What is down-home cooking here?" She finally set her pack on the floor and fastened her seat belt.

"Chicken fried steak." King hit the gas. "Thanks for trusting me, Anna. You won't be sorry."

* * * *

Anna *was* sorry. Not that the lunch hadn't been delicious. It had. King Sanders had clearly been determined to charm the pants off her. Unfortunately, it was working. The sad truth was that Anna had been lonely in Austin. This man, with his tall good looks and easy smile, made her want to do something foolish, like invite him upstairs when he drove into her apartment complex.

But she didn't know him. Yes, he'd told her about his ranch and his family, even his twin sister. He'd shown a real interest in getting to know her as well. So she'd laid it on a little thick about her big brothers, all in law enforcement back home. Yes, she had a local lawman on speed dial now, but he wasn't the only one she could call if King Sanders tried any funny business. Her brother Chance was FBI. What did King think about that? Actually, he seemed to want to know more. Like she was fascinating. Which she wasn't, sitting at a computer all day. Crap. A handsome man totally focused on her? She was finding it downright seductive. Oh, this was trouble.

No, no, no. She wasn't that easy. Was she? Anna gave him the gate code, then directions to her building. It was a big contemporary complex and impersonal, as different from her old apartment in an aging brownstone in Boston as it could be. The only reason she'd rented here was because it was literally across the street from her office. She'd never learned to drive, thanks to the great public transportation system back home, and she wasn't eager to learn now. A bike was perfect for her. She kept it chained on her balcony.

He slowed the truck. "Building C? This it?"

Anna dragged her gaze from the way his hands rested on the leather-covered steering wheel. Strong, competent hands with neatly trimmed nails. Tanned, masculine. She could imagine...

"Uh, yes. Pull into one of the unmarked spaces."

The truck jerked when he braked suddenly. "Damn it. Who lets their dog just run loose like that? I could have killed the little thing. Squashed it like a bug."

Anna sat up straight. There were rules. Leash laws. Then a white ball of fur raced past and stopped at the bottom of the stairs to her apartment. It started barking, obviously upset.

"Oh, my God! YoYo!" She grabbed the handle and tried to open the door. Locked. "Let me out! Now!" She released her seat belt.

"What the hell?" But he unlocked the doors with a click.

Anna almost fell out as she jerked the door open and jumped down. "YoYo! Come here, boy!" She ran toward him and scooped up the dog, frantically checking him for injuries. "How did you get out?" She realized King was right behind her. "I locked up tight when I left. He was inside."

"Which apartment is yours?" King held out his hand and YoYo licked his fingers.

"Top of the stairs. Two C." Anna hugged the dog and started up. She could see the door was closed, just like she'd left it. This didn't make sense.

"Stop! Stay here. The only way the dog got out is if someone let him out. You did say you live alone, right?" When she nodded, King ran to the truck, then came back with a handgun.

"Are you kidding me?" She gawked at him. "Put that away!"

"What if someone is still inside? They could be loading up, robbing you blind." He gently moved Anna aside and started up the stairs. "Who else has your key?"

"Just a friend from Boston. She's here for work too. But she'd never leave YoYo out in the parking lot. And I didn't expect her. She'd text if she was coming over." Anna stayed on King's heels. "What are you going to do?"

"Depends on what we find. Call the police, of course. Hold the thief till they come if someone is still in there." He looked all business, like he was ready to take on whoever had dared leave her dog at the mercy of big trucks and the heat.

"I hope they are here. YoYo could have been killed the way some people race through the parking lot. We need speed bumps." Anna felt sick thinking about it. She reached for the trowel she'd stuck into a bag of potting soil next to the door. "Guess this is better than nothing. It's got a good point on it." She set YoYo down and told him to stay. Not that he'd do it. He'd flunked obedience school, twice. The poor thing was panting like he was feeling the heat and needed water.

"You should wait at the bottom of the steps, Anna. Go ahead and call the police." King stopped like he thought she was really going to just stand meekly in the parking lot while he did his macho maneuvers.

"My phone's in the truck, in my backpack." Anna didn't want to think about why someone might have broken into her place. All her work, notes, things she'd brought from home were in there, along with her computer system. They were the only things of value. "The dog's not barking now. That's a good sign. If someone is still here, I think YoYo would be going crazy. Look at him."

King reached down to pat the tiny dog who sniffed his boot, then scratched against the door. "I hope you're right. I don't hear anything. Stand back anyway." He tried the door and the knob turned easily. "You did lock this when you left?"

"Of course. I have a computer system worth a fortune in there. It's my livelihood. I do a lot of work from home." Anna stayed close. No way in hell was she just going to obey him.

"Last chance to wait by my truck." He gave her a look, still not opening the door.

"If you're scared, hand me your gun. I'll use it on whoever might be lurking inside. I know how to shoot. Remember those brothers I told you about? They taught me." Anna tried to push past him.

"Now you're scaring *me*." He threw open the door. "Police!"

Anna gasped when she saw the chaos inside. Whoever had let out her dog had obviously been looking for something. Her gaze went right to her dining room table. Her computer was gone. Her heart sank. At least she'd taken precautions with her work. But to break in like this...

King stalked through the house, gun out in front of him as he searched every room. It didn't take long since there was only one bedroom off the living room, a tiny kitchen, and the bathroom. She heard him open the closet door before he shouted, "Clear!" just like in one of those police procedurals on TV.

"No one's here. What's missing?" He glanced at the empty dining room table she'd used as her desk. "Is that where your computer sat?"

"Yes." Anna blinked back tears. "My TV is still here. No surprise. It's not that big. My friend mocks me for it." She trailed into her bedroom. The drawers had been pulled out from her bedside table and her chest. Underwear was strewn across the mattress, which was off the bed frame.

"They were obviously looking for something. Money?" King picked up the mattress and slid it back on the box springs. "You keep cash here?"

"No. I don't fool with much cash. I'm all about my debit card." Anna grabbed a laundry basket and stuffed the clothes that had been dumped on the floor into it. She shuddered as she left the room. She was washing everything that the cretins who'd invaded her space had touched.

"Stop cleaning. The cops should see it like this." King picked up a bowl and filled it with water. His new best friend licked his hand, then drank greedily as soon as he set it on the floor. "Wish the dog could talk."

"You and me both." Anna picked up a sofa cushion, dropped it in place, then fell onto it. "I guess I should call the police. I have renters insurance." Her lower lip quivered but she refused to give in to it.

"Hey, talk to me." King slapped the other sofa cushions next to her then sat. "You want to get a hotel room? I know you probably don't want to stay here tonight. If these guys come back…"

"What?" Anna stared at him. "Why would they do that?"

"I don't know. You tell me." He glanced around the room. "They were searching for something. Did they find it?" He gave her a penetrating look. "You've been guarding your backpack since before I met you. I have a feeling there's something in there that's valuable. To you, and maybe to the assholes who broke in here. Or am I imagining things?"

Anna took a shaky breath. She'd already figured out that King was sharp. And she hadn't exactly made a secret of the fact that she wasn't going to let her pack out of her sight or her reach during their time together. It had even sat between her legs at the restaurant. Thank God she was careful, because she'd be in tears, and in jeopardy of losing her job, if she hadn't taken those special precautions before her little sightseeing jaunt today.

"No, you're not imagining things. I'm pretty sure whoever broke in here was looking for what's in my pack." Anna realized that, in her fright about her dog, she'd left the thing sitting in King's truck. Unguarded. She jumped up and ran outside her door. The truck was still there.

"Did you lock it?" She turned to him as he walked up beside her.

"No, but I will now." He pulled his key fob from his pocket and hit the command that made the lights on the truck flash as the locks engaged. "Why don't you tell me what's going on, Anna? Whoever broke in here knew what they were doing. They didn't have a key, but there are no signs of forced entry. So they were professionals. You carrying gold bars in that backpack? State secrets? What?"

"You know that joke, if I told you I'd have to kill you?" Anna tried for a smile but couldn't twist her mouth into one.

"Oh, come on. I don't believe you." He shut the door and turned the dead bolt. "You're a computer geek. And I don't mean that to insult you. What's in the backpack? A new revolutionary program?"

"Got it in one, King." Anna collapsed on the sofa and YoYo jumped in her lap for a cuddle. She buried her face in his soft fur for a long moment before she felt the couch move. King sat beside her again, waiting for more.

"You didn't insult me. I'm proud to be able to create computer software. It's what I do. And I invented a program that has the potential to save lives. It's why that huge company across the street paid big bucks for the little Boston company I worked for, and why I had to move here." Oh, hell. Tears. There was nothing she'd like better than to be in her mom's kitchen right now, surrounded by her older brothers. Safe. Instead she was telling this to a stranger. Could she trust him?

Wait a minute. She didn't believe in coincidences. Never had. So why had this man been the one to rescue her when she'd been about to faint today? And he'd been so determined to stick with her and keep her busy for hours. Was it so his buddies could break into her place and steal her computer? She faced him and looked into his dark eyes. He looked back, all innocence and interest. That in itself was suspicious. Men didn't fall for her at first sight, and certainly not men of his kind. Rich cowboy types were as foreign to her as that lunch in the diner had been. Yes, at first it had been delicious, but now it was sitting like a greasy lump in her stomach, making her wish she'd never taken the first bite.

He still held his gun, resting it across his knees like he was just a little too familiar with it. Why? Did all ranchers in Texas carry guns in their trucks? She had no idea. But her brothers had warned her to be careful here. And her boss had cautioned her about the program she was working on. It was valuable. Worth millions, maybe more. She was the brains behind it. Which meant taking her computer could be just the first play in a clever plot to steal her software. The second play? Well, there was no play at all without her to solve the glitches in it.

"Anna?" King shook his head. "You going to tell me what's going on? I can help you."

"I just thought of something." She ran into her bedroom. Was it possible the thieves had missed her hiding place? She'd brought her heavy-duty snow boots to Texas even though her brothers had teased her about it. The boots had been just right for slipping what she needed inside. Sure enough, they were where she'd left them, lying on the floor of her closet. They'd obviously not been thoroughly searched, and when she stuck her hand deep inside she hit pay dirt.

Anna walked back into the living room ready to confront King. She took a deep breath, determined to stay calm despite the nerves that threatened to make her sick and shaky.

"What the hell?" He stared at the gun in her hand she aimed at him. "Is that a .38 Special?"

"Sure is. It's loaded, and I'm not afraid to use it either. Now why don't you try to convince me you're not in on this." She waved her free hand at the mess around them. "I wasn't born yesterday, King. It seems a little too convenient that you came to my rescue today, then managed to keep me busy while someone broke in here and stole my computer." If he went for his gun she hoped like hell she had the nerve to blow him away. But he wasn't a paper target and she'd never aimed at anything else. Please, God, don't let it come to that.

Chapter Two

"You're nuts. Why the hell would I need to do that?" He left his own gun where it was and pulled out his phone. "You work for Zenon, right?"

"Yes, I told you that over lunch. But maybe you already knew that. Maybe that was part of your plan. My computer program is worth millions, King. I'm not kidding. I'm calling the police and I hope they find fingerprints that will help them figure out who did this. Will it show a link to you?" Anna knew she was getting worked up but, damn it, if this had all been a setup then she'd been played and it made her furious. Just when she'd thought she might have attracted a good-looking guy, made a connection, and possibly had something to look forward to here in Texas...

He was ignoring her, on his phone. He glanced at her, then she heard her name. Whoever he was talking to must have reacted to it, because his eyebrows rose. He finally handed the phone to her.

"Listen to this." He was solemn.

"I'm not putting down my gun." Was this a trick? Would he try to grab her gun when she reached for the phone? She backed up a step.

"I didn't ask you to, it's on speaker." He held out the phone.

Anna watched him closely, waiting for him to make a move. If he did, she'd have to shoot him. She swallowed, focusing on keeping the gun steady. Who had he called? That policeman at the capitol who might have been fake? Oh, she didn't know what to believe. He just watched her and aimed the phone in her direction.

"Anna Delaney?" The deep voice sounded vaguely familiar.

"Who is this?"

"Ron Zenonsky. King says you've been robbed. Are you all right?" He sounded concerned.

"Mr. Zenonsky, is it really you?" Anna glanced at King. He wasn't smiling but she could see he wanted to. Had he actually called the owner of her company? "Prove it to me. How many plants are in your office? What color is your iPad?"

"Are you kidding? No plants. I kill them. My secretary, Mona, finally forbade me to bring in any sacrifices, as she calls them. I have a pink iPad because my daughter Lea gave it to me for Father's Day last year. My dog's name is Zero and I drive a Tesla but keep forgetting to charge it so I usually arrive at the office by Uber. Does that convince you I'm the real deal? I know King. He and I go way back. You can trust him."

"Yes, sir." Anna finally let the gun drop and grabbed the phone. She held it tight because her hand was shaking. "I'm sorry about the robbery. But I've got everything backed up on my laptop, which I've kept with me at all times. And the program is on a thumb drive in my pocket. The other computer is heavily encrypted and password protected. Whoever came in here didn't get anything worth stealing."

"Good girl. Now put King back on for me. I'd rather you didn't shoot him. He's a friend, and happens to be one of our investors, Anna. You're lucky you ran into him when you did."

Anna walked over and set her gun on the kitchen counter. What were the odds? "That's a coincidence."

"King has fingers in lots of pies. You'd be hard put to find a successful business in town he doesn't own a piece of. The guy has a nose for a good investment, and Zenon is about to hit it big with your program. I've told you that before."

"Yes, sir." Anna studied the man lounging in the ruins of her apartment. She'd known the minute she'd been able to focus that King Sanders was not an ordinary man in a cowboy hat. Now it seemed like he was a high roller in the business world. Mr. Z had been pressuring her to finish her program fast because he knew it would make Zenon a fortune.

"But it was wise of you to be leery. Obviously we're dealing with corporate espionage here. Don't call the police. I'll cover your losses personally. I don't want news of this theft to get out. We have other investors. This kind of threat to our security could cause some concerns we don't need."

"Yes, sir. Here's King." Anna handed him his phone then ran to her bathroom. She barely made it before she threw up that delicious lunch. God. What had she fallen into here? Ron Zenonsky was a billionaire, so King Sanders must be one too if they were buddies.

When King's hand landed on her back, she wanted to scream. She did not want or need company right now. But all he did was hand her a wet washcloth, then step out and close the door. Okay, so maybe he understood. Good thing one of them did. When she finally emerged from the bathroom, King was roaming her apartment, his gun stuck in his belt.

"You need to pack." King issued it like an order.

"Excuse me?" Anna wasn't in the mood to take orders. She'd brushed her teeth after running scalding water over the toothbrush she'd found on the floor. Savages! What the hell had they thought they'd find in her bathroom drawers? But they'd dumped them anyway.

"I'm taking you out of here. You don't want to wait to see if they come back, do you?"

"No, of course not." Anna wasn't sure she ever wanted to come back to this impersonal and now defiled apartment. But where would she go?

"I'm taking you home with me. I have excellent security. Ron and I talked about it. He's going to have a new computer delivered there." King had the nerve to dump the contents of her laundry basket onto the bed. He carried the empty basket into the kitchen and opened cabinets until he found dog food, then began clearing the shelves.

"Hold it." Anna had lived with managing males all her life and had decided during the move to Texas that she'd never endure another one. "*Your* house? In what universe is that a good idea?"

"There's no way anyone should connect you and me. Until today we'd never crossed paths. It's the perfect solution." King had cleared out the dog food cabinet, found YoYo's leash, and clipped it to his collar. It hadn't been difficult—the dog was following the man like he was covered in beef gravy.

"Would you put down that basket for a minute?" Anna stomped over to King, kicking a throw pillow out of her way. "Drop me off at a hotel. I can call Mr. Zenonsky and have the new computer delivered there. I have no intention of bunking at your place, King."

"I can see you're getting worked up about this. But listen, my house has space for you to work and is on Lake Travis with limited access. I can't imagine you want to use public Wi-Fi like you'd find in a big hotel for the kind of sensitive information you deal with."

"What do you know about the information I'm dealing with?" Anna tried to wrap her head around this. Yes, she'd need to retrieve pieces of her work from where they were stored in the cloud, so Wi-Fi was essential. But King shouldn't know that. What she did for Zenon was so secret only her boss and very few other trusted high-level people had any idea what she was working on. Friend of Mr. Z or not, King was making this move too fast.

"Relax. Ron trusts me. He knows I'm not interested in his tech breakthrough but I do have the right to know, since I invested heavily in his company. I'm doing this for you. Look around. You really think I could leave you like this? And it'll count as a favor to him. A personal favor. Z and I go way back. We keep score. He'll owe me. I'll have fun collecting on this."

Anna bit her lip. When he put it like that... She knew men well after growing up with four older brothers. Payback was a big part of their games with their buddies. She almost believed him until King smiled and looked her over with the kind of slow assessment that made her tighten up in all the wrong places.

"Of course, maybe the whole idea of being alone with me in my house makes you uncomfortable, Anna. You afraid the big bad cowboy will try to jump your bones?"

"*Afraid?*" She got in his smirking, way-too-handsome face. As if she was so hard up she'd turn a terrifying situation into an opportunity to get laid. Oooh, but she wanted to slap him, stomp his boots, kick his shins, do *something* violent. She took a breath, and damn if he didn't watch the rise and fall of that too-snug T-shirt while she inhaled something spicy, male, and way too interesting. That did it!

She crossed her arms over her chest and counted to five. Didn't help. She went on to ten. Finally she saw the humor in his taunt and backed up. If he was trying to get her mind off the disaster that was her apartment, it had worked. He was either damned clever or an irredeemable horndog.

"I know I'm irresistible, cowboy, but you'll just have to tie a knot in it." She was rewarded when he laughed so hard he almost dropped that dog basket. Damn, why did he have to look so good, with his eyes twinkling and his white teeth flashing?

Anna pressed her hand over her heart. "You think that's funny? I admit it. I came to Texas with all kinds of fantasies. If I'm afraid, it's not of you. It's of me, King." She shoved aside that basket to slide one hand down his chest and the other up to where his hair curled over his ears. He could use a haircut.

"I've been so *lonely* since I moved here. And you came to my rescue. Big, bold Texan, complete with cowboy hat and boots. Why, all that was missing was you riding in on a white horse. Please tell me you have a big white horse somewhere." She gave a gusty sigh and sagged against him, batting her eyelashes. Too bad she'd sweated off her mascara.

He just grinned. "Would a black one do?"

"In a pinch." She walked her fingers up his shirtfront. "Honestly, cowboy, I've been fighting the urge to throw myself at you ever since I came out of that bathroom at the capitol building." She pressed closer, her elbow hitting that basket of dog stuff. "Why, if we're staying together at your place, I don't know what might happen. You might have to beat me off with a stick."

He dropped the basket to the floor, barely missing her dog, who scampered out of the way. "Beat you off? Sugar, that'll never happen." His arms went around her, pulling her so close not even YoYo could find space to wiggle in between them where their legs tangled. "You feel the urge to try the horizontal Texas Two-Step, say the word."

"No?" She pushed him back. He was a handful, no denying that. And the chemistry was off the charts. "Let's get out of here. If your place is the safest for me and my program, then that's where I'll go. Temporarily, anyway. And just to work." Anna surveyed the mess around her, not sure where to start with her packing. She grabbed the framed picture of her family and laid it carefully in the dog basket.

"Why not leave everything else here?" He dropped a hand on her shoulder. "Your backpack is all you need and it's in the truck. You know you don't want to wear stuff those assholes have touched. You can order new clothes online and Ron will pick up the tab. I guarantee it."

Anna nodded. "You're right. I don't want anything those assholes have touched. Let's move." She grabbed her gun, then headed back into the bedroom to get her extra ammo. She stuck them both into a tote her grandmother had decorated with needlepoint and given her as a going-to-Texas gift. A quick look around and she really couldn't see anything else that she treasured. She'd left most of her personal things back in Boston in boxes in her parents' basement. Her mom was convinced this move to Texas was a temporary aberration and had insisted she leave them there. God, her family would freak out when they heard about the break-in. She wasn't sure she'd tell them about it. Not anytime soon, anyway.

"I'm ready." Anna picked up YoYo, leash and all, then gestured toward the dog's bed, a big fluffy pillow he loved. "Add that to the basket. I'll get his favorite toy." She found it under the dining room table, then headed for the door. King was right behind her.

Anna could almost feel his eyes on her butt. He was definitely a man who liked butts and breasts. Well, she had plenty of both. She ran down the stairs toward King's truck and stood next to the passenger door, waiting for him to unlock it. She was glad she didn't have to stay in a hotel alone. Whoever had come after her computer and the program she'd written might actually break her encryption. But they'd soon figure out it wasn't going to be quite that easy to steal what had taken her years to create. Would they come back and try again? Want her the next time? The idea that she could be a target sent chills through her. Security wouldn't be tight in a hotel and he was right about using their Wi-Fi. It could be easily hacked and she'd never use it to work remotely.

"I hope agreeing to go to your place isn't a mistake. I do need to work. Mr. Z is really anxious for this program to be finished fast. He has a big investment in it." She heard the locks click and opened the truck door, setting YoYo inside. A hand on her shoulder kept her from following right away.

"Anna, I'm a gentleman. I know you've had a bad scare, and my only intention is to set you up in a safe place. Like I said, as a favor to my friend Ron." King turned her to face him. "I get that you were kidding with all that nonsense about jumping my bones. But, to be honest, I am attracted to you." He smiled at her. "Taking advantage of your shot nerves right now wouldn't be cool. I can be a good friend." He ran a finger over her cheek. "Or an enthusiastic lover. Just let me know which you need."

Anna decided that didn't deserve an answer. She just turned and began the awkward climb into the truck. He seemed to know all the right things to say. That was the most disturbing thing about this man. Smooth, way too smooth. The tongue-tied geeks she was used to had been so much easier to manage. King was going to be impossible. Best to leave him in the friend zone. Too bad she'd felt the touch of that rough fingertip all the way down to her own zone—the one that friends didn't make melt, much less throb with dangerous urges.

She settled into her seat and realized he still stood there, watching her, waiting. She faced him. "Thanks, King. For offering me safety. You're right. My nerves are shot. The only decision I'm up for now is that I want to get out of here." She glanced around the parking lot. It seemed empty, harmless, but you never knew. "This place is giving me the creeps. Can we go now?"

"Absolutely." He slammed the door, then paused to look around. He finally shook his head and walked around to climb into the driver's seat after tucking the basket of dog essentials into the back seat. YoYo scampered between the seats and attacked the basket, knocking it over and dragging out his bed so he could settle on top of it. He sighed and curled up, obviously ready for a nap.

"Poor little guy. I can't imagine what he went through, trying to protect our home from invasion then being left out in the heat. I'm surprised no one saw what happened, heard him barking, or called the police. But then

I haven't met any of my neighbors and the apartment below me is vacant."
Anna realized King hadn't started the truck yet. "What?"

"Give me your gun." He opened the glove compartment and slid his own
inside. "We keep them locked up when I'm driving. That's my personal rule."

"Oh, sure." Anna pulled hers out of the tote at her feet. "There's probably
a law about that."

"I have a permit to carry concealed in Texas. Do you?" He locked the
compartment, then started the engine.

"No, I don't. I've been too busy working." Anna realized King was
driving slowly, watching their surroundings as he exited the apartment
complex. "Do you think we're being followed?"

"Not that I can tell, but I'm going to detour until I'm sure there's no
chance of it." He pulled out onto the street across from her office building
and hit the gas.

Anna checked behind them. A silver compact car came out of the security
gates not long after they did. Coincidence? It was a huge complex. When
the car turned and followed them, she tried to see who was inside. Man?
Woman? No, it was a couple.

"I see them. I'm getting on the freeway. We'll see what happens." King
reached over and patted her hand. "Relax, Anna. Don't you think having
your computer will be enough for them?"

"No, I'm afraid not. You heard me talking to Mr. Z. It's password
protected and I use a special encryption program." She looked down at
his hand covering hers but didn't snatch it away. It felt good to have him
here, knowing Austin freeways and ready to do something for her. Okay,
so maybe managing men had their uses. "Yes, they'll break through the
password easily enough if they're pros. I could. But the encryption…
That'll take a while."

"So why would they follow us?" He took his hand away when they got
into some traffic that required careful maneuvering.

"Because the program I'm working on is complex. Someone else might
be able to finish it, but I doubt it. It's my brainchild. And it still needs
tweaking. The only way it will be worth anything is if I get it done and
done right." She lowered her makeup mirror and tried to see the traffic
behind her. Was that silver car still there? It was hard to tell with the dozens
of other vehicles on the road. Half of them seemed to be silver compacts.

"Impressive. I know Ron paid a fortune for the rights to your company
in Boston, mainly to get that program you're working on. He said you're
the brains behind it." King frowned. "I'm suspicious of that silver Toyota
back there. Hold on, I'm doing a quick exit and it's not going to be easy.

But it's the only way to lose them if they're trying to follow us." He jerked the steering wheel and she heard the squeal of brakes before they suddenly hit an off ramp at high speed.

"Oh! This is why I have no desire to learn to drive. These highways. Did you see the cars swerve to keep from hitting us?" Anna gripped the armrest as she looked back. No one had been hit, but at least one driver was giving them a one-finger salute. No sign of the silver car at least.

"You don't even know how to drive?" King wheeled into the parking lot of a large shopping mall. He cruised up and down aisles and finally pulled into an empty slot but left the engine running.

"No." Anna looked longingly at the department store just a few feet away. She needed new underwear, a couple of shirts, and new jeans. Ordering online was fine but she couldn't wait for delivery. She was desperate for a shower and would need something to change into after that besides the tight tee. "What now?"

"I figured we could get you a couple of things to tide you over." He glanced around. "It looks like we're in the clear. No sign of a tail."

"What about YoYo? We can't leave him in a hot car." Anna also hated to go in alone. She was still spooked.

"He's coming with us. Anyone gives us a hard time, we'll say he's your emotional support dog." King reached between the seats. "Hey, pup, wake up. Your mama needs you."

"I do. I'm still jumpy." She was happy but hesitant when King placed YoYo in her lap. Claiming something like that was cheating. Real working dogs were highly trained, even though running her hands through YoYo's soft fur soothed her and made her realize why little fluffy dogs made such good candidates for emotional support. She was having second thoughts about even going into the store when King jumped out of the truck and came around to open her door.

"Come on. I doubt you'll have to lie. I'll keep him in my arms and we'll be spending money. You really think anyone is going to try to stop us?" He held out his hand. "Give me the dog and grab your backpack. I know you don't want to leave it here."

"You've got that right." Anna handed over YoYo, who seemed to have adopted King, then climbed awkwardly out of the truck. Shrugging into her pack, she followed King into a store where she rarely shopped. She would have been happy with a discount big box store. But this guy was obviously used to the best. He was also right that no one seemed to care about the dog as long as YoYo stayed tucked in King's arms.

She made quick work of grabbing extra underwear and a sleepshirt. She pushed King toward the purses where he could still keep an eye on her. She was glad he didn't want to let her out of his sight, but he didn't need to see her bra size.

"You sure I can't help you pick out some nightgowns or something?" His wicked grin told her he had some experience in that department. He lifted a lacy confection that was pure sin. "Red. It's a good color for you."

"You're right. Do they have it in flannel?" She ignored his wink and set her pack on the floor to pull out her debit card. A woman bumped into her from behind, her hands full of panties.

"Oh, sorry. Great sale." She reached past her. "Do you mind? I need to set these down so I can go back and grab a few more." She dumped the pile on the counter.

Anna smiled but was busy scanning her receipt. No wonder she didn't usually shop here. Two bras and six pairs of panties plus a nightshirt had cost more than she'd expected. She shook her head, then let it go. The quality was good and they were pretty.

"Anna, are you done yet?" King walked up behind her. "This pup is getting antsy. I think we need to find a tree or some grass pretty quick."

"Yes." She took the bag and reached down for her pack. Gone. She looked around. That woman... And she hadn't even really looked at her. "My backpack. Did you see the woman who came up next to me?"

"Older woman? Dark hair?" King looked around the department. "No sign of her. What the hell? She grabbed your pack?"

"Obviously. I thought you were watching me." Anna knew she was wrong to blame King but he had insisted...

"I was. Then a fella came over, asking about YoYo. Not that the dog liked him. Growled something fierce. Which should have been a sign, now that I think about it. Son of a bitch!" King stalked around the underwear department and toward the exits. "They were probably working together. That silver car. There was a couple inside."

"Well, hell." Anna held on to her debit card. It was the only thing she had left. That and the bag of underwear. Now whoever was after her program had her laptop too. It wouldn't really help them but her notes were in there. Hopefully no one would be able to figure out her peculiar shorthand and crappy handwriting. Damn it! Tears filled her eyes and she blinked them back. Crying wasn't going to help. The clerk had come out from behind the counter.

"Do you want me to call security to report this?" She was young, probably working part-time on weekends while she went to college. "I'm so sorry."

"Not your fault." Anna dredged up a smile for her. "I'm having a bad day, and this just capped it off. Don't worry about it. You didn't do anything wrong. We'll notify the authorities." She looked around. "Do you have security cameras? We could use the footage if you have it."

"Everywhere else in the store, but not in underwear. Store policy." She smiled apologetically. "But the security office on the second floor might be able to help you. Maybe you could spot them leaving the store."

"Do we want to take the time to do that now, King?" she asked him when he came back from checking the closest exit. "Go to security?"

"We can get Ron's people to follow up on that. They can get the footage and we can look at it later." He took the bag from her and handed her the dog. "You look done in. Let's get out of here."

Anna had to admit she was tired. Between the heat outside, which was ridiculous in January, the stress of being a target, and relying on a stranger, she wanted nothing more than a hot shower and a nap. Maybe that seemed cowardly, but it was all she had the energy for at the moment.

"There are other things I'll need. Female things." God, she hated to say that.

"My twin stays at the house when she's in town. I bet you can find whatever you need in her bedroom and bath." King ushered her toward the truck, stopping first at a patch of grass for YoYo to do his business. "Karen's taller than you are, and bigger in spots." He glanced at Anna's chest. "That just means the clothes she left will be loose, comfortable. She always leaves behind plenty of makeup and hair stuff. She'll never miss it."

"Says a man who has no idea how a woman feels about a stranger digging through her things." Anna sighed. "But it beats trying to stop again. I just hate to take advantage…"

"Hey, if it'll make you feel better, keep track of what you use and we'll make Ron reimburse Karen for whatever it is. She'll get a chance to go shopping for replacements. Trust me, my sister lives for shopping." King started the truck, constantly looking around the parking lot as if he thought they might be followed again.

"That does make me feel better." Anna settled into her seat, curious about this lake house and King, who had a sister he let stay with him and talked about with affection. "Your twin. Do you look alike?"

"We used to. But she's always messing with her looks. I'm a big hairy guy, she's a tall beautiful woman. For some reason, she doesn't believe she's fine as she is and keeps having this plastic surgeon 'fix' her. Makes me crazy." He drove out of the lot, checking the rearview and side mirrors frequently. "You see anyone following us? I'd love to run into the sons of bitches that snatched your pack."

"You and me both. Now I don't have ID or even a hairbrush." Anna pulled down the makeup mirror again. Good thing King liked natural, because that was what he had riding with him right now. Her makeup was gone and her hair was an uncontrollable frizz.

She used the mirror to scan the street behind them. No sign of the silver car. Not surprising. The couple probably took off thinking they had all they needed to hack into her computers. Well, they'd be disappointed. She never wrote down her passwords. Not like her dad, who kept all his passwords in a notebook next to his computer at home. And they weren't very imaginative. Her name and birthdate. Her brothers and the same. Then there was the dog's name. At least she'd talked him into moving on from one-two-three-four.

She glanced at King. What would he use for a password? The name of his horse? His favorite cow? She caught him glancing at her.

"What are you smiling about? I figured you'd be in tears by now." He reached over and patted her thigh. "It would be nice if you'd rigged that laptop in your pack to blow up when those assholes turned it on."

"Wish I'd thought of that." Anna leaned back in her seat, suddenly too exhausted to fight the depression that had been threatening to take over since the pack vanished from right next to her feet. "How far is this house of yours?"

"It's a ways yet. About twenty minutes if the traffic doesn't hold us up." He picked YoYo off his lap with one hand and set him in hers. "I don't see any signs that we're being followed this time, so why don't you close your eyes and rest until we get there?"

"Thanks, King. I will." She rubbed the dog's head and endured YoYo's pacing over her stomach until he found a spot to settle in her lap. "And don't think I don't appreciate your taking me home with you." She touched King's hand where it rested on the gearshift between them. "I don't know what I'd do if you hadn't come along when you did. If I'd gotten off the bus and walked into that apartment and that mess alone…" Oh, shit. She was not going to cry. Not now, when she was safe and on her way to a bazillionaire's lakeside home away from home.

"I'm glad I was there for you, Anna. Fate brought us together. Fate and a hell of a heat wave for January." King held on to her hand. "Now, don't you turn on the waterworks. If you do, I'll have to pull over. Nothing like tears to make me go all to pieces."

Anna looked at where their hands were joined. His hand was tanned, strong, and made two of hers. She gave his a squeeze, pretty sure nothing made this big Texan go to pieces. She sniffed, then eased her fingers out of his grip.

"I'm okay. Just tired. I'm calling Mr. Zenonsky. I can't believe those assholes got my laptop. At least you made me put my gun in your glove compartment or they'd have that too." Anna sighed. But her phone was in that damned pack. She let her head flop back on the leather head rest. It was the last straw. Yes, her numbers were saved in the cloud, but until she got a new phone...

"Here, use mine." He pulled it from his shirt pocket. "Last number I dialed. Remember?" He dropped it into her hand. "Unlock it." He told her his code, just like that. Trusting her.

Anna shook her head. Not even her parents knew the code to unlock her phone. She made the call. Her boss answered on the first ring and listened while she told him about the latest disaster. He quickly agreed to send her a new laptop, cell phone, and credit card to cover any expenses for personal items. If Anna needed any reassurance that the project she was working on was important to the company, she got it in that call. By the time she hung up, King was steering them off the freeway and taking a winding route into the hills surrounding one of Austin's many lakes. This was high-dollar real estate, which didn't surprise her.

"Everything all right?" King stopped in front of an iron gate and hit a button on a remote clipped to the visor above his head. The gate swung open slowly.

"It's fine. He told me to call him Ron." Anna still couldn't believe that.

"He's a good guy. The computer delivery people can call us from the gate when they get here." King steered them through then stopped the truck, waiting until the gates were securely closed before heading down the gravel drive.

There were trees on either side and no sign of the lake, though Anna knew it had to be nearby. She leaned forward, eager to see the house. The road became steeper. Clearly he had built on top of one of the hills this area was famous for. Gravel changed to brick pavers when the road turned again, and there was a large garage big enough to hold four cars. Behind it was a sprawling house that hugged the hilltop. It was made of the local stone and natural wood, with windows everywhere. The landscaping consisted of trees and drought-tolerant plants. Anna had learned that was important in a part of Texas that was always one dry season away from a problem with water conservation.

"Oh, it's beautiful." She tugged at the truck door handle, eager to get out and explore.

"Wait till you see the view." King helped her climb down from the truck. "Leave your stuff and YoYo's. Conchita or Doug will get it."

"You have staff." Anna let YoYo down, holding him close with his leash. She could imagine him chasing a squirrel in this wilderness and she'd never see him again.

"Caretakers. I'm rarely here, and they keep the place ready for me when I need to use it. They have a little place through the trees there." He pointed to a narrow path.

If Anna concentrated she could just make out the shape of a building through the trees. "Looks like a nice-size home."

"They don't complain. Though Conchita says it's pretty far to the nearest grocery store." King walked up to the front door but it opened before he got there.

"King, I saw you on the security camera. I didn't expect you until late this evening." A smiling woman looked past him. "Hello."

"Conchita, this is Anna Delaney. She'll be staying with us for a while. She's going to need to borrow from Karen because she was robbed. We bought her a few things at Nordstrom, but she'll need a change of clothes after her shower and might want to have a look in Karen's bathroom"—King grinned at Anna—"for some feminine stuff."

"Aw, you poor thing. Come on in here. And who is this?" Conchita bent down and spoke rapid Spanish to YoYo. "What is his name?"

"YoYo. We brought his food and bed." Anna was glad to see her dog was behaving, tail wagging happily.

"He's a pretty boy." Conchita picked him up. "Wait till my husband sees him. He will spoil him, you can be sure of that." She got a lick on her rosy cheek. "Now follow me. You look tired, and no wonder. Robbed. Once, I was robbed. It's like a violation. A man snatched my purse at the Fiesta store. I chased him and threw a cantaloupe at him, right there in the produce department."

King watched Conchita lead Anna away. As usual, his housekeeper had plenty to say and knew just what to do to make a guest feel welcome. He'd heard the cantaloupe story. Conchita had hit the thief square in the back and security had rescued her purse and arrested the man. You didn't mess with that lady. He pulled out his phone and called Ron.

"This program Anna is working on must be worth a hell of a lot. Whoever is after it sent pros."

"King, thanks for taking care of our girl. It's crazy how you ran into her like that." Ron wasn't telling him what he wanted to know.

"Cut the bullshit. What am I guarding here? If these people don't get what they want from her computers, Anna claims they'll need her to finish the project. Is that right?" King walked over to stare out the window that looked over Lake Travis. The view of the massive lake was why he'd bought this piece of property and why he'd built this house. Right now, though, it didn't soothe him like it usually did. The silence on the other end of the line was ramping up his tension. "Ron? You owe me an answer. I have her in my home. That means I'm at risk and so are my people here if someone comes after her."

"All right. Here's what I know. There are several possible groups that want that software. Has Anna told you what it can do?" There was the tinkle of ice dropping into a glass.

"Are you fixing yourself a drink? Glad one of us can relax." King wanted to reach through the phone and throttle his old pal. Shit. Of course Ron could chill, he'd passed off his problem. But then again, King had volunteered. Maybe he should be rethinking this.

"I'm not relaxing. Far from it. This is serious."

"I get that. FYI, Anna hasn't told me a damned thing about her project. She's guarding your secret like it's more important than her life." King looked longingly at his own bar, built into the wall next to the window. "Which it is not. I can't think of anything that I would put before a woman's life, Ronald. Now be straight with me. Who is after this so-called big-deal project?"

"Could be the Russians. Or the Chinese. There are even some local bad actors who probably think to make some large cash by acting as middle men to either of those buyers." Ron obviously took a deep swallow. "You know I'm into healthcare now, besides the usual computer hardware and software. Right?"

"Yeah. It's a solid area for the future. Aging population. Blah, blah, blah. You talked me into being one of your investors and I haven't regretted it. Until now." King gave in and walked over to pull down a bottle of his favorite scotch. He twisted off the cap and poured an inch into a tumbler, tossing it back. The smooth heat was welcome but didn't dissolve the knot in his gut.

"This one program is set to make us millions, maybe more."

"Go on." King eyed the empty glass then walked away. One was enough.

"So we know in my business that drug interactions are a big problem. People die from them all the time. At the very least, they can cause confusion, inaccurate diagnoses, and unnecessary hospital stays." Ron was chewing ice now. When had his friend gotten so damned irritating?

"So?"

"So Anna created a program that can and will be used with a scanner. Each patient's records are put into it, every drug they're on. Then, when the patient is prescribed a new drug, the data is entered and checked automatically for interactions. If there's any danger of complications, a red flag goes up. No way can the new drug be administered if there is any possibility of a problem. The beauty of this is the program can be loaded into something as small as a hospital bracelet, King."

"That sounds interesting." King tried to wrap his mind around such a service. All that information crammed into a little piece of plastic. But then why not? His little phone could do the job of a giant computer now. And he'd seen for himself how Ron had innovated other tech and made a fortune. That's why he'd put money into Zenon.

"Imagine. People with health issues will be begging to own these for themselves, but the real bucks will come from pharmacies, hospitals, of course, and, get this, those emergency room clinics that are springing up everywhere. Totally helps with their liability claims." Ron sounded excited. "I'm thinking even insurance companies may start requiring this program for doctors before they'll write a malpractice policy. All you'll need is one of those scan guns and a computer and you're in business." Ron laughed, he was so high on this thing. "It'll save lives, King, and make us a butt load of money. Brilliant, absolutely brilliant."

"What's the catch? Seems like there always is one." King sat in his leather recliner.

"Yeah. Security has to be tight. People are right to want their medical records confidential. Plus, if anyone can break into the program, substitute the wrong meds? Well, it can be a killer." Ron crunched ice, nervously, King thought. "Trust is everything. That's why I sent Anna to some special training. To the National Institutes of Health for one, so she'd understand the pharmaceutical side. Then to classes in cybersecurity. So she could be sure this program is safe as houses. We can't take a chance anyone can subvert it."

"I see that." King couldn't sit still and got up again. More and more it seemed that Ron had put this all on Anna's shoulders. "So Anna came up with the idea. Did she insist on doing this all on her own?"

"I wouldn't say that. But she's motivated. Has been working on it for years. The fewer people who know exactly how the program works, the better. The idea's been around awhile but she figured out how to make it come together. She's just weeks away now from the first test run, then we'll take it to market. I put out feelers and the orders are going to be off the charts. Everybody wants it, especially if we can get the price right. We've already got the copyright in the pipeline." Ron sighed. "What can kill us is if someone steals our software and gets it out there first. That's why it's so important to keep this under wraps. To keep Anna safe until she can finish her program and we can get it into production."

"Well, you were doing a piss-poor job of it before I ran into her." King was back to staring at the lake. "She was wandering around Austin alone, riding on a public bus, for God's sake. Her apartment had such feeble locks my grandmother could break into it."

"Your grandmother is one clever lady. I wouldn't put anything past her." Ron cleared his throat. "But you're right. I just didn't foresee that anyone would be this bold. Would actually take such a step."

"Well, they did. The woman who took Anna's backpack was close enough to touch her, Ron." King opened one of the French doors to breathe in some fresh air. "Right then she and her partner could have made a move and we would have been hard-pressed to stop them."

"You want me to send a security team over there? When I send the computers and phone?" Ron was finally sounding serious.

"Yes. To sit at my gate. Once the bad actors figure out they can't get into her encrypted files, I would expect them to come after Anna herself." King turned when he heard a gasp behind him. "Now get the lead out." He hung up and saw Anna standing in the doorway. She'd obviously taken a quick shower and wore what he recognized as his sister's workout clothes.

Anna's hair was wet and slicked back from her face. The tank top clung to her breasts and she wore yoga pants that flopped around her bare feet. What Karen called comfortable Anna made look sexy. King realized he'd just terrified her with what he'd said to Ron.

"Hey, I'm sorry you heard that." He walked over to stand in front of her.

"I'm not. I need to know the truth." She nodded toward the bar and his empty glass. "Can I have one of those?"

"Scotch?" He picked up the bottle he'd poured from.

"I'd prefer whiskey." She moved around him and reached for the bottle of Jameson he kept on hand. "I'm Irish."

"Well then." King pulled out a glass and watched her pour a healthy measure before he gave himself a refill. "Have a seat. Ron is sending what you need and some security. I don't know why it's taking him so long."

She sat then sipped her drink. "Oh, that's good. It's Saturday. Maybe that's why. We just added a laptop and phone to the order too." She took another sip then tucked her legs under her on the leather sofa. "I feel safe here. Maybe that's stupid but I'm going with it."

King just swallowed his own drink and watched her. Strong whiskey and she didn't even flinch. Interesting. And the way that tank slid around on her shoulder, it was obvious she hadn't bothered with a bra. Hot damn. Was she sending him a signal? Doubtful. He wasn't taking advantage of her after the trauma she'd gone through today, even though she was tempting as hell. When her dog scampered out from the kitchen, Conchita close behind, he was glad he'd stayed on his side of the living room.

"Snacks. Then I will take this sweet pup outside for a little walk on the grounds." Conchita set a tray of crackers, cheese, and a few of her special nibbles on the coffee table between them. "Anna told me you're expecting a delivery, King. I will tell Douglas to wait by the gate for it."

"Be careful, Conchita. And tell Doug that there will be a security team setting up outside the gate. They're being sent by Zenon, Anna's company. No one is to come through, not even the delivery guys. Doug should have them set the computers inside. The people who robbed Anna might think she's the real prize here." King got up and took a plate, loading it with cheese, crackers, and a couple of stuffed jalapeños. When YoYo begged for a bite, sitting up on his hind legs, he dropped a piece of cheese into his mouth.

Conchita put her hands on her hips and looked fierce. "I'll get my gun right now and tell Doug to strap on his. No one gets past us and your security system, King. So you both can relax and enjoy your drinks. We will take care of you here. Never doubt it." She told the same thing to King in Spanish using stronger language, which made him smile.

King answered in the same language, ignoring Anna's raised eyebrows. He didn't want either of his employees, who he'd known for years, taking chances.

"Thanks, Conchita, and thanks for walking my dog." Anna rubbed YoYo's ears. "Maybe I should go somewhere else. I don't want anyone getting hurt on my account."

"Nonsense. King wants you here and we are happy to have something to do. There are too many days when we are alone here. A little action? Doug will be in his element, fighting off bad guys. You will understand when you meet my man." The housekeeper picked up YoYo, then disappeared out the way she'd come.

"I hope you told her in Spanish not to take any chances." Anna sighed and reached for the plate of snacks.

"I did. Now you be careful of those green things. They're spicy." King bit into his, enjoying the burst of heat and flavor but not sure someone from Boston would like it.

Anna seemed to take that as a dare and raised one of the peppers to her lips. One bite and she flushed, gulping down the rest of her drink. She fanned her face. "You weren't kidding. What did I just eat?"

King told her then took her a glass of water. She drank it down then stood and walked over to look out the wide glass doors and the view of the lake.

"Thanks. You have a beautiful home, King. I appreciate this."

He stood beside her. "We'll eat outside later, when it's cooler. Winter will come back, you know. I'm sure Karen has left a jacket or coat in her closet. You're welcome to whatever you need."

She turned and looked up at him, her eyes shimmering with unshed tears. "I'm sorry you've been dragged into this. It's sounding dangerous."

He brushed the tank top strap that had fallen off her shoulder back into place. Too tempting, too soon.

"I'm glad I came along when I did. You didn't need to go through this alone." He turned her back to face the lake, holding her against him. "Now look out there where the sun is starting to set. I always find it soothing just to stare at that beautiful sight for a while. There are steps down the side of the hill to the boat dock. It's a long way, but I wanted water access. I have a runabout. I use it more in the summer when I'm in town."

"You're right. It's very nice." She swayed against him. "That drink wasn't my best idea. I'm fading fast, despite the jalapeño jolt."

"Why don't you head to your room and lie down for a while then? I'll wake you when the computers get here. Or later, when it's time for dinner." King kept his arms around her. She fit just right.

"Thanks, I will." She brushed her hand over his shirtfront. "See you later, cowboy." She patted him, just like she would her dog, then staggered away, down the hall toward her bedroom.

King watched the sway of her hips until she was out of sight and he heard her bedroom door close. He turned to stare out at his million-dollar view again. For once, it didn't soothe him at all. Water access. Yeah. Someone could bring in a boat and climb up those stairs. He had alarms on all the doors but disabling those was child's play for a professional. Shit. Now he had something new to worry about.

Chapter Three

"Delivery just arrived." Conchita came in carrying a laptop with a phone balanced on top. "Douglas is still down at the gate. You might want to get the other four-wheeler and meet him. There are quite a few components to the computer system. Guess Anna needs all of that." She set her two pieces on the coffee table. "I'm getting dinner started. Anna told me you two had a big lunch on Sixth Street. Any preferences for dinner?"

"Whatever you have on hand. She's new to Austin, so she might like to try some of your good Mexican food." King strode toward the garage. "Let's set her up in the library. I bet she'll like the view from there if she ever looks up from her keyboard."

"Where will *you* work?" Conchita frowned.

"Don't worry about it. I came to town to meet with a few legislators about that agricultural bill. At least one of them is playing hard to get. When I'm sure she's safe enough here, I'll head back to the capitol and get in some faces, make my pitch. I won't even be here all the time." King had already tried setting up a new lunch date with the senator and been given the runaround. He was afraid the ag bill was going to have to wait awhile. "I can put my laptop anywhere if it comes to that. I'm sure Anna does need a big rig. She writes complicated programs."

"You're really putting yourself out for a woman you just met." Conchita glanced down the hall. "Not that she doesn't seem nice." She smiled. "And very pretty."

"I've got a lot invested in Zenon. Ron Zenonsky should have done a better job protecting that investment." He frowned because he sounded like an asshole.

Gerry Bartlett

"Is that what Anna is, an investment?" Conchita stared at him like she didn't know him.

"She's the brains behind one." King gave that lake view one more look. Yes, he lived well and made a lot of money, but he'd never been obsessed with the bottom line and wasn't now. "Okay, it pisses me off that he didn't protect Anna like he should have. It was careless. He knew damned good and well that what she was working on was important. Not only is she valuable to the future of the company, but what she's creating can save lives. Now we know other people want her program bad enough to steal it. What if she'd been home when those thieves came after her computer?" He shook his head, trying to imagine Anna and her little .38 against professionals who could have been ruthless to get what they wanted.

"They could have hurt her. I'm glad you brought her here, King." Conchita sighed. "So many bad people in the world. It's a shame."

"Yes, it is." He opened the door to the attached garage and realized it had cooled off since they'd come in. "I'm thinking Ron must have a leak at Zenon. As soon as I get this computer stuff inside, I'm calling him back."

"Oh, you won't have to do that. He's outside, talking to Doug. He brought the computer system himself. A security crew as well." Conchita smiled. "I think he's finally taking Anna's safety seriously now. I will see about dinner. I have plenty if you want him to stay." She headed for the kitchen.

King grabbed the keys to a four-wheeler from by the door and punched the automatic garage door opener. So Ron had come to see Anna. About damned time. He backed out and headed down the driveway. Doug and Ron were standing next to a pile of boxes right inside the gate. He didn't think Doug's own four-wheeler would hold it all. It looked like Ron had brought an entire freaking computer lab.

There was a parked car outside the gate with two men keeping watch. The security team. They should have been out, patrolling the fence line. Maybe they were waiting for instructions. Ron's Tesla, black, with all the bells and whistles, was parked behind them. His old friend wouldn't drive his car down King's gravel drive, afraid rocks would damage his precious undercarriage. King pulled to a stop next to the boxes and climbed out.

"We were about to call you to come help. Let's load up." Ron reached out to shake his hand. "Where's Anna?"

"Taking a well-deserved nap. I think she's in shock." King picked up a box. "I should make you walk to the house. What were you thinking, leaving Anna unprotected until something like this happened?"

"Surely you don't think I could have predicted a move on her place." Ron hefted a box. Doug was right behind him with the biggest box. "We've intercepted some attempts to hack our servers but they were easily blocked. There was no reason to think any major players were going to do something like they did today."

"But someone *had* made a move." King settled behind the wheel and Ron got in the passenger seat. "Where are you going?"

"To see Anna, of course. To make sure she's all right, personally, and to put this computer system together for her. She's a valuable employee. I thought I made that clear." Ron sighed. "You were right to ream me out. I should have provided security for her sooner. Trouble is, Anna is quiet, works hard, and I just assumed she'd be okay. I had other things on my mind."

"Like digging yourself out of a bad marriage. I get it, pal. But that's no excuse. You have a lot of investors, me included, who are counting on you to take care of business. And a woman who could have been hurt because you took your eye off the ball at Zenon." King was glad he'd never been trapped by a manipulative woman like Ron's ex. It could have dire consequences.

"At least I got a beautiful daughter out of that fiasco." Ron turned when Doug made a noise. "I'm sure you've heard the story, Doug. Everyone has. Lesson learned, my man, a very expensive lesson learned. I've sworn off marriage. Never again."

Doug was a man of few words, his wife doing most of the talking. He just rolled his eyes as he loaded the last of the boxes into the back of his vehicle.

"Wait. Are you paying those men in that car to sit and drink coffee?" King gestured at the black car and the two men inside. "They should be doing something."

"What?" Ron frowned. "I told them to watch the gate."

"They should take turns walking the fence line." King turned to Doug, a former Marine. "What do you think, Doug?"

"I'll talk to them, tell them Mr. Z wants them patrolling. That okay with you, Mr. Zenonsky?" Doug waited by the gate.

"Sure. Whatever you think will keep Anna safe." Ron watched as Doug punched in the code to open the gate then approached the car. "Man, I can't tell you how much I appreciate you bringing Anna here, King. I sure couldn't take her to my house. I get Lea every Wednesday and alternate weekends. If the creeps try to come after Anna again, how could I risk my baby girl?" Ron held on to the roll bar when King started the vehicle and Doug shut the gate again. "You've got the right setup here. Isolation, security fence. I can't match that."

"You should have done something about Anna's security sooner." King stopped the vehicle in front of the garage. "Seriously, Ron, looks to me like she's the key to the success of this billion-dollar program and you did nothing to protect her."

"You're right." Ron stared at the closed garage door. "If she'd been hurt, or taken… Shit, man, I'm not used to thinking like that. You've known me a long time. I've built this company on my brains. Those two goons by the gate? I hired them from the same company that wired my headquarters for security. Found it on the internet when I started Zenon years ago. I have no idea if they're any good or not because no one's ever come after us before. I sure as hell don't own a gun, and don't want to. Certainly won't have one around my daughter."

"Then it's a good thing you didn't invite Anna to come work at your place. She packs a .38 Special." King would have laughed at the look on Ron's face if this wasn't so damned serious.

"You're shitting me."

"Nope. She was going to shoot me before I called you to verify that I was one of the good guys. The woman is not to be trifled with. Keep that in mind, boss man." King climbed out of the four-wheeler. "Let's unload."

"She obviously has more to her than I realized. A dangerous woman. Am I crazy to think that's hot?" Ron grabbed a box and followed King inside. "Obviously my brain doesn't work where women are concerned."

Doug laughed as he carried his own load inside. "I can tell you, strong women can be a handful." He shut up when Conchita came out of the kitchen and directed them to the library.

"What is so funny, *mi amor?* I am worried about Anna. We must keep her safe." She took King's laptop when he handed it to her. "Look at all of this new equipment. Don't scratch King's desk. Wait! I will put a tablecloth over it. That is zebra wood. Very expensive." She hurried out of the library.

Doug pulled out a knife and began cutting open boxes. "She means it. Don't scratch the wood. She takes pride in everything in this house being perfect."

"Was that sarcasm, Douglas?" Conchita was back and covered the desk with a snowy tablecloth. "There. That's better. Anna won't have to worry about what she does here." She walked over to her husband and patted his back. "Of course I take pride in my work. And I expect every bit of that packing material to be taken out to the garage to the recycle bins when you men are done. *Sí?*"

"Of course, my love." Doug stood and kissed her cheek.

"Conchita, you can relax. You know I don't care about the desk." King handed Ron each piece of equipment as it was unwrapped. He had no clue what most of it was for. He used computers for their convenience but didn't have a love affair with them. Not like Ron did. His friend started to describe details about the equipment as he hooked it up, but King held up his hand to stop him. "Spare me, Ron."

"Ha! I do care about your furniture. Will Mr. Ron be staying for dinner?" Conchita leaned over to where the computer expert had crawled under the desk to plug something in. "Mr. Ron?"

"Sure. Count me in." He gestured and King handed him a bundle of wires. "This may take a while."

"Dinner will be ready whenever Anna wakes up." Conchita hurried out of the room.

Ron was in his element, putting together the complicated system for Anna. He had them leave her replacement laptop in the living room, intent instead on setting up the desktop computer with backup and a printer that could interface directly to his office.

"Your Wi-Fi is fast, but I'll jack it up even more. Then I'm adding firewalls. Even so, I'm leery about her sending out anything over the internet that might be hacked." Ron soon had the computer up and running.

He worked the keyboard so fast King turned to stare out the window. He used two fingers on his own keys and still made mistakes.

"Maybe she shouldn't work here. You can keep her safe in your office, can't you?" King asked when the keyboard had gone silent.

"Yeah, but these computer geniuses work odd hours when they get struck with inspiration. Anna did her best work at home. She'd come in with a problem solved after she'd been up in the middle of the night and worked for hours." Ron laughed. "It's weird, but sometimes we solve problems in our sleep."

"He's right." Anna spoke from the doorway. "Mr. Z, uh, Ron. You brought all that here?"

"Sure did. Sit and see what you think." Ron got up from behind the desk. "How are you, Anna? I'm sorry about your place. I hope you know I'll cover your losses. Everything that was damaged or even touched by those thieves. My fault for not taking your safety seriously." He nodded toward where King still stood next to the window. "King's already ripped me a new one for failing to provide you with proper security."

"King! How could Ron know this would happen?" Anna had approached the computer layout and stroked the forty-inch monitor like it was a diamond bracelet. "This is a beauty—4K."

King just watched the two computer geeks talk bits and shits as Ron explained what he'd brought. Anna had changed clothes, wearing her jeans again and a loose blue shirt that he recognized as one of his sister's. It matched her eyes. Not that he got to check that out up close since she was totally engrossed in computer talk with Ron. He was clearly forgotten. Then he heard his name.

"I can't stay here with King. You wasted your time bringing all this. We're strangers, and I'm imposing on him. Surely we can figure out someplace for me to crash that's safe enough for me to finish the program." Anna took one more longing look at the computer then faced her boss. "Seriously. I'm not comfortable with this arrangement."

"Get comfortable, Anna. King has offered his home and I think we should be grateful for it." Ron walked over to slap King on the back. "Where else would you have such security? Did you see the coded gate? His fence? Is it electrified, King?"

"No, there's too much wildlife in these woods that would be harmed for that. But the house is wired to alert us to intruders, and we have cameras that we can monitor at the gate and around the perimeter. You're safe here, Anna." King hoped so, anyway. He was counting on no one knowing she was here. But then Ron had arrived in that flashy car. If someone at Zenon was working for the bad guys, they might have put a tail on him.

"See? And you've got a world-class cook like Conchita in the kitchen." He sniffed. "Do I smell her enchiladas?"

"I think you do." King realized Anna wasn't happy. "We'll talk over dinner. If you can come up with a better solution, I'll personally help you move." He took her elbow and eased her out of the library. Of course she gave that computer setup a last glance. She was obviously dying to try it. "You need to eat first, work later. Unless we have to waste time finding you a new place to crash."

"I'm not trying to be difficult. But this is an imposition." Anna stopped at the open French doors then walked to the dining table set up on the deck outside. "Oh, look at the lights reflecting off the water. The view is spectacular, King. I don't think I really appreciated it earlier. I wasn't myself."

"Yes, he has quite a place here." Ron greeted Conchita. "You fixed my favorite, *Señora*. Enchiladas. And I see guacamole, rice, and *frijoles*." He gave her a hug. "We're trying to persuade Anna to work here. Your food should win her over."

"It certainly smells good. What are *frijoles?*" Anna slid into a chair.

The air was cool and King saw her shiver. He grabbed a throw from the living room and draped it over her shoulders. "Beans. Conchita makes some of the best. I can't say *the* best or my *abuela* would kill me."

"*Abuela?*" Anna smiled and pulled the throw around her. "Why do I feel like I'm in a foreign country?"

"*Abuela* means 'grandmother' in Spanish. King's grandmother is from Mexico. She's a wonderful cook." Conchita hovered next to the table. "I didn't know what you wanted to drink. You want to open a bottle of wine, King? I can make some margaritas. Or I have iced tea."

"No alcohol for me. I want to work tonight. If I don't move." Anna smiled at Conchita. "I'd love some iced tea. That's a Texas thing I'm getting used to. But not the sweet kind. Just with lemon, please."

"Sounds good." Ron pushed the dish of enchiladas toward her. "Eat. And think about how convenient this will be. King is one of our investors at Zenon. So he has a vested interest in seeing your program become successful."

"You told me that before." Anna stopped filling her plate. "I'm still finding it hard to believe. That I met him accidentally and he's connected to the company."

"Call it fate. Two people who happened to be in the right place at the right time. A dozen other people walked past you when you were about to faint and ignored you. I couldn't do it. I was raised to help anyone, man or woman, who is in distress. The fact that we have something in common, like the company you work for, is a bonus." King took a glass of tea. "Thanks, Conchita." He stared at Anna, willing her to believe him. Why the hell this was so important to him, he didn't know. But the idea of her in some unknown place, vulnerable, made him uncomfortable. Okay, maybe that word wasn't strong enough.

"It's weird." She put a timid spoonful of beans on her plate.

"Whatever it was that brought us together, you're here now, and it would be silly and maybe dangerous for you to look for another place when you're comfortable here. I won't bother you while you work. I have my own things to do while I'm in town." King passed her the guacamole after taking a big portion for himself. There were fresh tortilla chips on the table and he piled them on his plate. "Relax. You think I get meals like this every night? Conchita pulled out all the stops for you." He dipped up the green avocado dip with a chip and bit into it. "Delicious."

"I'm happy to have someone besides King to cook for." Conchita smiled and set a bowl of sliced lemons on the table next to Anna. "King is out too much when he is in town. You stay and work and I will have fun feeding you. Douglas will help guard the gate and we will play with your dog. Right now, your YoYo is out on the grounds with my man, looking for squirrels to chase. It is good for them both to have something to do. Please stay."

Anna dipped her fork into the beans, tasted, then smiled. "I guess I'd be stupid to say no. I wanted an adventure in Texas and it looks like I have one. Count me in."

* * * *

Anna had to admit, being served a delicious meal while looking at a million-dollar view was something she could get used to. But then there were distractions here she sure didn't have in her bland little apartment.

First, there were the two men who clearly had nothing better to do than to fix themselves an after-dinner drink and talk about the ongoing basketball season. When they'd seen her grab her replacement phone, they'd given her privacy to get her numbers restored and catch up with texts and emails from her friends and family back home. She decided there was no reason to explain her move or the delay in answering any of them. She just sent them a quick response, enough to let them know she was okay. For now, anyway.

Ron Zenonsky kept watching her, probably worried she'd have a meltdown and be unable to continue her work. She'd noticed King, on the other hand, had zoned out when she and Ron went over the new equipment. Clearly her host wasn't into tech.

Too bad her boss was off limits. He was just her type, smart and able to talk her language. Ron wore neatly pressed designer shirts and jeans and had his medium brown hair professionally styled. Cute. No surprise that he was pale compared to King Sanders. If Ron ever got out in the sun, it was only because his four-year-old daughter dragged him out to watch her play in his pool.

"Are you all right, Anna?" Ron finally asked what he'd obviously been wondering.

"Yes, no, I don't know." She fell onto the couch next to King. "I feel like my world has been turned upside down." She tapped her phone. "Crooks have my old phone. They'll probably break into it and…"

"Nothing. It was deactivated as soon as you called me. Mona saw to that. It's nothing but a paperweight now." Ron smiled. "You think we didn't take care of that? How do you like your new one? The latest upgrade. Facial recognition."

"It's cool." Anna meant it. She loved tech. She felt King looking over her shoulder and handed it to him. "Just came out. I'll have fun exploring all the features."

"Anyone worried about you, Anna?" King frowned at it, clearly mystified by the fact that the familiar buttons on his phone were missing and it was smooth glass. He passed it back with a shrug.

"No. My family is used to me ignoring my phone when I'm in the zone. They know this program is my priority right now." She sighed and leaned back against the soft leather. "I'm so close to finishing too. It's important to all of us. I got interested in it because of my grandmother. She almost died because of a drug interaction. We thought she had dementia. Turned out her confusion and other symptoms were caused by the combination of drugs she was taking."

"No kidding!" King stared at her. "So this isn't just a job to you, it's personal."

"That's right." She stood. "Which is why I'm anxious to get back to it. My notebook had some things I'd jotted down last night that I want to try tonight, so I have to recreate my notes." She rubbed the back of her neck. "Do you think I could make some coffee? It helps me stay sharp."

"Conchita will fix you a pot. We can set it up in the library for you." King was on his feet, close beside her. He told her the security code for his Wi-Fi. It was ridiculously simple and made Ron smile.

"Bud, no one should use their phone number for access like that. Tighten up." Ron stood and headed for the bar. "At least throw in a word or two."

"He's right. After I get in, I'll change it to something stronger and write it down for you. Now, surely Conchita goes off duty after dinner. I hate to bother her." Anna turned to Ron. "Thanks for bringing the computer system here. It's even better than what I had before."

"You deserve the best, Anna." Ron set his empty glass on the bar. "Don't work too hard. You've been through a traumatic experience. You should take a night off."

Anna was tempted to take that night off. She was so tired. No, a jolt of caffeine would fix her. "I can't. The sooner this is done, the sooner people can be helped. My grandma is fine now, but she could have died or ended up in a nursing home because of her meds." She headed toward the kitchen. "I'm going now. Good night, gentlemen."

"Good night."

She heard the rumble of male voices and the front door close, then the roar of a four-wheeler. King must be driving Ron to his car. She found Conchita cleaning the kitchen and arranged for a pot of coffee and a mug for the library. It took some persuading, but she finally got the housekeeper to leave for her own place.

"I can't believe Conchita didn't insist on setting up a coffee service in here." King almost startled her into dropping the mug.

"She wanted to. I had to bully her to go home. By tomorrow I'm sure I'll have a mini kitchen at my fingertips in here." Anna carefully set the mug next to her keyboard. Her fingers were itching to explore this new gear. She hoped King wasn't going to make a pest of himself. But then, she *was* in his office. "Do you need to get something? Am I in your way? This isn't going to work, is it?"

He stared at her for a moment. "It's fine. Except I'm worried about you. Have you dealt with today's trauma? Where's your dog?"

"YoYo's with Doug and Conchita." Anna felt a stab of guilt. "Honestly? I think it makes her nervous, having the dog in here with your expensive rugs. They love him already and she really wanted to keep him out there so I agreed. I'll get YoYo in the morning for a walk. My work schedule isn't kind to him. He doesn't rest well when I pull an all-nighter."

"You're pulling an all-nighter?" King shook his head. "After what you've just been through?"

"I have to, King. I want to try to recreate my notes while they're fresh." She sipped her coffee. Yes, that helped, even though exhaustion made her lean back in his ergonomic chair and wonder where and how to start.

"You're crazy. How productive can you be after the day you've had?" He stood beside her and pulled her to her feet. "Come on, admit it. The notes can't be that important. They're just notes!" His hands tightened on her arms. "Ron does not expect you to push yourself so hard. He told you as much."

"I push myself." Anna jerked out of his grasp. "This is important to me! Don't you get it? I've spent years on this project. Years. I'm close, really close, to finishing. I have to keep going."

"What I get is that when you're tired you make mistakes." He wasn't backing off. He just stood there, so sure of himself, so tall and strong and masculine.

Anna inhaled. And swayed, almost falling back into the leather office chair. Well, hell. He was right. She couldn't run on fumes and expect to produce any quality work. And as for those notes? Her brain was mush. The only thing in her head right now was this man in front of her smelling like something spicy and delicious. Okay, that was proof enough that she might as well call it a night. She didn't have the energy to even lift her hand to her keyboard, much less explore the arms that reached for her again and lifted her into—

"What the hell are you doing?" Her head fell against his chest. He'd picked her up, his arm firm under her butt as he carried her out of the room.

"Taking you to bed. Do you realize your eyes were closing? Woman, you need a keeper. And, for now, I'm it." He kicked open her bedroom door and laid her on the queen-sized bed. "Do I need to undress you?"

Anna stared up at him. She found a smile. "Try and I'll pull my gun from this bedside table drawer."

"All right then." He did reach down and jerk off her tennis shoes. "See you tomorrow." He dropped the shoes beside the bed and walked out, quietly shutting the door behind him.

Anna lay there, mustering the energy to get up and take off her clothes, brush her teeth, and put on her new sleep shirt. By the time she was in bed again and enjoying a truly great mattress and high-thread-count sheets, she realized she could never have accomplished a thing on her computer after the day she'd had. She ran her hand over the pillowcase, a pretty pink, then pulled the extra pillow to her and hugged it close. Comfort. She needed it. Because her life was a mess and there was no denying it.

* * * *

"Your phone is ringing and ringing." Conchita stared down at her. "I think someone may be worried about you. You're getting texts too. You'd better answer."

"What time is it?" Anna sat up, feeling like she'd been flattened by a semi. Crazy, when everything that had happened to her yesterday had drained her emotionally, not physically.

"After ten. You needed the sleep so King said to leave you to it." Conchita handed her the new phone. "I'm fixing waffles. I hope you like them."

"Sounds delicious." Anna glanced at the texts. "Oh, it's Sunday!"

"All day. I'll bring you coffee."

"Thanks." Anna hit the last message and realized her friend was frantic. She hit speed dial.

"Anna, where are you? I came by for our usual brunch date and your bike is here but you didn't answer the door. So I got worried and used the key you gave me. Your apartment is a disaster! Were you robbed?" Scarlett Hall sounded breathless. "Do I need to call the police?"

"I'm okay. But, yes, I was robbed."

"Where the hell are you?" Scarlett sounded mad now. "Why didn't you call me?"

"I just got a phone. It was stolen too. I'd like to explain it all but you have to calm down. Don't call the police, it's been handled." Anna reached out for the mug of coffee Conchita handed her. "Thanks."

"Why are you thanking me? Explain. Handled? How? I can't calm down. I'm sitting in what used to be your place and it's been destroyed. Your beloved computer is gone and so is your precious dog. Is YoYo okay?" Scarlett's voice broke.

"Hold it. For God's sake, don't cry. YoYo's fine. Though those creeps who broke in left him loose in the parking lot. He could have been run over." Anna realized her coffee mug was shaking and she set it on the nightstand. What might have happened to her dog still made her heart stutter. As if she'd called him, YoYo jumped on the bed and sat in her lap. She rubbed his ears and kissed the top of his head. He'd obviously had a bath in some kind of herbal shampoo. Conchita's idea, no doubt. Or had it been Doug's? Tears filled her eyes at their kindness.

"My God! Where are you? I'll come get you. You can stay with me." Scarlett was in fix-it mode now. "We can ride into work together tomorrow."

"I'm staying with one of Ron's friends. The boss bought me a new computer setup and I'm working from here. The guy is an investor in Zenon and it's a beautiful place with good security on one of the lakes. Obviously this theft was espionage. Someone wants to steal my program." Anna picked up her coffee and leaned back against the padded headboard.

"Ron? You mean Mr. Z? You're calling him Ron now? How did that come about? Who is this friend?" Scarlett kept firing questions. "Anna! Answer me. I want to see you. Hear every little detail. Give me an address. I'm on my way." Scarlett sounded very determined.

Anna didn't know what to say. Was she allowed to give out King's address? Could Scarlett be followed here? She looked up and King stood in the doorway.

"I don't know, Scarlett. I don't think I can tell you where I am. I'm here to work on my special program. I won't be coming into the office, it's not safe." She saw King nod.

"What the fuck, Anna? Are you being held prisoner? I don't like this one little bit. If I don't get to see you with my own eyes, I'm calling your brother, you know the one. First you're robbed and now you've disappeared? I'm sorry, pal, but you're not allowed to vanish. I'm not going to just let that go, you hear me?"

"Scarlett, calm down. You can't make waves like that. Talk to Mr. Zenonsky tomorrow at the office. He can explain everything."

"I'm not waiting until tomorrow. Not when I'm sitting in your place where there's drawers emptied and underwear strewn from the bathroom to the living room. Plus you won't tell me where the hell you are!"

"Okay, okay. I'll give you Mr. Z's phone number. You can call him right now. Would that make you feel better?"

"I'm not sure. I really want to see you, pal. We were supposed to have this Texas adventure together. And now you're missing?" Scarlett's voice had gone up several octaves and she sounded like she was hyperventilating. "We've only been here a couple of months and I don't know Mr. Z from Adam. I swear I'm calling Chance and getting the FBI on this if I don't get some answers pronto."

"I get it. I love you too, Scarlett. Let me see what I can arrange. For God's sake, leave Chance and the FBI out of it." Anna looked down and saw King holding out his phone, Ron's phone number displayed for her. "Here's Mr. Zenonsky's cell number. He'll answer, I'm sure of it." She rattled it off. "Call him. Listen to what he has to say. He's been terrific about the break-in. He's paying for all my stuff to be replaced and has already brought me a new computer system, a fabulous setup."

"I don't want to hear it. I know you. Buy you a tower with a bunch of RAM or whatever and you'd follow a man anywhere." Scarlett was near tears again. "Damn it, Annie, this reeks. You'd better be okay."

"Call me again after you talk to Ron. I swear I'll keep my phone by my side. Okay?"

"Okay."

Anna ended the call.

"Sounds like you have a good friend there." King stepped back from the bed. He took YoYo with him. "Breakfast is almost ready."

"Good, I'm starved. Yes, Scarlett is an old and dear friend. She came with me from Boston and is an office manager at Zenon. Our old boss made a special deal when he sold the company. Zenon had to take a certain number of employees with the purchase. Scarlett's not into computers like I am but she's an organizational whiz."

"Then I'd probably like her. We have a lot in common." King grinned. "You and Ron made me feel pretty damned dumb last night."

"Sorry about that." Anna waved him away. "Leave so I can get ready for that breakfast."

He did and took her dog with him, closing the bedroom door behind him. Not into computers. Why did that suddenly seem like a good thing?

Her former boyfriends had shared her love of all things that go click in the night—which had made for lots of screen time and little between-the-sheets time. And that time spent horizontally hadn't exactly been full of fireworks. Was she crazy for imagining that King would know his way around a woman's body with a heck of lot more finesse than a guy who got most of his experience from videos on the web?

Anna shivered, imagining King's big tanned hands roaming over her and finding spots that could make her scream. She'd never thought of herself as particularly passionate, not about anything but the latest software. But suddenly she was very aware of what she'd been missing, stuck in her cave, working too much and rarely playing.

Her pal Scarlett certainly never denied herself pleasure. She'd had at least two boyfriends in the months since they'd hit Austin. Both relationships had been flaming hot but had burned out quickly. Of course, that was Scarlett's pattern. She tended to leap then look, figuring out later that there was chemistry but little else to hold her to a man. Anna was the opposite. She was slow to commit, needing that connection to be solid before she'd give a guy a real chance. So what was she doing daydreaming about hitting the sack with the stranger down the hall?

Her limited wardrobe wasn't exactly going to help her cause if she did decide to break her cautious pattern and hit that hottie. She put on her new bra and a loose orange University of Texas sweatshirt. Her jeans were too far gone and she ended up tugging on some knit workout pants King's obviously tall sister had stashed in a drawer in her bedroom, rolling them up at the waist. Conchita had encouraged her rummage through those drawers, though Anna had hated doing that. Everything she'd found had been expensive and looked new.

The full-length mirror in the attached bathroom convinced her that she wasn't going to have King chasing her around the house for a fling in this outfit. Just as well. She had work to do and he had his own business to deal with. Good. But makeup from Karen's stash and an effort to tame her hair was just a matter of personal pride. Her mother would have insisted.

Anna decided she'd stalled long enough and headed to the kitchen with her empty coffee mug. Conchita gave her a refill and looked her over while Anna added cream and sugar.

"You look better, *chica*. You must have slept well." Conchita patted her shoulder.

"I passed out. That bed is very comfortable. Where are we eating? Not outside again."

"No, it's cold this morning. This crazy weather. In the breakfast room. Through there." Conchita picked up a platter of bacon and pointed at a door. "You will see. It is a beautiful view. King likes to look at the lake."

Anna held the swinging door open and Conchita preceded her. There was a round table with six chairs. Placemats were set for two and a coffee carafe sat in the middle of the table, along with butter and syrup. King stood when he saw her and pulled out a chair.

"Finally. I waited for you." He snagged a piece of bacon and fed it to YoYo, who sat beside his chair.

"You shouldn't have waited." Anna grabbed a piece of bacon for herself. "This is a treat." She chewed, sighing when Conchita brought in a platter of Belgian waffles. "Surely you don't eat like this every day. You wouldn't look like you do if you did."

"And how do I look?" King grinned as he speared a waffle with his fork.

"In shape." She took her own waffle and reached for the butter. "How do you stay that way?"

"I run most mornings. You have the shoes for it, I noticed them yesterday. Do you run?" He grabbed the syrup and drizzled it over the waffle.

"Sometimes. My friend Scarlett bought them for me. She's trying to motivate me to get out in the fresh air and exercise. Away from the computer. Since we haven't heard from her, I guess Ron talked her off the ledge." Anna smiled thinking about Scarlett. "She's always been protective of me. We met in junior high, in physical ed." Anna could laugh about it now, but then it had been the worst day of her life. "I was the slowest runner in class. Even fell down at the start of a race, if you can believe it." She glanced at King but he just sipped coffee, waiting for her to finish her story. "I just lay there, wishing I could die. You're so dramatic when you're thirteen."

"Hey, anyone can trip. Was your shoelace untied?" King put down his mug.

"No such luck. I was trying too hard. Tripped over my own two feet. So I lay there, spitting out gravel, the kind they put on those tracks, and praying for invisibility. Then here came Scarlett. She was one of the fastest runners in the school. She pushed everyone else aside, even one of her teammates on the track team who was taunting me. 'Anna Banana, slipped on her own peel.'" Anna laughed again. "That was actually pretty clever coming from that bonehead. Anyway, Scarlett helped me up and took me to the nurse to doctor my bleeding knees. Oh, yeah, I was scraped up good. Then she asked for my help in math, making a big deal later about her pal, the brain. We've been friends ever since."

"I can see why. And don't worry, I won't make you go running with me." King grinned. "You want to discuss that phone call? You really had to talk fast. She was obviously upset."

"Scarlett threatened to call my brother in Boston if I don't meet with her and show her I'm all right." Anna took a bite of waffle and savored it. "I should probably do it."

King worked his way through one waffle and started on a second. "Maybe you should warn your family, let them know you're okay."

"And have them go into protective mode?" Anna almost choked. "Chance, my oldest brother, is in the FBI. That's all we need, to bring the FBI into this."

"I don't know. The Feds can provide some powerful resources. Ron is against asking for help because he's afraid the competition or our other investors will get wind of it, but I'm more concerned about your safety." King laid down his fork. "Seriously, if you'd been in the apartment when they'd come after that computer, Anna…"

"I wasn't, and I think they planned it that way." She stabbed the waffle, her appetite gone. Damn it. He'd better stop bugging her about this. "Clearly they'd been waiting for me to leave, King. I'd been holed up in that apartment for days, working nonstop, then the one day I go somewhere, they hit it. Don't you think that's how they wanted it?"

"Maybe so." He picked up his fork again. "I'm changing the subject since this one has you riled up. So. Tell me something."

"Good. I don't want my family involved. That subject is closed." She swirled a bite of waffle into syrup and tried to decide if she wanted it or not. "What do you want to know?"

"Why you don't have the accent? I've known people from Boston before. They talk with a broader 'a,' you know what I mean. 'Pawhk the cawhr.' Instead of 'park the car.'" He smiled. "You sound more Midwestern."

"That's an easy one. My mom is from Kansas City. She arrived in Boston at eighteen to attend college. She met my dad when she was protesting for women's rights and he arrested her. Dad is a cop. Believe it or not, it was love at first sight. Mom insists we speak Midwest English. She's a professor now, at Harvard, brilliant. Dad's a captain with the Boston PD. My brothers are all law enforcement in one way or another, very protective. If I called them about the break-in, I guarantee at least one of them would show up here and try to drag me back home." Anna gave up on eating. "That would make it difficult, if not impossible, for me to finish my project."

"You don't have to do what they say." King put his hand over hers. It was warm, comforting. But a little sticky from the syrup.

"You have no idea the kind of pressure they can bring to bear." Anna pushed back from the table. "I need to get to work. We may have to arrange for Scarlett to come here, to see for herself that I'm okay. Otherwise, she may well call one of my brothers. She's known them most of her life and is just as protective of me as they are. She'd see it as her duty to call them if she's afraid I'm in trouble."

"You *are* in trouble, Anna." King jumped to his feet and walked with her to the library. "Ron has been busy this morning, even though it's a Sunday. I asked him last night if there could be anyone inside the company who might be working with the thieves. You know, someone jealous of the attention you and your program are getting. Seems like Ron's pouring a lot of money into this one project. But he laid off people in another department last fall."

"I don't know about that." Anna thought about it. "I really don't know many people there. Only four of us came from Boston. Scarlett is in the office and the other two are hardware people. Not my area." She'd been surrounded by strangers. No one had been particularly welcoming, but not nasty either. "He's let me work from home a lot. Then he sent me out of town to those special classes. Scarlett said that caused a bit of an uproar in the office. Some of the long-time employees have been asking for special training for years and he never sent anyone else."

"There you go. Motive. Do you think she can come up with names for Ron? He's checking out every Zenon employee anyway. Looking for cash payoffs in bank records, expensive purchases, things like that. He's into it. Playing detective." King frowned. "Jealousy is a powerful motive. People have done some really bad things in the name of it."

"Call Ron and tell him to check with his secretary. Mona knows everyone and everything happening at Zenon." Anna put a hand on her stomach. She'd enjoyed her new role in Texas, happy to be appreciated. It hadn't occurred to her that someone might think she was getting perks that they deserved. "Do you really think it could be someone at the company who broke in to my place?" Could it be someone she knew? Someone who'd worked side by side with her?

"He just started looking. But he's hired more security, and I'm going to post someone to watch the boat dock at the back of the house." King glared out the wide window with the view of the lake like he hated it.

"Seriously? Isn't that a little extreme?" Anna felt her phone vibrate in her pants pocket and pulled it out. Finally, Scarlett calling her back. She answered. "Hey, pal, you convinced I'm okay now?"

"You may be okay, but your little friend isn't." The male voice was deep and had the same Texas drawl King had.

"Who is this? Where's Scarlett? How did you get her phone?" Anna hit the command for speaker and held the phone so King could hear.

"Think you're so clever, don't you, Anna Delaney, with your heavy-duty password and encryption? We got your backpack too. Bet that got your goat, computer gal."

"I don't care about that." Anna's hand was shaking so hard she would have dropped the phone if King hadn't grabbed on to hold it steady. "What have you done to Scarlett? Let me talk to her."

"You want to talk to your gal pal, give us the encryption key for that program of yours."

"Not until I hear her voice." Anna swallowed bile. Scarlett, so brave. She'd probably do something to make these people mad. Make things worse. Calm, she had to be the voice of reason here. Anna had a brother in SWAT. This was a hostage negotiation. Oh, God. "Prove to me she's all right. I want her safe and away from you before you get access to my program."

"As if we're letting you call the shots." The voice was nasty and sent shudders through her. "Here's your proof of life. For now."

"Anna! Don't give these assholes anything!"

"Scarlett!" Anna heard a scream, a clatter, and the phone went dead.

Chapter Four

"Oh God!" Anna stared down at the phone. "I have to…" She hit Recent and called Scarlett's number. It was answered immediately.

"Your friend is a real bitch. Send the fucking thing right now or I'll carve my own key into her lily-white cheek. You can guess which one." There was another scream.

"No! I can't. But don't hurt her." Anna reached for King but he'd stepped away and was talking rapidly on his own phone.

"Too late. She'll live, for now. But she'd better learn to control that smart mouth." His nasty laugh made chills go through Anna.

"I swear to God, you'll never get that encryption key if you keep hurting her." Anna realized King was waving at her. He mouthed a question. She jotted down the number on a piece of paper and threw it at him. "Scarlett Hall is my best friend in the world. You kill her and you'll get nothing from me except the FBI and the entire Boston Police Department on your ass for the rest of your worthless life." Anna saw King nod. Apparently he was having someone locate the signal coming from Scarlett's cell phone. The police, of course. She had to keep this creep talking while that happened.

"Hollow threats." A different voice took over, no drawl this time. "My cohort has a temper. Ms. Hall shouldn't keep testing him. Now give me the encryption key and we'll dump her pretty ass at the nearest big parking lot. We're wearing surgical masks to protect our identities, so I doubt the woman will be able to pick us out of a lineup. You see? We've planned well and are perfectly willing to release her safely."

"I don't trust you. That cohort, as you call him, sounded like he *wanted* to hurt her. I bet he gets off on inflicting pain." Anna saw King give her a thumb's up. Progress. She had to keep these men talking. "I heard Scarlett scream again. Put her on the phone. I want to be sure she's still alive and in one piece before I give you anything."

"You aren't in any position to make demands. I sense a hidden agenda here. We've been on the phone too long. Not trying to pinpoint our location, are you?"

"How could I do that?" Ann sobbed. "Damn it, leave Scarlett alone and let her go. She doesn't know a damned thing about my program."

"Oh, I realize that. Your very best friend in the world? She's leverage, Anna. Now give me the encryption key, or shall I turn this woman over to my violent companion? Time is running out."

"No, please. Here." Anna rattled off some of the digits. Of course she'd memorized the complicated sequence. She'd used full disk encryption, which required her complicated password key to even open her computers. Without the key, her entire system, even her laptop, was worthless. The thieves must have been livid when they'd found that out. Oh, God. What were they doing to Scarlett?

"Do you think I'm as dumb as your friend here? That's not all of it."

Anna heard a scream and a sob. "Stop! I told you I need to hear Scarlett's voice again. When she tells me she sees the parking lot where you're going to release her, then you'll get the rest of it. It's a long sequence. As a sign of good faith, here's another section." Anna gripped the desk chair armrests. She forced herself to take steadying breaths. She couldn't afford to hyperventilate now. The digits in her key ran through her mind. She couldn't make a careless mistake either.

"Repeat what you've given me so far," the man demanded, then echoed them back. "Here's your friend. Son of a bitch! She bit me." There was the sound of a slap.

"Anna! Don't give these bastards the fucking key. This means too much to you. I'm fighting. They'll be sorry they ever—" Scarlett sobbed. "Sirens! Police are coming. I don't know how—"

"Clever, aren't you? Give me the rest of the key right now and we'll throw this bitch out in the parking lot. Fail me and you'll never see her again." He meant business, Anna didn't doubt it. "The sirens are approaching. We're leaving in ten seconds, with or without the woman. Ten, nine, eight..."

Anna gave him the rest of the code. The man repeated the digits back to her.

"There we go. Worked like a charm. And your friend has just done a face-plant on the parking lot of an abandoned Food Mart. Hmm. That had to have hurt." The phone went dead.

Anna fell back, panting like she'd run a race and lost. Scarlett. Was she really in the parking lot? Or on her way to God knew where? Her phone vibrated in her hand and she almost dropped it.

"Annie! It's me. They threw my phone out with me." Scarlett was crying. "I can't believe you did that. Gave up your program for me."

"Forget that. Where are you? Are you all right?" Anna waved King over. "It's Scarlett. Are you really in a parking lot? Are the police there?"

"Yeah. Cops just pulled up. Two cars. I'll call you back." The phone went dead again.

"She didn't say how she was. If she's hurt." Anna pressed her hands to her eyes, her phone in her lap. "Oh, God, I hate this fucking program."

"Hang on. Mike's talking to one of the cops on the scene." King was still on his phone. "Tell me what's happening. How is she?" He paused. "She's hurt, but nothing life threatening, Anna."

"Thank God!" Anna bowed her head. But there had been those screams. So there *had* been injuries, horribly painful ones.

"She said it was a white panel van, no markings. Gone before the cops got there. That narrows it down to about a thousand. A woman was driving?" King glanced at Anna. "Yeah, a woman took Anna's backpack. So three of them in the van." He listened. "She won't? Are you sure?" He glanced at Anna. "Then can someone bring her here after she's made a statement? Yeah, thanks, Mike."

Anna jumped to her feet. "I want to go to her. Right now."

"Not a good idea. Officers on the scene say she's been roughed up. They called an ambulance but she's refusing anything but basic first aid." King slipped his phone into his pocket.

"What does that mean, roughed up?" Anna kept imagining something horrible carved into Scarlett's backside or, worse, her face.

"She's got a bruise on her face, some cuts on her arms, stuff like that. They used zip ties on her hands and feet. Those left marks."

"Oh, God." Anna hugged herself. "She needs me. Let's go." Scarlett was in Texas for their great adventure. And look what had happened.

"We'd only be in the way, Anna. Mike's going to meet her at the station and personally help her through her statement. He says Scarlett's claiming this was a random abduction. That there was talk of selling her to a brothel. She couldn't identify the men because they kept on surgical masks and caps. The woman never turned around, so she couldn't see her face, and she wore what was obviously a bad wig. Scarlett told the cops she got away because she made so much noise and fought so hard that they finally got sick of her and just tossed her out."

"You're kidding. And they're buying that?" Anna got up and stared out the window but didn't really see anything.

"Guess so." King came up behind her. She could feel his presence. "She hasn't mentioned the computer program even once. Can you believe that?"

"Of course I can. She's been protecting me since the seventh grade!" Anna was shaking and couldn't stop. "This is all my fault! I had to come here to finish my program when the old company was sold, she didn't. But she took the transfer too because she was worried I'd never get out from behind my computer if no one from home came with me to Texas. This all started because of my obsession with that damned program."

King pulled her into his arms. Anna let herself lean into him for just a minute. It felt good, to sink into his strength, to feel those strong arms around her.

"Come on now. Your friend is an adult. If she didn't want to come to Texas, she wouldn't have. Look at how tough she is. And loyal. She's protecting you and the company with that story, and keeping a lid on the leak at Zenon." King ran his hand up and down her back like she needed soothing. Maybe she did, but it seemed wrong. Who was soothing Scarlett?

"Fuck Zenon!" Anna shoved away from him. "The company and the program are the last things on my mind right now." She staggered back to the desk chair. Anna still thought she should be with Scarlett. Damn it, maybe it was time to learn to drive. If she had her own car, nothing and no one would stop her from getting to her pal's side.

"Mike. He's your police buddy, the one at the capitol. But he's not with the Austin Police Department. He's with the state police. They let him help with this?"

"He has connections at the APD. He can grease some wheels. Get her through the statement process as quickly as possible." King pulled out his phone again. "He's doing this as a favor to me. And because he's a good guy, Anna. He'll make sure she is taken care of properly. I guess we should call Ron and let him know what's happened."

"Wait." Anna got up and grabbed his arm. "Thanks, King. I really, really appreciate your help with this. I guess Mike was also the one who arranged to track Scarlett's phone signal."

"Yes. You can thank him when he gets here with your friend." He squeezed her hand. "I'm just sorry Scarlett got caught up in this. And that you lost your program."

Anna slipped her hand from his, then sat again to frown at her monitors. "Lost the program? Not really." If she couldn't go to Scarlett, there was one thing she could take care of, and she might as well get started. She began typing. She had to install security on this computer right now, some even more complex than what she'd been using. "Do call Ron. He needs to get over here. Now that Scarlett has been drawn into this and hurt, we need security on her too. Because when those creeps realize the program they got is a dummy..." She was glad something had gone right today. "Well, they won't be happy."

"Damn it, Anna, what the hell did you do?"

"Protected my work. It's that important, King." Why couldn't he look a little proud of her? Instead, he hit the desk, making her monitors wobble.

King frowned at her. "Damn it, they'll come back again, meaner than ever."

Anna froze. Could he be right? "Maybe. Or maybe they'll realize stealing software is harder than they thought and go on to an easier way to make money."

"Crooks don't think that way. You essentially made fools of them, Anna. They're going to want revenge." King stared until her fingers stopped on the keyboard. "I'm serious. You've made nasty enemies. They were looking for a big payday. Scarlett just found out the hard way that they can be as mean as snakes. Now they know they need *you* to get to the program and to finish it." He sat on the edge of the desk. "Quit gloating about outsmarting them and start thinking about how you can stay safe until this is in the marketplace. I assume you're doing something that will keep it from being knocked off once it's out there."

"Oh, sure. If I didn't, once it's for sale, anyone could clone it and make a cheaper version. Tweak it a bit and they can claim it's different enough not to violate copyright. I'm building in all kinds of safeguards. That's why they want my code. The original code." Anna sighed and leaned back. "There are ways this program can be subverted too. I want to use it for good. But if you have a different agenda..."

She did that thing she always did when she felt overwhelmed. She covered her eyes as if looking inward could help. It never did. In the wrong hands her program could hurt people. Seriously hurt people. Was that why someone wanted it? King was silent, waiting for her to look at him. She finally did.

"You're trying to scare me, aren't you?"

"Damn right I am. Is it working?" He looked solemn.

"Yes." She pulled out her phone. "Enough that I'm making a call I really don't want to make. Ron won't like it but I think it has to happen." She hit speed dial. Of course he answered on the first ring.

"Annie. What's shaking?"

"I am. Chance, I think I need the FBI." To her horror, she burst into tears.

* * * *

King decided to give Anna privacy for her call, but he'd heard enough to know he had to get Ron in the loop—and fast. This situation had escalated and his friend was not equipped to handle it.

"You need to get over here." He didn't waste time on hello.

"Why? What's happened?" Ron was obviously watching sports on TV. Must be nice.

"Turn down the volume and I'll tell you." He waited, then filled him in.

"Anna had actually set up a dummy program?"

"That's all you got out of that? Her friend Scarlett was kidnapped, Ron. Hurt and terrified." King shouldn't have been surprised. Technology first. Ron always had his head in the computer cloud. It had made him rich but didn't make him the most aware guy when it came to practical matters. "Your employees are at high risk. Those bastards are going to be livid when they realize they don't have what they wanted."

"Yeah. But how genius of her." Ron was all admiration. "A shadow program. She must have also used disk encryption. Cool."

"Here's the bottom line, bud: she's calling in her brother with the FBI. So you're going to have the Feds crawling up your ass anytime now." King almost took pleasure in the groan that he'd pulled from Ron.

"Seriously? She called him? Without checking with me first?"

"I think having her best friend held hostage and hurt was provocation enough. She's still on the phone with him, telling him what happened. She's understandably upset, Ron. Hell, devastated. And damned lucky she has the FBI on her speed dial. Scarlett is at the police station giving her statement right now. I don't know how the fuck you deserve such loyalty, but Scarlett hasn't mentioned the company or even computers to law enforcement. She's claiming sex traffickers took her, held her at knife point, and finally threw her out of their van when she raised too much Cain."

"No way. Is she seriously hurt? What did they do to her?" Ron was finally taking this seriously. "Scarlett's a great woman, has totally whipped my front office into shape. Even Mona listens to her."

"She was knocked around but refused to be taken to the emergency room to be checked out. I've got a buddy in the state police who's guiding her through her statement before he brings her here. Naturally, Anna wants to see her. And then we have to figure out security for Scarlett. Know what I mean?"

"Man, where does this end? Do I have to put guards on every person Anna might care about?" Ron took a deep breath. "Shit. I'm definitely making sure my own baby girl Lea has protection. I'd hand over the world to keep her safe."

"Of course you would. Just like Anna was willing to give up the key to her program for her best friend. Lucky for you she had a backup plan." King could see Anna had ended her call and sat with her eyes closed, leaning back in the desk chair. "Listen, I've got to go. Make a call and get a guard on your daughter, then get your butt over here. Watch your back while you do. Make sure you're not followed. Maybe the thieves haven't figured out yet that the program they're looking at isn't the right one, but we can't take that chance. You got something to drive besides that flashy Tesla?"

"Oh, yeah. An old hybrid in the garage. I might have to jump-start it." Ron sounded distracted.

"Then come in that. Pay attention and make sure you aren't followed here. You getting this?" As Ron reassured him he understood, King felt a bump on his leg. YoYo had joined them. "See you soon." He ended the call then picked up the dog and set him in Anna's lap.

"Oh, my baby." She opened her eyes and stroked the dog's head. "I zoned out there for a minute. My brother had some startling news. He quit the FBI a couple of months ago. Right after I left Boston."

"What does that mean for this situation?" King pulled up a chair.

"He's started his own security company. He insists on flying down here right away to check out what he calls my 'clusterfuck' before I end up in a van like Scarlett did." She took a shaky breath.

"A security company run by a former Fed. I like the sound of that." King hoped she was done with the tears but he could see she was close to starting up again. "We could use that kind of help."

"Ron should be happy we won't have the actual FBI involved." She picked up the dog and let him lick her cheek. "I can't believe Chance left the Bureau. He said my dad is freaking out about it."

"It's a big decision. Did he say why?" King didn't care, but he knew talking was keeping Anna's mind off Scarlett and her injuries.

"Too much bureaucracy. They were going to transfer him to a place he didn't want to go. He felt like his boss wasn't respecting him, and a few other reasons he said he didn't want to go into on the phone. My dad told him to man up. That's what you do in law enforcement. Do the job, take your lumps, and keep your nose to the grindstone, all of the clichés Chance didn't want to hear. So they had a big blowup." Anna put down the dog and looked at her computer screen. "I need to work on this security but I can't concentrate. And I don't understand why no one in the family told me what was going on with Chance."

"What could you do about it? From way down here?" King let YoYo scramble into his lap. "When is he going to get here? We need better security. Doug told me that he could see on the video that the night shift at the gate slept through most of it."

"Well, hell." Anna pushed back from the desk and stood. "Do you think it's safe for me to go outside and look at your million-dollar view from the deck? I want to see if it soothes me."

"Sure. I'll bring my gun." King followed her.

"Somehow that's not making me feel better." She frowned, then stuck her phone in the waistband of her pants. "No pockets. Chance will let me know when he can get a flight and what time it'll arrive. He said he'll rent a car at the airport. You'll have to give him your address when he gets here. I don't have any idea where we are, if you want to know the truth."

"I'll be glad to meet your brother. Tell me more about him. Though I already like him better than the slackers we've got." King knew his house was hard to find in the best of circumstances, and that was deliberate. He followed Anna out to the deck.

"He went into the military after college and did a couple of tours in Afghanistan. I can tell you we were all terrified about that. Thank God he came out safely and almost in one piece. Then he went to law school." Anna leaned against the railing and looked out at the lake.

"Interesting choice." King stood next to her. The breeze was cool today but Anna seemed warm enough in her borrowed sweatshirt. He wanted to put his arm around her, but every time he tried to comfort her, she ended up pushing him away.

"Chance always had trouble figuring out what he wanted to do. The FBI seemed right for him but I guess it was just too buttoned up. He's more like my mom than my dad. She was always the rebel, protesting, doing things most women didn't." Anna smiled. "She and Dad are opposites. He's all about the law. They're madly in love, though, and we are always catching them in a clinch around the house. It's cute and embarrassing." Anna glanced at King.

"Sounds nice. My parents went down in a plane crash when Karen and I were little. My grandmother raised us." King stood next to her. There were a couple of boats out on the lake. He watched them for suspicious activity but neither seemed to be coming toward his dock.

"Oh, I'm sorry." She bumped shoulders with him.

"Thanks. So do you think Chance could take over our security here?"

"Definitely. He's going to whether Zenon is willing to hire him or not. That's our family for you." She sighed and leaned against the railing. "I trust him to do a good job. He said he's got good contacts in Texas. Buddies he knew in the service. He can set up a team that will keep us safe."

"Zenon will hire him, I promise you that. I'll put the screws to Ron if he hesitates." King turned to her. He saw her relax, just a little.

"Thanks, King. Chance has always been a very take-charge guy. All of us kids shoot well and can defend ourselves, Dad made sure of that, but my big brother Chance was family champion. I'm the family klutz. I'd rather outthink an attacker than use karate on them."

"You took martial arts?" King tried to imagine Anna taking down an opponent with her small wrists and delicate hands.

"For a little while. My moves aren't pretty." She collapsed onto a chaise. "I wonder how long it will take Scarlett to get through her statement. I can't wait to see her for myself. Make sure she's all right."

"It could be a while. I'll call Mike and see how it's going." King almost stepped on YoYo, who was dancing around his feet, and pulled out his phone. It didn't take long to find out that things were moving at their usual turtle pace at the station. Scarlett was asking for coffee, talking a mile a minute and showing signs of shock. Mike was campaigning for her to hit the emergency room when they were finished there. King hung up, pretty sure it would be hours before they'd see Anna's best friend.

When YoYo started barking madly and ran into the house, he knew they had company. Anna bolted into her bedroom and emerged with her gun. Her face was pale and her eyes wide, but her hand stayed steady as she aimed at the front door.

"Do you really think the creeps who took Scarlett would ring the doorbell?" King did stop and check the video screen next to the door. "It's Ron. He must have broken the speed limit getting here."

Anna's hand fell to her side but she didn't give up the gun. "Make sure there's no one with him. He could be a hostage, you know."

"Doug's watching the gate today, Anna, and he's armed. I don't think he'd let anyone past him we would have to worry about." King didn't smile though. "But I understand your caution." He opened the front door.

Ron stopped in his tracks when he saw Anna's gun. "Holy shit. What's going on here?" He held up his hands. "Would you put that thing away?"

"Are you alone?" Anna peered behind him. "Sorry, Ron, but we can't be too careful."

"I get that. So I sent Lea and Terri to my ex-father-in-law's house in Houston. The place is built like a fortress and has excellent security. I told them to stay there until I give them the all-clear or this program is on the market." He sighed when Anna laid her gun on the bar.

"Good idea. Can we all go?" Anna collapsed on the sofa.

"No. I'm not exactly A.J.'s favorite person. But he'll do anything for his granddaughter." Ron sat beside her and picked up her hand. "I am so sorry about Scarlett. Any news on how she's doing?"

"No. She's still at the police station." Anna nodded toward the library. "I bet you're dying to know how I did that shadow program."

"Of course. Will you show me? We might as well get to work. Nothing else to do until Scarlett gets here." Ron jumped up.

"Hold it." Conchita stood in the doorway to the kitchen. "I know I am not supposed to know what is going on, but I can see you're upset, Anna. Douglas told me we are on what he calls 'lock down.'"

"This is supposed to be your day off, Conchita. I'm sorry about this." King knew his housekeeper wouldn't be blasted out of here in a crisis.

"Ha! Where would I go? But I make it easy on myself. Lunch will just be sandwiches if anyone is hungry. I am putting some together now and will have them on the bar for when you want them. Help yourselves." She glanced at the gun and her eyebrows went up. "Anna, you want to put this next to your computer? Or back in the nightstand?"

"I'm sorry, Conchita. I'm freaking out. My friend has been kidnapped and hurt." Anna's eyes filled with tears. That got the housekeeper next to her, and soon she heard the whole story.

"Well, you mustn't forget to eat. You need your strength." Conchita wiped her own eyes. "I hope this computer program is worth all of this trouble, Mr. Ron."

"Oh, it is, Conchita. Anna is absolutely brilliant; she created it. Let me tell you what it can do." Ron walked with her to the kitchen, talking fast.

King watched them go. He was hungry but knew from the way Anna put her hand on her stomach that she wasn't going to eat.

Ron was soon back, a sandwich in his hand and full of questions for Anna about her shadow program. King didn't follow them to the library, instead taking his laptop out to the deck. He doubted Anna had noticed that it was a beautiful day. The sun was shining and the air was chilly but not cold. He had just decided he should check email when his phone rang. Mike.

"You're not going to believe it but we caught a break on the case."

"What kind of break?" King slammed the laptop shut, startling YoYo, who'd decided to keep him company outside.

"Scarlett Hall is one feisty lady. Just before she started downing coffee, she asked for a toothbrush or mouthwash. Because she had bitten one of the perps. Can you believe it? She had evidence in her mouth and hadn't even thought to mention it. So we examined her and got a bit of skin from between her teeth. DNA, my man. Now all we have to do is run it and pray for a hit." Mike sounded as excited as if he'd found a diamond in a dirt pile.

"No kidding. Tell me more." King stroked the dog. Why didn't he bring one of his hounds with him to town? They were damn good company. "How long does it take to run down that kind of thing?"

"Depends. Ex-military, pretty quick. Same with a perp with a criminal record. But otherwise…" Mike cleared his throat. "Shit, she didn't bite the one she should have. There were two men. One of them she described as pure Texas asshole. He used a knife, tied her with those zips and cut her a couple of times. Mean bastard. She said he obviously got off on it. Grabbed her privates, breasts."

"Oh, hell." King wanted to hit something.

"Yeah. The woman's covered in bruises, King. Makes me sick. Asshole would have done more but the other one kept a tight rein on him. He was the one who knew what to do with the laptop. Swore mightily when he realized what he called his usual clever tricks couldn't open the thing."

"So he was the brains of the operation and the other one was hired muscle. The woman driving the van say anything?" King was trying to remember the people in the department store. That man had asked about the dog. Of course, looking back, he'd worn a bad toupee, obviously a disguise. He'd sported a gray mustache and beard as well. Fake of course. Even if they looked at store video it wouldn't help much, but he mentioned it so Mike could pass it on.

"She said the woman just drove. The panel van had a mesh screen between the front and back. They gave her directions through it." Mike cursed. "We're almost finished here and then we're definitely stopping at St. David's for her to be examined. That bastard cut her on her butt, King. She was bleeding through her skirt. They took pictures of all her wounds, of course. When she had to expose her ass, she finally lost it. Scarlett's such a feisty gal. She had kept it together until then. I swear it broke my heart to hear her crying, King." He took a breath, like maybe she hadn't been the only one to tear up. "I want those fuckers. I want them bad."

King swore along with his friend. "That son of a bitch threatened to carve something special on her cheek. What did he do?"

"Initials. LT. APD is running them through their database. Those initials, white male, about six feet, she thinks. Likes to hurt women and she saw a tat on his lower arm. Crude and obviously jailhouse shit. She sketched it out for us. So we're looking. I hope it's just a matter of time before we get him."

"I'm not telling Anna any of this. It'll be hard enough when she sees Scarlett. You get that woman to the emergency room. We'll see you here later. Thanks, Mike."

"I'm glad I could help. Man, this makes me hot. We're going statewide with this APB but a white panel van is just too damned common. She didn't see a license plate of course. She was facedown on broken concrete when they drove away." Mike coughed. "Here she comes. We'll see you in an hour or two, depending on the wait at the hospital."

King heard a woman yelling at his friend.

"We're going, Scarlett. Shut the hell up. And don't bleed on my car seat. My wife will kill me," Mike said just before he hung up the phone.

"Eat, King. Anna's friend going to be all right?" Conchita set a loaded plate next to his laptop. She put a dish of dog food, or her idea of what a dog should eat, on the deck. Chopped, cooked chicken breast.

King brought her up to date.

"Oh, she'll stay here, won't she? Such a horrible thing. I will take care of her. I have a special cream for bruises. And we can put her in Karen's room. I'm sure your sister won't mind." Conchita wiped her eyes with a tissue then stuck it in her pocket. "*Cabrónes*! They should be dragged by their feet from the back of a truck until they are garbage."

King couldn't agree more. "Karen's room is fine. Scarlett might want some of her own clothes. We'll have to figure that out. I have no idea what she looks like. What size she wears."

"She's shorter than me. Has a fuller figure." Anna walked outside with a glass of iced tea. "I can't stare at that computer another minute. I told Ron what to do and left him to it." She smiled at Conchita. "I heard what you said. If a *cabrón* is a bastard, I'm all for it. I'd drive the truck if I knew how."

"I'll drive and you can sit in the back to throw rocks at them." Conchita gave Anna a hug. "I am so sorry about your friend. I want to help. Do you think my clothes would fit her?" She patted her full hips.

"Yes, you two are about the same size. Thanks, Conchita. That would be very generous of you." Anna pulled up a chair before King could do it for her. "Since she doesn't run very often now and has a desk job, Scarlett has rounded out. I think she looks great but she's always dieting. Claims she needs to lose twenty pounds."

"Aye. The story of my life." Conchita frowned at the glass of tea. "I'll make you a plate. You must eat."

"I couldn't." Anna frowned.

"Half a sandwich and some fruit?" Conchita picked up the empty dog food dish. "You do not need to lose pounds."

"I'll try to eat a little." Anna reached down and scratched YoYo's ears before he followed Conchita to the kitchen.

"I talked to Mike. He's taking Scarlett to be checked out by a doctor. I think it's a good idea." King took a bite of his sandwich. He and the dog were both getting chicken today.

"I'm glad. She was thrown out of a van. She might have internal injuries." Anna pressed her hands to her eyes.

King had noticed that was a habit of hers. Was she trying not to cry? "He said it would be another couple of hours. You might want to lie down for a while after lunch."

"I couldn't possibly." She smiled when Conchita set the plate in front of her. "This looks good. I'll eat it. I'm still getting used to the fact that you get such good fruit here in the middle of what you call winter." She speared a strawberry with her fork.

"Yes, we get it from Mexico." Conchita picked up YoYo. "I'm taking him with me to my house to find a few things for your friend to wear. I know she'll want to shower and change. After what they did…" She shook her head and walked away, muttering in Spanish.

"She is very kind." Anna abandoned the strawberry and stabbed a piece of watermelon but didn't put it in her mouth.

"Yes, she is. And she'll fuss if you don't eat a little of that." King finished his sandwich.

"I'll always feel guilty about what's happened to Scarlett. We've got to finish this program and catch those creeps." Anna finally put the bite into her mouth and chewed slowly.

"Mike had encouraging news. DNA from when Scarlett bit one of them, and another clue." King couldn't tell her about the cut. Just couldn't. That was Scarlett's story to tell or not. "From your friend's description, it sounds like one of the two was a computer guy. Can you think of anyone who knew about your program and might have decided to go after it? Maybe someone you knew in Boston?"

"Now that's an interesting question. A person from my past." Anna put down her fork. "It would have to be someone sharp enough to think they could understand the code, maybe even finish it once it was as far along as it is now." She leaned her head on her hand, obviously reviewing her past associations. "I should make a list."

"Maybe someone you went to school with. Or someone you worked with at your old company who wasn't invited to come along to Texas." King was grasping at straws and he knew it, but he didn't understand computers. What he did understand was business. He'd had problems with industrial espionage before. It pissed him off when people came after business secrets and wanted something without making efforts of their own. They watched you work hard and then tried to co-op it.

He'd had to be hypervigilant, watching his back every time he created special techniques for managing his land, marketing his products, and maximizing his profits. You didn't just grow a business and expect it to flourish without constant tending. It was like any crop. It needed all of his attention, all of the time.

"I have a couple of people in mind. But I can't imagine any of them would have the balls to pull off something like this. Most computer people are content to sit and work at home or in the office. To actually go out and kidnap someone, steal a computer? Well." Anna shook her head. "Come on, it's just way too aggressive for most of us. Sure, we might like to play Call of Duty until we've blown everyone to hell, but that's in cyberspace. To actually toss someone out of a van? Way too real, King."

"Not necessarily, Anna." The voice came from the living room.

King stared. How had he missed someone coming in his front door? Anna was on her feet, her face pale. Was she going to faint? He reached out, ready to catch her.

Chapter Five

King couldn't believe the man and woman had arrived and he'd been so focused on Anna he hadn't even noticed.

"Scarlett!" Anna jumped up and embraced her friend.

"Ow! Easy, pal. I have aches and pains like you wouldn't believe." Scarlett sniffled and kept hugging Anna.

Scarlett Hall wasn't anything like King had imagined. Of course he'd figured she'd be rounded, like Conchita, from their earlier conversation. Idiot that he was, he'd thought she'd be a redhead, because of her name. No, she was a blue-eyed blonde and very pretty. Or would be, if she didn't have the handprint on her cheek that was swelling and turning purple. Shit.

"I guess you know, Anna, your pal won't do anything she doesn't want to do. So no hospital." Mike watched the reunion from across the living room.

"I know." Anna had tears running down her cheeks. "Look at your face! Conchita, King's housekeeper, has some kind of cream to treat bruises. And I see bandages on your arms. Did that bastard really cut you?"

"Oh, yeah. Wait till you see the souvenir he left on my butt." Scarlett flushed, then sobbed, leaning her face against Anna's shoulder. "Oh, hell, I knew this was coming. That...that motherfucker."

Anna held Scarlett and looked helplessly at King, then Mike. King had no clue what to do. Finally, he helped Anna lead Scarlett down the hall.

"She can have Karen's room. If she can stand it, maybe she'd like a shower." King opened the bedroom door. To his relief, Conchita came hurrying down the hall, carrying a bundle. "Here are some fresh clothes for her." He'd already noticed that Scarlett's sweater was ripped and her short wool skirt had a patch of blood on the seat. Her leather boots were scuffed from where she must have hit the pavement when they'd thrown her out of the van, her knees above them raw. He wanted to put his fist through the wall.

Scarlett raised her head. "Oh, you must be King. Mike told me all about you on the ride here. Thanks for sending him to me." She looked down the hall. "Mike! You're not leaving, are you?"

"I've got to go, honey bunch. The wife is waiting. I'll call and check on ya later. Is that okay?"

She limped down the hall and threw herself into his arms. "Thanks so much, Mike. I couldn't have survived that police station without you." She kissed his cheek. "Tell your wife she's a lucky woman."

Mike hugged her carefully. "Soon as we catch those bastards, I'll have you and Anna to dinner. You can tell her yourself. How does that sound?"

"Like life back to normal." Her eyes overflowed with tears again as she pushed back. "Run along now. You know you're sick of watching me cry."

"Don't apologize for that. You've been through a traumatic experience. You deserve a good hard cry." Mike tipped his cowboy hat. "Miss Anna, take care of our girl. She was damned brave today, making her statement, giving evidence." He nodded toward the living room. "King, if you have a moment?"

"Sure." King waited until Anna and Scarlett were in the bedroom with Conchita and the door was closed. "Any news on that DNA or the tat?"

"The DNA? Nothing yet. I figure this is a first offender. Computer guy testing his luck, trying to sell something big on the dark web. But that tat? Got a hit or ten. It's common, a knife through a bleeding heart. With those initials and Scarlett's general description to help us, we should be able to run down a likely suspect pretty quick." Mike had worn his uniform on his day off and now he unbuttoned the top buttons and pulled off his tie.

King was sure he'd dressed up so he'd get cooperation as he'd walked Scarlett through police procedures. "I can't thank you enough for what you did today. I owe you. Tell your wife to pick out where she wants to go for the vacation of a lifetime."

"Save your money. You don't owe me a damn thing, King. I want these assholes. For what they did to that woman. Justice is what I'm after." Mike clasped King's hand. "I was glad I could be there for Scarlett. She's a sweet gal. Feisty. Reminded me of Brenda."

King swallowed. Mike's sister had been the victim of a serial killer who'd taken a string of young coeds when they'd all been at the university. Brenda had been a freshman, he and Mike seniors. The killer had been brutal, raping and torturing the girls before he'd finished them. A law enforcement task force led by the Texas Rangers had finally caught the man and, years later, he'd died by lethal injection on Huntsville's death row. Justice for Brenda was why Mike had become a cop after college and had eventually joined the elite Texas Rangers.

"I'll never forget Brenda, her great smile and take-no-shit attitude." King held on to Mike's hand then pulled him in for a quick hug. He stepped back and looked Mike in the eyes. "That man who cut Scarlett likes to hurt women. Bet she's not the first to feel his knife."

"Exactly my thought." Mike took a deep breath and straightened into the stiff posture of a man on a mission. "I'm sick of being a symbol of diversity at the capitol. I'm taking my black ass into headquarters tomorrow and talking to my commander. I want back out into the field. What happened to Scarlett is something I can't let go."

"You aren't just a symbol at the capitol, Mike. There have been terrorist threats. Your job is important." King had heard the rumors when he'd been twisting a legislator's arm.

"Let someone else do it. That asshole with a knife is going down. Hard." He was determined.

"Be careful, buddy. Going off when you're hot can be dangerous. Brenda wouldn't want that. And you have a little girl at home who needs her daddy to be around to watch her grow up." King walked him to the door.

"I know that." He stepped outside and looked around as if checking for assholes in the bushes, his hand on his gun. He'd driven the family car, a brown SUV that wouldn't draw a second look. "That security force you have at the gate isn't worth spit. They didn't stop me, check ID, nothing. Just waved at me as I stopped at the gate and punched in your code."

"You do have on your uniform, buddy."

"Shit. You can buy a reasonable facsimile down at any Goodwill. I'm talking to them. Will put the fear of God in them when I leave here." Mike's fierce look would definitely make the security team shape up.

"Thanks. I'm planning to replace them tomorrow. Got a new crew coming in. Anna's brother is former FBI. He's running his own security company now. She assures me he'll be on the ball." King couldn't wait to meet Anna's brother. He'd better be as sharp as advertised.

"Good. Since this is all about Anna and her program, he'll be on his toes. I know I would be for my sister." Mike ran a hand over his face. "Anyway, Doug's keeping an eye on your current crew. That's something."

"Keep me posted on the investigation." King liked that Mike was taking this case personally for Anna's sake, but hoped it didn't make him do something he'd regret. He almost said something but realized his friend wouldn't appreciate it. A man would do what he needed to do.

"Sure." Mike stopped next to his car and glanced back at the house. "You know, I could have sworn it was only yesterday that you and Anna bumped into each other at the capitol. Strangers. Now…"

King nodded. "Now we're tangled up in something I never saw coming."

Mike gave him a long look. "It's not too late to shove both of the women into a safe house and let law enforcement deal with them."

King knew that was the sensible move. So why couldn't he make it? He rubbed the back of his neck. Truthfully, Ron would certainly understand if he walked away.

Mike smiled wryly. "I get it. You always were a sucker for a pretty woman. You're a protective son of a bitch too. Goes all the way back to when I was the quarterback and you were on the offensive line."

"Hey, football is a rough game. Someone had to keep you from getting your bell rung. As it is, you had a few too many concussions, pal." King frowned at him. "So she's pretty. That's not why I'm helping Anna. Her program can save lives. Did you know that?"

"Scarlett mentioned it." Mike shook his head. "Don't joke about those concussions. Laura's threatening to take me to a neurologist to have me checked out. The news is full of stories about the hazards of football lately. If our next baby is a boy, she won't hear of him playing the sport we loved." He opened his car door.

"Wait. You guys expecting again?" King grinned when Mike nodded, glad to hear some good news. "Hot damn. I'm sending Laura flowers."

"She'd like that. I'm heading home." Mike tossed his hat into the car. "I guess for now the women stay here. You change your mind, let me know and I'll see about a safe house."

"I will." King stepped back when Mike took off down the driveway. Being protective. What was wrong with that anyway? He'd just entered the house and reset the alarm when Anna stalked down the hall toward him.

"Is Mike still here?"

"No, he just left."

"I might have a lead for him. I guess he'll pass it on to the proper authorities if he's not on this case himself." She paced the living room, her bright blue eyes blazing with excitement.

He stopped her with a hand on her arm. "Tell me."

"Let me show you instead." She picked up her laptop and sat in a chair with it open.

King stood behind her as her fingers flew over the keys. She was using a search engine and landed on a website. MIT. Someone from college then.

"Scarlett remembered a guy I dated briefly, very briefly, in school. Scar and I shared an apartment back then. She never actually met him but saw him once when he picked me up for a date. Anyway, it was the night I broke up with him. I'd decided there was something off about the guy and let him know we were done. He didn't take it well."

"I called him Ichabod. Tall, skinny guy. I couldn't believe she ever dated the freak." Scarlett had come out, wrapped in a terry robe. She waved the tie belt. "Sorry, but I can't stand to wear clothes right now."

"He wasn't that bad, Scarlett." Anna flushed. "He was brilliant. But the more I was around him, the more I decided he *was* a bit of a freak. Too intense. I was young and not feeling the chemistry with him, if you know what I mean." She glanced at King.

"Sure. Got to have chemistry." Did she feel it with him? He'd known there was some from the moment he'd led her to that concrete bench. But they were getting sidetracked. "So why do you think he's a suspect, Anna?"

"It's me, King. I'm thinking that might have been him in the van. The one who was on the computer all the time. He kept bumping his head on the roof. Really tall. The other guy, the one with the knife, didn't have that problem." Scarlett rubbed her wrist and King noticed the red marks. Mike had told him she'd been bound with zip ties.

"You called him Ichabod?" King waited for Anna to pull up whatever she was looking for on the computer.

"Isaac Crane." Anna hit a key and a picture popped up.

The man was ordinary—narrow face, sharp nose, and straight dark hair. There was really nothing to distinguish him. If you passed him on the street or in the capitol building lobby you probably wouldn't notice him.

"Let me show you a group picture so you can see just how tall he was." Anna hit another key. It was the Science Club and the same man stood in the back row. He was at least six inches taller than everyone else. Tall and very thin. Yeah, Ichabod Crane.

"Reminded me of a scarecrow back then." Scarlett peered over Anna's other shoulder. "I don't know why you ever went out with him in the first place, Annie. It didn't take you long, though, to realize he was a mistake."

"You're right. He did fool me at first. He was scary smart and could be charming. We were interested in a lot of the same things." Anna kept staring at that picture.

"Computers!" Scarlett obviously didn't share her friend's love of technology. "I bet King wasn't in Science Club." She looked him over. "With those shoulders, you played football, didn't you?"

"Yes, I did, but I wasn't just a jock. I was president of the Business Club too." He smiled. "Pretty dull stuff there."

"Stop it, Scarlett, this is serious. Look at the picture. Think. Did you see enough of the man in the van to think it could be Isaac Crane?" Anna was doing a search for more about the man in a separate window.

"I don't know. I told you they were pretty covered up. I guess the man behind the mask could have had Icky's nose." Scarlett limped over to the couch and sat down gingerly, rearranging pillows for comfort. "You should still make a list. Anyone who might want to steal your program. It's worth a lot of money. How about the guy in IT who wanted to go to cybersecurity training but you got to go instead? What was his name? Henry Littlefield." She snapped her fingers. "Yeah, I heard him complaining about you. Called you Mr. Z's pet."

King made a note of that name in his phone. He'd pass it on to Ron, who was so involved with the computer in the library he hadn't even come out to check on Scarlett.

"How long ago was this thing with Crane?" King studied Anna in the same group photo. She looked about nineteen, had long hair, and wore thick glasses. There were only two other women in the large group.

"More than ten years ago. Isaac was a senior. He was smart, but he never was that good at programming even though he hid it well. It would make him mad when I could figure things out in the computer lab faster than he could. He switched to medicine. I heard he became a doctor. Research was his specialty." Anna kept typing. "Actually I ran into him not that long ago. Though I pretended I didn't see him. It was when I was at the NIH, taking that pharmaceutical course."

"You didn't tell me that!" Scarlett leaned forward and winced. "How'd he look?"

"The same, only he'd filled out some. He worked in biological warfare, anthrax, things like that. Which gives me chills now that I think of it." Anna was into a new website.

"What does NIH stand for?" King hated for people to toss around initials he didn't recognize.

"National Institutes of Health. I heard he was fired after I left there. Don't know why." Anna moved so they could look at a new picture. "There's a more recent photo."

"Still Ichabod to me." Scarlett sneered. "Too bad I had my hands tied so I couldn't rip off his face mask and get a good look."

"No, that would have been the worst thing you could do. Hostages have been killed for stunts like that." King studied the photo of an ordinary man, a few years older now, his face fuller.

"The Isaac I dated back then knew a lot about me, too much. I realized pretty fast that he'd researched *me*. I became an obsession for him." Anna frowned at the computer. "I didn't recognize his voice on the phone today but he always spoke very carefully. Loved his big words. Cohort. That would be a word he'd use."

Scarlett wiggled, clearly very uncomfortable as she adjusted a pillow under one hip. "The man in the van was well educated. Not like Knife Guy who grabbed me outside your place. He never met an obscenity he didn't like. It would be hard for me to identify either one of them. They both wore long-sleeve white jumpsuits, those masks, surgical caps, and gloves. Computer Guy slapped me so hard I figured they could get some fingerprints off my face, even though he wore those gloves." She had an ice pack, which she suddenly remembered to lay against her cheek. "No such luck."

"How did you see the tattoo you told the cops about?" King hated to interrogate Scarlett again when she'd been through so much already. She sagged against the leather, then winced and shifted. "I'm sorry. You want to go lie down?"

"In a minute. I want to help catch those assholes." Scarlett sighed. "I saw the tattoo when Knife Guy pushed up his sleeves to work on my butt. It seems it was to be his damned work of art. Computer Guy was too busy trying to break Anna's encryption code to notice or he'd have yelled at him. He was all about protecting their identities and was obviously the brains of the operation. He kept reminding Knife Guy not to say anything incriminating."

"Oh, Scarlett, I'm so, so sorry. That must have been hell." Anna bit her trembling lip, clearly trying not to cry.

Scarlett stood, wobbling on her feet. "Yeah, you could say that. Now I'm going to bed, on my tummy. Nice to meet you, King. I can't remember if I said it before, but thanks for having me here. Conchita found painkillers in your sister's bathroom. I took one already but I think I need another one. See you later." She kissed Anna's cheek. "Don't you dare cry for me."

"This was all my fault." Anna stood, tears running down her cheeks.

"No, the two assholes are at fault. Being around your family of lawmen taught me that lesson years ago. Bad people do bad things because they're morally bankrupt, want something for nothing, or any one of a dozen reasons that make sense in a warped mind." She wiped a tear off Anna's cheek then thumped her on the arm. "Don't give them power over you, girlfriend. Finish that program. That's the best thing you can do right now."

King jumped up to help Scarlett as she turned toward her bedroom, but she waved him away. They both watched Anna's friend stagger down the hall.

"Good advice." But King knew, looking at her, that Anna was still wallowing in guilt. "Come on, she's right. You can't blame yourself because someone decided to steal your program."

"Can't I?" Anna frowned. "I didn't say this in front of her, but I have a feeling it *was* Ichabod. He had a personal reason for coming after my program, something besides money from the sale."

"Seriously?" King sat on the ottoman next to her knees. "This is important."

"The last time I saw him, in college, I humiliated him." She set the laptop aside and leaned forward. "I'm not proud of it but he just wouldn't take no for an answer, King. I tried being gentle, then logical. Told him we weren't suited for each other and that we had no future together. I wasn't going out with him again. He kept persisting, asking me out over and over again, insisting I give him another shot. He even ambushed me in front of other students. I guess he thought I'd say yes to avoid embarrassment. But I wasn't caving in to that kind of emotional blackmail. Finally, after about the sixth time he did it with other people around, I'd had enough. I turned on him, told him to leave me the hell alone and never speak to me again, then I walked away."

"Oh, man. I bet that made him mad." King could see why any man would want Anna, though, and maybe take it too far. She was beautiful, with her bright eyes and cloud of dark hair. Her mouth looked made for kissing. Her pale face flushed at remembering a bad time in her life. The thick glasses were gone. She'd probably moved to contacts or had some kind of corrective eye surgery.

Anna nodded. "You should have seen his face. I hated having to be that mean, but it seemed to work. He left me alone for almost a week. Then after class one night, I saw him waiting for me outside. It was my turn to shut down the computer lab and he knew it. Everyone else had left. I could see he was going to be trouble. My dad had drilled into me all the warning signs. I locked up, ignored Isaac, and kept walking, determined to avoid a confrontation."

"You should have called someone. Campus police." King didn't like where this was going. He took her hand. "Did he attack you, Anna?"

"You forget. I know how to defend myself. Isaac thought that, because he was bigger than I was, he could overpower me, teach me a lesson. That's what he said when he tried to push me against a brick wall next to the lab." Anna smiled. "Notice I said tried."

"What did you do?" King hated the thought of this woman having to defend herself against anyone, much less a man twice her size.

"I flipped that six-foot-six-inch weasel right over my shoulder. He landed on the concrete sidewalk flat on his back. Then I put my boot on his family jewels and pressed hard enough to make him squeal."

King barely stopped himself from cupping his own jewels protectively. "Seriously?"

"Very seriously. I told that creep that the next time he approached me I would be armed and ready to make sure he ended up with more than a few bruises. Then I hopped on his crotch to show him I meant business and headed home. He left me alone after that." Anna opened her laptop again and studied his picture. "We need to send this to Mike. Isaac is a viable suspect." She pursed her pink lips. "As a doctor, he'll know drugs. My program would be right up his alley."

"You say you think he was fired from the NIH?" King leaned closer, mesmerized by the way she bit her lip when she was on the hunt for information.

"That was a rumor. No one ever confirmed it. If you know Mike's email address, I'll forward this to him, Isaac's bio. His former employers might have his DNA on file. It's something they might do. Because of their work there." She looked hopeful, like she was really onto something. "I know Scarlett didn't tell the Austin police about my program, but she should have. This could help them catch the kidnappers."

King gave her Mike's email address. He hoped she was right. He sat back and watched her work. Amazing woman. He pictured her jumping on a man's privates and then walking away. Holy shit. The more he learned about Anna Delaney, the more she fascinated him. There was no way he was going to send her off to a safe house and leave her protection to strangers. Maybe he was crazy, but he wanted to see this shitstorm through to the end.

* * * *

Anna slammed her laptop shut and set it aside. She'd done all she could. If Isaac had been the one to try to steal her program and kidnap Scarlett, then it was only a matter of time until he would be tracked down. Yes, he was brilliant, but did he know how to disappear? Go off the grid? The

Isaac she'd known in college wouldn't have had that kind of knowledge. But then the old Isaac wouldn't have hired a knife-wielding psychopath either. She shuddered. Maybe she was steering them down the wrong path and it was someone else entirely. All Anna knew was that she needed to get back to work on that program but doubted she could concentrate.

King still sat near her knees, staring at her with a look she recognized but had a hard time computing in her rattled brain. He was interested in her. Really interested. This was not the time for that kind of thing, but, man, did he appeal. Remembering her brief insanity dating Isaac had reminded her why the tall egghead hadn't suited. Yeah, he'd been intelligent and interesting. But he'd soon crossed several lines that had made her uncomfortable.

Isaac's main problem had been his tendency to obsess over everything. He'd been compulsively neat, which she was not. She could have dealt with that. But then he'd started obsessing over her. He'd wanted to know where she was every minute and who she was with. Like he owned her. Definitely a deal breaker.

Now here was King staring at her like he could just gobble her up. Hmm. He was handsome, obviously very smart, and he fascinated her. Was it because his background was so different from hers? Maybe. He had a kind of cowboy vibe that made her want to see him in his natural habitat. King on a horse would be a sight to behold. Today he wore jeans that showed off muscular thighs and a butt that made her sigh. Little wonder that she was taking stock like this and imagining leaning forward and seeing how he tasted.

Oh, that would be insane. But he kept looking at her mouth. Yeah, the signs were there. What did they say here in Texas? This wasn't her first rodeo. Men had wanted her before. And she sure wasn't a virgin. Anna brushed her wild hair behind her ears and stood. King was on his feet immediately. A gentleman.

"I know Scarlett thanked you, but I hope you know I am really, really grateful for your taking us in. This has probably put you and your staff in danger. I'm sorry about that." Anna let him take her hand and pull her closer.

"I can't just abandon you, Anna. At least one of the men after your program has proven to be extremely dangerous." King rested his free hand on her shoulder. "I know we just met, but I have this urge to keep you safe. Is that crazy?"

"Maybe. But also very nice." She smiled up at him. His Mexican blood gave him a dark and exotic look. She could imagine guitar music, hot nights, and Spanish love words whispered in the dark. Now who was crazy? But she'd always been plagued by a scientist's curiosity. She wanted to know how his hair would feel between her fingers and if those broad shoulders were as firm as they looked.

"You know, every time I try to put my arms around you, you push me away." He ran a hand up to her neck, massaging it gently. "Why is that?"

"I didn't realize..." But she knew he was right. Knee-jerk reaction. Men in her past had thought they could push her around. Oh, not in an abusive way, just like she needed guidance. Because she spent way too much time problem-solving on a computer and not enough time on what they'd considered practical matters in the "real world." Damn it, just because she forgot to buy groceries or pay a light bill didn't mean she was helpless.

"You think too much." He smiled and pulled her so close her breasts brushed his chest. "What if all I want to do is offer you comfort? Can you deal with that? Can you just relax for a minute or two and let me comfort you?"

"It's not possible to think too much." He'd hit on one of her hot buttons. But then he felt so good against her. Her breasts ached, making her want to get closer and press harder to ease the building need that made no sense in the logical world she normally treasured. Maybe it *was* time to stop thinking. His hand kept moving on her neck, massaging her tension away.

Relax. Could she? Could she just let this thing between them flow? This thing? Chemistry. Not the kind they'd explored in Science Club, but the kind Isaac had insisted they had and which she'd known definitely wasn't there with *him*. Not when the tall geek had treated her like a possession to add to his collection of fossils and early Apple computers. With this man who wore jeans like they'd been invented for his muscular body? Spontaneous combustion wasn't just possible, it was becoming inevitable as heat flared between them.

"Anna." His eyes were almost closed as he stared down at her. "If I put my arms around you now, will you push me away again? Or toss me over your shoulder?"

She realized he'd stopped that wonderful massage and had lifted his hands away. It was her call. And wasn't that nice? Except... She wanted to be held. What had happened yesterday and today had been horrible, terrifying. She needed comfort. Since her family wasn't here and Scarlett was in no shape to offer any, King was her only option. She licked her lips. Oh, big mistake. His eyes darkened. Now he focused on her mouth, thinking about a kiss. And would it be such a bad move to kiss him? How would he taste? Suddenly she had to know.

"I guess you'll have to take your chances." She lifted her arms and linked them around his neck, spearing her fingers through his hair. Yes, it was thick and soft. Perfect. Then she pulled his head down and kissed him. Why the hell not? She wanted to know and this was an experiment. A logical move. But logic dropped out of the equation as soon as he growled and took her mouth with a control that left her breathless.

Their mouths were meant for each other. And when had that ever happened? Anna didn't have time to think at all. She felt, and tasted, and pressed even closer as King hauled her onto her toes and showed her how a Texas cowboy kissed. Oh, yes, it was deep and perfect and more than she could have imagined. By the time she was back on her feet and breathing hard, Anna knew she'd not been comforted. Oh, no, she'd been stirred and shaken. Like a dry martini. Except... She sure wasn't dry where it counted.

He held her for a long minute, his cheek on her hair, while her heart raced and she leaned against him. Comfort. And more than that on offer. But not now. She gently slipped out of his arms, her hand on *his* rapidly beating heart. He wore a soft sweater, a beige that made his dark skin look even more striking. She looked up, aware that things had definitely shifted between them as their eyes met. She wanted to analyze it, put it in perspective. Say something. But her usual logic had deserted her and she couldn't utter a single word.

"You all right?" King smiled and settled her back in her chair.

She nodded. But she wasn't. She felt off-kilter, her body humming with the urge to do something reckless. No, not now. They were in danger. She had a program to finish. What had her brother called it? They were in the middle of a clusterfuck. She picked up her laptop and opened it. Of course Mike hadn't checked his email yet. He was probably still driving home. She did have an email from her brother.

She had to clear her throat before she could speak. "Chance will be here later tonight. Much later." She read the lengthy message. "He's got men coming in from all over. Even a cybersecurity specialist from San Antonio. You may not know it, but, because of the Air Force bases there, that city is known for its cybersecurity. It's where I went for my special training." She didn't dare look up.

"That's good. I'm sure Zenon will pay for whatever he has planned to keep you and your program safe."

"Spending my money?" Ron walked into the room. "You need to check what I've done to the computer, Anna." He looked from her to King. "Something going on here? Anna, you're flushed."

"My brother's arriving tonight. And we have a lead on who's trying to steal our program." She told him about Isaac then carried her laptop toward the library. "Chance is assembling a security force. That's what you'll pay for."

"Good. And progress. I hope the Rangers catch the son of a bitch quickly." Ron glanced at King when he cleared his throat. "Something to tell me?"

"Scarlett arrived and you didn't even notice."

"I was hiding. What do you say in a situation like that?" Ron had the grace to look at his feet. "I'm sorry, Anna. I had no idea anyone would get hurt because of the program."

"Well, she did come up with a lead for you." King told him about the jealous coworker. "You need to check him out."

"I will." Ron headed for the bar and pulled out the bottle of scotch. "You know, we should probably move out of here, bud. What do you think?"

"I think it's only a matter of time before they figure out Anna is here. I know Mike was careful, but it's not impossible that he was followed from the police station when he brought Scarlett to the house. That may be why they let your friend go, Anna. So she could lead them to you." King paced in front of the sofa. "I have an idea about where to take the ladies, but I think we'll need to run it by our new security chief first."

"You think Mike and Scarlett were followed?" Anna stopped in the doorway to the library. She'd been feeling safe here but maybe that was stupid. If this was Isaac they were dealing with, then he'd be thinking one step ahead of them at all times. King was right. No wonder Isaac had been ready to dump Scarlett. If he'd changed vehicles, it would be a simple matter to stake out the police station then follow her friend when she left there. Anyone monitoring her social media could figure out that she and Scarlett had come to Austin together and were still best friends.

"It's the smart thing to do." King stood next to her, his hand on her shoulder again.

Anna didn't shrug it off. Maybe she should. She saw Ron looking at the two of them standing close together while he poured a drink.

"I've got to check out the new encryption Ron was working on." She headed to the library, King's hand falling away. What would they do if Isaac and his violent cohort tried to get inside the house and steal her computer? She had a gun, King and his staff were armed as well. She tried to imagine some kind of shoot-out. A modern-day Alamo with them barricaded inside King's beautiful home and bullets coming at them through the windows. "Do those French doors have bulletproof glass?"

King shook his head. "Afraid not. I never thought they needed it." He walked over and pulled the drapes closed, shutting out a spectacular sunset. "Is that better?"

"No! Worse. We need to see if anyone is coming. You did say there was a guard on the dock down below, didn't you?" Anna hugged her laptop. She had to face reality. Isaac, or whoever had taken Scarlett, wanted her program but they would also need her to finish it. Obviously they were willing to use torture to get what they wanted. She shuddered, thinking about a man who liked to cut women.

"Yes, there's a man down there. New shift comes on at seven." King exchanged a look with Ron. "I can double the guards. But I don't trust the people from Ron's old security outfit. Mike told me their attitude was lax when he came through the gate. I'm thinking of bringing Doug inside until your brother gets here with his squad, Anna. We can defend the house if someone tries to get to us. But there's just too much land around the house to keep an eye on every bit of it."

"You have the video feeds." Anna gestured toward the bank of monitors on the wall by the front door.

"If I were trying to break into this place, the first thing I'd do is cut the power. I don't know that much about security, but I bet the people after you know how to shut down the video feed." Ron paced the living room. "Shit. I don't like this. You really think they could make a run at us?"

"I don't know, but I want to be prepared." King got on his cell phone and Anna heard him order Doug to come to the house and bring Conchita with him, both of them with their guns.

"I don't know about you, but I'm not going to be caught standing in front of those big windows. I'd leave but what if they're waiting on the road to take another hostage?" Ron hurried back to the library. "Your thieves don't need me to finish the program, Anna. That means I'm expendable."

Anna looked after him as he disappeared inside. "I guess everyone here is except me." And they'd have to kill her before she'd give them one piece of code to finish that program.

King took her laptop and tossed it on the couch. "You look like you're prepared to be a martyr. Stop it."

"You think I should just hand over my program to those...those criminals?" Anna stiffened when he tried to take her in his arms.

"Listen to me. It's not worth your life." He held on, shaking her a little, as if to wake her up. "It sounds really fine to say you'll sacrifice yourself to keep your program from falling into the wrong hands, but think!" King was so deadly serious it was impossible not to listen.

"All right, I'm thinking." Anna put her hands over his. He was so strong, so determined for her to pay attention to what he was telling her.

"These men want to sell your program to people who will put it out there. Yes, they'll make a profit, as will Zenon. But it *will* be available to save lives. That's the reason you're so intent on finishing it, right?"

"Yes, of course. But I told you it could be subverted. It could be used for evil, not for good. And then there's Zenon. Ron has invested millions, no, make that a billion dollars in the development of this program. It's not fair to just let it go to these thieves." Anna saw his point but that didn't mean she was accepting defeat.

"You know fair has nothing to do with this." King stared into her eyes.

"I also know we can't give in to them, King." Anna squeezed his hands. "They'll want me along with the program. If it's Isaac, he'll need me to show him all the safeguards I've put in place. Even if it's not, there are very few people who can navigate this program successfully." He'd opened the drapes again and she glanced at the darkening sky. Stars were coming out. Night had fallen.

"It's that complicated." King shook his head. "You know I don't have a clue how this stuff operates."

"I'm not bragging when I say I believe I'm the only person who can make this program work the way it's supposed to. Taking my computers first was a pretty stupid move, if you want to know the truth. They should have waited and taken me with them. On second thought, I bet they were counting on finding me in that apartment when they went in yesterday. My bike was there. Honestly, I wouldn't be surprised if they were furious when all they got was a little dog when they broke in. Thank God they didn't take their anger out on YoYo."

Oh, shoot, here came the tears. Over a dog. But animals were helpless. At least she might have fought, maybe had time to go for her gun.

He pulled her close. "Damn, you're smart. Too smart."

"I've been told that before." She sighed and leaned against him, savoring the feeling of strong arms around her, his breath against her hair. "It's a blessing and a curse."

"Mostly a blessing." King kissed the top of her head. "So we'll just have to make sure these guys don't get hold of you or your program."

"You can still walk away, King." Anna rubbed his back, inhaling his fresh, clean scent and thinking here was another blessing. How strange that he'd been there in the capitol lobby when she'd needed him. A guardian angel had obviously been looking out for her yesterday.

"No, I can't walk away. You've hooked me, Anna Delaney." He lifted her chin and looked into her eyes. "Mike accused me of having an overdeveloped need to protect people." He rubbed her cheek with his rough thumb. "I want you to know it's not that. I admire you, Anna. And, God, you taste good." He leaned down and kissed her, making it world class.

Anna just let it happen, then held on to his shirt and almost climbed him. Good? No, great. He'd said he admired her. No more than she admired him. What kind of man opened his home to two women in terrible trouble? It was unimaginable. And damned seductive. By the time they pulled apart, they were both breathing like they'd just finished one of his morning runs.

Then the lights went out.

Chapter Six

It was so damned dark. Anna clung to King, not knowing where to move or what to do. An alarm shrieked, making her want to cover her ears, but she was afraid to let go and lose King as an anchor. A phone began ringing in another part of the house then the French doors rattled. Something thudded against them. Hard. The doors were stronger than they looked, and they were locked. Thank. God.

She tensed, waited for them to crash inward. Where was her gun? She couldn't think or see anything except for a red dot across the room. Phone charging. Hers. Next to the bar. Her gun was there. She started for it.

"Come out now, Anna, and no one has to get hurt." The voice came through the door and froze her in her tracks.

"Don't listen to him." King held on to her as he whispered. "Stay with me. The hall. Away from the windows." He held her hand and dragged her across the room. Glass broke in another part of the house. "Shit, that's the library. Ron! You okay?"

No answer. There was a sudden glow and Anna saw Ron holding his cell phone, using his flashlight app. He stood in the hall, steps away. He didn't say a word, just gestured. The bar. Anna dashed across the room to grab her gun. King had already pulled his own weapon from the back of his jeans. She pushed Ron behind the bar and gestured for him to stay there. Now what?

A noise from the library. Trying to take the computers? They could have them. A curse. Then light flared and moved into the hallway.

"Get your butt in here, Anna Delaney. You're coming with us or I'll kill every one of your fucking friends." A man wearing a surgeon's mask appeared. "Starting with this hot tamale." He had Conchita by the throat, the gun in his other hand pressed against her temple. Another man behind him held a flashlight and his own gun.

Anna froze, then aimed her gun at him. She had to keep it steady, with no sign of the nerves that made her knees weak. A wrong move and Conchita was dead. His sleeve slid down and there it was—the heart tattoo with a knife through it. The man who'd cut Scarlett. He liked to hurt women, and his grip on the housekeeper's neck was tight enough that Anna didn't doubt he could kill her, even without a bullet.

"Oh, God. Conchita. Let her go." Anna started forward. King's sudden grip on her arm stopped her.

"When you come here." The man shook Conchita to make his point.

"Anna's not going anywhere." King pulled her behind his big leather recliner as a shot rang out.

They were shooting at King. Anna peeked out to see the men. The shooter took aim and shot again, blasting a lamp next to the recliner.

"You hit the woman he wants and it's all over," the man holding Conchita growled. "Where'd you learn to shoot, kindergarten?"

"Shut the fuck up." The man behind him shot again, hitting the recliner on King's side.

"I'm sorry, King. He caught me on the way to the main house." Conchita's voice was hoarse, her eyes wide as she struggled, her hands bound together with a zip tie.

Anna stood and aimed her gun at them. They wouldn't shoot her. She could see Conchita trembling. Wasn't the housekeeper supposed to be armed? But maybe that was her gun Knife Guy was holding. At least he hadn't cut Conchita. She could see his knife, now that she was looking for it. The handle was sticking out of a sheath on a belt at his waist. If only Conchita could grab it and stab the asshole. But she was in no shape to do more than gasp for breath, her feet dangling and scrambling for purchase, as he pulled her up to cover his head. Yes, there were two guns aimed at him. What now?

The man in back who held the flashlight spoke, though he was clearly using the creep holding Conchita as a shield. "You're thinking, aren't you, Anna? The boss told us you would be. Think about this. How many people are going to get hurt before you give up and come with us? Boss has hired an army." A gunshot rang out and the man staggered, dropped his gun, and clutched his arm.

"Take a message to your boss. Anna isn't going anywhere." King aimed his gun at the man holding Conchita. "Let my housekeeper go." He ducked down behind the chair, his hand on top of Anna's head, when Knife Guy aimed at them and fired.

"Like hell." But he pulled Conchita up even higher, until she was covering him, the housekeeper gagging and on her toes.

"Tell your boss I'm thinking." Anna would give anything for a decent shot. If only the flashlight wasn't in her eyes and the man would stop moving. "What I'm thinking is that if I come with you, I'm as good as dead. Once my program is finished I'd no longer be useful to him. So forget this. You've failed." She might be able to wound Knife Guy, he was wider than Conchita, but it was too dangerous. He could snap the housekeeper's neck in a rage. Pull his knife and slash her throat. Oh, God.

"You willing to die for your boss?" King kept his head down. "You might get a shot off to take down the little woman you're holding, but that'll be the only one you'll take. I've got my gun aimed at your head now. You'll be dead before you can squeeze off another round."

"Big talk. But I bet you can't make the shot, not with the light in your eyes." The man did jerk Conchita up so high she screamed.

"You don't want to test me, man." King held his gun steady. "You really come here to die tonight for some egghead computer geek? The Rangers got his DNA from the woman who bit him in the van. They're running it right now. Bet they have an APB out for him by tomorrow. You'll be next. You ready to go back to prison?"

"Shut the fuck up." He shifted his feet when there was movement behind him.

"There goes your backup." King nodded at the man who was making a run for the door and taking the flashlight with him. "He's leaving you in the dark while he takes off like a jackrabbit."

"Fuck this." Knife Guy dragged Conchita with him as he bolted and slammed the library door behind them.

King pulled out his cell and turned on his own light, then rushed down the hall.

"We've got to get Conchita out of there." He tried the knob. When it didn't open, he handed Anna the light, then put his shoulder, then his boots against the door. He was finally able to break in after several hard kicks shattered the doorframe. The men had obviously left through the broken window. Conchita lay moaning on the floor. King pulled out a pocketknife and cut the zip tie. When they heard gunshots outside, he ran to look.

"Are you all right, Conchita?" Anna stayed next to her.

"The *hijo de puta* hit me in the head with my own gun." She rubbed her neck then staggered to her feet. "I am so ashamed I let them take me. Aye, my throat. I thought he was going to strangle me."

King came back to check on her. "How are you?" He glanced at the window.

"I will live. Go. See if you can catch those *pendejos*." Conchita waved him toward the broken window. "Douglas is out there. He needs help. They said they have many men."

"That must be Doug exchanging gunfire with them. How the hell did they get in here? Where's our security?" King was already halfway out the window. "Anna, you and Conchita stay out of sight in case they come back for you. Get behind the bar with Ron. Shoot if you have to." He disappeared before she could answer him.

Anna helped Conchita to where Ron was saying prayers.

"I heard shots." He was sitting with his back to the mini-fridge, a bottle of scotch in his lap along with his cell phone flashlight. He lifted the bottle and took a long swallow, then offered it to the ladies. "This is terrifying. What have we gotten into, Anna? Oh, God. Conchita! Your head! And you have fingerprints on your neck!" He scooted over and pulled a can of frozen juice out of the fridge. "They hit you? Put this on that lump on your head. Then, damn it, Anna, call the police. Conchita, do we need an ambulance too?"

"No, I'm okay." Conchita sighed when she put the cold can on her forehead. "No police. My man and King are taking care of it. I don't feel like telling the police my story tonight. I know how they are. It would take hours." She winced and closed her eyes.

"We have to call them. We need to catch these creeps." Anna pulled out her cell and hit 9-1-1. When the operator answered, she told her they had been—how to explain it?—attacked. That was the best she could do. The woman assured her that patrol cars were on the way. They sat in silence for a while. Anna thought the gunfire had stopped but she was afraid to move. When the lights suddenly came on, she breathed a sigh of relief.

"I think that's a good sign. Maybe King caught them or the bad men are gone." Conchita kept the juice can on her temple. The lump was big and ugly.

"If they're gone, that's not a good sign at all. I need to check on Scarlett." Anna kept her gun with her as she headed down the hall. Her friend was still asleep, lying on her stomach and dead to the world after taking two painkillers. Just as well. After what she'd gone through today, Scarlett really didn't need the trauma of another confrontation with Knife Guy. Especially since the knife had been replaced with a gun.

Anna stopped in the doorway to the library. That broken window was letting in cold air, the drapes blowing wildly. She shivered. What if those men circled back and came inside? Where was King? Sirens. That was fast. She should have asked for an ambulance but Conchita had gripped her arm when she'd started to say something about an injured party. Unfortunately, Conchita didn't look good and might have a concussion.

A leg appeared in the opening where the glass had been broken and Anna jumped behind the desk, aiming her gun and ready to do the unthinkable. Could she really shoot a man? She was about to find out. She didn't shout out a warning, thinking it was best to let them come in so she could finish this if she had to. She didn't want the assholes getting away to terrorize them again.

A hand flailed at the billowing drapes. Anna prayed as she braced herself, ready to take a shot. A face appeared from behind the curtains.

"Thank God." She let the gun drop to her side and put on the safety. "You scared the hell out of me, King."

He stalked across the room and took her in his arms. "You okay? You're pale, like you're about to faint again." He stared down into her face. "Thanks for not shooting me."

"My dad taught me caution. I don't shoot unless I'm sure of my target." She saw Doug climb in next. "Conchita's in the living room. She's staying behind the bar with Ron until we get the all clear."

"Damn it. I'd told her to wait for me in the house. Stubborn woman." Doug hurried past them, almost shoving King aside in his rush to get to his wife.

"How is she?" King finally stepped back.

"I think she may need to go to the hospital. But she didn't even want to call the police, much less an ambulance." Anna heard pounding on the front door and shouts of "Police!" "They're here. Got here really fast too."

"All the windows are wired. I'm sure the security company sent them as soon as the windows broke and we didn't answer the landline." King headed to the front door, checking the video monitor, which was up and running again. "Yep, Austin's finest." He threw open the door.

Anna quickly put her gun out of sight, then spent the next few hours answering questions along with everyone else involved. Conchita protested, but Doug bundled her off in his car to the emergency room to have her checked out. Two more police cars arrived and there was a thorough search of the grounds. No sign of the men who had invaded the house. When Mike drove up, she was glad to see him.

"I'm sorry they managed to get past your security, King." Mike had talked briefly with the officers from the APD. He'd heard about the break-in on his police scanner. "But not really surprised after what I saw earlier."

"They found one man knocked out next to the fence. Drugged. He was actually patrolling the perimeter like he was supposed to be. The other was in his car. He was obviously surprised with a syringe in the neck, his cup of coffee still in his hand. Both of them are groggy and just now coming around, but they're unemployed as far as I'm concerned." King looked thunderous. "The man stationed at the boat dock came running when the alarm went off, and he also got laid low. You'd think these guys had no training at all."

"You'd be right. I ran a check on this so-called security company you had guarding you. They are fine installing security systems for the home." Mike waved at the bank of monitors.

Anna could see the policemen gathered by their cruisers in the driveway on one screen, talking before they got in their cars and drove away. "But?" She knew there had to be a "but." She'd heard it in his voice.

"But they hire poorly qualified rent-a-cops to do patrol and guard duty. Obviously they weren't up to the job. Sitting ducks." Mike walked over to look out the library window. "Want me to help you board this up?"

"Yes, thanks." King patted Anna's shoulder. "Isn't it about time for your brother to be arriving at the airport? Do you need to text him my address?"

"No. I've already heard from him. Once I gave him your name he knew way more about you than you probably wanted him to know." Anna smiled. "Down to the size of your underwear and whether you prefer boxers or briefs." She sat on the couch. "He and his team are meeting at the airport and caravanning here in several vehicles."

She couldn't wait to see Chance. He'd always been a rock in her life, though he had that Delaney male tendency to want to throw a blanket over her and shield her from life. Well, right now a blanket would feel pretty good. Safe. Cozy. But she'd have to keep her eye on her brother—that blanket should still let her breathe a little.

"Okay then." King walked over to the door to the garage. "Mike, there's plywood in here. I think I've got a piece that'll fit without having to get out a saw."

"Good." Mike turned at a noise from the hallway. "Scarlett, did you get any rest? They had quite a ruckus here earlier, from what I hear."

She staggered into the living room and collapsed on the couch next to Anna, then yelped and stood again. "Damn it, I can't even sit without a pillow or three." She took one from Anna and sat very gingerly. "What are you talking about, Mike? And why is it so cold in here? Ron's in the library with the windows open."

"They're not open, pal, they're broken. We had a visit from Knife Guy and a pal of his while you slept." Anna kept a hand on Scarlett's arm and felt her friend stiffen. "No worries, they're gone."

"You let them get away?" Scarlett watched King and Mike walk through the living room with a big piece of plywood between them. "Is that why you're back here, Mike? Are you going to stay this time? To protect us?"

"No, I just came to check in. And to give you some news. Anna tells me you've got a serious security crew on the way." Mike nodded. "Put down the plywood, King, and let me tell you what I found out." He helped King lean it against the wall, then got out his cell phone.

"What is it?" Anna leaned forward. Mike looked grim but strangely excited.

"We got a hit on the DNA, Anna. Your information about the National Institutes of Health in Isaac Crane's background was the key. They don't put their studies in a national database, but they did have his DNA on file for one he participated in. When Scarlett bit him, she got just enough tissue to get a good sample. It was a match." He showed each of them the picture on his cell phone. "This is his latest photo ID from when he worked there. No criminal record. But he's going to have one now, as soon as we catch him."

"So it *was* Icky." Scarlett held on to Anna's hand. "I'm so sorry, Anna."

"Sorry? You got us key evidence!" Anna studied the picture. Yes, that was the Isaac she'd glimpsed at the NIH. He'd matured since college. He looked harder, more serious. The glasses were gone, just like hers were. His hair was short, no nonsense. It was one of those photos that had no refinement, no airbrushing. He looked bored, impatient, and almost halfway out of his chair.

"How on earth did you bite him hard enough to get DNA, Scarlett? You said they wore long-sleeve jumpsuits and gloves." King took the cell from Anna and gazed at the photo as if memorizing it, then returned it to Mike.

"I caught his glove with my teeth and ripped it, got his wrist bare, and just let him have it." Scarlett showed them her perfect white teeth. "My mama used to fuss at me for opening things with my teeth, especially after I wore expensive braces for years. I can rip open just about anything—bags, stubborn containers. When that asshole tried to force me to talk into his cell? Well, I was going to make him pay." Her eyes filled with tears. "I hope this helps you catch him."

"You did a great job, Scar." Anna patted her shoulder. "Let the men repair the window in the library and I'll tell you what happened while you slept. We scared them off. King shot one of them. The police took a blood sample from the hall hardwood floor and I bet we have an ID for another of the gang after me."

"That's something, but I should have done more. Conchita got the worst of it." King gestured at the plywood. "Come on, Mike, let's get that window boarded up. You never know when those assholes might make another run at us. We can't make it easy for them."

Mike nodded. The men grabbed the wood and left the room.

"Ron! Would you get off that damned computer? Go out to the garage and grab a hammer and the box of nails off the work bench." King bellowed from the library door.

"Yes, sir!" Ron came hurrying out and waved at Scarlett and Anna. "You slept through the gun battle, Scarlett. Lucky you. I was so scared I was about to wet my pants." He wore a sweater he must have found in King's bedroom because it hung to his knees. "I was going to check our computer, Anna. Doesn't look like they touched it. I guess they've realized it's just hardware. What they really need is you to finish the program." He made a face then darted into the garage and came out with a hammer and nails. "I shouldn't have said that. But that's what comes of being a computer genius, lady. Just means we have to catch those bastards. I'll pay whatever it costs to keep you safe and that's the truth."

"Thanks, Ron. I'm not stopping until the program is out there where it can do the most good. If it gets on the black market, I'm pretty sure decent people won't be able to afford it. I sure don't want some psycho using it for God knows what. We will always have to keep the code under lock and key. There's no excuse for lax security." Anna had been thinking about that a lot. Isaac saw a big payday with this theft, as well as revenge. Whoever he'd lined up as his buyer would employ him to keep the program going. Probably a foreign company. The kind of fairly cheap and easy accessibility she and Ron had planned wouldn't happen. No, the thieves would be all about profit.

Then again, Isaac might have his own ideas about how to use her program. It could take a patient's records, change them, and make someone vulnerable when they were in the hospital. For people who wanted someone out of the way? How easy it would be to make that happen with her program.

Substitute a drug in the record and, oops, the patient would be dead before anyone caught the error.

"I see that now. I followed up on your tip about Henry Littlefield. He had suspicious activity in his bank accounts. I couldn't believe it. Not that it would be enough to prove he's involved in anything, but when I tried to call him, I found out his phone's been disconnected. I touched base with Mona and she says he hasn't been into the office in a week. Littlefield is a quiet guy with not much going for him that I could see. Which makes me pretty sure he's working with our bad actors. I just never dreamed I'd be betrayed like that." Ron swung the hammer he was holding like he imagined a man in front of him. "I've passed the name on to the Austin police and to King's pal with the Texas Rangers. They're looking for him now to ask him some questions."

"Henry. I barely knew him. But then I haven't really mixed much with the Texas people in the IT department." Anna realized that was a problem. No one who'd been at Zenon before had any reason to feel a bit of loyalty to her.

"Hey, you aren't thinking this is your fault, are you?" Ron shook his head. "That man has worked for me for five years. But he wasn't getting promoted or sent to special classes because he did the minimum. No initiative. When you and a couple of other new people showed up with bright ideas, he probably got jealous. So he was open to a bribe. I wouldn't be surprised if he tried to access your work computer." Ron grinned. "Bet he cursed when he came up against your encryption."

"What else would they pay him for?" Anna opened her laptop and looked up the man. She recognized him as someone who'd hung around the lab, had tried to talk to her and even invited her to a Friday happy hour. She hadn't had time to visit. Had he resented her attitude? All work and no play.

"He could tell them when you came to the office and when you worked from home, stuff like that. He may have exaggerated his accessibility to your work. Then he couldn't deliver." Ron shrugged. "Now he's taken off. He may be running from the likes of that thug with the tattoo. I sure would if I'd let him down." Ron winced when King called his name again. "Bossy, isn't he?"

"He's freaked out." Anna realized yelling and ordering around Ron must be King's way of showing his frustration. He'd thought *he* was keeping her safe. The fact that he hadn't... Well, he sounded pissed and unhappy.

"Freaked out? Aren't we all?" Ron hurried into the library.

"You going to tell me what I missed?" Scarlett leaned back carefully. "Those were obviously very strong pain pills."

Anna gave her the highlights. "Now we're waiting for Chance and his new security team to arrive. They should be here soon." She heard the signal that she had a text coming in and picked up her phone from the coffee table. "Here he is now." She walked over to the video monitors. "I should probably text him the code for the gate." She started to call for King when she saw a man dressed in camo get out of the truck and put some kind of device against the keypad next to the entrance. The iron gate swung open.

"That was pretty cool." Scarlett spoke from behind her.

"Not cool if those were bad guys." Anna held on to her friend's arm. "It explains how those creeps got in earlier though. They must have had one of those devices. Clearly King's security here was a joke."

"I love hearing that." King was back in the room. "Your brother arriving?"

"Yes, and his team just got through your gate without the code. Makes me nervous." Anna helped Scarlett limp back to the couch. "I knew there were high-tech ways to bypass systems like that, but I haven't made a study of them."

"Obviously your brother has." King opened his front door when they all heard vehicles approaching down the long drive. "I don't think he rented those at the airport. He must have connections with the military."

"I'm sure one of his new team does." Anna walked over to stand next to King. There were a couple of all-terrain vehicles, large, dark, and ready to climb mountains or ford streams. There were also several black SUVs. When her brother leaped out of the passenger side of the lead car, she ran to him. He pulled her into a hug that almost crushed her. Then he let go and looked her over under the porch light.

"You want to tell me what the fuck you've gotten yourself into, little sister?" he growled before looking over her shoulder at King. "And who the hell is this?"

"King Sanders. Behave, Chance. He's been a lifesaver." Anna pulled Chance into the house. "And he's an investor in the company that's hiring you for this gig."

"Lifesaver? We'll see about that. Shots fired here. Police called. My sister in the middle of a shitstorm that includes the kidnapping of her best friend." Chance looked King up and down. "Is this an amusement for you, Mr. Sanders? Rich guy thinking to play with the lives of ordinary people to see what happens?"

"You think I'm playing, Delaney?" King's scowl should have made most men think twice about a confrontation. "And if you think your sister is ordinary, you haven't been paying attention."

Anna waited for the explosion. Her brother wasn't most men. Chance Delaney was a decorated war hero and a former FBI agent who'd led men into a raid on one of the most infamous drug compounds in the backwoods of Tennessee and lived to tell about it. He'd gone undercover to catch white-collar crooks and then done the same to bust open a Russian sex-trafficking ring. So when King Sanders glared at him, he shrugged. No big deal.

"I know my sister is something special, Sanders. Wasn't sure you knew it. I see you've got a gun in the back of your jeans. You know how to use it?" Chance kept his arm around Anna.

"He protected me with it, Chance. Shot one of our intruders." Anna had to admit it felt good having her brother close.

"That so?" Chance nodded. "Glad to hear it. Where's your gun, sis?"

"On the bar. I used it earlier. You would have been proud." Anna walked over to pick up hers. She handed it to Chance. He sniffed it.

"You didn't fire it. Why not?"

"She didn't want to hit my housekeeper, who was being used as a shield." King seemed content to watch as half a dozen people crowded the doorway. At a signal from Chance, three men peeled off to check outside, the other three, one of them a woman, walked inside and began to methodically search the house. He used the time to introduce Mike to Chance. The two put their heads together, exchanging information and business cards with contact information.

"If you need anything, give me a shout." Mike seemed impressed by her brother. "I've got to go. I'll be in the field starting tomorrow or I'll be looking for a new job."

"Come see me if you need one." Delaney shook his hand then told someone at the gate that Mike was coming out. "So we know who's behind this now."

"Isaac Crane." Anna shivered. "A blast from my past." She still couldn't believe he was haunting her like this.

"Sure you didn't have a shot?" Chance gave her back her gun.

"I don't think so." Anna heard her voice quaver. Damn it.

"She didn't. It was a hostage situation. You should have seen her, standing up in front of those two fuckers with guns aimed at her. She never backed down. Told them she wasn't going anywhere with them, no matter what the hell they did." King sounded sure of that. "Don't give her a hard time, Delaney, she's been through enough."

"Hey, what about me?" Scarlett spoke from her place on the couch. "I was kidnapped, taken hostage, carved like a Thanksgiving turkey, for Christ's sake."

"Hey, Red. You did have it rough. But you look like you're hanging in." Chance walked over and kissed her on the mouth. "But then, you always have been able to take it as well as dish it out."

"You bet I can." She wiped her mouth with the back of her hand. "Save your kisses for someone who cares. Now leave King and Anna alone. King's letting us stay here and we're basically strangers. Look around." She pointed to broken glass where a lamp had been knocked over next to the recliner that had bullet holes in it. "Those thugs have trashed his place. Prove this new gig of yours is a good idea and keep us safe." Scarlett waved at the team members that had come back to the living room. "A woman? What did she have to do to qualify to join your team? Kiss your, um, feet?" Her eyes swept over something closer to his belt buckle.

"You want to test my skillset, bitch?" The woman was short and curvy, her black jeans and sweater designed to show off her assets. She had a belt strapped around her slim middle with lots of loops and pockets that held, among other things, a gun and heavy-duty knife that added an edge to her look. She walked over to the couch and leaned down to put her face close to Scarlett's. "You got an issue with Delaney, fine. But don't pull that shit with me. Got it?"

"Whoa." Scarlett grinned and held up a hand. "I'm now a fan. What's your name, girlfriend?"

"I'm not your girlfriend but you can call me Madison." She straightened and sauntered over to the bar.

"First or last name?" Ron had come out of the library and was giving the woman the once-over.

"Wouldn't you like to know?" She smiled, then snapped to what looked like attention. "Sorry, boss. What's next?"

Chance frowned. "We set up here until we have a plan for removing these targets to a safer place. Madison, you take that exterior door in the kitchen. I want men on the dock and the deck outside these French doors." He turned and issued orders to a man who appeared behind him on the front porch. Then he slammed that door and locked it.

"Chance, this is Ron Zenonsky, my boss. He's head of the company footing the bill for security." Anna pulled Ron over to face her brother.

"Fine." Chance nodded. "Then Zenonsky, you and I have to talk. Privately."

"Whoa." Ron shook his head. "If it's to do with security, deal with King. I'm paying, not playing." He headed to the bar. "Seriously, you two are in charge. I'm strictly a computer guy. Anna and I are working on the program the bad guys are so keen to steal. That's my priority. To help her any way I can with that. Yours is to allow her to finish in peace." He poured himself a double from the bottle of scotch, then looked around as if hoping someone would join him. Finally, he shrugged and took the glass back to the library.

"As you wish." Chance frowned then glanced at Anna. "I'm not inviting you to the parlay, Anna. Stay here." He gestured to King and they walked down the hall.

"Bossy as ever. The Delaney men never change." Scarlett sighed and put another pillow under her hip. "I have not missed that."

"I have. Thought I'd never say it, but I have." Anna settled next to Scarlett and picked up her phone. "I wonder if he told Mom and Dad he was coming here and why. Must not have. No texts from them or phone calls. That's a blessing anyway."

"No kidding. If he'd spilled the beans, we'd have a crowd of Delaneys here." Scarlett patted Anna's thigh. "Not that they couldn't each protect themselves, even your mother, but I wouldn't want any of them to become a target for Icky and his thugs."

"Me either. I need to thank Chance for keeping this from them." Anna started to get up then thought better of it. When he'd ordered her to stay put, he'd meant it. Of course, she didn't have to obey him, but why start out causing problems? Chance definitely needed to work on his people skills. If he was going to be running a security company from now on, he couldn't treat clients the way he'd just treated her, as if she were a moron. He didn't have the power of the U.S. government behind him anymore.

* * * *

The library didn't exactly provide a secure location for a private meeting. The door wouldn't close since he had knocked it off its hinges. But letting Delaney see the aftermath of the confrontation with the men trying to take his sister wasn't such a bad idea. After all, he'd won that skirmish. King sent Ron to take a shower. His friend needed to sober up after hitting the scotch too hard.

"You want to bring me up to speed here?" Chance Delaney walked over and pulled back the drapes to take a closer look at the plywood covering the broken window. He was a big guy, dressed in black. No camo for him, just high-quality slacks, a designer sweater, and a cashmere blazer. He looked fit, not only ready to rumble but eager to take someone on. Of course. Because his sister was in danger. King could relate. He'd feel the same if someone wanted to hurt his twin.

King told him what had happened and that Anna's lead had helped identify Isaac Crane as the suspect behind the threat. Crane had had a hired gun with him in the van when they'd kidnapped Scarlett, and that same man had come back with another in a second attempt to take Anna.

"Your Ranger friend told me most of this. You wounded one of them. Too bad they got away." Delaney frowned and sat in the leather chair to study the computer system that covered King's desk.

"Yeah, I really wanted to catch at least one of the assholes. We needed intel on the scope of their operation." King got a feeling his effort to use military language was what made one side of Delaney's lip quirk. "I imagine Crane has a buyer lined up. If we take him out, who's to say another, more dangerous crew might not be sent in his place?"

"Russians or Chinese? Is that what you're thinking?" Delaney hit a key and then shook his head. "You don't have to tell me that what Anna is working on is valuable. Her little company went for big bucks because of this program. Otherwise she'd still be at home where she belongs." He got up and walked over to face King. "Well?"

"Zenon is an investment of mine, sure. Because Ron Zenonsky is a friend and has a nose for what's coming next in technology. But the computer business isn't my area of expertise. As far as Russians or Chinese? Shit. I'd hate to think we'd have to face either one of those."

King liked Delaney's vibe and the look of his team. They meant business. Didn't matter what they cost. Zenonsky should be able to afford it. He'd said as much.

Delaney nodded. "Look, I'm here to protect my sister. I don't know how you and she are connected. Maybe you met yesterday or have been dating since she hit Texas. I don't know and don't give a shit. But you gave her a place to hide. I appreciate it. Just sorry they found her so quickly. I'd like to know how they managed it." He glanced at the doorframe. "Obviously we need to move her and her computer gear out of here. You're going, everyone in this house is going. Because the people after her will assume you're all important to Anna. They took Scarlett as leverage, so taking someone else might still seem like a good way to get Anna to cooperate." He moved to the door, grim as he concentrated on planning.

"First thing I do is get everything there is to know about this Isaac Crane. That can help us catch him, put him behind bars. I know I'm not FBI anymore, but my goal will always be to get the assholes off the streets. That's the best way to keep a client safe." He stopped and looked King in the eyes. "I already know a hell of a lot about you."

"I just met Anna. We haven't—" King didn't know why he felt the need to set Delaney straight. The look he got made him shut the hell up.

"Didn't I just say I don't give a shit what's between you two?" Delaney stopped with his hand on the broken doorframe. "Understand this: Our family closes ranks fast. We protect each other. But I know my sister. She resents it. Doesn't want anyone getting into her personal business. So I'll stay out of it. She's an adult. She wants to take a lover, six lovers, male or female, that's on her." He swept King with a hard gaze that made him want to protect his family jewels for the second time in recent memory. "But don't hurt her. She doesn't deserve it. And I won't tolerate it. You hear me?"

"Loud and clear." King smiled. "Glad to know you won't be a problem as I get to know Anna better." He bit back, *you asshole*. "You have any idea where we should go from here? A safe place for her to work? Because I've been thinking about that."

"I know you have a ranch outside San Antonio. I've got a couple of men scouting it out right now. Is that what you're thinking?" Delaney nodded when King stiffened. "The reports I've received so far are promising. I'll have to strengthen your Wi-Fi and put up some serious firewalls. But I have a cybersecurity specialist who can meet us there."

Fucking mind reader. But then the man was obviously good at his job. He should be, for the small fortune he was charging for this protection. King felt the knot of tension at the back of his neck begin to relax. He followed Delaney out to the living room.

"The ranch. Yes, it's isolated enough to be easy to protect. Of course, Crane seems to know as much about me as you do, so I'm sure he's got plans of it on his computer already." King couldn't sit, his eyes going straight to Anna, who still sat on the couch. She watched her brother, clearly confident he'd take care of them.

King pulled out his gun and checked it, reminding Anna he could protect her too, before sliding it back under his shirt. Lame. But she did look his way and smile.

"I doubt Crane has the manpower I have. Not that we know of, anyway. If he's that well-funded, then we *will* be facing off against a foreign power. Somehow I think he's reluctant to bring them in." Delaney sat beside his sister and picked up her hand. "From your description, sis, I think he's an arrogant son of a bitch. Imagines he can handle this with his own little gang of local hired guns." He glanced at King. "The two here ran scared when Sanders shot at them. They don't sound reliable to me."

"Isaac would believe he's capable of outsmarting anyone. But I can't imagine that he's used to running with criminals who have their own agendas. He'll be pissed that his people ran and didn't come away with what he wanted: me."

"We can't let them have you, Anna!" Scarlett sat on her other side and clutched her other hand. "That animal with the knife. I wish you could have killed him tonight." She was shaking. "Promise me you'll never go with them just to save one of us."

"Relax, Red." Chance looked across at her. "We're not going to let it come to that. I'm here. We're going to keep both of you safe. I promise." He frowned. "I heard what that asshole did to you. Let me alone in a room with him and he'll find out what pain is."

"Thanks, Chance." Scarlett sat back and wiped her wet cheeks.

"I'm going to do research. See if I can find out how he hired those people, especially the one with the knife." Chance nodded toward his laptop. "From what Anna tells me, Crane may be clever with some things, but I'm sure he's out of his element with kidnapping and robbery."

Anna squeezed her brother's hand. "I'm glad you're here, Chance. Thanks for coming." She looked around the room. "Where'd you get all of your people?"

"Here and there. I had a few connections from my army days. And then I'm not the only one who got fed up and left the FBI. Sam there is one of them." He smiled at the man stationed by the front door, watching the many video monitors. "Now I think you all need to go to bed. We have you safe for now. We'll discuss where we're going in the morning." He leaned over and studied Scarlett. "I'd like to look at your butt first."

"Excuse me?" She jumped to her feet, then wobbled.

"It's a clue, Red. I know the cops are having trouble finding the man in the van who cut on you. Those initials along with the tattoo aren't panning out. Come on, Anna will stick with us. Show me your butt. Purely for investigative purposes." He winked. "Not like I haven't seen it before."

"Fuck off." She flounced, with a limp, down the hall toward her bedroom.

"Sis, I'm not kidding. There's something off here. Go persuade her. I'm sorry if she thought I wasn't being serious. Old habits. But this is evidence I need to see." Delaney pushed Anna to her feet. "At the very least, take a picture of the wound. Ask her if he was interrupted. Like maybe these aren't all of his initials. I have a hunch…"

"Fine. But she won't let you look at her. You didn't exactly end up friends." Anna picked up her phone and walked after Scarlett.

King could use some sleep. He found Ron behind the bar, catching some Z's with the bottle of scotch in his lap instead of hitting the shower.

He kicked him awake, then ordered him to bunk on the pullout couch in the library. Why not? He'd be close to his precious computer.

"You and Scarlett have a history?" King asked Delaney as he settled into his recliner that now wore a bullet hole. Hell, he'd leave it like that. A reminder of his first and hopefully last gun battle.

"Yeah. Years ago. Scarlett hasn't forgotten how it ended. I had an assignment out of town and didn't bother to tell her. Couldn't really." Delaney ran a hand through his dark hair, which was cut short, almost military style. "I had to disappear. That came with the job. You aren't allowed to tell friends and family where your assignment is taking you, and sometimes you get no notice. You feel me?"

King nodded, though he thought that sounded like the job from hell. No wonder Delaney had moved on from the FBI.

"Anyway, it fucked things up with Scarlett. And a couple more women who might have turned into something long-term." Delaney got up and walked over to pull aside the drapes at the French doors. "You have a sweet setup here. I can see the lights on the lake. I don't even own a condo." He faced him. "When you hit thirty, then thirty-five, you start thinking about wanting more." He studied King, like he was figuring out they were more or less the same age. "So I pulled the plug. I decided if I was ever going to do it, it was time to leave my government job and start my own company. Eventually I hope to be able to stay in the office and send out teams. Just be the boss."

"Sounds like a dream, bro. Though I can't see the control freak in you letting go of the reins that completely." Anna came down the hall with her phone in her hand. That hand was shaking. "I like the idea of you out of danger. Mom and Dad will be thrilled once they find out that you're even thinking about a wife and kids someday." Anna sat on the couch and gestured for him to join her.

"Dad thinks I made the mistake of the century. I gave up a solid pension plan for pie in the sky. His words." Delaney held out his hand. "What did that bastard do to her?"

"It's horrible. We had to take off her dressing but it needed changing anyway. It makes me sick to see how that creep treated her. Look at this!" She passed over the phone.

Delaney took one look then swore with the inventiveness of a man who'd spent time under fire. His face grim, he gestured for his guy at the door to come see the photo. "What do you think, Sam?"

"Obviously it's LT but I think he started to write something else. Another letter." Sam hit a fist on his thigh. "It'll be a pleasure to bring down that motherfucker." He glanced at Anna. "Sorry, ma'am."

Anna waved off the apology.

King studied the photo over their shoulders. He hadn't had a glimpse of Scarlett's bum, of course. Hadn't wanted to. But he could see now that the angry red knife cuts were defacing what had been a pale, perfectly round butt cheek. Sure enough, there was a curve next to the T that might have been the start of another letter.

"I think it could be the bottom of an S." King stepped back when Delaney jerked his serious-looking laptop closer and opened it.

"Don't tell me you have access to police databases." Anna kept her eyes on his computer screen.

"I won't tell you, but of course I do. What good would I be to my clients if I didn't?" He was hitting keys fast, almost as fast as his sister did when she was working.

King just stood back and watched. Were they onto something? And what good would it do? Obviously the man was an ex-con. It would be too simple if he had a known address and still lived there.

"Leroy Thomas Simms." Delaney turned the laptop so they could all see the screen. A man's mug shot appeared. They'd never seen his whole face but his description was dead-on. White male in his thirties, he was about six feet tall, had dark hair, and had a tattoo of a bleeding heart with a knife through it on his right forearm. He'd been incarcerated for aggravated assault with a deadly weapon more than once. His favored weapon? Knives. He'd been released from prison a few months ago. He'd never reported to his assigned parole officer but had an address in Luling, a few miles outside of Austin. When an arrest warrant had been issued for violating his parole, the address was found to be a vacant lot.

"I think we've found our guy." Delaney smiled. "What do you think, sis?"

"You are a genius." She leaned against her brother. "That could definitely be him. Do you have video of him anywhere? Could we hear his voice? Just to be sure."

"That's a good idea. Yeah. Says here he gave a deposition after a run-in while incarcerated. It was taped." He got busy and in moments hit a key so a video started playing. The voice that came from the computer made them all shudder.

"That's him. I'll never forget that voice." Scarlett was back, her eyes big. "You found him. Because of the picture of my butt?"

"That's right. Maybe next time I ask you to do something, you'll do it without whining like a little girl." Delaney got up and put his arm around her. "That sadist is going down, Red. Count on it."

"Thanks, Chance." She sighed and blinked but didn't let a tear fall. "I'm going back to bed. There's a painkiller waiting with my name on it."

Delaney watched her go. "Shit." He went back to his laptop. "I'll email this to the Austin PD, and to your friend at the Texas Rangers, Sanders." He got busy typing. "They can start a search for him right away."

"That was good work, Delaney." King saw Anna yawn. "I think we could use some rest. Anna?"

"Yes, I'm going." She kissed Delaney's cheek. "Thanks, bro. And thanks for not alerting Mom and Dad. I really didn't need a Delaney posse coming to my aid, just you."

"I hear that." He hugged her, then glanced at King. "This is a job, sis. I sure wouldn't drag the family into it. Good night." He gently pushed her toward the hall. Soon he was back on his computer.

King nodded, then followed Anna to her bedroom. "You all right? The last forty-eight hours have been hell for you."

"Not so great for you either." She glanced back at the library door Ron had leaned closed when he'd gone to bed. "Your house will never be the same because you got involved with me. That's your reward for coming to my aid when you saw me about to faint in the capitol building."

"Seems like fate, doesn't it?" He rested his hand on the door next to her head. "But I keep thinking about what would have happened to you if I hadn't insisted you stick with me. Crane and that knife-wielding bastard would have you now. Even if you tried to resist finishing the computer program, could you really hold out when Simms started trying to persuade you with his knife?"

Anna shuddered. "I thought I could. But then I looked at Scarlett's wounds and realized the pain she suffered. I'm not sure I'm that brave."

"You looked pretty brave when you were holding that gun earlier." King smiled. "I was waiting for you to blow a hole in one of those men."

"If I'd only had a shot." Anna shook her head.

"It's a lot easier to shoot at a paper target or a bottle on a fence than it is a living thing. They don't pose for you." King couldn't resist touching her, skimming a finger along the curve of her jaw, then tucking her hair behind her ear.

"Hmm." She slid her hands up to rest on his chest. "No, they don't." She leaned against him. "You ever killed anyone, King?"

"No, hell no." He pulled her closer. "Just rattlesnakes. Believe me, when one comes across my path on the ranch, I blow his fucking head off." He liked the way she felt in his arms, soft and vulnerable, not the tough woman who'd stood up to men with guns. That sight had made his gut squeeze. "If Crane or one of his assholes comes after you again, I promise to happily blow him away."

"Isaac reminds me of a rattlesnake. Long snout, flicking tongue." She shuddered. "As I remember, that's how he kissed. Oh, God, I was so damned stupid back then."

King lifted her chin and looked into her blue, blue eyes. "You were never stupid. Just young. What you need is a kiss good night. One that I hope you won't regret." He leaned down and his lips met hers. He didn't push it, just tasted her, waiting to see if she was into it. Thank God, she was more than into it, twining her hands around his neck and pressing closer. There were tongues involved but they were mutually engaged, playful. By the time he raised his head, King realized he'd pushed Anna against the bedroom door and they were both breathing fast.

"You want to come in?" She reached behind her and opened the door.

"Hmm. Tempting." He ran a hand along the curve of her hip. "How quiet can you be?" King glanced to where he could just see that laptop and a dark head. "I'm sure your brother has ears like a bat."

"Do things right and I'll scream this house down." She sighed and kissed King's grin.

"Believe me, I plan to do things right again and again." He pulled her up and in, savoring her mouth for a long minute before she let him go. "You sure you can't be quiet? I could stick a sock in your mouth."

She tugged on his hair, her smile wicked. "But I plan to use my mouth to make *you* scream, cowboy. Rain check?"

"God, yes." He backed up when he felt a presence nearby. "Delaney? You need me for something?"

Chance Delaney stood silently as he frowned at his sister. "You need sleep. I can tell you're operating on adrenaline. Sanders, your housekeeper and her husband, I believe he's your man of all work here, are back from the hospital. They told my guy at the gate that they're going to their own house, to walk and feed the dog. That would be YoYo, sis?"

"Oh, yes. I should—" She flushed.

"The dog is fine. Anyway, the couple is down for the night. Conchita claims she doesn't have a concussion, the doctor cleared her. She insists she will be here in the morning to cook breakfast for everyone." Delaney obviously had a comm in his ear. "Oh, yeah. She wants you to know that

Doug was careful but they think they could have been followed back from the hospital. So our perps have not given up. My people are on high alert." He nodded. "I believe you were on your way to your own bedroom, Sanders."

"Chance! Thanks for the report." Anna poked him in the middle of his chest. "Really. Now go back to your computer. Or your team or whatever."

King liked Anna's attitude. He would have liked to have added his own pokes, a little harder. Delaney's timing sucked. The big man just kissed his sister on the cheek and then, after giving King a warning look, ambled back to the living room.

"It's good to have caring family, but"—King pulled Anna to him and glared at Delaney—"not as an audience."

"Caring can be taken too far." She frowned at her brother who still watched them from the living room. "I'm a grown woman. If I want to drag you into this bedroom, I will."

"I appreciate that. In fact, I have Delaney's permission to become your lover, but was warned not to hurt your feelings." King grinned at the look on her face. "Hey, he brought it up, not me." He stepped back when she fisted her hands. "He's right about one thing. We need sleep. So I'll take that rain check."

"I hate men. I really do." With that she stepped into the bedroom and slammed the door.

The door across the hall opened and Scarlett peered out. "She shoot you down?" She frowned. "Don't give up. My best friend needs to get laid. Badly." With that she shut her own door.

King laughed when he heard the growl from the end of the hall. Yeah, there was a psychopath or maybe a sociopath—who knew the difference?— after them but he was feeling energized, alive. And challenged. Anna was the most interesting woman he'd met in a long time. And he had a feeling it was only a matter of time before he would know her much, much better.

Chapter Seven

Anna woke up when a ball of fur landed on her stomach. It was such an ordinary way to start her day that it took her a moment to realize where she was. Then the smell of bacon hit her. It reminded her of home in Boston. If only. She cuddled YoYo for a while, trying to get the nerve to climb out of bed and face the day. The bedroom door was ajar. She could hear masculine voices in the hall. Reality. She would love to pull up the covers and postpone, but it was not to be.

"Are you going to keep hiding in here?" Her brother walked in with a cup of coffee. "I thought you were hot to finish this program of yours." He looked eager to get going, dressed in khakis and a formfitting shirt that looked military. No designer duds this morning. He was taking this job seriously. Somehow that made her feel worse. What had she started with this program of hers?

"Is that coffee for me?" Anna sat up while YoYo greeted Chance with a happy dance.

"If it'll get you moving." He passed it over. "I heard from my team at the Sanders ranch. We're going out there today. You and Zenonsky need to break down the computer system so we can load it into the back of one of the vehicles. I want to be gone from here by noon."

Anna sipped the coffee. Conchita must have fixed it for her. It was just right with cream and sugar. "Where is this place?"

"The Rocking S, that's what he calls it, is a big spread, not far from San Antonio. About two and a half hours from here if the weather holds. It's overcast and may rain. Don't know if that turns into sleet around here or not. It's going to be easy to defend, and we should be able to keep you safe while you concentrate on what you do best." He sat on the side of the bed, the dog in his lap.

"I hope we're not putting anyone else in danger." Anna leaned against the padded headboard. "After what happened to Conchita..."

"That was rough. You should see her neck this morning, bruised all to hell. She's making light of it, but that bastard did a number on her. Good on you and Sanders to run them off." Chance stroked the dog's tummy when YoYo rolled over on his back. "Listen, there are people on the ranch that Sanders cares about. So it's my job to keep them safe. The guy understands the risks but he's all in on this, Anna." He set YoYo aside, ignoring the paw scratching his knee. "I ask myself why." He gave her a searching look.

"I don't know. Maybe he's just a stand-up guy. Seriously, Chance, we barely know each other." Anna's face was hot and it wasn't from the cup of coffee she was sipping.

"Maybe you're right. Some men get off to being a knight in shining armor." Chance smiled. "Of course, he does have that investment in Zenon. Not that I think losing a few million would cause him much pain. I ran his financials. The man's worth on the north side of a billion dollars."

Anna wasn't surprised. King had the confidence of a rich man and this house wasn't shabby either, with staff. But a *billion?* She was so out of his league. She managed a smile. "Look in his closet. You'd die for the suit he had on the day I met him."

"I wouldn't doubt it." Her brother patted her knee through the covers. "Then again, there's the personal angle. You've done something to make him think he's got a shot with you."

"Have you seen him in boots and jeans?" Anna laughed. "Why wouldn't a tall Texas billionaire have a shot with me?"

"That's my girl." Chance leaned over and kissed her cheek. Then he pinned her with a stare that made her squirm. "Listen, Anna, I don't care what bedroom games you play but this threat is serious as hell. A home invasion? Crane may not have a criminal past, but he's obviously lost his mind over your program."

"I know. Look at what he let that monster do to Scarlett. The Isaac Crane I knew in college didn't have the guts to plan such things, but clearly he's changed." Anna decided sweet coffee wasn't such a good idea and she set it on the nightstand. "If my rejection of him is why Isaac has focused on my program, I'm here to tell you, he's taken revenge to a whole new level."

"Yeah, Sanders told me your theory." Chance set YoYo on the floor. "He's not the first guy to be dumped and certainly won't be the last. It's not a bad motive, but money is always a stronger one. And power. As for Simms?

He's a wild card. Isaac Crane is obviously the brains of the operation but he needed brawn. He may regret hiring someone like the ex-con to do his dirty work. Guys like that are unpredictable when they get mad. And it sounds like Simms is not as easily led as Crane had hoped. Carving his initials on Scarlett was damned stupid."

Anna waited until her brother stood before she threw back the covers. If he was trying to scare her, he was doing a good job of it. "You think they're going to follow us to the ranch?"

"I wouldn't be surprised." Chance frowned then picked up YoYo. "But I'll have plenty of men guarding the place. I'd like to see them try to get past us."

"Forget it. I'm not going to put anyone else in danger. Certainly not King's sister and grandmother. And then there's Scarlett." She dug her toes into the plush carpet, determined to lay it all out now, while they were alone. "Here's the way it has to be."

"You trying to tell me how to do my job?" Chance advanced on her.

"Just listen." She stopped him with a hand on his chest.

"I want you to take Scarlett somewhere safe. You personally. You owe her that."

"You're crazy. I've been hired to make sure you're protected, Anna. You." He set the dog on the floor and put his hands on her shoulders. "You're not calling the shots, sis. I am. I have a team, I'll deploy it as I see fit."

"I brought you in, and I can get you and your fancy ass team fired like that." She snapped her fingers. "There are other security companies that have been around a lot longer than you have. I'm sure my new billionaire boyfriend can tap some of his rich friends and find one."

"Now wait just a minute." Chance backed up. "Are you fucking threatening me?"

"You need this gig, don't you?" Anna knew she was onto something. His jaw was set. Oh, but she'd pissed him off. "New business. Lucrative contract. If it was canceled the word would get around. You wouldn't get a reference either if you didn't please the customer."

"I don't need it so badly that I'll risk your life." His glare could have melted ice.

"I'm not trying to screw you over, Chance, I'm not. But it seems to me you said all your men are good and able to keep me safe. And I believe you. So I need for you to do as I say. Take Scarlett to a safe house somewhere, watch over her and let her heal. You, no one else. She's freaked out. Do you think she'll let some stranger take care of her? She would be a basket case." Anna had woken up during the night when she'd heard Scarlett screaming.

A nightmare. She'd met Chance in the hall and he'd watched her go in to comfort her friend. He knew Anna was right. She saw it in his eyes.

"But—"

"No buts. You can send me to a safe house with an armed guard, your most trusted people, where there's no one else who can be collateral damage." Anna touched his rigid jaw. No, no tears. She sucked them back, fought them.

"Please, please, do this for me, Chance. What happened to Scarlett is killing me. I won't let anyone else get hurt because of me and my damned program. If you trust the team you've assembled then this shouldn't be a problem for you."

"Fuck!" He stalked around the room, almost tripping over the dog. "I don't like this. Let me stick with you."

"No. You owe Scarlett. We both do." Anna couldn't get that mutilation out of her mind. "I mean it, Chance. You let her down once and broke her heart."

"Get real. That was years ago." But he wouldn't look at her.

"I'm sorry, but I won't feel comfortable unless you're the one that takes her away from here." Anna backed up when he came at her again.

"She acts like she's okay." But, again, he wasn't meeting her eyes.

"You know that's all it is. An act. Scarlett's always been good at putting up a brave front. She needs a familiar face to protect her. She may hate your guts for running out on her years ago, but she trusts you to keep her safe, Chance." Anna laid a hand on his shoulder. "Do this for me. And for a woman I know you loved once upon a time."

"Do you hear yourself? You're not making any sense, Anna. I should put other guards on you, but not on your best friend? Shit, this is nuts." He looked like he wanted to shake her. "I love you, kid. If something happened to you on my watch, I'd never be able to forgive myself, not to mention figure out how to face Mom and Dad."

Anna could see how hard this was for him but she was determined. Scared, but determined. "Nothing is going to happen. I trust you to figure this out. Your best team can take care of me. This is what I want and you're going to give it to me." She knew she'd made her point when he looked heavenward and cursed.

"And what about your friend King? Where is he in this plan of yours?" Chance narrowed his eyes.

"I'm grateful he's allowed us to invade his home and even offered to move us onto his ranch. But it's time for us to part ways. I won't risk him either. They already shot at him and made a mess of his house. That stops

now. Maybe you can send a team with him wherever he decides to go."
She looked around at the luxurious suite that was just one of several set
aside for guests. She'd like to see more of King. And not just to tell him
goodbye and walk away. It would hurt. She'd felt there could be something
between them. More than that chemistry. After this was over, after the
program was done or Isaac and his thugs were caught, maybe then... If
he didn't decide she wasn't worth the trouble. She wouldn't blame King
if he ran like hell, relieved she'd let him off the hook.

"You're going to tell him to kiss off?" Chance laughed. "Good luck with
that. I'm pretty good at reading people. I don't think your Texan is one to
just walk away from trouble. Especially not trouble involving a woman
he wants in his bed." Chance took her by the shoulders again. "I've got
one more thing to say, then I've got to go figure out a whole new plan. So
pay attention."

"Yes, sir." She snapped off a salute, then realized he was not amused.
"Okay, I'm listening. What?"

"Sanders told me you managed to flip Crane over your shoulder, once
upon a time." Chance shook his head. "A six-foot-six man, kiddo."

"Wasn't that amazing? I bet you didn't think I had it in me." Anna felt
a little guilty that she'd never told her family about that run-in with Isaac.
Of course, her father would have wanted her to press charges back then.
She'd decided to forget about it, satisfied when Isaac had left her alone after
that. "But I'm sure it's one reason why Isaac is so hell-bent on stealing my
program now. You should have seen how stunned he was that I managed
to lay him out on the sidewalk then threaten his baby-maker."

"I admit I'm proud that you took him down. The bastard had no business
trying to force himself on you. But that's not my point." His hands tightened
on her shoulders. "Surely you realize it was a fluke, Anna. No way in hell,
under ordinary circumstances, could you successfully make that move on a
man his size. Obviously you had the element of surprise working for you."

"Of course. I knew that at the time." Anna stepped away from him.
"Why do you think I started carrying a gun? I surprised myself that night.
The physics were all wrong for me to manage that maneuver, not with the
few classes I'd taken."

"Glad you see that. You need serious training to do martial arts. Granny
Delaney could take you down."

"Thanks a heap, bro." But Anna knew he was right. She'd never been
into fitness routines, despite Scarlett's nagging. "Don't mock Gran. She's
tougher than she looks. And hell with pepper spray."

Chance pulled her in for a hug. "Promise me you won't try hand-to-hand with anyone else, Annie. Use your weapon. And don't choke. You get a shot, you take it." He said this into her hair, his voice rough. "I don't want to lose you, kid. Don't want to lose anyone I love, ever again."

"Chance? Is there something you're not telling me?" Anna rubbed his back but he wasn't having it. He reared back, suddenly his tough and unreachable self again. "Who did you lose?"

"Ancient history." He picked up the dog before he tripped over him. "YoYo and I smell bacon and are going to get our breakfast. Get moving. Right after I hear that promise. No more Ninja moves from you, Anna."

"I wouldn't dream of it. I was never very good at that stuff and hated the lessons. My idea of a workout is opening a new blister pack of double-A batteries." She waited but her wisecrack didn't even get a smile out of him. The family had seen little of Chance in recent years because of his demanding job. Apparently there was a lot she didn't know about her big brother.

She picked up her gun from the nightstand. "Taking you seriously. Even carrying my gun into the bathroom with me. And I'm hurrying. The smell of bacon frying is a great motivator. Right, YoYo?" She reached over to rub the dog's ears.

"Good. Then pack your gear and meet me in the breakfast room." He moved out with purpose, shutting the door behind him.

Anna did hurry, but not before she called home. She had a doomsday feeling and needed a touch of what Scarlett called "back to normal." Talking to her mother, who was so happy to hear from her, made her have to clear her throat before she could speak. "I thought I'd let you know Chance is here, Mom. He came for a visit."

"In Texas? He must have business there." Her mother hummed, a signal she was figuring things out. "Are you in trouble, Anna?"

Anna dodged answering that one. "I'm so close to the end of my program, the one I told you about, that I took a day off to look around Austin." Anna shared a few details about her work. She kept them just technical enough that she knew her mother was probably already playing solitaire on her own computer while she pretended to listen. "Anyway, it's nice to see a member of the family. I think I'll be through with the program by Easter. I want to come home then. To see everyone and enjoy your baked ham." Oh, God, did she want that.

"I'd love to see you. You know I check the weather there every day. Was it really over eighty last weekend? In January!" Her mother laughed. "How did you deal with it?"

"Not well. I told you I went sightseeing. I had on a wool sweater—that pink one you gave me last year for Christmas—and almost fainted from the heat. But I met a new man when he kept me from hitting the floor in the state capitol building rotunda. He even bought me a short-sleeved T-shirt." Anna described King, though she left out a few details, like the fact that he was a billionaire rancher. Her mother was thrilled she was dating. Dating? Could you call hiding in his house dating? It did make the call end on a high note. "Got to go, Mom. I'll call you in a few days."

"You'd better. And tell that brother of yours to check in. Dad is still upset with him but wants to know all about his new security business." Her mother laughed. "A new man. I'm so happy for you, Anna. I'm going to send you a surprise package. I saw the cutest dress at Macy's the other day. Perfect for a date. You never think about your wardrobe." It was a refrain she'd heard from her mother all her life.

"You're right. I'm hopeless. I'd love a new dress, especially one you pick out. Same size, just make sure there's room in the hip department, I'm doing nothing but sitting in front of my computer, as usual." Anna sank down on the side of the bed. "Wait. I forgot. I may be moving. They're renovating the apartments in my complex. Let me see where I end up. I'll send you my new address as soon as I know it." She finally hung up after agreeing to let her mother mail the package to Scarlett's address. Great. She'd lied to her mother about her apartment. And then she'd gotten her excited about this new man in her life. Ha! Once she told King to take a hike for his own safety, she'd probably never see him again. Too bad that new date dress would go to waste.

She fell back and stared at the ceiling. The trashed apartment she never wanted to see again had left her basically homeless. She'd have to deal with that eventually. Later. Once she knew she was safe and that program she was beginning to wish she'd never thought of in the first place was safe too.

Anna headed into the bathroom. It always made her a little homesick—no, make that a lot homesick, to talk to her mother. But it was a good reminder to take her time with makeup and her hair after a quick shower. A woman should always look her best, even when she was running for her life. Could she persuade King to go with Chance and Scarlett? With that on her mind, she decided to raid King's sister's closet again.

She wrapped herself in a towel and peeked into the hall. Coast clear. She dashed into Karen's room, expecting to find Scarlett still in bed but the room was empty. She held on to her towel and rummaged in the drawer that held workout gear. Nothing interesting. But the closet was a treasure trove of designer jeans and shelves of sweaters in jewel tones that would look great with her hair.

A red pullover felt wonderful to the touch. High-dollar cashmere. Did she dare? Why not? There were half a dozen similar sweaters in other colors. And there were leggings stacked next to it. Black. Because, like she'd reminded her mother, she had computer hips.

"You finding what you need?" The deep voice startled her into almost losing her grip on her towel. Almost.

"More than I need." Anna turned to face King. "Your sister has beautiful clothes. I feel guilty raiding her closet like this."

"Don't. She has more of the same at the ranch." He leaned against the doorframe. "That towel looks good on you." He didn't touch her, but his eyes swept over her like he was imagining untying the knot between her breasts.

Anna shivered. "Is Karen at the ranch?"

"Yes, she's there. I thought about having her take my grandmother to San Antonio, maybe all the way to Mexico to visit relatives. But Chance advised against it. Crane has used people we are close to as leverage before. All we need is for him to intercept them and take a pair of hostages for this to turn into a real clusterfuck."

He straightened and moved closer. "Red. Good choice."

"Um. Yes, I've always looked good in red." Anna didn't back up, just pressed the sweater and leggings against the knot that threatened to slip. Did she want it to? The idea of what would or could happen next made her nipples tighten and ache.

"I'm not going to your ranch, King."

"What?" He dropped his hands on her bare shoulders. "Why not?"

"I told my brother I'm not risking any more innocent people on my account." She raised her chin. "You should go. Take a couple of Chance's people with you and protect your family. Chance is taking Scarlett somewhere safe."

"And what about you?" His fingers slid up her neck and into her hair. "Where the hell will you be, Anna?"

She had to fight the distraction of those hands on her. "He'll find me a safe house. Send me there with some of his best men." Anna couldn't breathe. He was so close, so all male and so…angry.

"Think you can get rid of me that easily?" He jerked her to him. "I faced gunfire for you, lady. I saw what those animals did to your friend. Why the hell would I leave you alone after that? Walk away to leave you to their mercy after that?" His hands had moved down her back, hot, insistent.

"You don't know me, King. This is crazy." Anna's fists were trapped between them. "You could be killed."

"I'm not letting you go without me. And I'd appreciate a little confidence in my ability to help protect you." He stepped back. "Not to mention a little gratitude for what happened last night. I shot one of those assholes. Stood up to them. They shot at me."

"Seriously?" She grabbed at her slipping towel. "I'm ungrateful?"

"Yep." He reached past her and picked up two more sweaters. "The blue and the purple. Take those. Karen won't care and sure won't miss them." He dropped them on her pile. "Some more bottoms." He added gray and navy ribbed leggings. "Too much?" His smile was wicked as he took the growing pile from her. "Get some socks from that basket." His hand brushed the knot and it gave up.

"King!" Anna caught the towel just in time. The flap opened and gave him a flash of her stomach and what was below. At least Scarlett had talked her into a spa visit on one of their recent Sunday outings and the darkness between her legs was tiny and tidy. Her best friend had insisted, calling it positive thinking. There was bound to be a Texas lover in her future. Was King, this maddening cowboy who wanted to protect her, the one?

His eyes were dark and knowing as he braced one hand on the shelf behind her head. "Anna." He slid the other hand inside that flap. It was warm against her skin as he gently tugged her closer. "Come here."

"You're making me crazy, King. Did it ever occur to you that I want to protect *you?*" Anna sighed, the feel of that big hand smoothing over her stomach irresistible. Sweaters hit the floor and the basket of socks tumbled along with them. She wanted to touch his skin too, and shoved up his dark sweater to feel the roughness of his stomach above his belt buckle. He'd never let some woman wax away what made him masculine. The difference between them delighted her and made her ignore the towel as it fell away.

"God." He groaned as he tugged her closer. "You drive me wild." He let go of that shelf and cupped her butt, pulling her up as he kissed her. He was hungry, but no hungrier than she was.

Anna hooked her leg around one of his, needing more of his skin, more of him. She almost ripped his sweater getting it up and off of him so she could feel that hard chest against her breasts. Yes. She needed the friction, the pressure. She didn't care if the bedroom door was open or closed. If her brother walked in or if Scarlett was outside acting as cheerleader. It had been forever, maybe never, since anyone had been able to light her fire like this. The taste, the feel, the everything, was too right, too perfect. She wasn't going to—

"Stop." He ground it out, easing her away and handing her the towel. "I'm supposed to be in here telling you to hurry. Chance wants to talk to us together. Now I know what it's about." He ran a hand through his hair. It was already wild and starting to curl. "Not the time, not the place."

"Another fucking rain check?" Anna couldn't believe she'd said that. She looked down while she tied the towel and gathered the clothes and socks. Idiot. Fool.

"Anna." He stopped her with a hand on her arm when she tried to leave the closet. To get past him. "I want you. We *will* get together. And you deserve better than a rush job, standing in a fucking closet." His voice was hoarse and he coughed to clear it.

"I hope this isn't why you're so determined to stick with me, Mr. Sanders. Just for the promise of sex." She gripped those clothes so hard she was making permanent wrinkles. Of course he was sure of *her*. She'd thrown herself at him. Acted desperate.

He stared at her until she flushed and looked away. "First of all, I want you safe. Then I'd like to get to know you under normal circumstances." He smoothed a rough hand over her shoulder. "You're high on the rush of facing danger and coming out alive, just like your brother said. It's not fair to take advantage of that."

Take advantage! She wanted to scream it. But settled for patting his cheek.

"I'd like to get to know you too. I just wish you'd take me seriously." Anna turned that pat into a gentle exploration when he shook his head. He'd shaved recently and his jaw was smooth. He smelled nice. Clean, like some kind of tree.

"King, run while you have the chance."

"No way in hell." He made his answer clear, then turned his head to nip her palm. "End of discussion."

"Stubborn man." She'd tried, that was all she could do. And she couldn't deny that the idea of having him with her made the next few hours, days, however long it took, seem a little less frightening. "Then forget the circumstances. I'm old enough to know that this chemistry we have between us *is* natural and normal. I can't ignore it because it's damned rare in my experience." Anna decided she'd laid it out as best she could. "Soon, King. This needs to happen soon."

Yeah, she was desperate. He probably had chemistry with legions of women. If he laughed right now she'd hit him with that basket of socks. Of course, it would bounce off his hard chest. The one she wanted to touch, taste, and—oh, she wanted him in the worst way.

"Glad to oblige." He pulled her hand to his lips and pressed a hot kiss into her palm, then picked up his sweater, the one she'd ripped off him, and dragged it over his head. Noise from the hall. Probably her brother wondering what the hell was taking her so long. Anna kept the clothes she'd chosen clutched to her breasts as King stepped out of her way. But he made sure to touch her as he did, sliding one of his clever hands under her towel to caress her bottom. She shivered, so terribly turned on she wanted to jump him again.

King was right about one thing. Not the time. A leisurely pace was definitely better than a quickie in a closet. She dashed across the hall to her bedroom to get dressed.

* * * *

King had to admire a woman who knew what she wanted. The fact that he was hard and aching meant he'd hang out in the closet until his body calmed down. No way was he letting her brother see him like this. Not that Chance seemed to give a damn what his sister did in her bedroom. Which was the kind of enlightened attitude King appreciated. He and his own sister had figured out long ago that was the only way two adults could coexist. Karen certainly didn't allow him to interfere in her love life. She wouldn't judge him either.

When he felt presentable, he headed out to the breakfast room where Anna was sitting down to a full plate. The red sweater looked damn good on her, especially when she saw him staring at her breasts and flushed. He wanted to touch her, say something, but she wasn't alone.

"You really think Douglas and I have to go to the ranch, King?" Conchita was settled at the table with a cup of coffee.

"I can't take a chance that Crane might send people back here to try to take another hostage." King grabbed a cup and filled it. His throat felt raw, like he'd been gargling cactus. He didn't have time to get sick. The hot coffee soothed it. "Mike called and said they have a statewide APB out for Crane and his thug Simms, but no luck catching either of them." He had more news but knew it wasn't going to make anyone at the table feel any safer.

"I guess that would be too easy. For them to be caught running a red light." Anna wasn't eating, just sipping from her own cup.

"Mike said the Austin police offered protective custody for Anna but, when they heard Zenon had hired a private security firm, they withdrew the offer. Budget concerns." It made King furious to see the bruises on his housekeeper's neck and the goose egg on her forehead. "How are you feeling, Conchita?"

"I have a headache. It hurts to swallow and I would rather sleep in my own bed." Conchita patted Anna's hand. "Anna has fussed at me for making breakfast but it is my job here. At the ranch, I won't be sorry to see your grandmother, King. She will never let me take over her kitchen, and I admit the rest will be welcome. Yes, we will be safe there. Anna's brother and his people are very professional. I trust them."

Anna glanced up at King. "First Scarlett, then Conchita. It makes me sick that both of them have suffered because of my program. Maybe I should forget it."

"You aren't the problem, Anna. And you have nothing to be sorry for." King saw one of Delaney's people walk past the window, patrolling outside. "Ruthless people don't care who they hurt to get what they want. You really going to let them scare you into abandoning what you say you've been working on for years?"

"If it hurts the people around me, maybe it's the smart thing to do." She had picked up her fork. Now she used it to stab her eggs.

"And what about all those lives you were hoping to save?" King knew that was on her mind. "People like your grandmother." He glanced at Conchita. "Anna's program is important. It protects people from taking drugs that can harm them."

"That's wonderful." Conchita leaned forward. "What a blessing to know how to create something like that."

Anna sighed and gave up on her eggs. "I know. I wanted... Never mind."

"No, you need to stick with it. You said you were close to the end. And now that your brother is here, you have a chance to finish your program in peace." King was glad Ron was in the library, breaking down the computer setup. If he'd heard Anna just now...

Ron Zenonsky had invested a hell of a lot in her program. The future of his company, really, on the success of it. If he knew Anna was thinking about abandoning her program, he'd have a heart attack, if he didn't lock her up somewhere and put a gun to her head himself and demand that she complete the damned thing.

"I say the next one hurt will be that asshole who is trying to steal something that doesn't belong to him." King was determined to make that the truth.

"You are so right." Chance Delaney walked up and glanced at his sister's plate. "But Anna's determined to change my plans. I've been on the phone. I have some ideas about where to send you, Anna. I'm taking Scarlett to

San Antonio where I've got a place lined up. Conchita and Doug can go on to the ranch with a couple of my men. King assures me his hands there can help with the security. I doubt anyone will be interested in following through with taking people you hardly know hostage, Anna."

"Sounds good so far." Anna played with the food on the plate in front of her.

King hadn't heard what her brother had planned for her. He waited. He didn't doubt that was top of mind for Chance Delaney.

"The cars are packed. Zenonsky is taking care of your computer. Did I tell you we found a few clever devices near it when we first got here?" Chance got a cup of coffee and sat at the table, then gestured for King to sit with them. "Of course, we scanned the entire house. Crane had his men plant a listening bug in the desk and a device to capture your keystrokes, Anna. That home invasion had more than one purpose. He probably didn't really think he was going to get you to come with him. He just wanted information about your program and your movements. He didn't count on your calling in someone who could find his little toys."

"No way." Anna looked horrified. "I'm so glad you got rid of them, especially the keystroke capture. You did, didn't you?"

"Of course. I'm sure the bastard is frustrated about that. We found something else too. But I'm still thinking about how to use it." He glanced at King. "Sit, Sanders. Let's talk logistics. Did you tell her about Littlefield?"

"No. She has enough to worry about." King pulled out a chair.

"What about him?" Anna glanced at Conchita. "Ron told us he was trying to find him. That he was a suspect. He would know how to put those kinds of devices on a computer. I bet he tried to do it at work." Anna frowned. "I never thought to check..."

"Whatever he did wasn't enough for Crane and his crew. Rangers found his body last night." Delaney ignored his sister's gasp. "Throat cut. Probably by Simms. He likes using his knife."

"So they're into murder now." King wished Delaney had kept that to himself. Now Anna was shaking as she put down her coffee cup.

"Afraid so. Littlefield probably would have spilled his guts if he'd been captured by the police. Guy like that, no record, trying to make some money. He was over his head with people of that sort." Delaney shook his head. "It's too bad we couldn't have found him first."

"He was just an ordinary guy." Anna's face was white and she was clearly fighting tears. "I brushed him off when he tried to be friendly. Now..."

"Now nothing, sis." Her brother got up and pulled her into his arms. "This is not on you." He looked into her eyes. "Understand? The man got greedy and paid the ultimate price. I've seen it more times than I want to admit. He was weak." He hugged her and patted her back.

King watched them and wished he'd been the one to comfort her. But what did it matter as long as, when Delaney finally put her back into her chair, Anna did look better, calmer? Then the man was back to business.

"Now, Conchita…" Delaney took the time to make Conchita feel valued and assigned her the duty of taking care of Anna's dog. As much as Anna wanted to keep YoYo with her, she seemed to realize that he was safer with the housekeeper. Conchita left to pack the dog's things.

Delaney had a tablet with assignments on a spreadsheet and outlined everything for King. While he went over his plan, Anna stayed silent. She did speak up when Delaney got to the arrangements for the cybersecurity at a possible safe house for Anna near Dallas.

"Wow, you are really on top of things, Chance." She laid down her fork. "I had no idea you had such a big crew either. How many men are you using for this operation?"

"I'd rather not say." Delaney smiled. "Zenon will get the bill when this op is over."

Anna pushed back from the table. "How good are your cybersecurity people? Where did you find them? I hate to ask this, but you know that's got to be a concern for me."

"Don't you trust me, sis?" Delaney wasn't amused. "I stole them from good government jobs, if you must know. Offered them big bucks to work for me."

"Seriously?" She stared at her brother. "Where did you get the money for such a big play?" She flushed. "I mean, we aren't from a rich family. This seems—"

"Stop. I have a client sitting at the table. What the hell are you doing?" Delaney stood and picked up his tablet.

"Those are legitimate questions. But I know how to do my own research, Delaney." King glanced at Anna. "Cut him a break, Anna. He's well financed. You don't start a business like this without a backer, and I know who's bankrolling him." He smiled. "You'd better make a success of this venture or you'll be sorry, Delaney."

"You think I don't know that?" Delaney sat back down. "I needed capital. Trent had it. His terms are interesting but he had faith I'd be able to do the job and was my first client."

"Yes, Adam Trent always needs security." King wasn't smiling. The billionaire was into everything from owning a sports franchise to casinos in a nearby state. He seemed to have no problem skirting the law, which was probably how he'd met an FBI agent. "So you have more than one team."

"Of course. I've got several people with Trent at all times." Delaney looked ready to change the subject. "Now forget all that. My security is the best. I've had years of experience, which you know, Anna. So trust me, you and your program will be safe."

"I do trust you. And I'm glad you found someone who believes in you enough to invest in your business." Anna reached out and squeezed her brother's hand. "I'm sorry if I sounded like I didn't. There's no one I'd rather have in charge of my safety. Are we good?"

"Kiddo, we're always going to be good." Chance nodded. "All you have to do is put your butt in one of my vehicles and go where I tell you to go."

"You need to work on your people skills, brother mine. Most clients would appreciate a little more tact than that, but I hear and obey." Anna pulled her hand from Chance's grip and settled back into her chair again.

"No, you're not obeying that order." King got both Delaneys' attention with that comment. "Anna's riding with me. We already decided I'm sticking with her. How are you going to keep us from being followed?"

"With you. All right. Then here's my plan. We're springing a trap." Delaney frowned at his tablet. "Crane put a tracking device on your truck, Sanders. I've left it there and am using it to plant a decoy. We're daring him to make a move." He held up a hand when Anna almost jumped out of her chair. "Don't worry, I won't risk Scarlett."

"You promise?" She sat back down. "Who's this decoy going to be?"

"Madison. She's about your size, only of course she could bench press you. The woman is a monster when it comes to self-defense. Not a cream puff like you." That dig earned him a sisterly poke in his arm. "Anyway, she found a black wig in Karen Sanders's closet. I'll put her in King's truck with a couple of my men. We'll have a convoy. Very well protected all the way to San Antonio. It's a busy highway. Crane would have to be an idiot to try anything there. But then I'm thinking he might just be that desperate, especially if he's working with someone else, a foreign group, and they have a timeline." Chance stared at his tablet.

"I'll be with Scarlett in one place, as my sister asked. Madison will be in another, well-guarded. It's outside the city. We'll be waiting for him to make his move and then we'll have him." He looked up, apparently satisfied with his plan. "Of course, I'll be in touch with every member of my team at all times."

"We know that the only person Crane really wants *is* Anna though, right?" King finished his coffee and set down the cup. "Where will she be?"

Anna reached for his hand. King liked the fact that she'd wanted to touch him. Liked it a lot. He just hoped he could keep her safe.

"Trent has a hunting cabin outside of Dallas. Some of my people are already there. And, believe me, his security, cyber and otherwise, is airtight. I'm thinking it would be perfect." Delaney got on his phone. "Yeah, it's me. Is Trent there? He's not? Perfect. Expect some company. I'll clear it with him. Two packages coming in tonight and one of them is my sister. So anything happens to her, say your prayers." He ended the call. "Now let me tell you where you're going, Sanders. I saw an old truck in your garage. Doug says it'll start, what do you think about driving it?"

"Yeah, I can do that." King leaned in. The beater in the garage was one they'd used to haul things on the ranch. Karen had driven it in as a joke, then left it there. Adam Trent's hunting cabin. The place where Trent made private business deals. King had even been to a barbeque there once. The isolation made it good for this and easy for Delaney's team to guard.

"I figure it'll be inconspicuous on the road. Trent's place is outside Dallas, north of there." Delaney showed him a map on his computer. "Straight shot northeast up Thirty-five through Waco, then you go around Dallas up to his place. My men will meet you there. No one gets in or out without checking in at the gate."

"Got it. I know exactly where it is. We can sneak Anna's computer gear into the bed of the old truck." He wanted her able to finish the damned program. He didn't think they could start something real between them until that monkey was off her back.

"I know you have a plane here, Sanders. Trent has a landing strip. I'd say fly in but the weather report doesn't look promising. What is it, three, three and a half hours to drive?" Chance was looking things up on his tablet. "And, you're right, my sister wants her big ass computer, I'm sure."

"Right now, I'm not sure of anything." Anna stared out at the lake through the windows, her hand still gripping his.

"It's an easy drive, Anna. You'll see." King was feeling more and more respect for Delaney. He had thought of every possibility. Brains clearly ran in Anna's family.

"I don't know about these plans, Chance. Don't you think we should take one of your guards with us?" Anna pulled her hand free and threw her napkin on top of her plate.

"Oh, you're taking guards. Plenty of them. But they won't be obvious." Chance smiled. "I wouldn't let my little sister go one block without my best men on the job. We just have to make sure they're invisible. Crane can't know you're still here after we leave with our decoy. He may keep an eye on this place to make sure we weren't pulling a fast one, so it's important that your leaving is very low key."

"Both of us will be armed too." King liked the idea of actually being alone with Anna, even if it was just for a drive to Dallas. "Madison can show herself at the safe house from time to time to keep the game going in case he's got eyes on her. That should give us plenty of time at Trent's place."

"If he makes a move, we'll take him down, sis. I promise you that." Delaney stepped away from the table to make a phone call.

"Fine. I guess that's what we're doing then. I'll just load the dishwasher for Conchita and then grab my bag." She took her plate into the kitchen then came back to gather the coffee cups.

"Slow your roll, sis." Her brother was off the phone. "Trent has given the go ahead." He smiled. "He's decided you'll owe him one, Sanders."

"He definitely keeps score." King wasn't surprised. Powerful men like Trent enjoyed giving and receiving favors as long as it didn't cost them too much. The loan of his cabin wouldn't make a ripple in his empire.

"Anna, you and Sanders are going to have to wait here until dark before you leave. Give us a good long head start. I've got a team set up along our route that's going to report if they think we're being followed. When I think it's safe for you to leave here, I'll text you." Delaney stood and walked around to give her a hug. "I meant what I said earlier. I don't like to let you out of my sight right now, but this is actually for the best. Believe me, I trust the people I have at Trent's place and the men who'll be with you or I wouldn't think of leaving."

"You keep Scarlett safe. That's what I want from you, bro." Anna kissed his cheek.

"You really think he'll have people watching the house for activity after you leave?" King had been trying to think like a criminal. Would Crane figure out that they would use decoys, try this kind of scenario? Anna claimed Isaac Crane was brilliant but that had been as a student. Hiring a volatile ex-con wasn't so smart. But he'd thought to plant devices in the house and on the truck. He was obviously taking to his life of crime with enthusiasm. "And what did you say to Anna earlier? Not to trust me?"

"Why would I say that?" Delaney popped King on the biceps. "As far as I can tell, and, believe me, I've done a deep dive on you, man, you've been a lifesaver for my sister. No, I told her to shoot next time she gets the chance to take Crane or his sidekick out. No hesitation."

"Yeah. Good advice. Unfortunately, neither of us seems to have the guts to take out a hostage when a piece of shit is holding them." King wasn't ashamed to admit this. He didn't doubt that Delaney had won medals for taking down bad guys to keep people safe.

"I get it. I've been in combat, trained for it. And I do have nightmares about seeing the light fade from men's eyes. Sometimes innocent bystanders pay the price." He turned his back on them and looked out the window then took a noisy breath and faced them. "Killing is not something I want my sister to ever have to do. So I pray this plan works. But when it's kill or be killed, trust me, you'll both find the will to do what needs doing."

"I can see that." King sure wouldn't let Crane or his henchmen take Anna away from him. Yeah, he'd shoot to kill then.

"Now I'm gathering the team and explaining the change. You two find a place where you can hunker down. No lights in here. Set the alarm system and make as few moves as possible once we leave. Then stay away from windows and make this place look abandoned. We'll load that truck for you and pull it out of the garage, like it was in our way, then leave the keys under the mat. When you get the all-clear, take it down the drive with the lights off. Reports predict a winter storm toward Dallas. I hope to hell that doesn't materialize but it may work out in your favor. It'll make it hard for you to be tracked. Not for my men. They know what they're doing. They won't lose sight of you. Guaranteed."

"I wonder how many people Crane has." King took a rag from Anna and wiped down the table. "We keep thinking there are just a few of them, but he can get a crew together just like we did."

"Exactly. I don't know how well-financed he is, his financials that I've been able to track down aren't that solid. But maybe he's hidden his assets well. He could have moved money overseas. Which is a red flag that he's dealing with a foreign entity." Delaney frowned. "Anyway, my guys haven't spotted anyone and they're looking, believe me. So I hope I'm wrong that the house is being watched. But sneak out of here anyway, like you've got eyes on you. Got it?"

"You be careful, Chance." Anna ran to her brother and hugged him. "Thanks for taking my wishes to heart. I know Scarlett will be safe with you." She turned when that very woman walked into the room.

"You're an idiot. Do you know that?" Scarlett gave Anna a hug. "Chance should stick with you, Annie!"

"No, he's taking you somewhere safe. And I don't want to hear an argument about it. Are we clear?" Anna held Scarlett away from her. "You need to heal. Far away from here and from me. He's promised he's found a good place." She glanced at her brother. "It had better be nice."

"Sure. Five star." He shook his head. "Well, it has good Wi-Fi anyway. But we'll be sharing a room, Red. It's the only way I can be sure you're protected."

She sniffed and limped over to the door. "Come near me with that certain look in your eyes and I'll hurt you." Scarlett stopped and hugged King then glanced down at his boots. "Thanks again, cowboy, for taking care of me and my friend. I won't forget it." She left the room, her shoulders sagging.

"That situation promises to be a pain in my butt." Chance grimaced like he realized how insensitive he'd sounded. "Okay, we're out of here. Don't you dare get hurt, sis." He pulled her in for a final hug. "Sanders, take care of her." He strode out of the room, on his comm to his team.

"Let's clean up Conchita's kitchen." King carried the rag in there and picked up Anna's plate to scrape it and set it in the dishwasher. She hadn't eaten much. He hadn't either, the soreness in his throat a damned worry. If his grandmother were here, she'd make him gargle with warm salt water. Instead, he finished the last of the coffee in the pot then rinsed it out. "We should fix a couple of sandwiches now. For when we have to lay low."

"I couldn't eat a thing." Anna rinsed out mugs and began to load the dishwasher.

"Well, I'm sure I could. And you should try." He handed her the plate and then got busy making a couple of sandwiches and throwing them into a mini-cooler. He could tell Anna was about to lose it. When she accidentally dropped a mug, they both jumped.

"Sorry." She held up the broken handle.

"Toss it." King took it from her and dropped it in the trash. "Come here." He pulled her into his arms. Yes, she was shaking. "We'll be okay. Wait until you see Trent's cabin. The man likes to live large. He owns one of the most successful football teams in Texas. Too bad we just missed the playoffs or we'd have him, some of his players, and a few cheerleaders there to keep us company."

"Then I'd never get any work done." She was holding on tight then looked up. "Is there anyone important in Texas you don't know?"

"A few. But guys like Trent are good to tap for charity donations. My sister and I like to get involved in some special causes close to our hearts."

"Really? What are they?" She leaned against the counter. "I don't know you at all, do I?"

"No, you don't. Just like I don't know you." He smiled. "But we'll have time to talk while we wait and in the truck. I have to warn you, it's a ranch truck. Torn seats, broken radio, and it smells like hay and manure."

"A real treat coming up." She began putting away the sandwich fixings. "Now about those charities."

"My *abuela* is a breast cancer survivor. Karen and I help raise funds for the cure. And then there's animal cruelty. Can't stand it." He picked up YoYo when he ran into the room. "We donate to support no-kill shelters. You'd better say goodbye to your fur baby. He has to go with Conchita."

"Yes, we're going. And, look, you cleaned my kitchen for me. Thank you." The housekeeper and Doug walked in with their bags. "We heard you're not going with us, Anna. This pup will miss you but I promise to take good care of him."

"I know you will." Anna held YoYo for a long moment, then passed him off to Conchita. "Take care of yourself. And thank you for watching over my dog."

"I'm happy to do it." She left, a squirming dog in her arms.

Scarlett was next, wandering into the kitchen in search of one more cup of coffee. "Your brother is going to make my life miserable. Are you sure you won't change your mind?"

"This is the best way to keep me safe. I'm sorry if it's a trial for you." Anna used the coffee maker to make enough to fill a travel mug for her friend.

"Oh, Chance and I had to declare a truce. I'm over him, he's over me. It's all good as long as he keeps his hands to himself." Scarlett eyed King. "Take care of my pal, King. She tends to get lost in her computer crap and forgets to take care of herself."

"I'll do my best." King slung his arm around Anna. "Can I ask you a burning question?"

"Me?" Scarlett stopped in mid-sip. "What?"

"Where did you get the name Scarlett? I swear I thought you'd have red hair when I first met you." King felt Anna's shoulders shake. He looked down. She was laughing.

"If you ever met Scarlett's mom, you'd understand. She's from Atlanta, home of *Gone with the Wind*. Scarlett O'Hara is my pal's namesake." Anna laughed out loud. "She has a brother named Rhett."

"No kidding." King loved to hear Anna laugh. She hadn't done much of it since he'd met her.

"My mother is a real southern belle." Scarlett sashayed up to King and batted her eyelashes. "I've learned a few things from her. Like how to make a mint julep. And bake a killer cornbread."

"Valuable talents, Miss Scarlett." King bowed in her direction. "A man will do a lot for good cornbread, especially in Texas."

"You hear that, Annie? Watch yourself. If you blow this with King, I might have a shot." Scarlett gave them a finger wave. "Anna can't boil water. Of course, you do have housekeepers, don't you? So that might not be a deal breaker." She blew them a kiss. "I'm taking extra pillows. But it's going to be a painful ride to San Antonio. Take care, you two." She ran back and kissed Anna on the cheek. "I mean that. Take care." And she was gone.

Ron was next. "I put a hard drive with what you'll need in the back of that truck, along with the big monitor and ergonomic keyboard. It's all wrapped in a waterproof tarp." He handed her two thumb drives. "Everything's here. I always like an extra copy. Keep it in a safe place. Don't put anything in the cloud if you don't have to. Too vulnerable. Delaney's people brought us satellite phones that are safe to use. Call me if you want to brainstorm. I know my coding isn't up to yours, but sometimes I can see things..." He grabbed Anna and gave her a hug. "You two be careful. I don't like this, don't like it at all."

"We'll be careful, Ron. You're the ones with targets on your backs. I want you to watch out." King shook his friend's hand. "You happy with Delaney's security?"

"You bet. The man exudes competence. He's set me up at the same hotel where he'll be with Scarlett in San Antonio. He's thought of everything, as far as I can see." He glanced at Anna, who had tears in her eyes. "And I'm not just saying that because he's your brother. And to have a connection to Adam Trent? I'm impressed he can get into that guy's place on a moment's notice."

"You're right." King looked down at Anna. "Anna?"

"Ron, I *will* call you. You believed in my program and have poured so much money into it." She sniffed and King handed her a paper towel. "I can't wait to finish this. You won't be sorry for the faith you've had in me."

Ron hugged her, his own eyes bright. "We're going to save lives, Anna, that's all that matters. Now I know your brother is chomping at the bit to leave. Your new SAT phones are on the bar out there. Keep your guns handy. If you get a shot, take it. I admire you so damned much." He ran out of the room before he could say more.

"Anyone else we need to have in here for a farewell speech?" King was trying to lighten the mood but it didn't work. Anna sobbed and leaned against him. "Well, hell." He patted her back and tried to think of something to say.

"Would you two get away from the windows and hide? We're leaving in exactly five minutes." Her brother barked that order from the door. "Anna, dry up. We don't have time for feminine hysterics."

"I'll have hysterics if I want to." She straightened and punched on the dishwasher.

King didn't bother to remind her that they hadn't added detergent yet. He didn't think she'd appreciate it. He just grabbed his cooler and a bottle of water and followed her. Where did she want to hide? Not behind the bar. He liked the mini-fridge but there was no way they could both fit back there. They each grabbed a new phone with their name on it as they went past.

She marched down the hall toward his bedroom. Oh, good idea. Except he had big windows with a view of the lake. When they got there she pulled the drapes closed until there wasn't a bit of view left.

"We can't turn on a light." It was a gloomy day and the room was dark. If they closed the door to the hall, it would be pretty hard to see.

"I'm fine. We can hide out here, can't we, Chance?" She turned to face her brother, who had trailed them.

"Sure. But pay attention to your surroundings. I'm setting the house alarm but I heard that Crane cut the electricity last night. You need to be alert to noise. And keep your guns close." He frowned at King. "If someone comes in here after my sister, shoot him."

"I will." King put his gun on the nightstand, then stood with his hands in his pockets. "I think this will work. We'll be quiet and wait here. You sure it's okay to use the satellite phones?"

"Yes, and they're on vibrate. I'll call or text you when it's time for you to leave. Remember what I said." Chance huffed when Anna kicked off her shoes and climbed onto the king-sized bed. "This is not the time to fool around. You get that, little sister?"

"Of course. I'm just getting comfortable. We're waiting. I don't have to stand on my toes while I do it. Or even sit in the upright position." She smiled at him. "I've freaked out enough. So go. Lead the assholes away from us. King and I will just lay here and take a nap. I could use one. For some reason I haven't been sleeping well. Imagine that."

"Okay, do what you want. But I've got guys watching the house just in case. Anything hinky happens before you leave, one of them will call me and the local police. So you're not abandoned here." Chance moved over to double-check that the windows were well covered.

King breathed again. Anna's brother *had* seemed to have thought of everything.

"Now I'm gone. And thanks for calling Mom, Annie. She interrogated me about my trip to Texas. So now she knows I have Trent for a client. She's making big plans for next year's football season. You know how she is about the game. She wants some primo seats for when Trent's team plays the Patriots in Foxborough." Chance stopped next to her side of the bed. "I got even. I told her I met your new boyfriend. She was already on Google when we hung up."

"Thanks a heap." Anna held out her arms. "I love you anyway. Now one more hug. Watch your back, Chance."

"Love you too, kiddo." Delaney held her for a long moment. "Sanders, she's all yours. Do not fuck up."

"I'll do my best." King sat on his side of the bed. All his. The idea had his imagination in overdrive. But it wasn't the time for fun and games. Anna just stared at him with big eyes. Did she trust him to take care of her? See her safely to Dallas? The idea that it was on him made his stomach twist. All he could do was his best. Would it be enough?

Chapter Eight

When the phone vibrated under her hand, Anna was surprised to realize she'd actually fallen asleep. She answered quickly, aware of King's arm around her. No wonder she'd been relaxed. He'd given her a feeling of safety when he held her close.

"You're good to go, sis. No sign of anyone watching the house now, though there was someone earlier." Chance sounded excited. He really got off to the chase and obviously thought he was going to spring his trap on Isaac Crane wherever he had set it. "We've fooled them, kid. Put Sanders on the phone."

Anna passed it over, then climbed out of bed. She knew Chance was repeating the same instructions he'd told them earlier. She was glad he was so thorough but right now she just wanted to get this trip over with and finish her program. The house was chilly. Apparently the thermostat had been lowered as if King really was leaving town. She walked into Karen's bedroom and decided to pick out a warm coat. The temperature outside must have really dropped for it to be cool in here and Chance had mentioned a possible ice storm toward Dallas. Real winter in Texas. King had called it a blue norther. Who knew?

A beautiful red, tan, and black plaid wool coat with a fur-lined hood would match her sweater. If she was going to a billionaire's cabin, she wanted to fit in, though King had never commented on her lack of style. Of course, he'd known her for about five minutes. The only time they'd been seen in public together had been at lunch, the day they'd met. The restaurant had been casual. Good thing, since she'd been a strange sight in that too-snug pea-green tee eating with a man in a very expensive suit. At least he'd taken off the jacket and tie.

Why was she worrying about what to wear when people were trying to kidnap her? She had to get her priorities straight. Warm gloves were stacked on one of the shelves. If she doubled up on socks, she could fit into some beautiful black leather boots. Better. By the time she got back to King's side, she was so warm she was almost sweating.

"You look good." He shrugged into his own suede coat and added a wide-brimmed cowboy hat. All black.

Definitely better for sneaking out of the house and, boy, did *he* look good. The ranch look suited him just as much as his expensive suit did. But now she wondered whether her red was too bright. She said as much.

"Delaney assures me no one is watching the house. No one from Crane's side anyway. But why don't you throw a dark blanket around you so you'll blend in with the shadows? I'm sure your brother thinks he's got us covered, but it won't hurt to be cautious." He stuck gloves in his pocket.

"You're right. Your sister has a black coat—" Anna shut up when he touched her chin.

"Don't change." He kissed her lips. "You look beautiful. Red is definitely your color. Now let's get going."

"Thanks. Be patient with me. I'm nervous." Anna smiled at that giant understatement.

"You have a right to be." King shouldered a bag that must have held his clothes and headed toward the kitchen. "Delaney says the weather has deteriorated between here and Dallas. We're going north. It's always colder in those parts of Texas than it is here."

"I forget how big this state is. But cold weather? Just like home." Anna found a navy throw in the hall linen closet and covered her head with it. They'd been talking in whispers. Maybe they were being paranoid, but she was glad to be cautious. Isaac might have run all kinds of possible scenarios in his mind and taken precautions. Had Chance's caravan been too obvious? Was leaving the tracker on King's good truck with Madison in it a little too heavy handed?

Anna carried a bag she'd also pilfered out of Karen's closet. It bulged with the clothes she'd borrowed. The SAT phone and her gun were in that needlepoint tote her grandmother had made for her. Ron had already made sure her laptop had been shoved into the old truck. One thumb drive with her work went in her coat pocket since she was determined to keep it close, the other was deep in her bag of clothes. She waited for King to disarm the alarm.

When he cautiously opened the back door, she could see that storm clouds had blocked out the half moon and it was very dark. A cold wind whipped the trees and made her glad for that warm coat as she waited for him to reset the alarm before she followed King around the house. They stayed close to the shadows as they hurried to the waiting truck. Oh, it really looked like a hunk of junk, a mud-colored two-door with dents, scrapes, and a beat-up bumper. She was surprised a billionaire owned such a thing but stayed silent as King pulled open the passenger door and helped Anna climb inside. Someone had disabled the inside lights. Clever.

To her surprise the hinges worked smoothly and silently. Anna waited while King pulled the door closed, then set her stuff on the floor next to her feet. A spring poked her in the butt and she realized the torn upholstery had given way on her side of the bench seat. Wiggling around finally helped her find a semi-comfortable spot.

"Don't be fooled by the exterior or upholstery. This truck has a new engine and is good to go. It's perfect for the ranch. It wouldn't be here except I dared Karen to drive it into town wearing one of her designer outfits. We do that. Dare each other to do stupid things. Last time she dared me to fly my plane naked to Houston. You should have seen the ground crew when I landed." King chuckled quietly as he reached back to set his own bag in the small back seat, along with his hat.

"I'd liked to have seen that." Anna knew it wasn't the time or place but she was so nervous, she giggled. "My brothers play tricks on me, but I can't imagine..." Lie. She could imagine King naked. It was better than thinking about creeps who used guns and knives and...

"Hey, ranch life can be a drag. Our dares keep things interesting." He drew off his gloves and stuck them in his pockets, then pulled the key from under the mat. "We get where we're going, you won't have to imagine me naked, and that's a promise." He grinned and pulled her over for a quick kiss. "Now this engine's a V8. Hope it doesn't wake the dead." He turned the key and the engine rumbled to life.

To Anna it sounded loud, too loud, despite the noise from the wind through the trees. But King nodded, like he was satisfied that it hadn't caused too much of an uproar. It had certainly started easily enough. He put the truck in gear and drove slowly down the drive, lights off. Anna held on to the overhead handle as it bounced down the gravel road like the demented tea cup ride she'd despised on a visit to a theme park when she was a kid. She'd disgraced herself by throwing up when the thing had finally stopped.

Now she felt nausea making her gulp and looked for a bag. Nothing. Doug obviously kept the interior vacuumed, so why did it smell like YoYo had left a present behind her seat?

She needed air. Hand crank windows. She rolled hers down one inch, then two, and gulped as she leaned against the cold glass.

"You trying to freeze us to death?" King glanced at her as he pulled out a remote control.

"Trying not to hurl." Thank God they'd stopped at the gate and he punched a button. The gate opened silently.

"I needed air." Anna left it down. "Turn on the heater if you're cold." She shivered but her stomach had settled. "This poop smell is killing me."

"Sorry. Guess I'm used to it." He spared her a sympathetic smile. "No guarantee the heater will work. And we have to drive for a while before it'll put out warm air." Once they were through the gate, he hit the remote again. "If there's anyone watching the house, the gate opening and closing just gave us away. Where's your gun?"

"In my bag." Anna reached for it. "I'll get it out if you think I'll need it." The thought of having to arm herself made her head swim. Or was that the smell again?

"Keep the safety on but leave it on the seat. I hope like hell you won't have to use it." King pulled his own gun from his coat pocket and laid it on the seat between them.

"You and me both." He'd started driving again but at least the road was smooth now and Anna's stomach calmed down. "It's one thing to watch gun battles in the movies. That shoot-out last night was way too real for me. If we're being chased and I have to shoot from this truck, I can't guarantee I'll be able to hit a thing." Anna decided it was better to stick the gun in the door's side pocket. Bad enough his gun was lying there. When they hit a bump, it slid next to her hip.

"See if you can tell if a car is following us." He turned the truck onto the private road that led away from his house and still didn't turn on the headlights. It was only when they came to the intersection with the highway that he flipped the switch.

Anna had been watching that road behind them. "I don't see anything. Of course, if they're driving dark like you did, there could be someone back there and I wouldn't be able to tell."

"I don't know if that's good or not. Your brother is supposed to have people tailing us. Maybe they're just really good at staying out of sight." King glanced at her. "Fasten your seat belt. I'm going to hit the gas now. Five more minutes and I'll see if the heater works." He reached over and patted her hand. "You look like you're about to jump out of your skin. Try to relax. We'll be on the road for hours."

"Sure. I'll do that. Maybe take another nap. This is just a casual drive to Dallas, which I've never seen, by the way. What fun." Anna rolled the window down another two inches. "If I don't throw up first. This is the most foul-smelling truck I've ever been in, King. I'm surprised your sister went through with that dare."

"Karen complained about it. She even gave away the designer outfit she wore during the drive. She swore she could never wear it again, though she's used to this smell, grew up with it." He sniffed, like he was finally noticing the reek. "That's the sweet perfume of good, honest manure. Home grown. Just like the tons of spinach I cultivate on my place. It's a good cash crop. We appreciate the manure from our chickens and cattle. But we age it before we put it in the soil. Our spinach is organic. There's a big market for organic vegetables right now."

"I know. I have friends back home who won't buy anything else. But I don't envy your people who have to shovel your shit." She flushed. "Was that politically incorrect?"

"It is what it is." He reached for her hand. "A rancher has to get his hands dirty."

Anna looked down. His hand was big and strong and made hers feel delicate. He'd obviously had a decent manicure since he left his ranch. "I hope you pay your workers well." Anna silently counted her blessings. A good education was on the top of her list.

"I pay top dollar. That way I keep the same crew year after year. It's a shame how migrant workers are treated. But that's another one of my causes. Don't get me started." King kept glancing in the rearview mirror.

Anna's phone rang. Her brother calling. She showed King the caller ID. "We're on the road."

"I know. My men are with you, though you probably can't see them." Chance was all business.

"You're right. We haven't noticed anyone tailing us." Anna checked behind them again. "And I looked."

"I thought I caught a glimpse of a black SUV but it's gone now." King nodded. He could hear the conversation since Anna had put the phone on speaker.

"That was one of my guys. We're pretty sure you're in the clear. Relax and keep going. No sign of Crane's people. So far my plan has worked."

"Thanks, Chance. Let us know if anything happens on your end." Anna realized her brother had ended the call. No time for a chat, obviously. Okay, now she really could relax and get to know King.

"Your brother is good at his job." King coughed and reached for a bottle of water someone had thought to put in the drink holder on the driver's side. "Now can you relax?" He took a drink.

"I'll try to. Yes, Chance is impressing me." Anna had a bottle of water too but ignored it. "So you raise spinach? Seriously? I assumed you were one of those big-time cattle ranchers. Isn't that what Texas is famous for? Beef?"

"I run some cattle and a few chickens. *Abuela* insists. She loves fresh eggs. But the little town near the ranch is known as the spinach-growing capital of the world. We even have a statue of Popeye in the town square." He was grinning now, and wasn't that a good look on him?

"Popeye the sailor man. Like in the old cartoons. I'd like to see that statue." Anna noticed he was getting on a freeway. It was starting to rain and he'd turned on the windshield wipers.

"I'd like to show you the town. Though it would take all of five minutes. I thought I'd get to take you around the ranch. Too bad your brother decided that wasn't a good idea." He reached for a knob on the dashboard. "Let me try this heater. No guarantees. My ranch is southwest of here and we don't get much really cold weather. I doubt this heater has ever been used." He sniffed when a blast of stale air hit them. "It's warm, but it doesn't smell much better than the manure."

"I'll take it." Anna rolled up her window. She didn't tell him she'd been the one to nix the idea of going to his ranch. "What else do you grow on that place of yours?" She kept him talking about his spread, as he called it. King was a practical man. And apparently his crops were big business. Then there were the oil wells and his other investments. He did know a lot of important people in Texas and had connected with them to form different companies and make money. More than a billion dollars. He didn't brag or mention a number, but Anna couldn't forget what her brother had told her.

The farther north they drove, the worse the weather got. King kept both hands on the wheel, calming Anna with his assurances that they had good tires and that he'd driven this highway to Dallas many times. But the thunder sounded ominous. Rain turned to sleet. Now Anna knew what a blue norther was. The cold front had hit Texas hard. She looked at the radar on the handy radar app on her new phone. It didn't look good the closer they got to Dallas.

Several times the truck skidded on patches of ice and King had to fight to keep them on the highway. There were other cars on the road, but the gas stations and restaurants they passed were packed with cars and trucks, travelers who'd decided the conditions were too poor for driving.

"Do we have plenty of gas?" Anna thought to ask.

"Yes. Doug keeps all my vehicles full and in good shape, even this one." King had slowed the truck to a crawl. "Look at the light show."

"When it's lightning like that, I have to turn off my computers." Anna hated lightning. All important work had to stop even if she was in the middle of solving a problem. The thumb drive in her pocket made her feel better about the safety of her program. Not even Ron had seen how far she'd managed to get. Since the robbery, she'd realized it hadn't been paranoia that made her so careful with her work. It was the right thing to do.

King gripped the steering wheel with both hands as the weather worsened around them. "I lost a great TV once to a lightning strike." He glanced at her. "That hurt. It was in the middle of a football game."

The sky lit up right in front of them and a loud clap of thunder rocked the truck.

"Wow. That was really close." Anna clutched her seat belt, suddenly scared even though King was proving to be an excellent driver.

"No, that one hit us." King sounded funny. Lights on the dash went out and the road in front of them was suddenly dark. The heater fan had quit and King struggled with the steering wheel. "We've lost everything electrical, Anna—power steering, brakes, lights. Shit, even the windshield wipers. The lightning must have fried it all. I've got to try to steer us over to the shoulder before someone comes up on us and slams into the back of the truck. The icy road is helping us with a downhill skid, but I'm having a hell of a time steering or stopping this thing."

"What? How *are* you going to stop?" Anna tried to see through the front window that was rapidly fogging. Rain mixed with ice made it impossible to tell what might be just a few feet ahead of them.

"I'll pull the emergency brake when we're where we need to be. We have to get off the highway. The truck is now invisible to oncoming traffic. Thank God there aren't many cars on the road tonight. They were smart enough to get off in this weather." His voice sounded hoarse as he peered ahead of them. Without working wipers, ice built up rapidly on the windshield and he had to be driving blind. "All I can do is keep steering right, toward where the shoulder must be though I sure as hell can't see it."

"Oh, God. What can I do?" Anna unlatched her seat belt and grabbed his arm to help him pull the steering wheel to the right.

"Pray. We need to be seen by the other cars on the road. That's my main concern." King's arm was hard, every muscle tense.

Anna looked around them and pulled out her phone. Thank God it had that flashlight app and she turned it on. Could it help them be seen?

No, not nearly bright enough, not with the back window as fogged and frozen over as the front. But at least now she could see King's face. Not encouraging. He looked determined but grim.

"Is there anything we can use to help coming cars know we're here? What about the horn?" She saw King stomp the brake pedal, as if he could force it to work to slow them down as they skidded toward the unknown. His teeth showed in a grimace while he strained for control, his hands clamped on the steering wheel. He leaned his whole body toward the side of the road, using one hand for a moment to whack the horn. Nothing.

"There's your answer. There's probably an emergency kit in the back of the truck but we can't get out and try to find it in this weather. It would have flares. Not sure how they'd work in this rain and sleet." King was almost standing on the brake pedal. "Fuck. Nothing's working. What are the odds we'd be hit by lighting?" He was back to putting everything he had into manhandling that steering wheel.

"What can I do, King?" Anna looked behind them. Was that big truck bearing down on them? She knew they were barely coasting because King hadn't been driving fast to begin with. Only an idiot would be speeding in these conditions. But then she'd seen idiots on the road before. A horn honked long and loud, then the truck changed lanes and blew past them, the draft from it rocking them. Close, too close.

"Damned fool! He almost hit us." Anna waved her cell phone in the back window. Stupid waste of time with such a feeble light. No one coming down the highway would see it.

"I can't let go of the wheel. Hit the emergency flashers, see if they work." King grunted and the steering wheel actually moved an inch. "We're almost there. I can feel the truck slipping faster." But he might have been saying that to make her feel better. His face hadn't changed. He looked as if he was trying to *will* the truck over to the side of the road.

Anna didn't know a damned thing about cars. "Flashers? Where the hell are they?" She shined her little light across the dash.

"Red triangle in the middle of the dashboard. Do you see it?" He swore as the truck lurched and bumped over something big, swaying them in their seats. "Shit. I hope that wasn't a culvert we ran over and we're headed into a ditch. I can't see a damned thing ahead of us."

Anna finally spotted a button with a red triangle and hit it. A clicking sound and red lights started flashing outside the truck. Thank God. At least they weren't invisible now. Though why that had worked when everything else was dead was a mystery. Weren't they electric? She started to ask King about it but figured this wasn't the time.

"Okay, I think we're off the road." He reached down and pulled a handle. The emergency brake. They jerked to a halt. He looked at her, his face hard to see in the weird glow of the on again, off again red flashers and her cell phone light. "Are you okay? Did you feel that lightning when it hit?" He flexed his fingers, looking at them like he wasn't sure what to think.

"I'm fine. Didn't feel..." Anna realized her ears were ringing. "Uh, well, now that you mention it." She swallowed and her ears popped. She told him. "How about you?"

"Mine are ringing too. And my hands tingled when it hit. Like I'd hit my funny bone in both elbows. They're still feeling a little strange." He kept working his hands. "Hit by lightning. What are the odds?" He picked up his satellite phone. "I wonder where the hell we are. We've been driving for about two hours. We passed Waco, that's the halfway point, about fifteen minutes ago. Which means we're making piss-poor time."

"Of course we are. It's the weather. You can't drive eighty in these conditions." Anna looked out the back window. A truck slowed but obviously decided it was too dangerous to stop. She didn't blame him. "I'm calling my brother." She picked up her own phone. When she got a signal, she sighed with relief. It hadn't occurred to her that the phones could have been fried. Thank God she hadn't plugged hers in to charge, that would have probably been the end of it.

"What are you going to tell him? That I fucked up?" King leaned back. He looked exhausted and coughed, then drained his water bottle. She silently passed him her unopened one.

"Of course not! You did a great job getting us off the road. Thank you. I had visions of some eighteen-wheeler smashing us flat. You were right. We were basically invisible out there." The sleet was coming down harder, thunder still rumbling but not as frequently. At least the lightning seemed to have moved off.

"Let me make the call. Delaney said his men are tailing us. One of them should be here any minute. We need to give them a heads-up before they drive right past us." King reached out and laid a hand on her cheek. "You sure you're okay?"

"As okay as I can be under these circumstances. That was scary as hell." She pulled his hand to her lips.

King hooked a hand behind her neck and pulled her closer. He kissed her long and deep. "I promised to keep you safe. This wasn't part of the plan."

Anna pulled on his ear. "Act of nature. You're my hero. Again. Make the call. If he gives you grief, hand the phone to me. I can sic my mom on him. She can turn him into a quivering bowl of Jell-O. You'd enjoy seeing that."

"I sure would." King kissed her once more, then sat back and made the call. He laid out what happened while Anna watched him. He *was* her hero. She'd like to give him a parade. A very personal one.

* * * *

King had just hung up from a difficult conversation with Anna's brother when flashing red lights showed up in his rearview mirror. State troopers. They'd obviously been alerted by a passing motorist. Which was a good thing. He told Anna to put her gun in her bag while he stuck his back in his coat pocket. No need to get the cops excited about their weapons. Anna didn't have a permit to carry in Texas. She'd have to do something about that. Later. What he needed now was a tow into Waco and a different truck, one that ran and didn't smell like the back forty in his spinach fields. He rolled down the window when there was a knock on it.

"Officer. Hell of a night, isn't it?" King pulled out his wallet and passed over his driver's license and insurance card without being asked.

"What happened here?" The trooper, who had on a slicker over his uniform, scanned his ID with his flashlight after looking him over then Anna. "Mr. Sanders?"

"Would you believe the truck was hit by lightning?" King kept his hands on the steering wheel. "First time it's happened to me and I've been driving around my ranch since I was thirteen."

"I've seen it more than you'd think." The trooper spoke into his radio. "I'll be right back. Guess you'll want a tow. Back to Waco?"

"That would be great. Thanks, officer." King rolled up his window as soon as the trooper headed back to his car. He knew they were running his record and license plate. If by some chance Isaac Crane was monitoring law enforcement channels, this would give away his location. There would be no mention of Anna, but Crane wasn't stupid. King had taken Anna home with him, protected her during the home invasion. It wouldn't be a stretch to think he'd want to stick with her now. But why would Crane be checking the Highway Patrol channels?

King decided not to mention any of his thoughts to Anna. Instead he tried to distract her, telling her about his family—his grandmother and his sister's love for fancy dress balls. Karen was on several committees that planned fundraisers for the charities they supported.

"I saw her ball gowns in her closet. I've never worn anything like that." Anna flushed. "I've been a nerd all my life. I usually dress as Einstein on

Halloween. Brush out my hair and spray it gray. I wore black to my prom during my Goth period."

King would like to see her with the wild hair on Halloween and said so. "I'm trying to picture you Goth. Black lipstick. Combat boots. Bet you were cute."

"Not so much. I had a boyfriend who was into that and thought dressing in his style would help me fit in with his crowd. After we broke up, I realized having all black clothes made it easy to get dressed every day. So I stuck with the look way longer than I should have." She smiled. "Do you like those galas? Dressing up in a tux and drinking champagne?"

"If it's for a good cause." He could picture her in one of those barely there dresses his sister wore. Designers were clever about charging a fortune for next to nothing. Anna certainly had the body for one. "There's an event coming up in Austin this spring. Once we get this behind us, I'll take you."

"I couldn't. I wouldn't know how to act. What to say to those people." She flushed and looked down at her lap.

"Give it a chance, Anna. The rich are just like you and your brother. Not as smart, maybe, but generous. Show them a dog who needs a home and they open their wallets. Their very expensive wallets."

"Really, King, you act like we have a future. I can't imagine—" She jumped when there was a knock on the window on her side. The trooper was there and gestured for her to roll it down.

"I want to show you something." He shined his big flashlight in front of them. "You people were lucky. There's a stream not five feet from where you stopped. It's running fast and deep tonight. You'd have been in big trouble if you hadn't stopped when you did. Up ahead a half a mile you'd have been caught on the bridge with nowhere to go."

King swore. Yes, he could see the fast-running water. He couldn't imagine trying to get Anna out of the truck safely if they'd landed in it. They'd had a close call. The cop probably thought he was doing them a favor, showing them the near miss. King wished Anna hadn't seen the terrifying possibility that could have been their reality.

"Thanks, officer. How's that tow coming?" King knew he didn't sound grateful but he didn't give a damn.

The man passed King's license and insurance card to Anna. "They're on the way. Should take about fifteen minutes, give or take. You want to come sit in the cruiser where it's warm?" He started to open Anna's door, then realized it was locked. "Ma'am?"

"No, we'll stay here and wait for the tow truck. Thank you, though." She smiled at him. "I've got a blanket and my coat. We're warm enough and I'd hate to get out in that rain."

"Whatever you say. I'll stay parked behind you in my car with my flashers going until that tow truck gets here. Unless I get an emergency call." He tipped his hat, then walked off.

"Do you think we were rude?" Anna nibbled at her bottom lip then, handed King his cards.

"He meant well, but you *would* have gotten wet just getting to his car. Not helpful. Let's see what your brother wants us to do." King wasn't surprised when his phone rang before he could call Delaney himself.

"Your name just came up on the police scanner." Delaney was not happy. "What the fuck?"

"Don't yell at me, Delaney." King was not about to be blamed for something he hadn't done. "Someone obviously decided we needed help when they saw us on the side of the road. It was the right thing to do. The trooper has already called for a tow. I'm going to get the truck towed into Waco."

"Be careful. Do not get into a tow truck or even into a patrol car. My men are trailing you. I'm not sure why one of them hasn't already stopped right behind you. Let me check." Delaney hung up before King could say another word.

"He didn't yell at you, did he?" Anna had wrapped that dark throw around her but she was still shivering. "I swear, if he is trying to blame you for this, I'll make him sorry."

"He tried. You heard me. I shut him down." King shivered and he put on his gloves again. Yeah, it was getting damned cold in the truck and having the windows down for even a short while hadn't helped. Maybe sitting in the back of a patrol car wasn't such a bad idea. But Delaney had warned them off that. Why? Surely the man was no part of Crane's network. Of course, he could be an innocent bystander if there was a showdown coming.

King turned so he could watch the highway for coming cars. The traffic was sparse and passing cars kept going at a snail's pace, avoiding the police car by a wide margin. Soon a black SUV pulled over to the shoulder in front of them and put on its emergency flashers. A man got out and approached their car. King could see that he was armed because he'd kept his coat unbuttoned. That was strange considering the weather. He tensed and pulled out his own gun. Whose side was this man on?

The state trooper jumped out of his car and approached the new arrival. Quickly, the man buttoned up and walked over to greet the cop. They exchanged a few words, then the policeman walked back to his car with a wave and drove away.

When his phone rang, King was trying to decide what to do about the man who was waiting for him to roll down his window.

"Yeah? There's a man here. Should I shoot him or talk to him?" King only knew that he wasn't going to let anyone take Anna without a fight. A tow truck pulled up, distracting him. Bad timing.

"That's Sam. Look at him, Sanders. Don't you recognize him? He was guarding the front door last night." Delaney sounded impatient.

"My window's fogged up. I can't see shit. If he has one of your comms in his ear, tell him to take off his cap then put it back on." King wasn't eager to roll down his window again. All he could tell so far was that the man was big, bulky, and armed. To his relief the man took off his knit cap, stroked his bald head, then slipped the cap back on. "Okay, it must be Sam. I'll call you if I need you." King hung up and rolled down his window. "What took you so long?"

"Sorry, Mr. Sanders, but I've had you in sight the whole time. Hung back until the cop was through with you." Sam leaned in. "You all right, Ms. Delaney?"

"Just cold. How's your heater, Sam?" She unlocked her door. "I'm willing to run through the sleet if I can count on a warm car when I get there. And call me Anna."

"Wait. Let me get an umbrella. And you're on a slope. There's quite a drop on your side of the truck. I'd hate for you to slide into that water. I'll give you a hand." He frowned toward the fast-running stream in front of them. He had a powerful flashlight in his hand and made sure they could see just how dangerous it was.

"Thanks, Sam. And it's King, not Mr. Sanders. Hell, I don't even know your last name." King unlocked his own door and reached for his hat. There was no help for it. He was going to have to talk to the tow truck driver, who was making his way cautiously toward them. The driver had on a slicker suit, smartly striped with reflective tape. Obviously the man had been caught in this kind of weather before.

"Sam Johnson. Now, Anna, you wait for me." He smiled and hurried to his SUV, returning with a big black umbrella. He slid once getting around the end of the truck but quickly found his footing.

King held up a hand when the tow driver started in with an explanation about how he'd have to pull out the truck. "Wait. Let me make sure my lady gets out safely." He hurried to Sam's side and took Anna's elbow, gesturing for Sam to take her bag. "Hold on to me, Anna. Sam, you keep that umbrella over her head."

"Really, it won't hurt me to get a little wet." But Anna did grip his arm when they both struggled up the slippery incline and had to step over the low concrete barrier that separated the shoulder from the grassy verge. The cars going past stayed in the far lane because of the tow truck's flashing lights. By the time Anna was settled in the back seat of the warm SUV parked on the shoulder nearby, she'd practically pulled King's arm out of its socket.

"Heated seats!" She reached out for her bag. "Thanks, Sam. Oh! Please rescue that computer from the back of King's truck before it gets towed away. And my laptop. I'll need it where we're going."

"Yes, ma'am." He handed the umbrella to King. "You keep this. I'll need both hands to unload the cargo."

King looked down at his coat, covered in ice. "I think it's a little late for that, but thanks." He closed the umbrella and stuck it in the back of the SUV. Didn't Sam know that a rancher relied on his hat to keep the rain or, in this case, the ice off his head?

He walked back to the truck driver. After a brief discussion, they agreed it could be taken to a dealership in Waco. Nothing could be done tonight about getting another vehicle. King looked back at Sam's SUV. It had been joined by another black one and Sam was being helped to move Anna's computer by the man who'd been tailing them. When a third vehicle drove up and stopped, he realized they'd also had someone ahead of them, watching for problems. The three men made quick work of emptying the old truck. Then they stood waiting for him to join them. In the icy rain. His phone rang.

"I just talked to Anna. Now I'm asking you. My men are waiting to hear where you want to go next. Any ideas?" Delaney waited.

"I think we should spend the night in Waco. I can get a new truck in the morning and your people can get rooms near us. So far the only issues we've had are weather related." King waited while Delaney digested this.

"I don't have a problem with that. One of my guys will put the rooms on a credit card that Crane won't recognize. Anna is exhausted after her near miss. Get a good night's sleep and you can head out in the morning. The weather is supposed to clear and you can be at Trent's place in an hour or so."

"Sounds like a plan. I can wait to get something done about the truck until later, if you think that might leave some kind of trail for Crane to follow. We can ride in one of the SUVs to Trent's place." King pulled out his wallet. He'd gotten plenty of cash out of his safe. Good thing.

"Excellent. The less you're on anyone's radar, the better. I don't like that you were on the Highway Patrol's radio, but maybe Crane didn't notice. You'll be well-guarded tonight no matter what."

"You had three men on us? I never saw even one of them." King stood aside when the tow truck started backing up toward his beater. He figured it was destined for a junkyard. Electrical problems were a bitch to solve and it had served its purpose over the years.

"Four. You still won't see him. He's my reserve. If you notice him, I'll fire him. It's always good to have an invisible man." Delaney cleared his throat. "Anna said you did some good driving there, Sanders. She says you saved her life. Thanks."

"I'll do whatever I can to protect her, Delaney. So you have five men taking care of her. Remember that." He ended the call and walked over to talk to the truck driver. He handed him half his fee in cash. "One of us will follow you to Waco and you'll get the rest at the dealership. Are you okay with that?"

The man's eyes widened. "This is a little more than we discussed."

"That's for hurrying the hell up. Hey, can you explain why the emergency flashers worked and everything else was fried by the lightning?" King stared at the truck, silently telling it goodbye.

"Works off the battery. If there's any charge left in it, flashers can work. It's a lifesaver. But then you never know with a lightning strike. I've seen airbags go off after one. You were lucky that didn't happen. Little lady might've ended up with bruised ribs." The driver nodded toward the SUV where Anna sat.

"Okay. Thanks." King swallowed and his throat let him know it. Damn it. The cold was getting to him, especially since he'd stepped in a low spot and icy water had sloshed inside one of his boots and wet the bottom of his jeans. He walked back to the SUV and the waiting men. "Would one of you mind meeting the tow at the dealership in Waco? I assume your boss told you we're spending the night at a motel there."

"Yeah, he told us. He's picked one out, texted me the address and reserved three rooms. He even let us know how he wants us deployed." Sam pulled off his cap and shook off ice crystals. "Chance is always one step ahead." He glanced at one of the men. "Buck, you want to take the tow?"

"No problem." The burly guy who could have been a linebacker held out his hand. "Chance said you're paying cash."

King gave him the rest of the driver's fee. "He's getting a bonus if he hurries. I'm sorry you fellas have to deal with this weather."

Buck shrugged. "Compared to some places I've been, this is paradise. Let me touch base with Cooter." He'd obviously read the name on the side of the tow truck. "Then I'll sit in my vehicle and thaw out my ass with the heated seat before I follow him into town. Piece of cake."

King shook hands all around, double-checked to make sure his bag was out of the truck, then climbed in the back seat with Anna.

He hadn't realized how freaking cold he was until he sat his own ass on the heated seat and adjusted the vent to blow warm air on his face. He opened the door again to shake the ice and rain off his good black hat before he set it by his feet. It would be fine once it dried. Then he took a deep breath that startled him when it turned into a cough. He managed to get it under control, then turned to face Anna.

"King! You're covered with ice!" Anna looked alarmed. "And your lips are blue." She pulled off her gloves and touched them. "What can I do to help?"

"Sleep with me tonight." He figured he might as well lay it out there. He'd take her pity. Hell, he'd take her any way he could get her.

"Sam told me we're going back to Waco." She moved her fingers over his cheeks, which, he had to admit, were numb. "Then Chance called back a few minutes ago and asked me if I wanted my own room. I said no, I'd share with you."

King wanted to shout, hit the back of the seat, do something to celebrate. A kiss would have sealed the deal. Too bad he didn't think his frozen lips could do a decent job of it. Just then Sam got into the driver's seat and turned to look at them.

"Buckle up. Bad roads, but I guess I don't have to tell you that. We should be at the motel in about fifteen minutes."

"Thanks, Sam." King settled for pulling off one of his gloves and wrapping Anna's hand in his. His chest was tight and breathing took an effort. Maybe he was coming down with pneumonia. He should probably take off that boot and dump the water out of it. Couldn't feel his toes on that foot. Didn't matter. Tonight was going to be special, he'd make sure of it or die trying. Anna squeezed his hand. He leaned back and closed his eyes, imagining how it would be. They were safe and the time was finally right. No rain checks. Nothing could come between them now.

Chapter Nine

They were lucky Chance managed to get three rooms in the motel. The bad weather had made a lot of travelers seek shelter. Sam wasn't happy that the rooms weren't next to each other and tried to insist that he stay with her and King. Anna put her foot down. She had a gun, King had a gun, and Sam was only two doors down with his pal Buck.

"One of us will stand guard outside your room then. You seriously don't expect us to leave you unprotected." Sam was determined. He looked out at the sleet that swept into the open walkway.

"I'll be with her. Isn't that enough for you?" King threw his hat on the desk.

"I don't know you. So, no, it sure as hell isn't." Sam wasn't smiling and ignored King's growl.

"Really? You're going to stand in front of my door? You know if the decoy didn't work and Isaac saw King's name on the law enforcement wire, he'll start checking local motels and hotels for us." Anna looked down at the parking lot. The other two bodyguards were on the floor below. They'd take turns doing surveillance on the parking lot throughout the rest of the night. Anna felt sorry for them but had shut up about it when they stoically insisted it was their job. "Your big black SUVs are so obvious, they practically shout hired muscle. All Isaac has to do is see them and he'll figure out we're here. Then he'll find one of you standing in front of my door. Might as well post a sign: Here she is, come and get her."

"First, I'm pretty sure that decoy worked, Anna. The guys scattered the cars here and they're covered with ice. They're only obvious to you." Sam sounded impatient with her. "I'm following orders. You want to call your brother and argue with him? Feel free." He tried to hand her his phone.

"No. He's probably already trying to figure out how to dump my friend Scarlett and join us here. I'm not bothering him." Anna realized King had been awfully quiet since that first outburst. He was letting her handle this. She handed Sam her phone. "Put your number in there. I'll call you if I need you. Surely that will be good enough. Please don't stand out there in the sleet all night."

"Buck and I will take turns. We have on thermal underwear. No big deal." He did put his number in her phone. "Good point about being obvious. I'll think about it." He glanced at the parking lot. "You want your laptop?"

"No, I'm not thinking about work right now." Her desktop computer was locked in one of the SUVs too. She had no idea which one because they looked like clones. She glanced back at King, who'd shrugged out of his coat and was sitting on the foot of the king-sized bed. No reaction to that remark? She was worried about him. Of course he'd swaggered into their room like he was aces. But now he pulled off one of his boots and water poured out. Oh, no!

"See you in the morning, Sam." She shut the door in his face. "What happened, King?"

"Stepped in a puddle." He held up a wet sock. "The boot will dry. Luckily only one of them got it." He took off the other one and set the pair next to the heater that was going full blast. He stood in front of it for a moment, shivering.

"You okay?"

"Sure. Nothing wrong with me that a hot shower won't cure." He looked her over with a wink when she took off her own coat. "You go first. I want to see you in a towel again."

"No, your foot was wet and you were out in that sleet for a long time. You first." She had to push him into the bathroom, and the fact that he let her told her he was really, really cold. Was it the lightning strike or standing around in the ice storm that had done a number on him?

He was in there a long time but finally came out of the steamy bathroom wearing nothing but a towel, a grin, and a naughty twinkle in his eyes. Tempting. But Anna was still chilled to the bone, despite the warm air coming from the vents in the room. So she scurried past him into the bathroom to take her hot shower. That's what it took to finally stop shivering. Taking her cue from King, she stepped out wrapped in a towel, only to find him sprawled on the king-sized bed—sound asleep.

She dragged the comforter and a blanket over him, then pulled on one of the oversized nightgowns she'd borrowed from his sister and climbed into bed beside him. Four men guarded them. No one except her brother knew where they were. She could finally relax and get a good night's sleep.

She hopped up and put their guns on the nightstands, one on each side, then lay down again. Okay. Now she could close her eyes and let her worries go. She was wrung out and exhausted. Hopefully she and King would wake up and be able to deliver on that promise in his sister's closet. She wanted to do more than snuggle against his hot body in this bed.

She moved closer. Hot, not warm. She sat up again and put her hand to his forehead. He definitely had a fever.

"King?" She nudged him gently. No response. Well, hell. King was really and truly sick. Now what?

She called Sam. He hit her door before she could say a word. She let him in, the extra blanket around her shoulders, and stared down the barrel of his gun.

"Whoa. Would you let me tell you what I need before you start shooting at shadows?" She had peeked out of the curtain first to make sure it was him who'd banged on the door.

"What is it? Did you hear a noise?" Sam strode into the bathroom, checking behind the shower curtain then looking in the closet. Buck stood guard in the doorway, leaving the door ajar. His gun was out, his face grim as he spoke into his phone. Cold air blew in, making her wish for socks on her bare feet.

"No, nothing like that. King is sick. He has a fever. Look at him. He hasn't moved despite all the noise you're making." Anna walked over to stare down at King's flushed face. It was true. Sam had banged doors in his search for intruders and King hadn't so much as twitched.

"False alarm. Stand down." Buck holstered his weapon and stepped inside, closing and locking the door. He hadn't bothered with a coat, so Sam must have taken the first watch.

"Can we send for a doctor?" Anna brushed King's hair back from his forehead. He was burning up.

"He was fine less than an hour ago." Sam frowned down at King's prone figure like he was faking it.

"I have a first aid kit in my car." Buck looked to Sam for permission. Obviously Sam was the man in charge here. At his nod Buck took off, closing the door quietly behind him.

Sam locked it again then walked over to lay the back of his hand on King's forehead. "I agree. He feels like he's got fever. Was he all right when you left the house?" He looked impatient, like he wouldn't have let a sick man come along on a mission.

"Sure. I guess so. He didn't complain. But he stepped in ice water out there, walked around with it in his boot." Anna felt guilty that they'd been so careful to cover her with an umbrella and had practically carried her to the heated SUV like she was made of delicate porcelain. "All of you stood around in the ice and rain way too long."

"Didn't bother me any." Sam walked to the door at a soft knock. He checked through the curtain then let Buck in. "What have we got?"

"Aspirin, penicillin, antibiotics. Everything I'd need if someone got shot. The usual first aid for the field." Buck opened a rather large metal box with a red cross on it.

In case someone gets shot? Anna shuddered. The casual way Buck said that reminded her of that gun battle at King's house. It had been a miracle the man behind Knife Guy hadn't hit King. That overstuffed leather recliner would never be the same.

This was how Chance's men prepared for a security gig. Her own first aid kit held little more than Band-Aids and alcohol.

"Buck was a medic in the Army. Let him see what he can do." Sam led Anna over to the desk chair. "Sit. Stay out of his way."

Anna didn't like being ordered around but knew nothing about emergency medical care. Buck stuck a digital thermometer in King's ear then swore after the thing beeped and he looked at the temperature.

"He's got a pretty high fever. Let's give him ibuprofen, then bathe him with some wet cool towels to help bring that fever down. Has he eaten lately?" Buck pulled away the comforter and stripped off King's towel. "Sam, bring me a couple of wet washcloths. Cool, not warm."

"Eaten?" Anna was staring at one of the most perfect butts she'd ever seen. Oh, she was ridiculous. King was sick. "Yes, he had a couple of sandwiches before we left the house."

"Good. Taking the meds on an empty stomach could make him nauseated. Bring me a bottle of water, Anna." Buck pointed to the makeshift kitchenette that held a microwave and small refrigerator.

"Oh, right. So he can swallow the pills." She tore her gaze from King's body and ran to get the bottle, twisting off the top.

"We don't want him dehydrated either." Buck dug through his impressive store of medication.

"Is he unconscious? I thought he was just sleeping. I napped during the day while we waited but I think he stayed awake, guarding me." Oh, shoot. Tears. No, she wasn't going to let them fall.

"Guarding you was the right idea, but if he exhausted himself, it left him vulnerable to illness." Buck rolled King over.

Anna looked away. Totally not fair to gawk at him when he was unaware. "You didn't answer me. Is he unconscious?"

"Doubt it. Just out of it. Finally getting the sleep he needs to get well." Buck lifted King's head. "Put the water to his lips as soon as I shove these pills in his mouth. Ready?"

There was no help for it, Anna was going to have to look while she moved to the side of the bed to position the water bottle against King's lips. King was a solid man with wide shoulders and narrow hips. He had the muscular build of a man who took care of his body by running and working out. She skimmed past that nest of dark hair where his...

Sam was back and laid a towel over King's private parts. Whether he did that to spare her blushes or not didn't matter. She had to concentrate on getting water into King after Buck shoved three pills into his mouth. She wasn't doing a great job until Buck grabbed King's cheeks and forced his mouth open, then held his nose until he swallowed.

King moaned and shook his head. But the pills stayed down.

"What does that mean? He's resisting us." She took the wet washcloth Sam silently handed her and wiped King's face with it.

"I think that means his throat is sore. That explains the fever. He probably has an infection. Do you know if he's allergic to penicillin?" Buck dug into his kit and came out with more medication.

"No, I just met him. Let me call Chance. He can check with King's grandmother at the ranch. I'm sure he has the number." Anna hit speed dial. Chance wasn't happy with what he called a "complication" but promised to get right back to her. In moments, he let her know that King had no allergies other than ragweed and dust.

"That cowboy better not slow us down, Anna."

"Shut up, Chance. Anyone can get sick. Even you."

"I'm telling you right now that if this is serious he's being left behind. I'm supposed to keep you safe. Zenon isn't paying me to worry about King Sanders." Chance was issuing orders.

Anna wasn't having it. First, she was worried about King and now she had to listen to her brother's threats? "Shut the hell up. I'm promising *you* right now that you'll have to carry me out of here screaming if you try to leave King behind. Understand? Isaac already used Scarlett as leverage. What if he thought King might work for that purpose? Are you saying you'd leave some of your men here with him? To guard him?"

"Hell no. They are there for you. But get real, Anna. You just met him. He can't be that important to you. Crane sure wouldn't think so. He's all about using you and what you know. Then God knows what will happen to you once you've done what they need doing." Chance blew out a gusty breath. "Sis, I'm not saying this to be mean, but check yourself. Sanders is a stranger. Get a grip."

"You have no idea what's important to me. Right now, I have to be sure King gets the medical care he needs." She ended the call, her hands shaking she was so mad at her brother.

"We're good on the penicillin." She let her gaze roam over King's flushed face. A stranger. Really? After what they'd been through together?

He'd been beside her when bullets were flying. They'd sat together in that truck when lightning had struck. Oh, not like in a romance novel but it had done something to them both and they'd survived. The other kind of lightning, the romantic kind, she'd felt the first time she'd kissed him. It was a connection, one she'd never expected to feel with any man. Rare, precious, and not something she'd just walk away from. Certainly not because her brother had ordered her to do it.

Buck was busy counting out some pills. "He'll really fight us this time if it hurts to swallow. You ready to try this again? Or Sam can take over."

"No, I want to do it." She sure wasn't going to stand by and let Sam have water-bottle duty. She had a feeling the man would be no nonsense, impatient, and rougher than she wanted him to be. She handed Sam the washcloth that had warmed way too fast and got ready to force down more water.

Buck was right, King fought them, flailing with his fists this time. He managed to hit her with a strong left but she dodged most of it and at least didn't spill water down his chest. When they were done, she gently touched King's hot cheek and murmured words of comfort. That seemed to soothe him and he settled down again.

"Okay, he swallowed them." Buck patted her shoulder. "Now we keep wiping him down. Every time the cloths warm up, we'll replace them with cool ones. As soon as the fever breaks, we can let him sleep it off." He studied her. "Sam and I can handle this, Anna. You should go sleep in our room. Rest. I'll call one of the men downstairs to stand guard over you."

"No, I want to help. Give me a cloth." Anna took a fresh cool washcloth and began to wipe off that same left arm that had tried to knock her into next week. He was still so hot. And now he mumbled as he lay there. What was he saying? She couldn't tell. Something about a horse, a dog, or was it a woman? She had no right to be jealous. But someone made him call out, swear, and then kick at the towel Sam was using on his legs.

After what seemed like hours, he finally seemed cooler. Buck took his temperature again, satisfied that the fever was going down. He gave

King a couple more ibuprofen with Anna's help. Then they covered him up and let him sleep.

"We could call down for fresh linens, but the fewer people who see us, the better." Sam felt the comforter. "Seems dry enough. I think he'll be all right."

Anna wasn't sure Sam really cared so she tested it herself. Okay, but the bottom sheet under King was probably damp. At least King wasn't restless now and seemed to be sleeping peacefully. She turned to Buck, who had impressed her with his calm competency.

"You think he's on the mend?" She was so tired she thought she could fall asleep standing up.

"I do." Buck smiled for a change. "Whatever it was has let loose of him." He looked at her as if inspecting her. "How do you feel? Chance says you and Sanders are getting close. Think you're coming down with this? It might be contagious. Swallow." He reached out and felt her neck and behind her ears.

"I'm fine. Just tired." Anna swallowed, relieved that, while dry, her throat wasn't raw. She told him so, glad he was conscientious. Buck was as impersonal as any doctor she'd ever visited as he took her temperature just to be sure. He handed her a bottle of water and told her to drink to guard against dehydration. Then he packed his thermometer and the pills away and snapped the kit shut.

"I agree. You're okay. You just need to go to bed." He nodded and picked up his heavy kit. "Stick to the dry side of that bed. Lie down and we'll leave you to it."

"I can sit here. Wait to make sure you don't need anything else." Sam glanced at the desk chair in the corner of the room.

"No. Go on." Anna sat on the edge of the bed, her legs giving out. "I couldn't sleep if I knew you were sitting in that uncomfortable chair, staring at me."

"It's what I'm paid to do, Anna." Sam glanced at Buck. "But I see your point. Follow me to the door. Lock up and put on the chain. It's feeble but every little bit helps. Put your phone by the bed, next to that gun. I like that you thought to keep a weapon there, close at hand."

Anna dragged herself to her feet again. "Thanks, Buck. You were a wonderful medic. Bet you saved some lives when you were on active duty."

He just grunted, clearly not willing to talk about it. Sam was right behind him and just nodded. Like he knew things but wasn't going to talk about them either.

"See you in the morning. Not early. I'll call you when I want breakfast." Anna stood in the doorway. The blast of cold air from outside woke her a little. And gave her an idea. "If this weather hasn't cleared, then maybe we can stay here a little longer. What do you think? We're using assumed names. Seems safe enough to me."

"It's a thought, but there are more men where we're headed. A more secure location with no strangers around us." Sam looked significantly at the room next door. A baby was crying, then a woman told it to hush. "Civilians can be a liability and at risk."

"I forgot about that." Anna started to close the door. Stupid to get chilled. And staying here had been a dumb idea. She hadn't thought it through. "Never mind. I should trust you and my brother to know what you're doing. The sooner we get settled in that secure location, the sooner I can finish what I started. Thanks, Sam." Then she shut the door and locked it, sliding the chain into place as well.

She hurried back to that dry spot on the bed but not before she pushed the thermostat up a few degrees. She might get too hot, but she was determined to finally at least get warm. It was tempting, once she was under the covers, to ease her icy bare feet over to touch King's legs. He was warm now, not hot, and it would feel so very good. No, that would be cruel and might wake him.

He mumbled something. She leaned closer, trying to hear what he said. Spanish. Well, that was disappointing. If a miracle happened and she did have some kind of future with King, she was going to have to learn the language.

Oh, he was calling for his grandmother. That made her eyes fill with tears and she rolled away from him, determined to give him privacy. He'd been a little boy when his parents had died. His *abuela* had raised him and his sister. What nightmare made him restless in his sleep?

She'd been lucky to have both parents, even two sets of wonderful grandparents, all her life. Her large family had given her a feeling of safety and security that never left her. Leaving Boston to start a new life had seemed like an adventure, but she'd always known there was a haven waiting for her if she failed here. She could go back and no one would think less of her. Some people weren't so lucky. King didn't have a large family but he certainly seemed well grounded to her. A success. This *abuela* of his must be a strong lady. Anna would like to meet her.

* * * *

King woke slowly, aware of a warm body curled up next to him. Too bad he felt like he'd been on the bottom of a pile on the football field. He swallowed. At least his throat seemed back to normal. For a while there he'd felt like he'd swallowed barbed wire. He turned his head and his nose brushed dark hair. Anna. She'd slept next to him and now was draped over him like a sweet, warm blanket. Hot damn! And he was naked as the day he was born. That would have cheered him up, except he could tell she wasn't naked, not even close.

If they'd finally had the night he'd been looking forward to, he sure as hell couldn't remember it. He tried to think back: They'd come to the motel, one of those ordinary chain things. She'd insisted he take the first shower. He'd come out of the bathroom and she'd hurried to take her turn. And then… It was a blank. Shoot. He must have fallen asleep. What kind of man does that? Crashes without making his move?

"You're awake." She smiled up at him. "How do you feel?"

"Let's see." He brushed her hair back so he could see her face. "Like I've been struck by lightning, thrown from my horse, and run over by a semi. Other than that, pretty damn good."

"How's your throat?" She sat up and stared down at him, a worry line between her dark brows. "You were really sick last night and had a high fever. Buck is a medic. He gave you some medicine. He left another dose by the bed. Take it."

King reached for the water bottle and pair of pills on the nightstand. "Whatever I had, I'm obviously snapping back. I must have passed out last night, but no fever now. My throat's a little scratchy but nothing I can't live with." He tossed back the pills. Yeah, his throat was raw. "Miracle drugs." He looked her over. Where the hell had she found that enormous flannel nightgown? She sure hadn't bought it at the department store. It covered every inch of her, even her hands. "What are you wearing?"

She grinned. "Don't you like it? I found it in one of your sister's drawers. You have to admit, the color is pretty." She toyed with a bow the color of raspberries tied under her chin.

"Oh, sure. My grandmother probably gave it to her. She's always telling Karen to *actúa como una dama*, that means 'act like a lady.' That's why that thing was at my house and not with my sister."

He reached for the bow and jerked the end of the ribbon, opening the top so he could see some cleavage. "That's better. Karen's into stuff that's more revealing. Thank God I've only heard about that. Never had to see it."

"Wait." She scooted out of reach, pulling the ribbon from his fingers. "I've got to brush my teeth."

King liked the sound of that. It promised a close encounter in his future. He realized he needed to use the facilities. When she appeared in the bathroom doorway, a very pretty vision in that huge nightgown with her bare toes peeking out, he wished he didn't have to heed nature's call at all.

"Hold that thought." He leaped from the bed and almost shoved her out of the way, slamming the bathroom door behind him. Relief as he peed like a cow on a flat rock. He hoped Anna couldn't hear. It wasn't a romantic start to their morning. At least he found his own toothbrush next to the sink. Too bad he didn't like what he saw in the mirror. He'd been sick and looked it. He had dark circles under his eyes and he'd gone to bed with his hair uncombed. It was hopeless, sticking up like that lightning had shot right up through it. Hey, it was an excuse.

Didn't matter. He remembered the look in Anna's eyes. She wanted him despite the fact that he looked like roadkill. He reached down and gave his buddy a check. Oh, yeah, he had some life left in him. He opened the bathroom door, refusing to bother with a towel.

Anna had lost that nightgown. He knew it because it was on the floor at the foot of the bed. She was under the covers though, her bare shoulders showing and leaving it to him to play treasure hunt as he approached the bed. He crawled from the foot up to where she lay. She stared at him like she couldn't wait for the games to begin, those blue eyes bright with eagerness.

He had to kiss her, to take her mouth and trap her under him, but carefully. She grabbed his shoulders, pulling him down, while their mouths learned each other all over again. He savored her taste of mint and Anna. She was so right for him, playful yet intense. God.

He rolled off her so he could get rid of that bulky comforter and then the sheet that was between them. He needed to see her. She was beautiful, every inch of her. He took a moment just to look his fill. She had full breasts, creamy skin, and a curve to her hips that made him hungry to explore all of her with his hands and his mouth.

"King." She linked her fingers with his and brought his hand to her breast. "No more rain checks."

"God, no." He learned the soft shape and curve of that breast, then the hard point of her nipple before he moved over her and pulled it into his mouth. Sweet, so sweet. She moaned and grabbed his hair to make sure he knew she liked what he did. She didn't need him to be too gentle either as she strained against him. He got the message and used his teeth, then sucked her deep, the pull making her come off the bed.

She slid her fingers across his chest, learning him and finding where he wanted to be touched. She made him hum with pleasure too. He ran his hand over her stomach, touching the small dark patch that had tantalized him since the glimpse he'd had in the closet that day. Oh, yeah, soft, already damp, and leading to the treasure below. She wanted him as much as he wanted her. She moved her hips and widened her legs, silently begging him to come inside and touch her there.

He raised his head and looked into her eyes. "Tell me what you want. Show me."

"You. Everything." She kissed him then guided his hand down until he slipped a finger inside her. He swallowed her gasp of pleasure. Her other hand was on him, tracing the shape of his cock and moving along the length of him until she dragged a groan from him.

"Easy. I want this to last." The rhythm *was* easy at first. But then she moved her mouth down to kiss his chest and nipped at his nipples, making him crazy. He slid another finger into her and increased the pressure. When she squeezed his cock and began to match what he was doing to her, he thought he'd come unglued.

"Anna, get on up here." He rolled them, sitting her on top as he kissed his way to her stomach, holding on to her hips.

"What are you doing?" She gripped his arms, her face flushed.

"Hold on to that headboard." He lifted her until he had her where he wanted her, then dove deep, tasting her while her back bowed and she gripped the shiny brass headboard.

"King!" She bucked against his mouth as she came with a surprised squeal. "God." She shuddered, then reached down and grabbed his hair. "Let me. I want you, inside me." She finally managed to slide down his body.

When she guided him where she wanted him, they both just stared at each other for a moment. Joined.

The wonder of it, the perfection, made King pull her down for a long kiss before he could even begin to move. Where had this woman come from? Had it really been only days since he'd met her? And yet, he couldn't imagine ever giving her up. She kissed him like she couldn't get enough of him and he felt the same way. Finally she sat up again and he held those perfect pink-tipped breasts in his hands.

"Move. Show me how you want it." He stared up at her. Waiting. He was as hard as he'd ever been in his life. If she didn't hurry, he might come anyway, and wouldn't that be a damned shame and disgrace. But he wanted her to know that her pleasure was what he was here for. So he kept still. Determined and forcing an iron control he'd never known he had. Not about this.

"I could sit here forever. Just like this. It feels…incredible." Her smile was wicked. Like she knew she was torturing him. Then she leaned forward and kissed him again. She braced her hands on his shoulders, her hair a wild nimbus around her beautiful face. "But I know better. I need you now." She began to move, taking him deeper, then easing off.

She set a rhythm that made King's eyes cross. He felt it coming and thanked the good Lord she was trembling, clenching around him as her own climax began to shudder through her. She moved faster and faster, her head thrown back, her dark hair even wilder than his as she shouted her release and took every bit of his. Her scream echoed through the room and King shouted her name when he couldn't hold it in another moment. She fell onto him, both of them spent.

A hard banging on the door threatened to break it down. "Anna! Are you all right?"

"Sam and Buck." She grinned against King's chest, then sat up again, still connected to him, flushed and satisfied. "I'm fine. I'm having sex, you idiots. Go the hell away."

King hoped that was plain enough for their bodyguards. But a phone next to the bed rang anyway. He reached for it, not about to break his connection with Anna, and answered.

"Yeah."

"My men are concerned. Will you verify that my sister is all right?" Chance Delaney was not happy.

"From here it looks like she's more than all right, but I'll let her tell you herself." King handed the phone to Anna. He could barely move and sure as hell didn't want to. He smoothed a hand down Anna's bare back as she told her brother that she was fine, better than fine, and to tell his men to go away. No, she'd need an hour, thank you very much. She handed the phone back to King.

"You need to stop the fun and games and get ready to hit the road in thirty minutes. Are we clear?" Delaney was in commander mode.

"We'll need breakfast. I've worked up an appetite. And didn't I hear your sister tell you an hour?" King grinned at Anna as she slid off him and walked over to the bathroom, her bare bottom twitching in a way that had him hardening and thinking about another round. She gestured for him to join her as she started the shower.

"Shit. What's next? You want Sam to bring you two breakfast in bed?"

King laughed. Her brother's foul mood wasn't about to bring him down.

"One hour. We'll be ready."

"Fine. I'll give the orders to stop for breakfast after the cars are loaded." Delaney bit off the words. "And, Sanders, remember what I said."

"What's that?" King was having trouble remembering his own name as Anna bent over to adjust the water temperature through the open bathroom door.

"Don't hurt my sister. If you do, I'll come looking for you."

"Don't worry. Concentrate your efforts on finding Crane and his people. I want this mess over and done." King had never meant anything more. "Anna is my top priority. She's in no danger from me." He ended the call and headed for the shower.

Chapter Ten

Sam had the door open. He'd already handed off their bags so Buck could load them into one of the SUVs. Anna made a sweep of the room, making sure she hadn't left anything. She was almost sorry to leave. She'd felt safe and had finally been as close to King as she'd wanted. The man sat on the foot of the bed, giving her a look that was pure masculine satisfaction. Why not? He'd earned it. She was feeling more than satisfied herself. Anna stopped in front of him and got trapped between his knees.

"You'd better put on your coat. You don't want to get sick again." She smiled into his dark eyes. She was happy. Didn't matter that bad things kept happening. For now, she was happy.

"In a minute." He pulled her in with two firm hands on her butt. "How are you feeling? About this morning." He didn't show a bit of insecurity but glanced at Sam. "Could we have some privacy?"

"You've had more than enough, Sanders. We need to get a move on." Sam turned his back on them and looked both ways before he leaned out over the balcony. "Weather's cleared. That's something. Should be an easy drive this morning." He glanced at his watch. "Uh, this afternoon. Housekeeping is working its way toward us, already taking care of the room Buck and I stayed in. It's checkout time. We need to get the hell out of here." He frowned at them both before he went back to studying the parking lot.

"Ignore him." Anna pushed King's unruly hair back from his forehead. "I'm feeling great. No regrets, if that's what you're asking." She leaned down to kiss him. Should she admit that what had happened between them had been a revelation? She'd never let go like she had with King Sanders. She'd forgotten to think. And Anna Delaney didn't quit thinking.

What started out as a quick kiss deepened. When she heard Sam curse she pulled back.

"What is it?" She reached for her coat and slipped it on, sticking her gun in her needlepoint tote. Her phone went in her pocket next to her flash drive. Sam stood rigid outside their door. King jumped up and shrugged into his own coat, his hat firmly on his head. They both joined Sam on the balcony.

"Anna, inside. Now." Sam gave Anna a look that made her scoot back into the room, but King didn't move. "Sanders. Tell me you didn't send Anna flowers."

"Are you kidding me?" Chin up, King faced Sam. "You must think I'm an idiot."

"Like I said before, I don't know you." Sam got on his comm. "Eyes on that panel van in front of the motel office. Betty's Buds, Waco. White female, gray hair, headed up the stairs toward me carrying a dozen roses. Hello?" He tapped his earpiece. "Comm isn't working. I don't like this." He pulled his gun and pointed it at the woman who was now on the walkway heading toward them. "Stop right there."

"Save me, Jesus!" The woman with tight gray curls and a long black coat stopped in her tracks then backed up a step. "I don't carry money. I swear it on my mother's life." Her hands were shaking so badly water sloshed out of the glass vase holding a bouquet. She took another step toward the stairs, her black Ugg boots slipping on the wet walkway.

"I said stop." Sam grabbed her arm. "State your business." He pulled a card from the bouquet. "Molly. Who's that?"

"I don't know. All I do is make deliveries for Betty's Buds. This classic Pink Lady rose bouquet is supposed to go to room 215. The lady in there just had a baby. See the plastic stork stuck in the middle of the arrangement?" Her lips quivered. "Please don't shoot me."

Anna watched all this from behind the curtain in the room. King stood in the doorway with his own gun out while Sam blocked the landing in front of their door, room 213. Okay, so the flowers belonged to the room next door. Where there had been a crying baby.

"Sam! Let her pass. You're scaring her to death." Anna squeezed past King and grabbed Sam's arm. The poor woman's eyes were wide behind her wire-rimmed glasses and she kept glancing around, as if looking for someone to call for help.

"Look. Room 215. We heard the baby crying last night, remember? I bet the woman's husband sent those beautiful pink roses and that the baby is a girl." She smiled at the woman, then tugged Sam until he released the woman's arm and moved back into the doorway so she could move past him.

"Thanks." Then, in a shockingly fast move, the woman pulled a canister from her shoulder bag and sprayed Sam, then King, in the face. They both dropped instantly. Anna opened her mouth to scream when the housekeeping cart slammed into her, knocking her inside the room and on top of the two unconscious men. Immediately, duct tape was slapped across her mouth and her hands were zip tied behind her back. Her feet were next. It was done with such efficiency she didn't have time to struggle. She ended up completely helpless, thrown on the floor next to the bed by the man who'd been pushing the cart. She lay there, heart pounding as she wondered what would happen next. Were King and Sam going to be all right? What was that spray? She could smell it, acrid and burning her nose. What on earth could it be doing to the two men?

The woman dropped the roses into the trash can then helped the housekeeper drag both men in far enough that she could shut the door. They weren't bothering to be gentle.

"How'd you like that, Billy?" She grinned and put her arms around his neck. "Worked like a charm. Just like the boss said it would."

"Yeah." He pulled her in and kissed her. "You're something else." He patted her bottom. "That gray wig does nothing for you, baby. I like you better as a blonde." Then he focused on Anna. "Boss is going to be happy. We finally got his computer hag. She looks just like her picture."

"I'm sick of hearing about her." The woman held that canister.

Anna braced herself. Was she going to be next to get whatever that was sprayed in her face? She held her breath.

"Don't do it; the boss won't like it. She has to be able to think clearly, you know. I have no idea how that spray shit works. The side effects might fuck her up." The man, Billy, who wore white pants and shirt with the motel logo, stared down at her. He stepped on Anna's stomach when she tried to wiggle closer to King despite the bindings holding her. "Search her. We need to find that thing with her program on it."

"Yeah. The thumb drive." The woman set the canister aside and squatted down, checking Anna's coat pockets. "Pay dirt!" She held up the tiny drive and Anna wanted to cry. "And look what else I found." She gripped the satellite phone. "You know how much these things cost?"

"Yeah. So what? This man had one in his pocket too." He'd been busy going through King's coat pockets and tossed the matching phone on the bed. "What the hell do you think you're doing?"

The woman stuck Anna's phone in her purse. "I'm taking it. You know reception at headquarters isn't worth shit. These things are great. I've always wanted one."

"Don't be an idiot. They can be tracked." He had moved on to Sam's pockets. His phone went on the bed too.

"Not if you turn them off. Don't you watch those CSI shows on TV?" She grabbed the phones off the bed and studied the buttons. "Yeah, this turns them off. I'll bet I can find something on the internet that'll help me figure out how to use it and keep it from getting tracked too. What do you bet?" She smiled and looked around. "I can sell the extras. People will pay top dollar for them."

"Francie, I don't care what you say. If the boss finds those, he'll shit a brick."

Anna was forgetting how to breathe as the two used their names. And they hadn't bothered with masks. Did that mean they knew she wouldn't be alive to tell the police who they were later? Or to identify them in a lineup? But they both were wearing gloves. They knew enough not to leave fingerprints for anyone else.

Oh, God. She stared up at the ceiling, trying to pray. What could she do to get out of here alive? And with King? She turned her head. He was unconscious. Breathing but not stirring. She wanted to *do* something. But what? She couldn't speak, to try to bargain with these people.

She studied them closely as they argued about the phones and then how to split the money they'd found on the men. Of course they'd taken the guns first. It was definitely the same woman who had stolen her backpack in Nordstrom. She was clever with her wigs, and now glasses. The long coat made her look dumpy but disguised a decent figure.

Her boyfriend could be the same man who'd shot at them at King's house. No, probably not. He didn't seem to have a wound. Both spoke with a Texas accent. Billy had a couple of crude tattoos on his neck. Mike would probably say they were jailhouse stuff. Maybe he'd met Leroy Simms in "the joint." Billy finally gave up on the phones when Francie told him to keep the cash. The credit cards he'd found stayed on the bed.

Francie held up the drive. "This is what the boss wants. He'll be over the moon when he sees we got it. No reason to tell him about the phones or the cash." She nudged King with her boot. "This guy must be her boyfriend. If we want her to cooperate, he can be leverage. Like that little blonde was before. The boss will be glad we thought of it. Might even earn us a bonus." She kicked at King's body. "He's really zonked. I love this shit." She caressed the canister.

"How long will they be out?" The man lifted King's eyelids. "What is that stuff anyway?"

"Boss says it puts them out for about an hour, so we have to hurry. I have no idea what's in it but, damn, did it drop them quick. We got quite a drive ahead of us. Your pal Leroy was supposed to spray those men downstairs but you know how he is. He's knife happy. As soon as boss messed with their comms, the men down there might have gone on alert and been ready for him. Look at the size of this one." She nudged Sam with her boot. "Leroy thinks he's tough but if he got into a fight and lost, we might have company. I only have a few sprays left."

When she picked up Anna's tote, she smiled. "Another gun. These people are well armed." She stroked the fabric. "I like the needlework on this. I think I'll keep it. I need someplace to put all these phones anyway." She laughed when Anna cursed her behind the tape on her mouth. "Oh, did your granny make it for you? Too damned bad. My granny has other uses for needles. Not pretty, but the shit she sells can get you going good, I tell you that." She stuck her canister in the tote, along with the phones. The gun went into her purse.

Anna tried to kick her. What a bitch. And how sad. Granny was a drug dealer. God. No wonder Francie had turned to a life of crime. It was all in the family.

Billy pulled Francie in for a hug. "Your grandma's shit is the best I ever had." He peeled off a hundred-dollar bill from the cash he'd just stolen then stuck it in her bra. "Give that to Granny when we get home. We'll have ourselves a party."

"Oh, Billy. You do know how to show a girl a good time." Francie gave him a kiss that lasted way too long.

Anna spent the time trying to get closer to King. Was he breathing? She hated the fact that he'd dropped so suddenly. That bitter smell lingered in the air; even the perfume of a dozen pink roses couldn't hide it. She was surprised breathing the fumes hadn't made her dizzy. No wonder Francie loved it.

"We got to go." Billy picked up King's gun and stuck it under his shirt.

"You think you can crawl to the door? Think again." Francie aimed a kick at Anna.

"Hey. Don't bruise the merchandise. At least not until that computer program is done to the boss's satisfaction and sold to the highest bidder." Billy frowned at Francie, then dragged Anna away from King. "Guess we put her in first, so if she moves, trying to attract attention, nobody will notice. But I'm not sure both of them will fit in that cart."

Anna could have cried in frustration. If she just could have touched King. He'd been so sick last night and now they'd dosed him with some horrible drug. What if it caused permanent damage?

"I don't think the boss would mind if we banged her up a little. All he wants is her program." Francie walked over and started dumping linens onto the floor. "It would help if you thought ahead, babe. When they're both in we can throw a sheet over the top, like you got a full load." She came back and took Anna's feet. "Okay, now lift."

Billy grabbed Anna's shoulders, then dropped Anna into the cart headfirst. "She was heavy. How the hell are we going to lift the cowboy?"

"You want to call Leroy up here?" The woman stood next to him. "He's big and strong."

"I can handle this. We don't want to interrupt that guy in the middle of whatever he's doing." Billy leaned over and poked at Anna. "It's going to be a squeeze though."

Anna twisted so she could lie on one side. If King was going to land on top of her, she needed to take up as little room as possible.

"At least we haven't heard anything yet. Like gunfire. That's a good sign, don't you think, Francie?"

"What I think is that you need to man up and quit stalling!" She must have hit him because he yelled. "Yeah, he's heavy. Get his coat off first. That'll help. Expensive coat. It'll look good on you, Billy. We can throw it on top of him in the cart and you can put it on when we're downstairs."

"Now you're talking."

Anna knew he was coming but it was still a shock when King tumbled headfirst into the cart to land on top of her. Air. She needed air. But her mouth was taped closed. She was seeing stars, sure she was going to pass out, when King's head shifted to land on her ear.

"There. Now I can see her nose. Hope she can catch a breath. If we kill her, we might as well shoot ourselves or make a run for the border." Billy held a fistful of King's hair. "What do you think?"

"She doesn't look so good." Francie studied her. "Reckon we smashed her?"

"There will be hell to pay if we did." Billy jerked King's head over some more. "There. I can see her whole face. Her boyfriend's still on top of her, but I bet it's not the first time." He chuckled and pulled Francie to him. "Am I right?" He gave her a big kiss.

"Enough of that. Time's ticking." Francie shoved him away, then slammed King's feet down on top of Anna's legs.

Anna grunted, the only sound of pain she could manage, as she struggled against King's dead weight. She had to do something about the pressure on her lungs.

"She looks peaked. I'm sure she's feeling the weight, but that's the best we can do for now." Billy tossed in King's coat. Apparently he had his priorities.

"Move the cart fast. We'll be dumping them out of there once we get downstairs to the van. Then she'll be able to breathe just fine." Francie didn't seem worried.

"Right. Get going. Pull the van around to the back. I'll take the cart down in the service elevator. Then we can lay them out side by side in the back of the van."

The woman smiled down at Anna, then dropped in King's hat. "There you go, Anna. Enjoy the ride. Because the boss is waiting for you and he is not happy. You've made it hard for him to finish this program and complete the sale." She shook her head. "He's been in a bad mood for days." She threw a sheet over the top of them, blocking out the light.

Anna took shallow breaths but they were painful. King on top of her now wasn't the same as when they'd been making love. He was a big man, tall and muscular. She loved that. Or had before, when he'd been careful to brace himself and keep his full weight from crushing her. Now she felt every pound squeezing the air out of her lungs. She tried to find a better position but, without the use of her arms, it was impossible.

Could she make a sound? Attract attention? She screamed behind that tape. Why not? Francie and her precious spray were downstairs moving the van. Too bad her muffled screams were pathetic, drowned out by the rumble of the cart's metal wheels rolling along the rough walkway. Anna doubted someone standing right next to them would have heard her.

The cart seemed to be going fast, bumping over pebbles after Billy slammed the motel room door. Cold air pierced the heavy-cotton cart and Anna shivered. King's body heat helped and she had on her coat but it must be below freezing outside. How much time had passed? Not much. If only they were wrong about the spray and King would wake up now. Had they zip tied his hands? Taped his mouth? She couldn't remember. She'd been too worried about what they'd sprayed on his face.

What had Isaac worked on at the NIH? Biological weapons? Germ warfare? Horrifying possibilities raced through her mind. Whatever it was had worked instantly. Big men like King and Sam had dropped unconscious without a sound. What other creepy things did Isaac have on hand that he could use to make her do what he wanted? He'd even had someone killed to get this program. Poor Henry Littlefield. He'd paid the ultimate price for his greed. She couldn't believe the Isaac she'd known so long ago had been willing to kill for her program. Of course he hadn't done it personally, the gutless geek. But he'd had enough nerve to hire a killer. The idea that Knife Guy was on a rampage against the men who'd been paid to protect her made Anna sick.

She had to think. Was there anything she could do to get away from these people? She had a feeling it would be impossible once she was at their "headquarters." The cart hit a bump, jostling her against King. The motion was making her queasy and the smell of dirty linens, probably years' worth, didn't help. Oh, no, she couldn't give in to the nausea. She'd choke if she threw up with that tape over her mouth.

Breathe through your nose. Right. If she could breathe at all. She was already lightheaded from the pressure on her lungs as King's body shifted and his elbow dug into her stomach.

Another noise. The hum of the service elevator coming. She heard the clunk of doors opening and then the cart lurched as it was shoved into the elevator. That extra movement made her swallow and pray for a steady ride down to the ground. But then they'd be on their way from here to Somewhere, Texas. It was a huge state, much of it wild and untamed. If only she could leave a trail, some way for them to be followed.

Was Francie right about the satellite phones? She knew there was a GPS locater in each of them. Maybe Chance could track them even if the phones were turned off. She knew nothing about them but her brother was so good with that kind of technology. The last call she'd made had been to Chance. Would that help him somehow?

When he couldn't reach his team Chance would realize that the worst had happened. He'd draw the awful conclusion that his sister was in the wrong hands. She kept praying as the elevator halted abruptly. First floor. Would Leroy, aka Knife Guy, meet them there? And what had he done to the men guarding her?

An hour. That was a good head start. Well, a bad head start from her point of view. As soon as that spray wore off, the guards would try to come after her. They'd left Sam lying on the motel room floor. God, he'd hate that he'd failed to keep her safe. But as soon as he woke he'd find a way to call Chance. Yes. Her brother would figure out how to follow her and find her. He had to.

* * * *

King opened his burning eyes and stared at the metal roof above him. Blurry. He blinked until it cleared. Definitely a car ceiling, too big for a trunk. No, the back of a van. God. He felt movement, a bump, and his head hit the metal floor under him. Damn, he had a headache. They were moving over rough terrain. He tried to sit up and realized his hands were bound behind him. He carefully lifted his head and saw his feet secured with a huge zip tie around his boots at the ankle. Huh. He didn't know zip ties came that long or that strong. *Focus.* He shook his head and pain hit him right between the eyes.

Let it go and think. Something moved and he slowly turned his aching head. Anna. Lying next to him. She had silver duct tape over her mouth. He tried to say her name and realized his own mouth was taped shut. Well, hell.

Her eyes were closed. Was she hurt? Drugged? Dead? His heart stuttered and he rolled toward her. Thank God her eyes popped open. She'd been resting then. He managed to get his head next to hers, then brushed her cheek with his. Shit. He felt the dampness of tears there. And he was fucking helpless.

He pulled at the restraints on his hands. How sturdy were zip ties anyway? Pretty damned sturdy. He wasn't doing anything but rubbing his wrists raw. One thing he could do, though, was sit up and maybe get his fingers to where he could pull the tape off Anna's mouth. He managed to put his back to her. Smart woman. She got the idea right away and scooted so her face was next to his moving fingers. In less than a minute he'd managed to rip that damned tape off her face.

"Ow! But that hurt so good," she whispered, then hit his shoulder with her head. "Now let me do your tape."

He could see how raw and red her cheeks were where he'd pulled that tape away. He hated that. But at least now they could talk. He waited while she wiggled to lie on top of him. Her soft breasts pushed against his chest before she managed to get her hands to his mouth. He closed his eyes, savoring the smell and feel of her as she tried to grip that tape. Just being this close to her was a comfort. He needed to enjoy this moment, because who knew what in the hell they'd face when they got where they were going.

"Shit fire!" He took a gusty breath of air when it ripped off. Well, practically yelling that probably hadn't been smart. Just a wire rack separated them from the two people in the front of the van. But they had the radio on or maybe a CD, playing a country song, and were singing along. Idiots. For kidnappers, they weren't exactly alert to what their captives were doing. Good thing. He rolled toward Anna and kissed her gently. If her mouth was as raw as his, that was all they could tolerate.

"We need to be quiet." She glanced at the front of the van. "Those two are taking us to headquarters. To the boss, they said." She laid her head on King's shoulder. "They got my flash drive."

"I'm sorry, but the worst thing is that they got you." King kissed the top of her head. "We need to find a way out of this van before we get there." He looked around the empty space. This was obviously the one that had sported the sign for Betty's Buds, Waco. Those peel-off signs were easy to slap on the side of a vehicle, then discard. It could have been the same van that had been used to kidnap Scarlett. It was probably too much to hope that the singers up there had left anything useful back here. He sure couldn't see anything he could use to get loose.

"There's a sharp piece of metal sticking out on my side, next to the wall. I've been working on my hands, sawing at the tie." Anna whispered this close to his ear. "Check your side to see if you have one like that. You can probably do yours faster. I'm frustrated that I'm so damned weak. I swear I'm going to work out more if I live through this, spend less time on the computer."

"You're perfect as you are. And so damned smart, I think I love you." King leaned to the side where the wheel well bulged into the cabin. Sure enough, there was a small piece of metal that hadn't been elegantly placed when the interior of the van was finished. He positioned himself with his back to it, hoping the couple up front didn't turn around to see that he was pressed against that wheel well and sawing like a fiend. Anna was right: he had the strength to make a serious effort to get free.

He glanced up. Anna hadn't moved. She stared at him, her eyes wide. What was wrong with her? She needed to get busy. Then he realized what he'd said. He grinned until his raw mouth hurt. Hey, it was too soon, but sometimes stuff happened like that. If she wasn't ready to hear it, he could wait. Could wait for her to decide if that was what she felt or might feel in time.

"Get busy." He mouthed the words and she finally moved, sliding back to saw at her own zip tie. His woman. He was pretty sure about that. He wasn't going to let that asshole Isaac Crane have her for even a minute. Not to steal her program and sure as hell not to hurt her. The zip tie gave and he shook out his hands, being careful not to let the people up front see that he was free. He stuck the broken tie in his jeans pocket. Now he had to work on his feet.

He slid one hand down into his boot. Had they thought to check there? He'd grown up on a ranch. An old cowhand named Shorty had taught him to always carry a knife. He'd had a trick that King had borrowed, having custom boots made with a sleek case for a small pocketknife sewn inside. Now King found it where it should be. Thank the Lord! He sent a thank-you upstairs to Shorty as he cut the tie on his ankles. The old man had been one of several hands who'd been like a father to him. Now Shorty's wisdom might just save his and Anna's lives.

He rolled toward Anna, the knife in the palm of his hand. He was careful to make it look like he was still bound in case their movements were finally noticed in the rearview mirror. He did a gut check. Headache was still there, but fading. Eyes had quit burning. Whatever had been sprayed at him and Sam had been fast and effective but hadn't seemed to do permanent damage. He would like to wash that poison off. He could smell it on his skin, a strange chemical residue. But he'd live, that was the main thing. He didn't doubt they wanted him alive so they could torture him in front of Anna and make her cooperate when they got to the damned headquarters.

"Come here, Anna. You can stop now."

"I've almost got it." She sniffed. "Damn, I hate not being better at stuff like this."

"Don't worry about it. Roll away from me." King quickly cut her hands free, then her feet. "Now we need a plan."

"I don't know where you got the knife. But I love you too." She kissed him, a quick one. She looked him in the eyes. "What did that spray do to you?"

"Froze me. It was cold and then I was out. Don't remember a thing after the hit." King slid the small knife back into his boot. His watch was gone. The asshole in the passenger seat was probably wearing it—King could see he was enjoying his coat. The man's girlfriend was driving. She thought she was June Carter to her man's Johnny Cash as they harmonized to an old song the couple had made famous. They were obviously in high spirits. Of course. Because they'd finally caught Anna.

"Now let me tell you what I heard while you were out of it. They're taking us to Isaac's headquarters. It doesn't get good cell service so it must be isolated. The woman said that when she took our satellite phones. I'm praying that somehow Chance can use the phones to track us, even though they're turned off." Anna was doing what King did, trying to keep her hands hidden but lying close beside him. "Leroy, Knife Guy, supposedly sprayed the men downstairs with the same stuff that took you and Sam down. Now he's following us in another car."

"I hope that's all he did. Sprayed the other guards." King still had the image of Scarlett's carved butt in his mind. He'd never forget it. Simms was the kind of loose cannon who would leave souvenirs on all the men just for the hell of it. But he kept that opinion to himself.

"If he did more to the men, he didn't tell Francie and Billy—that's their names. He helped Billy dump us in the van then took off. They left Sam in our room." Anna sighed and rubbed her arm against his in a silent gesture of affection. "How do you feel? I'm worried about that spray. It wears off in an hour they said, and that's about how long we've been driving. They thought they'd be at their destination by now but I think the weather worsened again."

"Headache, no big deal. It's about gone." King looked around again. No windows in the back. He could hear the windshield wipers going and, Anna was right, it was raining or sleeting again. They might be going farther north, but not necessarily. The heater was going full blast, which helped drown out his whispered conversation with Anna. He tried to picture the area around Waco. Not a lot of towns. There were some lakes, a few caves and parks. He told Anna what he could remember.

"They might be taking us back toward Austin. It would make sense for him to set up there. That's where you were working. He'd have his choice of little towns in the hill country between Waco and Austin where he could get the Wi-Fi he'd need." King wished he had his phone, even a map would help.

"Isaac had a real interest in geology. He loved fossils and he had a thing for caves. If he could find one fit for his headquarters, he'd grab it." Anna gasped when the van started hitting some potholes and rolled them around.

The woman driving turned off the music and yelled back to them. "Sorry, Anna. I hope you don't get carsick. We're getting close to the hideout." She laughed. "Yeah, that's what I call it. Why the boss liked it for a place to set up is a mystery to me, but then the man is unique, isn't he, Billy?" She laughed. "Anyway, get ready to see your old friend. Oh, will he be happy to see you. And this!" She held up that flash drive. "I'm betting this program of yours is worth a big bonus. He talked about putting a bounty on it."

Her cackle made King want to jump up and grab the steering wheel. Maybe that wasn't such a bad idea. Wreck the van. Get a jump on the man beside her. He stared at Anna. Could he keep her safe in that scenario? There was that heavy wire rack between them and the driver. They needed to get the woman to stop the van. He whispered his idea to Anna.

"They don't know what the spray could do to you. Can you pretend to have some kind of fit?" Anna's eyes gleamed. "Make a lot of noise. That'll get her to stop. We can put the tape over our mouths again and our hands behind our backs. We'll have the element of surprise when they open the back of the van."

"I don't suppose you'd stay out of the way and let me handle it." King would give anything to keep her out of this.

"King, they won't shoot me, I'm their prize. We can't let them take us to that hideout. If I get a chance to hurt that woman, I'm taking it." Anna looked fierce. "Now promise me you'll be careful. I have plans for you later." She winked, then carefully laid tape over her mouth, her eyes on the doors in the back of the van. She looked ready to rumble.

King wished he could kiss her just then. What a woman. He'd like to think later was not only possible but probable. "They need me. I'm their leverage. Just like Scarlett was. So hopefully they'll be careful not to hurt either one of us. Let's see if we can take advantage of them thinking we're helpless." King settled his own tape over his mouth, then started banging his boot heels on the floor of the van. His shoulders were next. He used his anger at being tied like a damned heifer to put some real muscle into each hit. The van floor was getting dents he was hitting it so hard.

Anna did her part, rolling as far away from him as she could get so he could make his "fit" King-sized. He writhed and kicked at the wheel well, getting even louder. He heard the man up front shout for the woman to pull over, that the man back there was going crazy. Okay, now it was on.

King's gut knotted as he got ready to throw himself at whoever opened the back door once the van stopped. He just hoped like hell it wasn't Leroy Simms. If they were lucky, Knife Guy had gone on ahead or wasn't following closely. Because one thing King knew for sure: his little sticker would be no match for what he'd seen Leroy Simms carrying on his belt. If it came to a knife fight, King was doomed.

Chapter Eleven

Anna worried about King. Yes, he was raising hell now with his boots banging hard on the van floor, but she knew he hadn't fully recovered from that high fever of the night before. He'd made love to her, sure. That last round in the shower had taken a lot out of him though. He'd collapsed against the tile wall once they finished. Well, *she'd* been finished anyway. He had simply run out of gas. Not that she let on that he'd been anything but a perfect stud.

Now he raised his poor aching head and thumped it on the floor. She wanted to reach out and stop him. No, his noise was working. The van screeched to a halt.

"What the hell is going on back there?" Francie screamed. "Billy, get out and check on them."

"In the freezing rain?" Billy obviously wasn't eager.

"Sounds like the man is having some kind of fit. What if he hurts the woman? You're gonna be the one to explain to the boss that you just let it happen."

"What am I supposed to do? Knock him out? He's bigger than me."

"Yeah, I noticed. So use the spray. At least it kept him quiet. And where's that cowboy's hat? Put it on."

"It didn't fit. I threw it in the back."

Anna heard the squeak of the door opening, then slamming. Okay, he was coming. If only she dared sit up and see what Francie was doing. Was she aiming her gun at them? As soon as the back doors opened King would jump out and knock Billy to the ground. With luck, he'd grab the spray.

Locks clicked and the doors began to open. King raised both legs, knees to his chest.

"Watch out, Billy!" Francie screamed from the front of the van.

Too late. When the doors were flung wide, King managed a hard kick that knocked Billy on his ass. The can of spray went flying while King leaped out of the back of the van. He landed on top of Billy and hit him with his fist. Anna jumped out after them. It was a shock to land in the cold. Icy rain buffeted her. A quick look let her know King had Billy under control.

She ran around to the driver's side. If she could surprise Francie before the woman had a chance to jump out, she might be able to grab her gun. She kept telling herself she was only valuable to them if she was alive and able to work on her program.

Of course, logic didn't keep her from wanting to run like hell in the opposite direction. She couldn't. Ignoring her churning stomach, she kept going, sliding as she hit gravel on the shoulder of the road. She glanced back. Leroy Simms was supposed to be following them. But there was no other car in sight, even though it was the middle of the afternoon. Thank God. She got to the driver's side door and stared into the barrel of a gun. Francie had found the smarts to lower the window.

"Stop right there. I can shoot pretty good. You think I won't?" Francie stayed inside the van. "How'd you like a shoulder wound? It would hurt bad. I know, it happened to me once, when I was robbing a liquor store. I think you could still do your computer shit with your arm in a sling." She waved the gun toward the back of the van. "Tell your boyfriend to quit whaling on Billy and come around here."

"Tell him yourself." Anna swallowed, then stiffened her spine. "You won't shoot me. If I can't work on that program because I'm hurt, your boss is going to be pissed. He might even refuse to pay you. You want to take that chance?" Anna darted back to where King was still with Billy. She felt a bullet whiz past her arm just as she put the van's back door between her and Francie.

"Bitch. I'm going to teach you a lesson." The driver's side door opened with a squeak. "Fucking weather."

Anna was glad to see King next to an unconscious Billy. Her man held that canister and grinned up at her.

"Got him," he whispered as he used the bumper to pull himself to his feet, shivering. "You okay? Did she hit you?"

"She missed. But she's coming and she's pissed. Give me the spray." Anna couldn't wait to use it. "Get your coat on."

"What are you going to do?" He picked up Billy and peeled off his coat. "Don't take any chances. Damn, I hoped he'd have a gun in his pocket."

"Watch." Anna peeked from behind the door then waved. "Don't shoot, Francie," she yelled at the woman who was picking her way carefully along the side of the van with her gun held out in front of her. "I give up." She held out her hands so Francie could see she was unarmed. "My man passed out again. Yours is on the ground next to him. King knocked him out cold."

"I don't believe you. How'd you get your hands and feet loose? Huh?" Francie stopped where she was with a few feet between them. "You're up to something."

"I'm up to getting into the warm van again. Please let me ride up front with you. We can leave the men here. What good are they anyway?" Anna had stuck the canister out of sight, in her pocket. "Come on, Francie, woman to woman. Let's work out a deal."

"What kind of deal?" Francie stayed out of reach. "What do you have to offer me?"

"I'm the one who invented that program your boss is so hot for. I'm sure you've figured out it's worth a lot of money. Right?" Anna stepped out from behind the van door. "I know who your boss is. We used to date, a long time ago. If there's any way Isaac Crane can screw you out of what's owed you, he'll do it."

"I've been screwed over before." Francie was thinking. "But Billy and I…"

"I get it. You've got a thing for him. It happens. But I heard you two talking. It's clear to me who has the brains. But does he listen to your ideas? Hell, no! He tries to order you around. Like with those phones. Why would you put up with that?" Anna moved closer.

"Hey. I tell him what to do most of the time." Francie frowned. "Why are you running him down? Thanks to him, I didn't kick the shit out of you."

"Oh, you're right. Billy must be the brains and you're the beauty." Anna hid a grin at Francie's curse.

"Shut up." Francie eased a little closer, her gun pointed at Anna's shoulder. "I can sure as hell make you sorry you stepped out here."

"I believe you." Anna nodded. "But forget Billy. Maybe he's good in bed, so you got hooked. But what's a little sack time compared to financial freedom? I can help you get some real money, Francie. Enough that you could leave whatever shithole you came from, where Granny is the local drug kingpin, and be set for life. Never work again." Anna was almost close enough. She remembered Francie had said she was low on spray. She had to make this shot right on target.

"He's not that good. How much money are we talking about?" Francie looked behind Anna. "You sure they're both out of it?"

"Yeah. King kicked Billy in the head when he opened the door. You saw him. Billy managed to spray my guy right before it was lights out for him too." Anna saw Francie was listening, her gun barrel slowly dropping until it was aimed at the ground. "I figure we could get a cool million apiece for that thumb drive you took off me. I'm sure Isaac was only talking four, maybe five figures pay for your work for him."

"A million?" Francie took another step closer. "Dollars?"

That was all Anna needed. She grabbed the canister and sprayed Francie in the face. She dropped to the ground instantly, her gun slipping from her hand to hit the gravel. Anna snatched it and carefully stopped beside the woman. She gave her a kick, not a gentle one either, when she remembered how they'd treated King. No response. So Francie was really out. There was that bitter smell again. It was really strong this time. If Francie woke up with a terrible headache, it was what she deserved.

She shook the can. It felt empty. Was it? She stuck it in her coat pocket anyway. She'd love to have what was in it analyzed once this nightmare was over.

"King! It worked!" She wiped rain off her face and stepped around the woman's body. She had to get into the van and find one of those satellite phones. She'd turn it on then call her brother. Chance would be able to follow the GPS signal and send someone to get them.

As far as she could tell, they were in the middle of nowhere. It was a paved two-lane road in rough repair, with shallow ditches on both sides and no houses around that she could see, though there were gravel driveways leading off it. A barbed wire fence kept sad-looking black cows from crossing the road. A couple of them huddled together under a tree. She didn't blame them; the cold rain was relentless.

Had she heard a car engine? Anna gripped the gun handle, about to look back when she felt something cold touch her neck.

"Drop the gun, sweetness." The voice was chillingly familiar. "Right now."

Anna opened her hand and let the gun fall. Leroy Simms had found them.

She realized King had never answered her. Had Leroy hurt him? Cut his throat? Oh, God, God. She didn't dare move as her stomach dipped and rolled. The cold steel at her neck made her afraid to breathe. When he slid it over her face, she couldn't help it, she shuddered.

"I'll take that spray can too." He pulled it from her pocket and tossed it under the van. "Now turn around slowly. I want to see your pretty face." He chuckled as she eased around to face him. "Look at you. Surprised you, didn't I?" He kept the flat of his knife next to her mouth. "Afraid I'm gonna cut a little souvenir here, Anna? Sure I am."

Anna gasped and braced herself for pain. What was this animal going to do to her? Carve his initials in her cheek? She bit back a scream when he turned the knife to its edge, then neatly sliced off a curl from above her ear. Her knees were so weak she almost fell to the ground.

"None of that now." He tucked her hair in his coat pocket, then grabbed her arm in a brutal hold and forced her toward the back of the van. "Look at this. Your boyfriend did just fine until I came along. He had Billy boy down on the ground and sprayed him good. Imagine how disappointed his highness was to get a spray from me then." He laughed. "King Sanders. King of what?" He twisted Anna's arm. "Let's go."

"No, wait! You can't leave him there. Lying on the ground in the rain." Anna cried out, horrified when she saw King collapsed beside Billy. If they left him there like that, wet and cold, would he end up with pneumonia? At least there was no blood. Thank you, God. Leroy hadn't cut his throat. Out of character, but such a blessing. As if he'd read her mind, Leroy jerked her closer to him.

"You should be down on your knees thanking me right now, missy. I didn't cut him, did I?" He frowned. "I wanted to. But the boss doesn't like what he calls my 'bloodthirsty ways.' He ordered me to stick with the spray. I'm following those orders. For now. But it's hard." Leroy slid the back of that huge knife across Anna's throat again. "It's so satisfying to feel the warm blood flow over my fingers."

He kicked at King's boot. "This fucking spray's a wimp's weapon. But I got a big payday coming so I'll play this the boss's way. Until I just can't help myself. Now be smart and don't make me mad. I can't cut you—the boss wants you too bad—but I could do one or two of these boys if I lose my temper."

"Please." Anna whimpered. "Don't." She could see the lust in his eyes. Blood lust. This man was crazy. He'd cut King, even Billy, just for the pleasure of it. She gagged, leaning over and throwing up the coffee Sam had brought her and King that morning.

Leroy cursed and jerked her away from the mess. "Stop that." He dragged Anna down the road to where he'd parked a dark sedan about a hundred yards away. It was hidden behind brush in one of those driveways. She struggled, desperate to stay with the van. With King. Of course, Leroy was too strong for her. He just picked her up and tossed her over his shoulder. When they got to the car he dropped her on the ground, pinning her there with a muddy boot. Then he opened the trunk and pulled out a piece of nylon rope.

"Fuck those zip ties. Never have liked them. Good old-fashioned rope, that's the way to keep a body corralled. I grew up on a farm. We knew the right way to take care of business: tie 'em up. Tight." He wrapped the rope around Anna's arms, then tied her wrists together. Another short piece of rope went around her ankles. Then he picked her up and dumped her in the trunk. He stared down at her while she tested his knots. Oh, they *were* tight. There was no escaping this.

"Give it up, Anna. When I tie something, it stays. You gonna scream? Of course you are. And I need to stop for gas. So here." He stuck an oily rag in her mouth. "I'd hate for you to catch a chill." He tossed a dirty blanket on top of her, then slammed the trunk shut. "Hang tight, Anna. It won't be long now."

Anna heard the engine start and then they were moving. She prayed that a car would come by quickly and find King and the others. They'd be unconscious for an hour. If anyone ever did come down this godforsaken road, they'd call the police immediately. The scene looked suspicious and no one would know what was wrong with the people lying in the freezing rain. Cops would think they'd taken drugs with those strange canisters lying next to them. Ambulances would take them to a local hospital. Who would wake up first? Francie? She'd take off, of course. Unless... There was still the hope that the satellite phones had been tracked somehow.

Why was she obsessing over King when she was tied up in a trunk and alone with Knife Guy? She had to stop shaking long enough to calculate the odds that Leroy had taken one of those satellite phones from the guards he'd knocked out of commission. Doubtful. He was actually playing things by Isaac's rules. Like keeping his knife clean. She could only be grateful for that or she'd be wearing Leroy's initials already. And as for King... God, she couldn't bear to think about that.

She closed her eyes and tried not to get sick again as the car bumped over uneven roads. Wherever they were going, it still wasn't on a main highway. She was so cold and terrified she was almost numb with it.

But Leroy had made a mistake. She suddenly realized Francie still had her thumb drive with the latest version of the program. What was Isaac going to say about that? Anna wanted to laugh out loud. Of course, the rank, oily rag prevented that. She was getting hysterical. Isaac still had her other laptop. It wouldn't be impossible to access her program and re-create the parts necessary to finish it, if she had to in order to save her life.

Was she strong enough to resist whatever persuasive tactics he or Leroy would use to get her to cooperate? Anna shuddered. At this point she didn't give a good damn about the program. She wanted King, her brother, home. Anywhere but this foul, cramped, and freezing trunk with a killer at the wheel.

Pining for the impossible was futile. She needed to *do* something. Leroy was going to stop for gas. So there was some civilization ahead. Could she kick out a taillight? She'd seen that on a TV show. People or the police would notice a broken taillight. Of course, it was dark in that trunk. And the blanket was over her face, a filthy blanket that smelled like dirty underwear. Ugh. She tossed her head until it finally fell away. She could just make out the red glass of the lights, on because it was a nasty, gloomy day.

She twisted, trying to get her boot heels in position. Firm kicks. What kind of glass were the lights made of? The things resisted her best efforts. She was frustrated with her lack of strength. Again. It made her mad. Which added some power to the next kick and, yes, she heard a crack. A few more hard kicks and the glass—well, maybe it was plastic—came apart. That was something. Now if only an eager cop would pull Leroy over, maybe she could thrash around and make noise so he'd order Leroy to open the trunk.

Then she thought about it. An eager cop could end up either sprayed into unconsciousness or dead with his throat cut because Leroy was sick of following the boss's rules. God, she hated what her program had brought down on everyone around her. Friends, lovers, and maybe innocent bystanders. She had to wonder where Billy had gotten that laundry cart. Was there a helpless worker stuck in a closet somewhere who was supposed to clean those motel rooms?

Stop it. She'd make herself crazy if she blamed herself for every bad thing Isaac had done or ordered done because he wanted something he didn't deserve. He was the bad guy here. This was not her fault, damn it. Not her fault.

* * * *

King woke up with another headache. He'd been sprayed again. Left helpless and out of commission. Where was Anna? He gazed up at the ceiling and realized he was in another vehicle. Moving. Not the van. This one was dark, black metal, not white. He was lying on something soft and covered with a blanket. He realized his mouth wasn't taped this time either. And his arms and legs weren't bound. What the hell?

"Anna?"

"He's awake."

King tried to sit up but a hand on his chest stopped him.

"She's not here. Stay there until we stop. It's crowded in here, no room to maneuver, and we're almost there."

"Where?" King had that damned blurry vision again. He blinked and the man crammed in next to him came into focus. Buck. One of Delaney's men.

"We're meeting up with Delaney. Simms got his sister."

"No!" King fought to get up, do something.

Buck pushed him back and handed King a water bottle and a pair of pills. "You know they need her unharmed. Now settle down. Take these for your head. Then drink as much water as you can manage. I was sprayed. So were the other men. Guess they got you twice. Head hurt?"

"Like a son of a bitch. But Anna—"

"We've got a man on her trail." Buck nodded at the water bottle. "I said drink. You want to be a hundred percent when we find her. Right?"

"Damn right." King took the pills. Even managed to get down some water in the moving vehicle as it hit some rough roads. Finally he passed the bottle back to Buck. "Simms has her?" He wanted to get his hands on that man who loved his knives. If he was cutting on Anna... He struggled not to throw up that water and breathed through the nausea. No, Anna was important to Crane. Surely he wouldn't allow that.

"What do you remember before you were sprayed the last time?" This voice came from the front seat. Apparently the passenger seats had been folded down to make this SUV into a type of ambulance. Sam was driving. "We found three bodies. You and two of Crane's people."

"Yeah. Anna said their names were Francie and Billy. Where are they now? I want to get my hands on them. They know where Crane's hideout is." King winced as the car hit a bump. This headache was worse than the last one.

"They're in custody. Your Ranger pal Mike is in charge of them. He heard your name on the Highway Patrol scanner and had been following the case anyway. We've been working with him. He's all over this. I'm sure he'll press them hard and get that information from them. He's meeting us where we're going right now."

King wanted to help. What could he remember about the van and what had happened?

"How did you get them to stop the van?" Sam was in interrogation mode. "There was nothing beside the road. No houses. No sign of car trouble."

"I pretended to have a fit. Anna's idea. Those two didn't know what the side effects of that spray could be." King took a steadying breath.

"Smart." Sam seemed to hesitate. "Leroy Simms stopped behind the van. He's the one who took you out. In case you don't remember."

"God, no. I hate like hell that he has Anna." King struggled to breathe while his heart seemed to have lost its rhythm. He looked up and saw Buck frowning at him. When the man who, Anna had told him, was a medic tried to take his wrist as if to check his pulse, he held up his hand. No fucking way.

"Yes. But our guy saw the whole thing. He said Simms didn't hurt her. He just tied her up and put her in his trunk."

"And your guy, as you call him, just watched this?" King sat up so suddenly the car went dark and spun around him. "Goddamn it, Sam. What kind of operation are you people running?"

"If we didn't always have an extra man, Sanders, we wouldn't know right now where Anna was heading. That she was safely tucked into that car trunk and on her way to Crane's headquarters." Sam said this calmly, but King heard anger underneath that statement. Yeah, it was a plan, but carrying it out wasn't easy on any of them. "He's our invisible man. That's what Delaney calls him. It worked like it's supposed to. You should be glad about that."

"Oh, yeah. I'm glad Anna is in the hands of a knife-wielding psychopath." King sagged back down. He might be sick. Buck, the mindreading son of a bitch, handed him a bag. No, he couldn't do that. Not in front of these stoic men, who carried out orders like they had no minds of their own.

"You think we like this, Sanders?" Buck handed King the water bottle. "First chance I get, I'm using my own knife on that bastard."

"You'd have to beat me to him." King took a drink, spilling half of it down his chest. Didn't matter. He liked Buck's support. "How long before we get wherever the hell we're going?"

"Ten minutes." Sam answered. "Delaney's having a hard time keeping his shit together too, if that makes you feel better. She's his sister."

"Nothing will make me feel better right now, except finding Anna and putting that nest of rattlesnakes down." King lay back and closed his eyes. He had ten minutes to pull himself together. Not enough. But he'd manage. He had to help or he'd lose his mind. Anna with Knife Guy. It didn't bear thinking about.

* * * *

Anna decided to stay quiet during the gas stop. Leroy was such an unpredictable crazy person she didn't dare anger him or involve a bystander. When she heard someone comment on his broken taillight, Leroy cursed and blamed an old girlfriend. Then he thumped the trunk so hard Anna felt the vibrations down in her stinking hole.

"Women. I got only one use for 'em," he told the man who apparently shared his views. "I can give 'em a good time, but if they want more than that, they can go somewhere else."

"A good time." Anna swallowed as the strong smell of gasoline was added to the other stenches in her cold prison. As if that creep knew how to give a woman anything but misery and pain. When the motor started again, she gave in to the tears that had been coming since he'd caught her.

Did anyone know where she was? Would police find the van and King? He was an important man with connections. Once he woke up, he could get them to call Mike and the Texas Rangers. Francie, at least, had admitted to having a record. Billy had those jailhouse tattoos. Now they'd added kidnapping to their crimes. Maybe they could be made to talk and would lead the police and Chance to Isaac's hideout. She quit sobbing and tried to invent rescue scenarios. It was the only way for her to stay sane and not give in to despair.

When the car slowed, then stopped, Anna braced herself. Whoever opened the trunk was going to get her boots in his face. She wasn't going meekly, that was for sure. She wiggled around, ready to react as she listened to people talking next to the car. The key turned in the lock and the trunk popped open.

Anna kicked as hard as she could. Her feet were grabbed before she could connect and she was hauled out, painfully. She ended up over Leroy's shoulder. Too easy. For him.

"Nice try." He slapped her butt after he slammed the trunk closed. "But my knots aren't giving you a bit of slack, are they, girl?" Leroy laughed as Anna's head bounced against his back while he walked up a path.

It was making her sick. No, she didn't have time for that. She had to see where they were going. He carried her toward what looked like a low slung modern building. The rain had stopped but it was still miserably cold. She was desperate to get away from him, struggling to shift off his shoulder.

"Settle down." His hand gripped her thigh. "Didn't I warn you not to make me mad?"

Anna had been working on getting that rag out of her mouth for what had seemed like hours. Her tongue was sore from trying. Hanging upside down finally made it happen and she spit it out.

"Get your slimy hands off of me!" She kicked him again, right in the chest.

"Son of a bitch!" He slapped her butt so hard Anna saw stars. "Kick me again and I'll do to you what I did to your girl Scarlett. You hear me?"

"Leroy, put her down." The voice came from the doorway they'd approached. "You're not cutting anyone."

"Listen, boss. This woman has disrespected me. You expect me to put up with that shit?" Leroy did dump Anna at his feet to land on a concrete slab.

She lay there, miserable, hurt and determined to fight whatever came next. She looked up and saw Isaac Crane standing there, glaring at Leroy. Isaac shifted his gaze to study Anna and she looked away. He'd changed, filled out and hardened into a man she almost didn't recognize. He was still ridiculously tall, but now he loomed large, dwarfing the bulky Leroy. He had a dangerous aura that made even Knife Guy pay attention when he spoke.

"I expect you to do what I say. I'm paying the freight, as you put it. Now untie her and escort her inside." Isaac Crane nudged Anna with an Italian loafer. "She looks a little worse for wear. Your trunk must have been filthy."

"Yeah, well, I got the job done." Leroy pulled out his knife and began cutting Anna's ropes.

She didn't say a word, just shook out her hands and managed to stand. It wasn't easy as blood rushed into her feet and ankles, making them tingle. She wobbled but would be damned if she'd reach out to anyone for support. She couldn't believe this Isaac was the same man she'd known all those years ago. Or even the one she'd run into at the National Institutes of Health. This Isaac was cold-eyed and confident enough to stare down Leroy Simms when he kept his knife out long after the last rope was cut.

"Bring her inside." Isaac turned his back on them and walked into the building.

"You heard the boss. In you go." Leroy finally put his knife away and took Anna's elbow in a bruising grip.

"Where are we?" Anna studied her surroundings. If only there was an obvious way to call for help or escape. The building looked like some kind of showroom or welcome center, long abandoned. It backed up to a stone mountain. A faded sign offered tours of a cavern.

"You can read, smart ass. This used to be a place where people paid to see caves. But there are more popular ones in Georgetown and around

San Antonio. So I guess this one didn't measure up. Anyway, it went out of business." Leroy jerked her arm as he nodded to two men guarding the front entrance with automatic weapons. "I got her. If she tries to escape, shoot her in the leg, not the head. Boss needs her brain."

"Got it, Leroy." One of the men checked her out. "She's a looker."

"Could be, once she's dry. Looks like a drowned rat now." The other man nudged his cohort. "Welcome to the cave, Miss Anna. We've all heard about you. Boss has got to cheer up now."

Anna ignored them, glad that at least this hellhole had heat, while Leroy chuckled as he hustled her past them.

"Boss picked this place out special. He loves that cave—oh, excuse me, cavern. He's in there all the time, looking at it. We have all the comforts. Wi-Fi, kitchen, even hot springs." Leroy sounded like a tour guide as he kept pushing her along a hall lined with faded pictures of a beautiful cavern and brown bats in flight. "Boss's lab and office is in the back. The viewing room, he calls it. There's a bunch of windows where he used to watch the bats fly out every evening. They don't do it now. Not in winter."

"How long has he been set up here?" Anna couldn't believe her eyes. They passed several rooms. Most of them were empty. One, though, had a stone fireplace with a roaring fire. She wished she could stop and thaw out her hands. Her gloves were in her coat pockets. She reached for them but Leroy wasn't having it. He jerked her along with his hand on her elbow.

"Since last fall. The boss is a planner. But he can tell you what he wants you to know." Leroy pushed open a glass door and they were in a huge room that featured a wall of windows facing a beautiful cavern. "See there? Boss loves those hanging things."

"For the hundredth time, they're called stalactites, Leroy." Isaac turned to face them. "Welcome, Anna." He gestured toward a group of chairs that faced the view. "Leroy, that will be all."

"Are you sure, boss? She's a feisty one. You should have seen her carrying on about that King Sanders." Leroy grinned. "I put him down with your miracle spray. Left him freezing his ass off in the rain."

"I can handle her, Leroy. I said that will be all." Isaac stared until Leroy backed toward the door.

"Don't say I didn't warn ya. And could I get a little praise here? I don't see Billy and Francie delivering her." Leroy stood in the doorway.

"Where's the flash drive?" Isaac held out his hand. "When I have that, I'll heap praise and a pile of cash on your head."

"I've got it. She had it in her baggage, in one of the SUVs. You think I'd leave it to those two Bonnie and Clyde wannabes?" Leroy dug in his coat pocket. "Here ya go." He stalked over and brushed Anna's cheek. "Aw, is that a tear I see? Bet you thought I forgot all about it. No way, sweetness."

Anna was fighting tears. He'd thought to search her luggage for that extra drive. Damn him. Francie had taken the one she'd kept on her, but Leroy, who was obviously proud of himself as he strutted to the door, had just earned his bonus and was crowing about it.

"I'm hitting the bar. I think I deserve a tall cold one." He winked at Anna when he stopped for a last word. "Unless you have orders?"

Isaac turned the thumb drive over in his hand. "Yes, by all means, have a celebratory drink. But don't get roaring drunk." He faced Anna, who had steadfastly refused to sit. "If Anna won't cooperate, I'll need you again soon. You are so good at making people do what we need them to, aren't you, Leroy?"

"Yes, sir, I am." He chuckled and pulled out his knife again. "Anna, see you later. Don't disappoint me now. I like women with a little fight in them. Your pal Scarlett got me all hot and bothered when she played hard to get." He turned and left them alone.

Anna's knees failed her and she sank into the chair. "Isaac, what's become of you?"

"I've become a man, Anna. I'm no longer the kind of boy you could toss over your shoulder. I would think you'd approve." Isaac walked over to a small kitchen and fixed a cup of coffee. "You must be chilled. Do you still take cream and sugar?"

Anna wanted to tell him to keep his coffee. Or toss it in his face once he handed it to her. But she was cold all the way to the tips of her ears. Her toes were numb too. So she just nodded. When he brought her a mug, she wrapped her hands around it and breathed it in.

"Yes, Anna, I matured. And learned that the world doesn't reward intelligence unless it is paired with guile. I thought I could just take what I wanted." He sat across from her and stared at her. "That certainly didn't work with you, did it?" He shook his head. "You surprised me that night. I vowed then and there to never be surprised again."

Anna sipped her coffee. She needed strength if she was going to get through this. Ahead of her she could see a beautiful cavern. She could understand why it had once been a tourist attraction. There were bound to be exits, places to hide, even a way to make a phone call if she was lucky. One thing she knew she needed to do was keep Isaac talking. Stall.

"Guile. Is that what you call this elaborate scheme to steal something that I worked so long and hard to create?" She got up and paced. She needed to see where the exits were. If there could possibly be a cell phone lying around. But she knew Isaac was a genius. He wouldn't be stupid about his security.

"We talked about your idea back when we dated. I daresay I gave you some valuable insights that helped you along the path to bringing the program to life." Isaac just sat and watched her. He was confident she wasn't going anywhere.

"What?" That statement stopped Anna. "You're claiming you helped me with my program?" She saw that he had actually convinced himself he was right about this. He wore a superior look that made her want to fly at him and dig her nails into his arrogant face. Calm. She had to be thinking about escape. She couldn't make him mad enough to get Leroy in here with a knife and more rope.

"Not just helped. I hope it won't hurt your feelings, but my buyers have no idea that anyone but me even worked on the program." He smiled as if he believed every insane word out of his mouth. "I was there, at its inception, older, wiser. You just had vague ideas. I saw the practical applications immediately. As a future doctor." He sipped his coffee. "I graduated top of my class at Johns Hopkins. Did you know that?"

"No. I didn't follow your career." Anna tried to breathe. The gall, the sheer nerve of the bastard. She'd never brainstormed with him. All she'd done was share her concerns about her grandmother back then. Talked about the need for monitoring meds for interactions. Vague ideas indeed. He was rewriting history. Suffering from delusions. Didn't they say there was a fine line between genius and insanity? She wanted to shout all those things at him. Instead, she kept walking the perimeter of the room, looking for an escape route.

"You should have. I've done quite well. I admit it was a pity the NIH didn't suit me. I had some interesting thoughts on the mission there." He got up to refill his cup. "Shortsighted people. They have always been a bane of my existence. But this program of mine that you have finally finished, that's a winner. My golden ticket. Cooperate with me now and I will give you credit, Anna. Someday." He actually preened as if he'd done something great.

"Stop. This program isn't *yours*. It's mine. When I knew you, I hadn't written one line of code. Surely you don't think a little conversation over coffee entitles you to steal my work now."

"You keep using that dreadful word, Anna. I can't steal what's mine. If you'd just answered my emails, my calls, this could have been ironed out between us." Isaac put down his coffee cup and stood. "I can't wait to see what's on this drive. The finished product. Oh, I know there are a few kinks left, but I'm a more advanced programmer than I was back then. I'm confident I can finish what you started even if you remain stubborn. Of course, it would be so much easier and pleasant if you helped." He walked over to the elaborate computer system he had set up on a standing desk in the middle of the room.

"Wait. I blocked your emails and calls years ago. I know nothing about any communication from you." Anna took a breath. She couldn't stand the thought of him opening her program now. "But it wouldn't matter. None of that belongs to you. I wrote it. It's mine. And Zenon's. Not yours."

"You're wasting your breath. I have a buyer lined up. This is my big play, Anna. When I sell this, I'll be set for life. I can do what I've always wanted. I'll travel the world exploring little known caverns. I can also use my money to fund special projects like the spray that worked so effectively on your boyfriend." He paused with the drive in his hand. "A cowboy. Really?" He raised an eyebrow. "You've really taken Texas to heart, haven't you?"

"You seem to be enjoying Texas yourself. This cavern is beautiful." Anna walked over to stare out the wall of glass. She had to keep him away from the computer.

"Yes, it is. I'm sorry the bats are hibernating now. You should see them when they come out at sunset in the fall. Incredible. Thousands of them." He joined her at the window, that small drive in his hand.

"Tell me about the spray. I saw it work. So fast and efficient when you need to stop someone in their tracks. Did you really create that?" She had a feeling it was another thing he'd stolen.

"I refined it. Some people just don't realize the potential of what they create. Like I said, they're shortsighted. I saw its possibilities immediately. Working at the Institute was interesting but so limiting. The scientists there were going to use the spray to treat wounds. Can you imagine? But use it in someone's face and you can knock out a person for an hour. You said it—efficient." He smiled at Anna, like she'd pleased him with her insight. "I'll use that word in my marketing. The application for warfare or even ordinary criminal activity is going to make it extremely valuable." He moved closer. "You were always so very bright. One of the few women worthy of me."

Anna barely kept herself from jumping away from him with a scream. Worthy? Of this creep?

"Aren't you worried that associating with criminals like Leroy can be dangerous?" Anna recognized the way he was looking at her. It was that obsessive gleam in his eyes, the same one he'd had in college. He was going to try to touch her, she knew it. "Isaac?"

"I can handle them. I've learned money makes a difference. I'm sorry Leroy was rough with you, but I needed to see you, Anna." He plucked a leaf from her hair.

Anna couldn't say anything. Sorry? Like that made it okay to send a killer to fetch her? She just stared up at him, trying not to let his size overwhelm her. She had to be as clever as he thought she was. Use her brains to figure out a way out of here.

"Anna, we could work so well together. I remember how our minds sparked off each other. And now I'm mature. I know how to please a woman like you." He set aside the flash drive and reached for her.

"Do you?" Anna looked him up and down, like she might be interested, then leaned closer. When she was close enough, she snatched that drive and dropped it into her coat pocket. Then she knocked a chair between them and almost leaped across the room. She looked for a weapon, anything that she could use against him. Wireless keyboard. She grabbed it and held it in front of her. "Save your moves, Isaac. I have a man who knows how to please me." Not smart to say that, but she couldn't hold it back. Arrogant ass. Like she'd ever let Isaac Crane touch her.

"King Sanders? Forget him. I can have him taken care of if he hasn't already died of exposure. Leroy said the last time you saw him Sanders was lying in the icy rain, unconscious. How do you think he's doing now?" Isaac threw the chair aside and stalked her. "Put down the keyboard, Anna, and give me the drive. I was so impressed with your martial arts before that I trained in them myself. I can take you down now without breaking a sweat."

"Of course you can, Isaac. You're a big man." Anna threw the keyboard at him and dashed toward a door she'd noticed in the wall of glass. She threw it open and sprinted into the cavern. Cold air slapped her in the face and the floor was slippery under her boots. Didn't matter. She was going to run as fast as she could and hide. It was dark. Which was a good thing. She could barely see, and that meant no one behind her could follow her until they grabbed some kind of light.

She heard Isaac call her name just before she ducked behind a rock formation and wedged herself into a dark crease in the wall. Damn her red plaid coat. She should have turned it inside out. No time. Isaac called for Leroy and other men to help him look for her. He sounded nearby.

She barely breathed as she hunkered down, determined to stay put as long as she had to. Lights flashed around her hiding place and over the rock walls above her. Footsteps and curses meant the hunt was going deeper into the cavern.

"Anna, you'll die of exposure if you don't come out. Don't be foolish." Isaac sounded irritated. "You're too intelligent for this kind of nonsense."

She couldn't move, not even to shiver, as the cold seeped into her feet and through her coat. She carefully eased her gloves from her pockets and slipped them on. The flash drive was small but solid. She'd never let him have it. Bastard. Thief.

Anna kept her hands deep in her pockets, one wrapped around that little piece of plastic and metal. If he did find her hiding place, she'd make one last run, then throw the drive deep into the cavern, hopefully making it impossible for him to find it in the slimy bat guano.

"I'll give you a few more hours to come to your senses, then I'm going to use a little gas I've been experimenting with. It will make you run out of there, my dear. You won't be able to stand it." Isaac sounded very close. "It makes you feel like your skin is crawling with a million bugs. You lose your wits and feel like you have to move. Sound delightful? I thought so." He chuckled. "So if you're planning to just hide and wait me out?" He sounded like he was pacing. "Well, it won't work."

More footsteps. "Woman, you are trying my patience." Leroy was so close she could smell the beer he must have just finished drinking. "I swear I'm going to cut a souvenir on you no matter what the boss says."

"You have my permission, Leroy. Anna is proving to be a disappointment." Isaac sighed. "I'm going inside. Stay here with a couple of men in case she tries to sneak out. I'm sending out hot coffee."

"I hope you heard that, Anna. Scarlett got my initials. I'm thinking something a little different for you. A Texas star? On your breast. I'd surely like to do some titty work." He laughed. "Damn, but it's cold as a well digger's ass in here. You'd better come on out or I'll be doing a map of the whole fucking state on your pretty body, and that's a fact."

Anna heard more grumbling then the smell of hot coffee. Her stomach rebelled and it was all she could do not to throw up. No, no, no. She didn't dare do anything but stay still and wait. Surely someone would find the van and make Isaac's people talk. Help was on the way. She had to believe that.

Chapter Twelve

"This is where he says she's being held?" King passed back the binoculars. He was ready to storm the place. He had his gun back, but what he really longed for was one of those assault weapons like Delaney's men were carrying. He'd never owned one, never even wanted one until now. But he was staring at the headquarters of the man who'd sent Leroy Simms after the woman he loved. Right now he'd do whatever it took to get Anna back. Things he'd never before imagined he was capable of doing.

"Get that look out of your eyes right now, Sanders. You aren't leading a charge. My men are handling this." Delaney was calm.

Too calm. King wanted to smash his fist in his face. Anna's brother had landed in a helicopter and started issuing orders. But he wasn't as cool as he pretended. He had Scarlett with him. It seems he couldn't manage to say no to that little gal. King took a steadying breath, reminding himself that Anna loved her brother, then faced Delaney.

"Look. I'm not hanging back here while your team does its thing. I was with Anna when this went down. I need to see it through. She would want me there." He hoped to hell he was right about that.

"You'll just get in the way." Delaney glanced at Scarlett, who was stuck like a burr to his side. "You can stay here and keep an eye on this one."

"Like hell. I can shoot straight. I'll remind you that, even after I was sprayed with that crap, I woke up and managed to take down Crane's man in the van." King was sick of arguing. Every minute they wasted here was one more minute Anna was in that asshole's hands. He reminded Delaney of that too.

"That spray. I'd sure like to know what it was. We'll have to be alert in case they try to use it on us. But look at who Crane hires, locals like Simms and those two who took you and Anna. They won't like getting close enough to use shit like that. They'll be all about their guns. Which we certainly know how to deal with." Delaney stalked over to his laptop, set up on one of the SUV's tailgates.

He'd arranged his own headquarters on a hilltop with a view of the Crane hideout. Almost a dozen men and half as many vehicles were clustered together. Trees shielded them from anyone glancing their way from down below. One team member had rigged up a tarp in case the rain started again, but so far it was just cold and cloudy. A portable generator ran a heater and equipment King didn't try to identify. He did recognize a mini satellite dish. Delaney's laptop wasn't the only computer in use.

"I hope you're right. I don't want to ever be hit by that spray again." King wasn't about to admit he had a nagging headache even now. He looked over Delaney's shoulder at the computer screen. "What have you found out about Crane's headquarters? Is that the layout?"

"I told you, you're not going with us, but yeah."

"I'm going. Let me help." King grabbed Delaney's shoulder and almost got a gun in his face. But he held on. "Better to let me in on this from the start than to take a chance I'll blunder in where you don't want me. Are we clear?" He wasn't backing down. "I'll do anything, anything, to see Anna safely out of there."

Delaney looked behind him. Sam and Buck stood there, no doubt ready to pull King off if their boss gave the signal. "She's obviously gotten under your skin."

"More than that, brother. Much more than that." King waited, ready to react in case he had a fight on his hands.

Instead Delaney suddenly nodded. "Okay. But you have to follow my rules. Do as I or my team members say. Understand?"

"Sure. You're the expert here. I know that."

Delaney turned back to the computer. "Here's the front entrance. It's bound to be guarded. The building's connected to the cavern. It was abandoned when the former tourist site and cavern were found to be unsafe. Crane is renting the building but the terms of the agreement prevent him from going inside the cavern. If he's as smart as Anna says he is, he'll abide by that."

"If Anna's right, he makes his own rules." King knew caverns. Texas was full of them and they could be beautiful and dangerous. Why the hell had Crane picked this godforsaken place? He answered that question himself. It was isolated. And only a few miles outside of Georgetown, a stone's throw from Austin. He could monitor Anna's progress from here, and had even set up a satellite dish on the roof to give himself modern communication.

King had counted eight vehicles, from pickups to jeeps, outside the low-slung building. And then there had been a dark blue four-door sedan parked at the door, which Delaney's "invisible man" had claimed was the car Anna had arrived in, tied up in the trunk. Damn it.

"What's the plan, Delaney?"

"There are doors here and here." Delaney pointed to the side of the building that was attached to what looked like a small mountain. "There's a viewing room with a wall of windows in the back of the building. Old records show it's made of heavy-duty glass. Not bulletproof, but it would be hard to penetrate. I'm thinking our best bet is to go in at the two sides. Maybe do a feint at the front to draw them off from there."

"Sounds good. Lots of other rooms in there." King wondered where the asshole would stash Anna. Delaney's spy had told them that Anna had been carried to the front by Leroy Simms, but she had been able to walk under her own steam into the building. He'd been relieved to hear it. "Any idea where Crane keeps his computers? That's where he'd want Anna."

"True. He'd put her right to work. But I doubt she'd do it willingly." Delaney enlarged the floor plan, then hit a few buttons. "Schematics show he's got most of his power going to the big viewing room. I'd guess he set up his office there."

"Then we need to get to that room." King realized Sam and Buck were flanking him. "Are these guys my babysitters? I told you, I won't mess up your game plan. You obviously know what you're doing."

"You're an amateur, Sanders. Amateurs make mistakes. We want Crane as badly as you do." Sam was grim. "He made us look like fools. His people sprayed us with his shit then took the person we were supposed to keep safe right out from under us. We won't forget that."

"We're going to take him down, Sanders." Buck was checking his gun. "And get Anna back. That's a promise. If Delaney says you can come along for the ride, fine. But we need this and we won't let you fuck it up."

"If you catch Leroy Simms, I want a crack at him." Scarlett had been staring at the building at the foot of that mountain of rock. "I mean it."

"Red, we've been over this. You're here to be a friend to Anna once we rescue her. Don't even think about going down there with us." Delaney took her by the shoulders. "I'll tell you what I'm telling Sanders. You won't be allowed to get in our way. We've trained for hostage rescues. We know what we're doing."

"Of course you do." She nodded. "But if he is captured, I want five minutes with him." She laid her hand over Delaney's. "And a sharp knife."

He pulled her in for a hug but didn't make any promises.

One of the men who'd been hunkered down at the edge of the trees ran up to Delaney. "Chance, our drone just sent back a report. Thermal imaging is suddenly showing activity coming out of the back of the building going into the cavern—a lot of it, and moving real fast."

King hurried to the edge of the hill. Of course, there was no sign of life on this side of the building. He reached for his gun that Delaney's men had found for him in the van. He could think of only one reason there would be rapid action in that cavern. "I bet Anna got a chance and made a run for it." He wanted to head right down the hill but knew that would be a fool's suicide mission.

"Shit. I think you're right. She has no idea how dangerous that place is." Delaney checked his weapon. "We've got to move. Now." He started issuing orders. A disgruntled Scarlett was assigned a guard and left behind in an SUV. The rest of the men got detailed instructions and King ended up with Sam and Buck again.

The ride was rough as they hit what was barely a trail in their four-wheel drive. The road wound down the side of the hill toward the facility that had been known as Mystic Bat Caverns. King tried not to think about Anna having to run for her life in what amounted to a huge cave that could fall in on her at any minute. He hoped like hell she'd managed to get away from Crane. Damn, but he was proud of her. Unless... Was she hurt? Terrified?

"Get ready. When we pull up, we're bound to meet resistance. Keep the car between you and the building." Sam gunned the motor so they went into a skid on the gravel as he braked hard and stopped the vehicle parallel to the door. He and Buck were out of the car fast, raking the door with gunfire when a man popped out and shot at them.

King hit the ground on his side and looked for a target. Another man ran out and used a pile of rocks to set up and start shooting. Buck darted toward the door, rolling and then shooting. A man fell out of the doorway to land unmoving in the mud. That brought the guy behind the rock up to look and King took the shot. He heard a grunt and knew he'd hit him. Had he put him out of commission? Only one way to find out.

King scrambled, running low and heading for that pile of rocks. Yep, he'd wounded the man, who lay bleeding on his side. The guy reached for his gun when he saw he had company but King kicked it away.

"Here." Sam jerked the man's hands behind his back and pulled them together with a zip tie. He tossed one to King. "Do his feet. This door is clear. Follow me."

King took care of those legs, then picked up the man's gun and stuck it in his coat pocket before he ran after Sam. Buck was right behind him.

They could hear gunfire from another part of the building. The men in front and probably the other side were putting up a fight. Was Anna really in the cavern? All they'd seen were hot spots. Those could be anyone or anything.

"Anna!" He couldn't help it. He had to call for her. That outburst got him a hard look from Sam. "What if they caught her again and she's locked up in here somewhere, Sam? What the hell does a drone know?"

"He's right." Buck nodded. "Anna! Can you hear us?" He began throwing open doors. Every room they checked was empty. But they kept going, getting closer to the big room where the windows would look out into the cavern.

When they'd gone pretty far, King held up his hand for silence. "We don't want to be heard if Crane and his men are in that viewing room."

The three men walked on, cautiously, until King thought he heard a voice from behind a door. He pressed close and knew they'd found the right room. Isaac Crane's voice was distinctive. He was a man who liked big words and hired killers to do his dirty work. He was also loud as he gave orders.

"It's obvious you need to make a stand here. Prove your value, Leroy, and take care of this intrusion. I'm going into the cavern. When Anna hears those gunshots she'll think she's being rescued and will come out of hiding. Then I'll have her."

"I've got your back, boss." Leroy Simms sounded confident. "You get that bitch and bring her to me. I've got plans for her."

"Of course you do. I may even watch you at work this time, Leroy." A door opened and closed.

"Spread out. It sounds like they brought a fucking army in here after her." Leroy issued orders. There was the sound of furniture being moved and a crash. "Yeah, like that. Boss won't like it, but we got to have a shield. We're taking a stand. Don't let the assholes through." There was a rallying cry.

"Ideas?" King could see a group of well-armed men through that dusty window set in the top of the door. It was obvious that he wasn't going to be able to get out to the cavern except by going through that big room where Leroy and his crew were setting up. King couldn't wait to take them down.

"I wish we had some of Crane's spray." Buck looked grim as he whispered. "Man, would I love to give Simms a taste of his own medicine."

"You and me both, brother." Sam tested the doorknob. It turned easily. "Time to let Delaney know we're ready on our side. He figured this would happen. We'll come at them all at once." He touched his earpiece and muttered into it. Then he nodded. "On his count." He paused, listening, then put up three fingers. One by one they went down until he threw open their door and started firing.

King found himself pushed back behind Buck. He didn't like it but he had a feeling those were the man's orders. Doors popped open in the middle of the room and on the other side. The three-pronged attack made quick work of Leroy's band of not so merry men. Some bleeding, they were rounded up and zip tied efficiently. King wanted a word with Leroy. So did Chance Delaney. But as they went through the piled up furniture it was soon clear that Leroy had made a run for it.

"Damn it. There's only one way out of here. He's in the fucking cavern." Delaney kicked aside a chair.

"With Crane. And Anna." King told him Crane's theory. "Surely she wouldn't come out. But she had to have heard the shooting. And now that it's stopped..." He stalked over and opened the door. "How dangerous is this cavern supposed to be?"

"Careful. You're presenting a clear target, standing in the door there." Delaney gestured and the room lights were turned off, pitching them into utter darkness.

"What the hell?" King couldn't even see where to step.

"Relax. I got this." Delaney called a name and there was a thump nearby. He thrust something into King's hand. "Night vision goggles. Put them on."

"Right." King slipped them over his eyes. The relief was instantaneous. The room around him was visible and so was the cavern in front of him in that eerie way night vision worked. He'd used them before, hunting. Shit. He'd told Anna he hadn't killed anything before—well, anyone. Did a wild turkey count? Or deer? He had to get his head on straight. Time enough to confess what every boy in Texas did growing up.

Delaney had been talking.

"Now, let's go." He called for Sam and Buck. "Stick with Sanders. You know firsthand how dangerous Leroy Simms can be. Not sure about Crane. But he's a big guy. Shoot to kill." He had handed out goggles to everyone. "Watch for the little one—that would be Anna. And it's unstable rock. Be careful."

King stepped out into the vast space. The glimpse he'd had before the lights had gone down had shown him the beauty of one of the state's natural wonders. But he couldn't appreciate it. He had to find Anna. Should he call her name? But what if she answered, only to fall into Crane's arms? Or worse, Leroy's?

* * * *

Anna knew something had changed. She'd heard distant sounds, popping. Gunshots? She could only hope. That would mean someone had found her and was attacking the compound. She wanted to scream for help but that might bring the wrong person.

Not just the noise was different. Once her eyes had adjusted, she'd realized the glow from the building had allowed her to see into the cavern when flashlights weren't raking the area around her. Now suddenly the lights in the building had gone out. Had she ever been in such complete and utter darkness? She closed her eyes again, trying to find her own night vision.

When she opened them she thought there was movement in the middle of the cavern. She'd discovered a break in the rock that let her have a line of sight and now she could see a silhouette of a man with a cell phone light. It was tempting to lean forward for a better look. But she'd been frozen in place too long. Her legs were numb. Hell, her entire body was like an ice cube. Sitting in a wet coat was probably going to kill her—if Leroy Simms didn't get to her first.

When a second man's form appeared, she could tell that one of them, the freakishly tall one, was Isaac. Their whispered conversation carried in the vast cavern.

"You failed."

"We were outnumbered, boss. Tell me there's a back way out of here." Leroy turned on a flashlight but it was quickly knocked to the ground and shattered.

"What the hell do you think you're doing? Lighting the way for them to find you?" Isaac's whisper was furious. "I've been exploring in here. There are a couple of possible exits, but I'm thinking that our best bet is to go through the hot springs."

"The place that smells so bad?" Leroy kicked at the broken flashlight. "I can't see my hand in front of my face. How am I supposed to find it?"

"Follow me. Get out your cell phone, turn on the light, and keep your body between it and the windows. We can't let those gunmen see us." Isaac grabbed his arm. "And, for God's sake, stay quiet."

"What about your woman, the precious Anna? She brought this hell down on us. You giving up on her?" Leroy turned on his cell phone light, following Isaac's directions.

"She's for another day. I'm not giving up. But an intelligent man knows when it's time to cut his losses and regroup. Since you failed to stop her rescuers, I'd be a fool to keep wandering around in here, hoping to find her before they do." Isaac turned to walk deeper into the cavern. "Stay close. You do have your gun, don't you? Watch my back."

"Hell, yes! I have my gun and my knife. I haven't been paid yet. I won't let you out of my sight until I see the money." Leroy was on his heels.

Anna sighed. They were leaving and she could finally get out of that tight space and make a run for it. She reached out for something to help her stand, grabbing the rock in front of her. It crumbled under her fingertips, sending shards to the floor.

"Did you hear that?" Isaac stopped. "I knew it. She was close all along."

Before Anna could do more than scream, he was on her, grabbing her arm and dragging her out of her hiding place. "No! Help!"

"Shut the hell up!" Leroy slapped her.

Anna's ears rang as her head hit the rock behind her. When she saw Leroy's knife gleam in the dim light, she didn't say another word. Blood rushed to her feet when she tried to stand and she collapsed. Leroy slapped her again and jerked her upright. The pain in her cramped legs made her cry out. He knocked her to the ground, then pulled open her coat.

"Shut up, bitch." Leroy cut a strip of cloth from the lining of her coat and used it to make a gag so she couldn't scream again. "Boss, this is a bad idea. She's going to slow us down." He yanked her to her feet.

"No, she's a bargaining chip. Come on." Isaac took her other arm and dragged her deeper into the cavern. "Hurry. The gunfire has stopped again. They'll be coming out here next."

Anna stumbled. He was right. She'd do whatever she could to slow them down. Leroy muttered obscenities, then hoisted her so high her feet no longer touched the ground. Her arms were almost torn out of their sockets. Not that they cared. They were running into the darkness along a path with worn arrow signs. Soon she smelled what must be the hot springs. Leroy was right, they were nasty. She recognized the rotten egg scent from a long ago chemistry class.

"Pee-yew! No wonder this place didn't make it as a tourist trap. Who'd want to bathe in that crap?" Leroy dropped Anna's arm and pulled out a bandana to wrap around his nose.

"Hydrogen sulfide, Leroy. When the springs were open, there were large fans for ventilation. We don't want to breathe this for too long or we'll suffer unpleasant side effects. You're right about that. But the water had medicinal properties."

"Save the lecture, boss. I want out of here." Leroy paced and waved his light around.

"Of course. As I recall, there was a shower area and a restroom. Workers had to come and go to install those. Look over there and see if there's an exit." Isaac forced Anna down on a stone bench. "I'm searching Anna. She has that flash drive you brought me earlier."

"Oh, yeah. You'd better get that." Leroy pulled down the bandana and grinned at Anna. "Bet you're wondering why I cut on your coat instead of using this to gag you." He chuckled. "Honey, I wanted to remind you about the knife. Worked, didn't it? You should have seen your face when I went to use it that close to your body. Which is smokin' hot, by the way. Can't wait for my turn to make you cooperate with the boss." He tapped that knife, which was back in its scabbard, then pulled up the bandana again.

Oh, Anna hated him. She eased her hand into her pocket. If she could toss that drive into the hot springs bubbling a few feet away, it would be out of Isaac's reach. His hand clamped down on hers before she even touched it.

"So that's where it is. I'll take that." Isaac smiled. The smell didn't seem to bother him. He jerked Anna's hand from her pocket.

Anna wasn't going to make it easy for him. She jumped to her feet and tried to run. Damn it, she'd fling herself into that hot spring if she had to. It wouldn't be poison for the short term, just a noxious pool that would probably help her aching muscles if she could get to it. Too bad the smell was already making her nauseated.

Isaac grabbed her, his long arms wrapping around her so tightly Anna struggled to breathe. She kicked, struck out, and tried to hit his chin with her head. But he *had* learned a thing or two since she'd thrown him over her shoulder. He gripped her arms, holding her against his chest while he stuck his hand in her pocket. As soon as he had the drive, he threw her to the floor.

Anna stayed down, panting, the smell getting to her. She had to stop breathing so heavily. She looked around. Isaac was gloating and Leroy was down a passageway, looking for the way out. She had one chance to run and she was taking it, along with Isaac's cell phone light. He'd dropped the phone during their struggle and didn't seem to have noticed as he ran his fingers over the drive to make sure she hadn't damaged it. She wished she'd thought of that. She could have used a rock to smash, scratch, or scrape it.

She snatched up the phone and took off. That left Isaac in the dark and her with an advantage. She heard him shouting for Leroy as she ran back the way they'd come, using those old signs that pointed to the main building. She heard sounds behind her, the men coming after her. No! She couldn't let them catch her. She slipped and slid as she turned a corner, pulling off the gag as she went. She was going as fast as she could when she ran into a man.

"Let me go!" She hit him as hard as she could. No way was she letting Isaac have her again.

Chapter Thirteen

"Anna!" King grabbed her and wouldn't let her go. "It's me, King. I've got you."

"Careful, Isaac and Leroy are right behind me." Anna's heart didn't quit pounding and she sure couldn't take a moment to relax into those strong arms around her. This was almost too good to be true. She pulled King toward the building. "Hurry. They have guns."

"Anna, get out of the way."

"Chance?" Anna was rudely plucked from King's grasp and shoved behind her brother. "Thank God!"

"Shut up and let us do the job." Chance wasn't sparing time for a family reunion. "Sanders, get back there with her."

"Right." King was suddenly beside her, his arms around her again. "Damn it, you're wet. And freezing."

"How can you see anything?" Anna shivered. When he put his coat around her she wanted to protest but didn't have the strength of will once his warmth and smell surrounded her. Heaven.

"Night vision goggles." He handed her a gun. "Here. Turn off that cell phone light. It's like a beacon to a shooter in here."

"Only if I get my own goggles." Anna felt something land in her other hand. Goggles. "Thanks." She turned off the cell light and put the phone in her pocket.

"Now be quiet, Anna. We're not letting you out of our sight until Crane is dead or captured." Sam's voice. "I'd take you into the building but they're still clearing it."

"Okay." She put on the goggles. Amazing. The men around her stood out in a green landscape. King pulled her behind an outcropping of rock.

It was the same place where she'd stayed hidden for what had seemed like hours. Chance and two other men advanced into the cavern. She prayed they would be careful. Isaac and Leroy were so unpredictable.

"They might not find them. Leroy was looking for another exit, by the hot springs." She said this as the team rounded a corner and went out of sight.

"We're supposed to stay here." King held on to her. She could feel him shivering beside her. He should have his coat back. But she knew he would refuse it. Macho man. She loved him. And hated what Leroy had done to him. It all came back to Isaac, though, and his orders.

"Come on. I have a gun, you have a gun. I'm not cowering here, waiting for my brother to rescue me." Anna slipped out of their hiding place. Of course King was right beside her. "Let's go this way." She headed the opposite direction from Chance's crew.

She loved those goggles. Now she could see where she was going and didn't have to trip over rocks like she'd done on her wild run away from Isaac. Sam was on his comm and waved at her to get back to her hidey hole. No way.

She'd taken one geology class long ago, when she caught the bug from Isaac. This cavern was beautiful, with many different rock formations and columns reaching up, as well as the descending stalactites Isaac had mentioned. She could hear running water as they cautiously moved forward. It wasn't the hot springs, but closer to the building.

Had Isaac found a way to escape? Or had he discovered a passage that would lead him back to his headquarters so he could shoot his way out? She got her answer when two forms emerged from behind a pile of flowstone. She knew instantly from his intimidating height that one of them was Isaac, Leroy beside him. King stiffened and grabbed her arm.

"Stop where you are." Anna loved saying that. She knew the one feeble phone light Leroy held was not enough for them to pinpoint where she stood.

"Anna?" Isaac sounded incredulous. "My dear. You waited for us? I knew you'd finally see that it's in your best interest to throw in your lot with me. We'll make a fortune together."

"Give it up, Isaac. My brother is here with a tactical team. He's already taken down all of your men except Leroy. He's all you have left. And that's not saying much, is it?" Anna waited to see how that would go over with Knife Guy. She wasn't disappointed.

"What the fuck does that mean?" Leroy must have had another flashlight, because it went on and he waved it around the cavern. "I'll cut you apart, bitch."

"Don't let her get to you, Leroy. That's her goal." Isaac grabbed the flashlight. "Quit making yourself a target."

Too late. King made a great shot and Leroy yelped, dropping his gun and falling on his ass with a shoulder wound.

Anna wanted to happy dance.

"My turn. Give up, Isaac. I hear my brother and his men coming. You might as well turn yourself in and hope an insanity plea will work in court. That's your best shot at avoiding hard time in a super max prison." Anna saw Chance and his men emerge from the side entrance. So did Isaac. He ran deeper into the cavern as gunfire erupted from both directions. Anna knew she couldn't hit a moving target. To her surprise, Chance ran toward her and grabbed her arm.

"We have to get out of here." He spoke into his comm and the lights in the building suddenly came on again. "Sam, Buck, get Simms as fast as you can then follow me. Sanders, you have my six?" Chance pulled Anna toward the building.

"Sure. Whatever the hell that means." King was right behind them.

"My back. You have my back." Chance wasn't slowing down while he dragged Anna with him.

"We need to go after Isaac. He's getting away." She tried to stop when they reached the steps up to the building.

"No, he's not." Chance ignored her resistance, picking her up and carrying her to the door. Then he stopped and set her on her feet. "Inside, then listen."

King's arm went around Anna while they waited and watched through the wall of windows. Sam and Buck dragged a cursing and bleeding Leroy between them. Buck finally stuck that bandana into Leroy's mouth. Anna heard rumbling from deep inside the cavern. As they stood there, it got louder and she saw the first of the sharp pieces of what geologists called drapery fall to the cave floor. They shattered on impact.

"What's happening?" She saw more pieces of the cavern ceiling fall as, behind her, Chance directed an immediate evacuation.

King stood beside her, holding her close. It was as if he had to make sure she was really there, safe. "I guess the noise of the gunfire caused vibrations that were too much for a cavern that was unstable to begin with. We need to get out. Unless there's an escape route deep in the mountain, Isaac Crane is about to be buried by falling rock."

"God." Anna shuddered as more and more of the cavern ceiling crashed with a mighty roar. Now the building itself, attached to the mountain wall, began to shake. She bit back a scream. Was the building next? "What a horrible way to go."

"Hell, it's what he'd want." Leroy Simms had spit out his bandana while he was getting first aid from Buck. "That man loved the cavern. If one of those hanging things took him through the heart? He'd die happy." Leroy cursed when Buck poured some kind of disinfectant on his gunshot wound. "I think you enjoyed that."

"Sure did. Want me to dig out the bullet with your knife?" Buck waved the knife in front of Leroy but held it out of reach while Sam kept a gun pointed at the man. "If I didn't think this building was about to collapse, I'd do it real slow."

"You think I couldn't handle it? Go ahead." Leroy threw back his shoulder. But when Buck actually looked like he was about to dig in, he flinched and demanded an ambulance and a lawyer.

"Wimp." Buck slapped a bandage on him, then bound his arms behind him, not gently either, and hurried him out of the room.

"Anna, come on. We've got to go." King urged her toward the door.

"I know." She was scared, but she had to see if there was any sign of Isaac among all those falling rocks. The floor under her feet cracked and heaved. "He has my flash drive."

"Crane's not going to be able to use it in hell." King pushed her through the building and out the door. The roof of the building buckled and parts of it began to fall into the cavern.

"Get in the car." Chance was at the wheel. "Don't inhale. This debris might be toxic. Crane had all kinds of shit cooking in that lab of his."

Anna and King got in the back seat and the SUV roared away. They had to hang on as he drove like a wild man up the hill. They'd escaped just in time. The building finally fell into the cavern with a huge boom. There was an explosion as they stopped on top of the hill.

Anna jumped out of the SUV in time to see thousands of bats emerge from the opening in the face of the mountain. She couldn't look away. Wave upon wave of bats kept coming. Dust filled the sky but the wind was thankfully carrying it away from them and the nearby town. It took more than an hour before there were no more signs of life. The sky had cleared as a patrol car pulled up and King's friend Mike got out.

"I hear you have a prisoner for me." He pumped King's hand and pulled Anna into a hug. "Been a hell of a few days, hasn't it?"

"I'll say." King and Chance walked him over to where Leroy sat sulking in the back of a car. Scarlett stood next to it, giving him a piece of her mind. Mike caught her arm just as she was about to hit him.

Anna couldn't tear her eyes from the ruins of that cavern. Every once in a while something would move—another rock formation crumbling or one lone bat finding its way out of the darkness. She hoped this disturbed hibernation wouldn't mean the end of the little furry creatures.

"Quit frowning." King had borrowed a coat. Now he brought her a hot cup of coffee.

Anna wasn't sure she could drink it. The last cup had been handed to her by Isaac. But the cup felt warm so she just held it.

"Seriously. You should be happy. We're safe. Your program is safe. And that asshole is obviously no longer going to be a problem for you." King led her over to the back seat again and settled her inside. Then he climbed in beside her and closed the door.

The motor was running and it was blessedly warm. Even the seats were heated.

"So this is the part where I go home and relax." Anna looked at him. "Except I don't have a home, do I?" She leaned back and stared at the seat back in front of her. Yes, it was all hitting her. "I'm wet, aching all over, and miserable." She realized something even worse. "For some stupid reason I feel guilty that a man died practically right in front of me."

"Whoa. No way should you feel even a bit of guilt over that conscienceless bastard." King grabbed her shoulders until she faced him again. "He had a man killed and Scarlett maimed. He was prepared to have Simms do his worst to you, just to get that program finished. And all for money." He pulled her close, his cheek resting on her hair, his hands on her back. "When I think of how he treated you..." He took a deep breath, the movement pressing his chest against hers. "I just wish I'd been able to get hold of him. I wanted to take him down myself."

Even through all the layers she wore, Anna could swear she felt his heart pounding. King was truly upset. At her close call. She could only imagine how he'd felt when he'd woken up and realized she was gone. She knew how she would have felt if he'd been the one missing.

She leaned even closer, determined to comfort him. She slid her fingers through his damp hair and brought his lips to hers. She needed his kiss just as much as he seemed to need hers. Their mouths met hungrily but it wasn't carnal. It was more of an affirmation. That they were still alive. That they belonged together. A knock on the window next to her broke them apart. She reached blindly for the control and ran it down.

"Hate to interrupt, but I need to know how you're doing, sis." Chance leaned against the car. He looked tired. Of course. She doubted he'd slept since she and King had disappeared.

"I'm okay." She reached for his hand and clasped it.

"How can you be? You look like the back end of hell." He frowned. "You had me scared shitless. Sanders was in bad shape too."

"I admit it." King exchanged looks with her brother. "Anna says she's okay, but I think she should be checked out. No telling how long she was stuck in that cavern, cold and wet."

"I agree." Chance opened the car door. "Let's go. I'll have Sam and Buck run you to the closest emergency room."

"No way. I told you I'm fine. But if it'll make you feel better, let Buck look me over. I saw him treat King. He's more than qualified to check me out." Anna wasn't about to be subjected to tests and what would probably end up an overnight stay in a hospital. Of course, her legs hurt from the unnatural position she'd held for way too long. She probably had a knot on the back of her head from whacking it on that rock. Damn Leroy Simms. Her throat was a little sore. No surprise. She was probably coming down with whatever had laid King low just twenty-four hours before. Or maybe that was from screaming for help. Yep, that could do it.

"You don't call the shots here." Chance tried to drag her out of the car.

"I do now that the crisis is over. I'm one of your clients, remember? And, for God's sake, don't manhandle me. I've had just about enough of that, brother." Anna saw another black SUV arrive. When the man climbed out, she knew she had an ally. "There's the guy who can call the shots. Ask him." She pointed.

"Oh, great. That's all I need." Chance let go of her hand and turned to face the new arrival. "He did nothing but drink and complain the whole time we were in San Antonio."

"He's paying you. Smile." Anna pinched her brother on his rock-hard arm.

"Anna! Are you really all right? The Rangers gave me your flash drive. I can't believe Crane almost got both copies of them." Ron Zenonsky slid in the mud on the way to her. He waved the drive as he almost fell into the car. "King! Were you in on the kill?"

"Please don't call it that, Ron. Hold on to the drive for me for now." Anna slowly climbed out of the car. She wobbled, not surprised when King was right behind her to help her stay on her feet. She leaned against him.

"Well, he is dead, isn't he?" Ron gazed down at the ruins of the building and cavern. "What the hell happened there? Did you bomb the place?"

"Not necessary, Mr. Zenonsky. Natural disaster. The cavern was unstable." Chance hustled Ron over to his bank of computers and smiled. "Very successful mission. Let me debrief you. Anna, I'll send Buck. There's a cot next to the heater under the tarp. Humor me and go lie down on it so he can check you out."

Anna started to argue then realized she wanted nothing more than to stretch out and close her eyes.

"You're swaying." King picked her up and carried her toward the makeshift tent where the heater was located. When he set her down, it was on a padded cot that had been set up close to that circle of warmth. "Now get out of that wet coat." He helped her shed it. "Your sweater is damp too." He looked around. "Did anyone bring Anna's bag? She needs to change out of these wet things."

"Sure thing, Sanders." Sam stepped up. "Buck and I will hold up a couple of blankets to give her privacy. Should have done that the minute she got here." He dropped the bag on the ground at the foot of the cot. "Give me her boots and I'll clean them."

Anna didn't care if anyone saw her in her underwear. But Scarlett came hurrying over and helped her shed everything down to her dirty boots. Shivering in her bra and panties, Anna slipped into a soft sweater, dry socks and leggings. A blanket, then two more, were wrapped around her before she lay back on the cot.

"Let me help you wash up." Scarlett brushed off King's efforts to take over. "This is what friends are for. I'll let you know when she wants you." Scarlett took a basin of warm water from one of the men. "Trust me, Annie, you don't want to look in a mirror right now." She proceeded to clean the mud and gravel from Anna's face and hands. She talked softly the entire time, complaining about Chance and his high-handed ways. Then she went on to assure Anna that Leroy was on his way to jail and a lifetime behind bars.

"He'll never see daylight again, Mike says." She sighed. "I'm so glad you got away from Ichabod and that he's dead and buried."

Anna shuddered. "You're right. He'll never see daylight again either. The mountain came down on top of him." She wiped at a tear.

"You aren't crying for him, are you?" Scarlett tossed away the dirty water. "I'll slap you if you are."

"No, no. It's just so surreal. Watching the cavern, that beautiful place, fall to pieces. Then all the bats flew out. How can they survive?" Anna closed her eyes. She kept seeing Isaac disappearing into the dark. He was gone. She kept telling herself that. But they hadn't seen a body. No exit. Of course, there was no way he could have survived.

"Mike says the bats will be okay. This cold front came after a warm spell, remember? There are insects the bats can eat in other caves near here.

So relax. Think about yourself. You're safe. And King Sanders is looking at you like you're the last cookie on the tray." Scarlett patted Anna's leg under that pile of blankets. "As soon as that medic gets through checking you out, I say you make sure that cowboy doesn't get away. If that's what you want."

"Can it really be that simple?" Anna opened her eyes to stare into her best friend's face. Scarlett always seemed to be optimistic. Even after what Leroy had done to her, she was bouncing back.

"Why not? Fate brought you two together. You always think too much. Isaac is gone. King is here and clearly wants you. Don't ruin this, Anna. You hear me?" Scarlett stood, picking up the camp stool that someone had kindly topped with a pillow for her. She tossed a lipstick at her friend. "The pale look is working for you, but a little pink wouldn't be a bad idea." She grinned and winked. "No thinking. That's an order." She walked away, still limping, but obviously well on the way to recovery.

Buck showed up next with his massive first aid kit. He looked into her eyes, then took her temperature, frowning and announcing that she was running a slight fever. That brought out a water bottle and a couple of ibuprofen. Anna took them obediently. She didn't want to get sick. Fortunately, that was the only symptom Buck could find.

Chance was there to help her sit up. "Buck says you're sore but unharmed. It's a miracle." He watched her sit up and put on her cleaned boots.

"Thanks for rescuing me." Anna kissed his cheek. "This should be a good payday for your new company, and a good recommendation."

"It is. But I hope I never again have a job involving a family member." He glanced behind him. "Sanders is waiting for you. But I'll set you up somewhere else if you don't want to go with him."

"Thanks. But he and I need to talk." Anna took his hand. "You really are good at this. I'm glad you left the FBI. I'll talk to Dad about it when I'm home at Easter."

"Thanks. I appreciate it." Chance stared at her. "Sanders is okay. He stepped up and showed he really cares about you. You could do worse."

"That's a ringing endorsement." Anna smiled. "Help me stand."

"You're going to be achy for a few days. You have any idea how long you were in that cavern?" Chance pulled her to her feet.

"None. But it seemed like hours." She saw King walking toward her. "Where are you going now?"

"Dallas. I got a call a few hours ago. Of course, I wasn't leaving here until I had you safe and sound." Chance put her hand in King's. "One of my men will take you wherever you need to go. Just say the word."

"That's up to Anna." King threw his arm around her. "She needs to rest. Recuperate."

"Finish the program." Ron was right behind him.

"When she feels like it, Ron. Quit pushing." King glared at his friend. "If this program is the only thing Zenon has to offer, then you need to take a hard look at how you're running things. And so does your board of directors."

"Hold up." Ron backed up a few steps. "We're diversified. We have a new tablet coming out next month. And the cell phone business is coming along. Androids are hot right now. We've got some accessories that millennials are going to go crazy for."

"Then quit pressuring Anna about this one program. Am I clear? Or do I have to contact the other investors and see about changing management?" King's arm tightened around Anna.

"No, hell no. I just told you what's in the pipeline." Ron turned to Anna. "Take a break. As long as you need. You've been through a bad experience. Relax. Gather your thoughts. Who could write code when you're stressed like you have been? I know I couldn't."

Anna didn't say that she hadn't seen Ron write a lot of code when he *wasn't* stressed. She just said thank you and let King lead her to an SUV with Sam at the wheel. They settled in the back seat again.

"Where to?" Sam had the heat going, and those heated back seats were toasty.

"Give us a minute." King turned to Anna. "You said you don't have a home to go to. I know that's a problem."

"No kidding." Anna waited.

"Would you consider going home with me? Not to Austin, but to my ranch. It's a good place to relax. You can bring your laptop if you wish, but you don't have to. You heard Ron. You can take a real break." King held her hand. "I'd like for you to meet my grandmother and my sister. See where I grew up. What do you say?"

Anna took a steadying breath. King's home. A ranch. With cows, horses, and, God help her, spinach. She suddenly realized it sounded like heaven. She leaned over and kissed him, needing to make sure he was still just as dear as she thought he was.

"I'd love that. But I do want my laptop. Sam? Is it in this car?"

"Sure, Anna. Scarlett even made your brother buy you a new backpack for it. That and your bag of clothes are in the back." He tossed something over his shoulder. "Here's your thumb drive. Zenonsky slipped it to me. In case you did want to get back to work."

Anna rolled the tiny drive around in her fingers. "Do you know what happened to the couple who kidnapped us? Francie and Billy?"

"They're locked up and trying to work a deal. They thought testifying against Isaac Crane might help them." Sam chuckled. "That won't work now."

"No, they should be punished. Kidnapping, assault. I guess Mike will make sure they get the book thrown at them." Anna leaned against King. She'd never forget how they'd tossed him in that cart on top of her. A man like King hated being helpless. "Of course, they could testify against Leroy Simms."

"I'm sure they'd be too scared to do that. Billy and Leroy could end up in prison together. I wouldn't want that asshole out to get me." King kissed her cheek. "Now would you give me that drive? When you want it, ask. But I don't want you feeling like you have to get back to work anytime soon."

"Thanks." Anna sighed as she pressed it into his hand. "I hope all of them cut some kind of deal. I don't want to have to testify in court. That would just bring back this nightmare."

"Your friend Mike will probably take care of it, Sanders, if you let him know how Anna feels. I like those Texas Rangers. Very professional." Sam tapped the steering wheel. "Waiting for driving instructions, you two."

"The Austin airport. Bergstrom." King told him how to get there. "I left my plane there. Since the weather's cleared, I'll fly us to the ranch."

Anna sat back and closed her eyes. Sam assured them it wouldn't take long. Relax. She tried, she really did. It was over. Isaac was gone. Why couldn't she believe it?

Chapter Fourteen

Whisked away to a Texas ranch. If Anna had been daydreaming about Texas, then she couldn't have imagined anything better than this. King had his own freaking plane, a sleek four-seater that he handled like a pro. He landed it at the airport in the little county seat, Sparkle City. It didn't sparkle, but it was cute. It had a square that, he was proud to show her, really did have a statue of Popeye next to the courthouse. Yes, this tiny town was the spinach growing capital of the world.

He had a truck parked at the airport and tossed their bags in the back. King kept up a running commentary about the town's colorful past. At one time almost every city official had been indicted for illegal gambling. He waved to a man coming out of a café on the square.

"That's Dr. Murakami. He's a good doctor. I can see you have a lump on your forehead. You know that's making me crazy, don't you? If you feel dizzy or have a headache, I'm taking you to see him." He glanced at her. "You going to tell me what happened?"

"I was slammed against a rock. Knife Guy did it." Anna squeezed his thigh when he cursed. "Hey, I'm fine. No headache. Well, not much of one. If you don't nag me about it, later I'll let you kiss it and make it better. Believe me, I'd take being knocked around over a souvenir carving on my body any day."

"If I could get my hands on that bastard…" He looked like he was chewing ground glass.

"Well, you can't. Let it go, King. How far to this ranch? The Rocking S, right?"

"Yes, it's been in the family for four generations. You'll see the brand when we go through the main gate. Karen and I inherited it when my parents died." He took a breath and grabbed her hand. "Nice way to distract me, woman." He talked about his place as he drove out of town.

Anna sat back and tried to memorize anything she should remember when she met his grandmother. God, she didn't even know her name. She should ask but didn't want to interrupt his flow. All he'd ever called her was *Abuela*, Spanish for grandmother. His sister had flown the coop, as King put it. She'd gone off to Houston to attend a charity fundraiser. Anna was glad. Meeting one family member at a time was enough for her.

King drove for what seemed like miles past grazing cattle, spinach fields dormant because of the season, and pumping oil wells. They even passed a grove of olive trees. She'd always known King was rich, but the sheer size and variety of what he had just in land overwhelmed her. By the time he parked in front of a sprawling one-story house, Anna wanted to beg him to take her back to Austin. As a woman raised in the city, in a place with barely enough yard for her mother's herb garden, she felt way out of her league.

"You're awfully quiet." King turned off the engine and looked at her. "I know this seems kind of isolated, but I swear we have good Wi-Fi and satellite TV." He grinned. "And the best food in Texas. Wait till you taste my grandmother's cooking."

"King, this is beautiful." Anna knew there was so much more she could say. For a man worth more money than she could imagine, King didn't show off his wealth. She could actually be comfortable here. It was a relief. Trees shaded the front and sides of the house. It wasn't a mansion, just large and welcoming. She could see a pool gleaming under the bright blue sky. No rain today.

"It's a nice spread." King hopped out of the truck and came around to open her door. He helped her down from the high cab. "There's the barn and the paddock where we work the horses. The bunkhouse where the hands live is behind it. The ranch manager has his own house. I'm gone so much, I had to hire someone to oversee the day to day. Randy's been with me for about six years." He walked her toward the side door. "Hope you don't mind but we never go in the front door. *Abuela* hangs out in the kitchen. That's where we'll find her. It's almost dinner time."

Anna realized she hadn't eaten all day, and delicious smells were coming from the house. Of course, her stomach growled.

"I heard that." King laughed and hugged her. "*Abuela* will be happy if you're as hungry as you sound."

"Now I'm embarrassed." Anna was smiling as she walked into a big, beautiful kitchen fitted with top-of-the-line appliances. The woman sitting at the large wooden table in the center of it was reading a best-selling novel. She had a cup of coffee near her right hand as she looked up in surprise.

"*Mijo*! I didn't expect you." She held out her arms to King for a hug. "And who is this beautiful lady?"

King did the introductions after he kissed her cheek. "This is Anna Delaney, the woman I told you about. She's starving. Is it time for dinner?"

"It can be. I was baking a cake for the church bake sale, that's what you smell. We can have it for dessert and I'll make another. It's your favorite—*tres leches*. I had no one to feed tonight so I was thinking about a sandwich, but now? I will pull out some things and make a feast for us." Her black eyes lit with pleasure. "Please, sit. Would you like some coffee?"

Anna realized she couldn't imagine drinking coffee. Maybe never again. She glanced at King. "Water?" She sat at the table and sipped a glass of ice water while she watched the small woman bustle around the kitchen. King's grandmother, whose dark hair streaked with gray was fashionably styled, wore dark pants and a colorful top over her generous figure. Soon a plate of the same kind of Mexican food she'd had at King's house in Austin was set in front of her.

"It smells delicious. Let me see if I can remember what I'm eating. *Frijoles* and enchiladas." Anna tasted and sighed. "This is even better." She glanced around. "Where's Conchita?"

"She and Douglas went to San Antonio. As soon as they heard the danger was over, they decided to take a little honeymoon." King's grandmother laughed. "I encouraged it. She means well, but Conchita was getting in my way in this kitchen."

"You could have let her help you." King was enjoying his own plate of food. "Teach her how to make enchiladas like this."

"It would insult her. She thinks hers are better than mine." *Abuela* sat with them and worked on her own serving.

Anna shook her head. "No, these are better. Though they are both delicious." She kept eating. Soon her plate was clean and she was turning down seconds. "I know this sounds terrible, but I'm really tired. Could I see my room? I'd like a shower and an early bedtime."

King smiled at her. If he had plans for sharing his bedroom, she was going to put a halt to that. His grandmother was standing right there! Maybe she was being a prude, but Anna couldn't imagine playing bedroom games in front of such a sweet lady.

"Sure, I'll show you to a guest room. It's right next to mine." King stood. "*Abuela*, Anna has very few clothes. She has had a hard time, as I told you on the phone. Karen's coat that she borrowed is in the back of the truck but it's in rough shape. Maybe we can donate it after it's been cleaned."

"I am so sorry, Anna. There is evil in the world, I know that." *Abuela* gave her a hug. "You must rest and get back your strength." She gave King a look. "And my grandson needs to give you time to decide what you want from him."

"Now *Abuela*, we are adults." King grinned. "Don't go putting rules on me."

"Did I say what you can and cannot do? But she is obviously exhausted. She has dark circles under her eyes. And it is clear to me that they starved her when they took her." *Abuela* shook her head. "Call me *Abuela*, Anna. I know I am not your grandmother, but I would be honored if you would see me as a family member, *chica*. Let me take care of you while you are here."

Anna blinked back tears. Such kindness. She *had* been terribly mistreated. By horrible people. She missed her own family with a sudden sharp pain. Maybe she should call her mother. Then she realized that, damn it, she didn't have a phone. She could borrow one from King but didn't have the energy for a call now anyway. And she was very afraid she'd burst into tears when she heard her mother's voice and scare her to death.

"Thank you. That means more than you know. I am used to being around a big, loving family. I didn't realize…" Anna stood. "Well, I'd be honored to call you Grandmother."

"There you go." King took her arm. "Now you need that shower and a bed." He hustled her down the hall. "Much more of that talk and she'll have you with her down at the church, taking vows of chastity."

Anna stopped him with a hand on his chest. Caught by his smile, she tugged his face down to hers. "Chastity? Not a chance, Sanders." Then she kissed him with all the love in her heart. God, she wouldn't have made it through this without him. Since the moment she'd almost lost it at the state capitol building, he'd been by her side, making sure she knew she could count on him. His hungry growl assured her that he was happy about that. Finally, she eased back.

"Get my bag, would you?" She grinned up at him. "Which door?"

"Guest room?" He pointed. "Or mine?"

"For *Abuela's* sake, make it the guest room. You can always sneak in later." She ran her hand down his chest to the bulge below his belt buckle.

"Now you're talking." He pulled her to the bedroom and flung open the door. "Queen size. Mine's a king. Come see me. It's more comfortable. Whenever you're ready. Or wait, if you're too tired. I'll understand. We've got a long time ahead of us together, Anna." He studied her face. "Maybe forever." With that he turned on his heel and strode down the hall.

Anna stared after him. Forever. Could he really mean...? She walked into the bedroom and looked around. It was the same kind of welcoming space with quality touches she'd seen in his home in Austin. The attached bath had all the bells and whistles and she started the water running.

She couldn't wait to wash her hair and get the stench of that hot springs out of it. She could swear she still smelled the scents of the past days whenever she inhaled—the acrid spray that had taken down King and Francie, the bat guano in the cavern, and then whatever had exploded when the mountain had come down at Isaac's hideout.

She quickly stripped and jumped in the shower, using the bottles that had been left out for guests. Organic body wash and shampoo with wonderful scents soon left her feeling rejuvenated. She wrapped her body in a large, soft towel then fluffed her damp hair. She walked into the bedroom and found her bag sitting on a bench at the foot of the bed, her laptop on a desk under the window. Winter hours, it was early but already dark outside with a million stars in the sky when she glanced out that window.

She dressed quickly in a warm sweater and leggings, then put on the same boots again. It was a bit warmer here than it had been in Austin, but it would still be cold outside. South Texas. That's what King called it.

Anna wandered out to the living area and found King on the couch, working on his own laptop. "Can we go outside? I got a glimpse and it looks like a beautiful night. There are so many stars in the sky."

"You're right. You can see them out here because there are no city lights to blind us to them." He closed his computer. "Come here." He pulled her down beside him. "You look great. And smell a hell of a lot better."

"Thanks a lot." She leaned against him. "I may have to raid Karen's closet here. I need a coat."

He gestured to a hall tree by the front door. "Take your pick. How about a poncho? Warm, and one size fits all."

"Perfect." Anna got up and picked a black and tan one, then threw it over her head. It was warm and he was right—size wasn't an issue. "Let's go."

They walked outside and he showed her the stars. Anna wished for a telescope since there were so many of them, and they were so bright and clear. No, how about a blanket so she and King could make love under the beautiful night sky? She held that wish inside, thinking about the future. Forever. Could it be possible?

"Had enough yet? I know you're tired." King kept her close.

"Will you show me your horse?" Anna was fascinated by her first visit to a Texas ranch. She'd been strictly a city girl all her life and most of it had been spent indoors. Her choice, of course.

"I can tell you're dragging. We'll make it fast." He led her to the barn.

She did get to meet some of his horses. "I thought a barn would smell more, um, 'horsey.'"

"Not one that's well-kept." He pointed out his favorite ride.

"I'm glad. I've had my fill of bad odors lately. And you know I'm an animal lover. I can't believe Conchita and Doug took YoYo with them to San Antonio."

"I guess they weren't thinking you'd miss the little guy. Conchita told my grandmother you were probably worn out from what you'd been through. YoYo is a little"—King grinned—"high maintenance."

"Don't you dare criticize my dog." Anna laughed. But he was right. And keeping her pup contained when there was an entire ranch to explore? Well, the housekeeper and her husband would be back in a couple of days. Time enough for a doggy reunion. "I forgive you. The horses are beautiful. Will you teach me to ride one?"

"Can't wait." He showed her a gentle mare named Blossom and made sure she knew how to approach the horse to pet her.

By the time they headed back to the house, Anna had to admit she was tired. Very little sleep the night before and more physical exertion than she'd ever had in her life had taken a toll. And then there were those aches and pains.

Abuela met them at the kitchen door. "Anna, I found this in that coat you wore. I guess you forgot it was in the pocket." She handed Anna the phone, then kissed each of them on the cheek. "I'm going to bed now. I know it's early, but I have a good book to read. Good night, you two." She winked and headed down the hall. "I won't hear a thing."

"She won't either. She's obviously decided she likes you." King grinned. "Whose phone is that?"

Anna stared down at it. "Isaac's. I picked it up in the cavern. What should we do with it?"

"It's evidence. Mike will want to see it. Maybe he can run down Crane's buyer. That would be a big get for the Rangers." King took the phone and set it on the kitchen table. "Tomorrow is soon enough to call Mike and let him know we have it. Come on, you need to go to bed."

Anna sighed. "I'm tired, but not too tired." She pulled him down the hall to his bedroom. "I need for you to hold me."

"I'm up for that." King kissed her at his door. "But that's all I'll do if that's all you want." He walked her inside and closed the door behind them. "This has got to go. Ponchos are warm but sexless." He jerked it over her head and tossed it on a chair. "I like the blue sweater. Matches your eyes. *Adios*." It went off over her head next. "This bra is very utilitarian. You should go underwear shopping with my sister. She likes skimpy lacy underwear. My grandmother complains, but Karen's boyfriends do not." He opened the front clip and the bra was added to the pile. "Beautiful. I don't know why you bother with a bra. Your breasts are perfect." He leaned down and took his time kissing each nipple with care. "*Mmm*."

Anna let her head fall back, lost to the sensation. He held her up with his hands on her back. "*Mmm* is right."

"I'll stop anytime. Just say the word." He laid his head against her breast. "I mean it."

"King." Anna ran her fingers through his hair. "You're making me forget that I'm tired."

"That's the plan." He kneeled on the floor. "Boots." He unzipped them then helped her kick them away while she held on to his shoulders. "Leggings next. And look at that, the panties came off with them. Handy." He grinned up at her. "And I'm right where I wanted to be." He pressed his lips to her stomach, then licked a path south. "Woman, you are everything I want. You know that?"

"I want to be." Anna fell back on the bed, her legs widening as he had his way with her. "Please!" He was driving her mad. "Take off your damn clothes. I want to see your body."

He looked up. "This old cowboy's body?" He stood. "If you insist." He'd shed his coat and hat in the kitchen, hanging them on a coat rack by the door like it was a habit. "Now here's the deal. I have a few scars, in case you haven't noticed." He pulled his sweater off over his head. Tonight's had been black and had matched his hair.

"This one is from a bull." He pointed to a jagged scar on his stomach. "Bastard got me when we were taking him to donate sperm. Seems he thought he should take care of business the old-fashioned way, by humping a cow. He took objection to going to the vet. I finally sold that son of a gun. He just wasn't worth the trouble."

"Oh, come here. Let me make it better." Anna grabbed his belt buckle and got him close enough to run her tongue across the old wound. "This is an interesting buckle."

"Earned it riding bucking broncs one summer. Never again. I threw out my shoulder." He smiled when she opened that buckle and pulled down his zipper. "You'll find another scar down there. A little north of, you know."

"Oh, I sure do know." Anna traced a fingertip over a pink line that went along his hip bone. "What happened here?"

"Fishing line got caught there. I was skinny-dipping as a teenager with some of the fellas. One of them thought it would be a hoot to drop his line in while we were getting some sun. Caught me way too close to... Well, doc said another few inches and I'd have never been able to make babies."

"Now that would have been a shame." Anna pushed down his jeans and that baby-maker sprang into view. She took it in hand, then lavished it with kisses, grateful it was still there. For her pleasure. "You want kids?"

"Sure. Do you?" He sounded like he was strangling as she pulled his cock deep into her mouth. "Anna?" His hands were in her hair. "Stop or you won't get your own satisfaction."

"*Mmm.*" She finally let him go. "Yes, I want kids. A couple at least. I come from a big family. It can be crazy, but a lot of fun." She shoved him away. "Take off your boots. Lose the jeans. I want you naked. Now."

"Yes, ma'am." He hurried to do as she said. Then he stopped and stared at her. "Listen to us. Talking about a family."

"Pillow talk. Relax, cowboy. I'm not holding you to anything." Anna's heart pounded as he kept staring at her. The last cookie on the tray, like Scarlett had said? Or was he wondering if this was too fast, too soon, too serious?

"Would you stop looking like I'm about to hold a shotgun on you and walk you down the aisle? I've had the day from hell. Right now all I'm thinking about is how much I need you. I want you inside me, King Sanders. Please?" She held out her arms.

"Anna, I want you and need you too. It was also the day from hell for me, thinking about losing you. I kept worrying about what those bastards might be doing to you." He pulled her up to stand in front of him, dragging her close until they were skin to skin. "I could kill when I see the bruises and scratches on your body." He kissed the lump on her forehead gently. "I bet you hurt all over."

"You're making me forget everything but how much I want you." Anna pressed closer, her legs riding King's muscular thigh. It was the most wonderful feeling in the world, to be so close to him. Had she ever had this strong and fierce connection with anyone before? She ran her hands along his sides, over his back, wherever she could touch him. She breathed him in and knew she'd always know the unique masculine aroma that was King Sanders.

"I love you." He said it into her hair. "Stay with me."

"I will. I am. I love you." She pulled him to the bed and lay with her arms open wide. She hoped he would ignore all those places where she knew she looked the worst for her experiences in the cavern. He noticed and kissed each injury, no matter how slight. The back of her knee, her elbow, both shoulders; there was no place that didn't warrant a gentle exploration and thorough inspection.

Anna was desperate to move this along when he finally came to those places where she didn't hurt, she ached—for him. He knew just how to make her cry out, to reach for him and pull him closer. By the time they were finally together, the way she wanted them to be, she was desperate for completion. He let her set the pace as she shoved him down to sit astride and take him the way she needed to. Then they were moving, making love and becoming one. It was glorious, tender, and so completely right. By the time the last ripple of sensation rolled through her, Anna knew this was what she'd always wanted. And she was never letting it go.

* * * *

"Your phone is ringing." *Abuela* handed Isaac's phone to Anna as she was coming out of her bedroom the next morning.

"Thanks." Anna just stared at it.

"Breakfast is ready." *Abuela* watched her. "You don't have to answer it. I understand. You're on vacation. King told me." She walked off toward the kitchen.

Anna could see it was an unknown caller. Should she answer it? Just to see who it was? It might be a clue to help the Rangers track down Isaac's buyer. But what if she said the wrong thing, scared off the caller? Better to let it go to voice mail.

"You look completely freaked out." King was right behind her. His hand slid under her hair in a familiar way that was instantly comforting. "What happened?" Then he noticed what she had in her hand. "Why are you holding that?"

"It rang. Someone called Isaac and *Abuela* brought it to me. She thinks this is my phone." Anna wanted to drop it, throw it away. It was like a snake that could strike at any moment, full of poison.

"Okay. First, turn it off." He took it and hit the right button. "Second, we'll call Mike and get him to come get it. Or send someone for it. He can have techs go through it. There may be phone numbers or voice mails they can use to track down the people who were going to buy your software. They need to be brought to justice."

"Right." She was glad it was off.

"Do you think they could still come after you and your program? Is that why you're so upset?" King pulled her to the living room and sat down with her on the couch. "Do I need to get Chance back here? With his crew?" He actually picked up his phone from the coffee table.

"No, wait." Anna sat back. "Believe it or not, Isaac claimed it was his program that he was selling. He bragged to me that he had the initial idea, when we were dating in college." She still couldn't believe it. "It was bull, but I let him rave about it. I was too busy trying to find a way to escape."

"Are you kidding me? Crane told his potential buyers that he wrote your program? Are you sure? He never mentioned your name to them?" King looked at Isaac's phone. "I don't suppose we can get into this thing. I'd feel better if we could make sure of that. Your brother was worried that there might be foreign buyers who were after it. They wouldn't be happy to lose out on the big bucks they could make with the program."

"Well, if Isaac is dead, then so is their deal. They will think the program died with him. As for me, I'm more scared that Isaac escaped from that cavern somehow, King." Anna put a hand to her stomach. "I can't stop thinking about it. He was obsessed. If there was a way out of there, he would have known about it."

"Mike and the Rangers are following up at the site. He'll let us know if they find out anything, Anna." King pulled her close. "I don't see how Crane could have survived that cave-in. Your brother kept people there afterwards too. I'm sure Crane is dead."

"Call Mike, call Chance too. I have to know for sure." Anna wondered if she was losing her mind. She was sitting next to the man she loved and surely no one could come after her here, at his ranch. So why couldn't she relax? "I need my own phone, you know. I've been going through phones like crazy lately."

"Ron will buy you another one and send it out here. I'll call him as well." King steered her toward the kitchen. "Let me handle it. Hungry?"

"I don't know. Maybe eating will calm my nerves. But no coffee. Isaac served me coffee when I was there and it's put me off of it."

"Fine. *Abuela* makes a delicious hot chocolate." He turned to his grandmother and said something to her in Spanish that made her laugh and she got busy.

"I don't feel right, being waited on like this." Anna headed to the counter. "May I help?"

"I have a helper. Carmelita is out gathering the eggs, Anna. Please, sit down. You are our guest." *Abuela* gave her a hug. "You will enjoy my *choco caliente*. I have a secret ingredient." She was mixing something in a saucepan. "I insist. Sit. I will introduce you to *huevos rancheros* this morning. Have you tried them before?"

"No. What are they?" Anna did sit at the table. King was already on the phone. She heard him talking to Mike. That was a relief. She couldn't wait to get rid of anything to do with Isaac Crane. King's grandmother explained the Mexican egg dish. "Not too spicy, please. My brothers tease me. I'm a wimp when it comes to hot stuff."

That led to her telling King's grandmother about her family in Boston. *Abuela* was happy to hear she had so many brothers and looked significantly at King. Then she told Anna about the tragic plane crash that had left King and his twin sister to be raised by her when they were toddlers.

"It was hard on them. I was glad I was able to be there for my grandchildren." *Abuela* pulled out a tissue and wiped her eyes. "They are my heart."

* * * *

King watched *Abuela* set a steaming cup of chocolate in front of Anna and waited expectantly. "Try it and tell me what you think."

Anna raved over the hot chocolate, his grandmother's homemade tortillas, and the salsa topping fluffy scrambled eggs until *Abuela* told her to hush or she'd get a big head. They all laughed at that. Anna even asked for tortilla-making lessons. He fell a little more in love with her on the spot. Damn, he had it bad.

He took Anna on a tour of the ranch in a four-wheeler while he tried to reassure her of her safety. Her brother's crew at the cavern site, working with the Rangers, claimed there had been no sign of Isaac Crane escaping. She finally seemed to relax after she talked to Chance herself. He was willing to come to the ranch if she needed him. But she insisted he take care of his obligations to Trent, who needed him in Dallas.

"Don't worry about me, big brother. King is taking good care of me." Anna hung up and handed King his phone. "I think I've been overreacting. Chance has calmed me down. He insists no one could have survived in that cavern."

"You've been through a lot. If you want to freak out, go right ahead."

"It's hard to stay tense when I'm in such a beautiful place." Anna smiled at him.

They were at the pond where he'd gone skinny-dipping as a teen. It was a beautiful day and they were bundled up against the cold breeze. A few head of cattle were nearby. King knew she was a city woman. This was as foreign to her as cold snowy Boston would be to him. Could she be happy making her home here? Not that he spent a hundred percent of his time on the ranch now. But he'd always figured there'd come a time when he'd want to settle down and raise his kids here.

It had been a great place to grow up, even though he hadn't had the traditional two-parent household. Was he really thinking about how Anna would fit into that picture? As mother of his children? He hadn't known her that long. But, somehow, it seemed right. She seemed right. He tried to slow down, think. But all his instincts, which were what had made him successful in business, were screaming at him not to let her go.

It was dinnertime before Mike arrived. He drove up in an unmarked car.

"I had to wait for a few things before I could leave Austin." Mike was greeted by *Abuela* like a long-lost grandson. She'd known him since King had met him in college. "Now I get to stay for dinner. Not bad timing."

"You're driving back tonight?" King urged him to stay over.

"Getting that phone back is a priority. Plus, I don't like to sleep away from the wife." He winked. "You get used to that warm body in bed next to you. And now that she's expecting again, well, I need to be there for her."

Anna looked thoughtful. "Thanks for bringing me a new phone."

"Zenonsky says to try to keep this one. You're busting his budget." Mike laughed. "Like he can't afford a few phones." He shook his head. "I've got a ton of computer equipment in the trunk of my car. King can help me unload it. Zenonsky insisted I bring it out here. In case you get in the mood to work."

"That—" King was about to go off when Anna laid her hand on his arm.

"It's okay. I probably will want to work. I'm not used to being idle. And I do need to finish the damned thing." She grimaced. "Oh, I did not just curse the program I've spent years developing."

"I get it." Mike leaned forward. "The phone you're giving us is important, Anna. So is the program, obviously. Zenonsky told me what it'll be able to do. I'm impressed. I can think of several of my family members, all of them elderly, who will benefit from something like that. Not everyone has a caregiver who can go with them to make sure their medications are right. Having a program to double-check that none of them can interact, well, that's a godsend."

"Thanks, Mike, I needed a pep talk." Anna was sitting next to King on the couch in the living room.

He felt her warm thigh against his and realized she was still a little depressed.

"So, still no sign of Isaac Crane in the ruins of the cavern?" He squeezed Anna's hand. "Anna's worried he'll rise from the ruins and come after her again." He felt her stiffen.

Mike sipped iced tea. "We sent in cadaver dogs, Anna, as soon as we were sure it was safe. Of course, we wanted to be certain Crane hadn't found an escape route."

"Did they find anything?" She was holding on really tight to King's hand now.

"Yes, they signaled that there was a body near the hot springs. Crane had clearly made a dash for that side, hoping he could get out or maybe find a safe place in the restrooms. His body was in one of the shower stalls, which proved to be strong enough to withstand the cave-in." Mike's gaze was steady.

"Wait. Are you saying he survived?" Anna tensed next to King and leaned forward.

"No, he was dead. ME's preliminary is that the fumes from the hot springs got him. We identified him from his picture and fingerprints. There really is no doubt it was Crane's body we found." Mike sat back, clearly pleased to deliver that news.

"Thank God!" Anna covered her mouth. "I mean…"

"No, you're right. He's gone. And now you have proof. He was an evil man and you don't have to worry about him anymore." King kept his arm around her. "Are either of us going to have to go to court for any reason? I know there's Simms and that Bonnie and Clyde duo to prosecute."

"If they're smart, they'll try to cut deals. The evidence should make it a slam dunk. Simms will do whatever it takes to avoid death row. He murdered Littlefield and probably others. If the DA offers anything that will get him life without parole, he'll grab it. He knows his day in court would be a disaster. Same for the other two and those kidnapping charges. You may have to give some depositions, but don't worry about it now. I told Scarlett the same thing." Mike sniffed the air. "Fajitas or I'll eat my hat." He stood. "King, your *abuela* is a treasure and I need a refill." He ambled off to the kitchen.

"Yes, she is." King waited until his friend was out of sight, then pulled Anna into his lap. "I see your face. Anna, don't you dare feel guilty for being relieved. That bastard Crane got what he deserved. No, he got off easy. He should be in prison for the rest of his life."

"I don't like feeling happy over anyone's death." Anna murmured this into his chest. "But I *am* relieved."

"Of course you are." He held her close. "I'm not letting you go until I feel you relax. Come on now. Deep breaths. In and out. That's my girl." He finally felt the tension drain out of her. Then her arms slid around him and her lips touched his throat.

"Howdy, cowboy." She kissed her way up to his mouth. "How do you know just what I need?"

"I'm making a study of you, Ms. Delaney. You're not the only thinker around here." He kissed her gently. "Now that we've got all the bad guys put away and the dust has settled, could you see your way clear to thinking about the future?"

"I don't know. I thought I was supposed to quit thinking so much." She bit his earlobe.

"Think about life in Texas. With me. Sometimes in the city, sometimes out here with the horses, the cattle, and the world's best grandma. Maybe raise a pack of kids." He chuckled when her bite got firmer.

"A *pack* of kids? How many is that?" She leaned back. "City, yes. Country? As long as there's good Wi-Fi." She tapped him on his chin. "But you're not the one popping out the pack, mister."

"There you go, thinking too much. Let's take it slow." King slid his hand under her sweater. "I haven't even put you on a horse yet."

"That's right. Slow. And you haven't met my daddy yet either." Anna laughed. "You start on that pack of kids before there's a ring on this finger and Daddy will get out his gun."

"Sugar, if your daddy didn't carry a gun, this wouldn't be Texas."

Keep reading for a sneak peek at the next dose of suspense in

Gerry Bartlett's Lone Star series

TEXAS TROUBLE

Coming soon from

Lyrical Liaison

Chapter One

Scarlett Hall was sick of feeling like a victim. She'd had plenty of time to heal both her mind and her body. There was nothing to be afraid of here. It was a beautiful spring day in Austin, Texas. No knife-wielding psycho was going to jump out of a doorway and drag her into a van like...

Stop it. Just go inside and get on with it.

Right. She'd done her research, a ton of it. This was the perfect place to wipe away the past. Scarlett took a deep breath and pushed inside. The place was clean. Good. And the woman was waiting for her. Because she'd made an appointment and she was late. Fifteen minutes of second guessing and worrying had made that happen.

"Ms. Hall?" The woman held out her hand. "Casey Evans."

"Oh! Did you do that?" Scarlett stared at Casey's elegantly colorful arm. The scene looked like the garden of Eden without the snake. Beautiful.

Casey laughed. "On my own right arm? I'm good but not that good." She waved at a man busy on a customer reclining in a chair who was getting a word written across his biceps. "This is Carl's work. My brother. We own Amuse Tattoos together. Isn't he amazing?"

"Yes. Can you do that art, too? I want something floral like yours, only smaller. Where we discussed on the phone." Scarlett looked around the shop. There was a pair of special chairs in the open where the tattoo artists could work and another man sat against the wall waiting his turn. He was young, probably one of the thousands of college students in town now that the huge University of Texas was in session. "You do have a private room, don't you? For situations like mine?"

"Of course. Come on back. I'm even better than Carl." That got her a grunt from her brother. Casey laughed. "He says otherwise. Anyway, let me take a look and then we'll talk." Casey had a friendly vibe. She was tall, toned and wore a muscle shirt to show off her body art. Her short white hair was buzzed on the sides and spiked on top. Her ears held multiple piercings and she favored silver and turquoise jewelry Scarlett immediately coveted.

"I'm still not sure..." Where was this wishy-washy attitude coming from? Of course Scarlett was sure. She had to get rid of the evidence from that one hellacious day and move on. She stopped and stared at the pictures on the wall. So many options for tattoos—everything from simple butterflies to an elaborate battle of the Alamo, a Texas icon. But she had a folder under her arm. More research. She knew what she wanted. Remembering Texas wasn't high on her to-do list. Her life here had been a nightmare so far.

"We can call this a fact finding mission if you wish, Ms. Hall. Ease into this." Casey opened a door to a private room where there was a table similar to a massage table. Just like the front, everything was sparkling clean.

"Call me Scarlett." She thrust her folder at Casey. "This is what I think I want. When you see what happened to me, you can figure out if it will work. Your resume on your website said you have extensive experience hiding scars with your art. Camouflage, I guess you could call it."

"Yes." Casey opened the folder. "Very pretty. A little similar to the sleeves on my arms. We have our love of nature in common." She smiled. "You're going to have to show me where you need the work. You said on the phone…"

"That son of a bitch carved his initials on my butt." Scarlett was reminded every time she got out of the shower and passed a mirror what had happened that horrible day. The monster was in jail now, for crimes even worse than what he'd done to her. She'd had to testify in depositions but, thank God, never had to face him after he'd been captured. She had told Casey some of this on the phone.

"Why don't you lie down on the table and pull down your jeans just enough to let me take a look? You did say you were completely healed. That's a requirement before I can do my thing." Casey waited for her to toe off her sneakers.

"I am. A plastic surgeon did what he could to repair it, but there is a permanent scar. He released me not long ago. You'll see." Scarlett unsnapped and unzipped her jeans. Her thong bared enough so her underwear wasn't in the way. Casey helped her climb on the table. The curse of being short.

Nerves made Scarlett fumble as she pushed down her pants. Damn it, she didn't show her scars to anyone other than doctors and nurses. She hadn't even dated since the attack. Her best friend had seen her wound when it had first happened but now Anna and her new boyfriend were off visiting her family back home in Boston. Anna was so in love, so happy, Scarlett hadn't wanted to tell her how freaked she still was or how many nights she woke up screaming.

So she held it in and pretended to be the same strong, together Scarlett, she'd always been. Now she bared her ass and waited. If Casey said the wrong thing, she didn't know what she'd do. A meltdown wasn't off the table, but she might be.

But that's why she was here. She was sick of being alone and scared.

The silence was almost worse than if Casey had said something like "Holy shit!" Finally, Scarlett couldn't stand it anymore.

"What do you think?"

"Do you mind if I touch it? The texture could make a difference in what I do." Casey's voice was gentle but entirely professional.

"Uh, sure. I guess." Scarlett kept her cheek on her arm, her fists clenched, as Casey touched the slight ridges where Leroy Thomas Simms had carved his initials.

"I hope he's dead or in prison."

"Serving life without parole." Scarlett was surprised her voice hadn't trembled with her hatred.

"Good." Casey walked around so she could see Scarlett's face. "I can do a very pretty floral over it and you won't be able to see a bit of what that bastard did to you. It might take a couple of sessions. And I want to offer you a discount. Covering scars is something I do to satisfy myself. I have one of my own." She pulled up her tank and showed Scarlett a tree climbing up from her navel. Bright red flowers bloomed from it. There was no sign of a scar. "Abusive first husband knifed me. There won't be a second husband unless I lose my mind."

"I'm sorry. You can't tell you were ever hurt." Scarlett lifted her head and clasped Casey's hand.

"Not on the outside." Casey smiled sadly.

"That's what I want. The outside pretty. I'm still working on the inside." Scarlett wasn't about to cry. Not in front of this strong woman. God, she admired her. "When can we start?"

"Right now. Let me get set up. I like what you chose—pretty colors, tasteful. I'll be back in a few minutes. Relax. It won't be painless but I'll do what I can to make it easy for you." She nodded at a music system and headphones. "See if I have some tunes you like. Listening helps you zone out while I work." She helped Scarlett climb down.

Then she left the room.

Scarlett went through the tall stack of CDs and loaded the changer there with a variety of music she hoped would help her chill. By the time Casey came back with a tool box and gear, she was lying on her stomach again, headphones on, and trying to relax to some slow tunes with a mellow vibe.

"Ready? I'm going to draw the design first. This is permanent marker so it won't wash off in the shower unless you scrub the hell out of it." She picked up a thin tipped marker. "Once I'm satisfied with the design, I'll start with the ink. We can make another appointment to finish when we see how much I get done."

"Fine." Scarlett closed her eyes. Casey was still gentle, careful. No worries. She almost drifted off to sleep as the artist went to work outlining the pretty design of flowers. When the whirr penetrated through the music, at first it didn't bother her. Like she was at the dentist. A minor cavity, no big deal. Then the needle touched her and she was back, in that van. The man loomed over her. He gripped her breast, pushed against her and breathed in her ear all the things he wanted to do to her. He'd violate her. What a pretty little ass she had. He would like to come inside it and make her scream. He sliced into her, hurting her...

"No!" She threw off the earphones and fell off the table. Jerking up her jeans, she had to get out of there. Scarlett didn't see anyone or anything. All she knew was that she had to breathe fresh air. Run and get that hand off her butt. No one was going to hurt her, ever again.

"Scarlett!" Someone reached for her.

Blindly she slapped at them, pushing out one door, then another, until she almost fell on the sidewalk. Where could she go, where could she hide that he couldn't find her? She heard him coming. A woman stood in her way, staring at her. Hell, no. Can't trust anyone. Footsteps behind her. A door. Closed sign. He'd never look there. The knob turned and she was in. She leaned against it.

Breathe. Turn the lock. She flipped the dead bolt and waited. Someone jiggled the knob but it held. God. God. She sagged to the floor. Safe. Please let her be safe.

"Are you all right?" A man's voice came from across the dark room.

No, she was not all right. What had she done? Locked herself in with him. Scarlett searched for a weapon. Shit. She didn't even have her shoes.

"Calm down. I'm not going to hurt you." He was coming closer.

"That's what they all say." Scarlett jerked her cell out of her bra. She'd started keeping it there after the attack. "Don't come any closer. I'm calling 9-1-1."

"And say what? That you broke into my bar?" He was too close. He hunkered down in front of her. "Ethan Calhoun. How can I help you?"

"You own this bar?" Scarlett hit reality. Hard. He was right. What was she doing here?

"Yeah, I do. Something scared you. Do I need to go outside and kick some butt?"

Scarlett checked him out. Tall, good-looking, a little young, but not too young. He looked like he could enjoy some butt kicking but would prefer something more civilized in his vintage rock band tee and jeans. She waited to see if he tried anything that screamed danger. Instead, he just sat there, patient and, damn it, kind. She took a steadying breath and made a decision.

"You can buy me a drink."

"That, I can do." He stood and held out his hand. "Usually, it's no shoes, no service, but I'll make an exception if you tell me your name."

"Scarlett Hall." Scarlett took his hand and let him pull her to her feet. "I have to warn you, I'm a head case right now."

"Honey, I'm way too used to those." He pulled her to the bar, then walked around and put two glasses in front of her. "Name your poison."

"Tequila. I've had a rough day, rough month, rough year." She sighed. "Told you I was messed up."

"Then you've come to the right place." Ethan smiled and poured them both a splash of top shelf tequila. "I think I've lost my mind too. Never owned a bar before. Now here I am probably about to lose my shirt. Moved to Austin because I loved going to college here. It's a common thing with Texas Exes." He picked up his glass, waited for her to pick up hers then clinked it. "Here's to crazy."

"Crazy." Scarlett threw back the shot. She wasn't about to turn to alcohol to solve her problems but she liked Ethan's smile and that was a start. She needed her purse and her shoes. She had to go back and apologize to Casey. And she wanted that damned tattoo. She shook her head when Ethan offered her a refill.

"No, I've got to go back next door."

"To Casey's? You getting a tattoo?" Ethan walked her to the door.

"If I can find my nerve." Scarlett looked around. The only light came from the dusty windows and a laptop on the bar. No furniture yet so obviously he wasn't ready to open.

"Want me to hold your hand?" He grinned.

Scarlett could imagine that. For the first time since the abduction, she didn't want to throw up a stop sign as soon as a man showed interest. And Ethan was definitely interested.

"No, thanks. This is something I have to do myself." She handed him her phone. "Can I call you if I need moral support?"

"Hell, yes." He tapped in his number. "Use that so I'll have *your* number, Miss Scarlett. And come back. I sure need moral support. I've spent years on the customer side of the bar business, but only six months learning about the behind the scenes part. I'm flying pretty blind here."

"I will." Scarlett looked around. It had potential to be a nice place but needed something to stand out. She was no stranger to bars—in front or behind. "When are you opening?"

"Next month, I hope. Obviously the place needs work. Furniture, staff. I hired somebody to help with that, but we weren't on the same page. She wanted to make it look just like every other bar on Second Street. I think it needs to be different. New. I fired her yesterday." He turned the deadbolt and opened the door. "I'm getting desperate enough to call one of my sisters and see if they know somebody to come help."

"What do you have in mind?" Scarlett tried to picture the place cleaned out.

"I've got a name, at least. Fuel. Fuel for the soul with live entertainment. Then there's fuel for the body—I stole the best bartender in Austin from down the street. Luckily she wanted to bring her brother, who is a chef. She's into those new craft cocktails and he's known for his creative way with bar food. They've always wanted to work together but never got the chance before. This opportunity, a pretty free rein, and my offer to pay them more than the going rate sealed the deal." Ethan was excited and it was a good look for him.

"I like it." Scarlett could appreciate the idea. "Austin has a great music scene."

"Yeah. I want a stage in here so we can feature up and coming artists on weekends." He pointed to what had been a raised area at one end of the large room. "I can see this working. I have some connections I can use to get some names in here too." He paced the length of the room. "My family thinks I'm nuts, but then Calhouns take chances. Daddy was a wildcatter."

Scarlett let that pass. She had no idea what he meant. "You've never run a business like this before? You do need support, moral and otherwise. I worked my way through college as a cocktail waitress. I can't tell you how hard it is to get and hold good help. You need a strong manager to keep things organized and to supervise your people." Scarlett realized his enthusiasm was contagious.

She'd been stuck in office work since college, thanks to her sensible business degree. Her organizational abilities had brought her to Texas with the tech company she worked for. She enjoyed what she did, but it didn't excite her. Would she be insane if she took the leave of absence her employer had offered her after her traumatic abduction and decided to help Ethan? Hey, she could do the research and then organize the hell out of him. He needed someone like her. And she did have those years of cocktail experience. The bar business in Boston and Austin couldn't be that different. Her research would let her know about that. She was about to say something more when her phone rang.

"Hello."

"Scarlett, are you all right?" Casey had decided to try calling her.

"Actually, I think I am. For the first time in months." Scarlett stood in the doorway. "I'm sorry I ran out like that but I'm coming back. Let's get this party started again." She turned to Ethan who was on his own phone.

He'd lost his smile. She decided to wait until he hung up to thank him for the drink. He finally laid his phone on the bar.

"Are you okay?" Scarlett walked back toward him. Casey could wait another minute. She didn't know Ethan, but she did know worry when she saw it.

"Not really." He reached for the bottle of tequila but stopped before he poured another shot. "Oh, hell no. Not going to try to drink this one away." His laugh was bitter. "Bar owners can't afford to do that, can they?"

"Nope. I've seen it happen and it doesn't end well. You soon learn to leave the drinking to the customers." She touched his hand. "Bad news?"

"The worst." He looked her over. "I don't suppose you want a job. I could use a woman with experience." He shook his head. "That didn't come out right. A waitress with experience."

"I have a job. Office manager at Zenon Technology." Scarlett stepped back and looked around again. She really would like to get her hands on the place. It had potential and Ethan seemed open to new ideas.

"Manager. Even better. Whatever you're making, I'll double it." He picked up his phone when it buzzed again. "Damn. I've got to take this. More shit hitting the fan. Think about it? The job? Quick. I'm in a time crunch."

"I will." Scarlett walked to the door. Behind her she heard Ethan curse.

"How could you let this happen? She's dangerous. Who the hell is this person with her?"

Whoever he was talking to clearly didn't have good answers because Ethan was cursing again when Scarlett stepped outside into the sunshine then shut the door behind her. She paused and looked around like she always did these days. Paranoid? Maybe, but then she had a reason to be cautious. No rough-looking men were hanging out between her and the tattoo parlor but that woman... Wasn't she there earlier? Just standing and staring. She looked straight at Scarlett. Or was she watching the bar?

Was there a Help Wanted sign in the window? No, nothing. When the woman noticed Scarlett paying attention to her, she glared and started walking rapidly away. Weird. For a moment Scarlett had felt like she'd received visual hate mail. Damn. Now she really was being paranoid. She could swear she'd never seen the tall thin woman before in her life. Forget her. She was gone and Scarlett had a serious step to take.

She took a steadying breath. Time to start erasing her past and thinking about her future.

About the Author

A nationally best-selling author, **Gerry Bartlett** is a native Texan who lives halfway between Houston and Galveston. She freely admits to a shopping addiction which is why she has an antiques business on the historic Strand on Galveston Island. She used to be a gourmet cook but has decided it's more fun to indulge in gourmet eating instead. You can visit Gerry on Facebook, twitter or Instagram. You can also check out her latest releases on her website at http://gerrybartlett.com where you can sign up for her newsletter or read her articles with advice for aspiring writers, The Perils of Publishing.

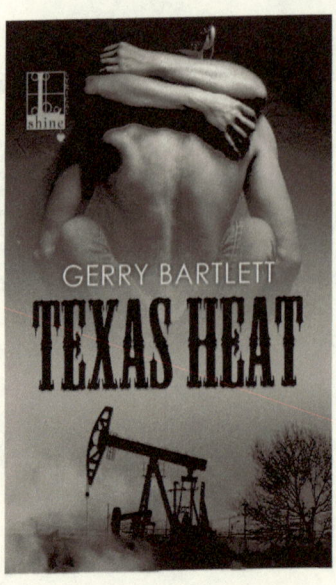

A surprise inheritance. A family of strangers. And a man she can't avoid...

Cassidy Calhoun can't believe she's the secret daughter of an oil billionaire. This small-town Texas girl with student loans by the barrel has never gotten a thing she didn't earn for herself.

The terms of her late father's will say Cassidy—and her newfound spoiled half-siblings—must work a year at the family's floundering business before they inherit a dime. Too bad the only thing Cass knows about oil is that it makes the junker she drives go.

Mason MacKenzie, the evaluator for their test, will help her get up to speed. Or will he? Mason is a boot-wearing, truck-driving Houston hottie who runs Calhoun Petroleum's biggest rival. The sparks between him and Cassidy could combust any minute. But the closer they get, the more strange near-accidents Cassidy seems to be having. And Mason has plenty of reasons to play up their attraction for his own benefit.

If she can trust him, the two of them working together might save a crumbling dynasty. But if she can't, Cass might just lose both her fortune and her heart...

Her father's dream. Her crossroads. And a man who sees just her...

Megan Calhoun doesn't stick with anything long. She's the daughter of a billionaire—why pretend to be somebody else?

Until she finds out her father's will says she has to. She has to last a year in the oil patch, in the dust and heat of West Texas, working for her daddy's company. Otherwise she's cut off without a cent—and no way to earn one.

The only upside is her new pal Rowdy Baker, ex-football star, Calhoun engineer, and grade-A stud. If she has to live in a trailer, his doesn't sound so bad.

Rowdy knows the roughnecks running the rigs won't take kindly to a smartass blonde rookie whose last name matches their paychecks. He can't control his attraction to her. And with everyone from the foremen to the stockholders spitting mad at the Calhouns, he expects trouble ahead.

But Megan has never been scared in her life. And with Rowdy to help her plot, she has the chance of a lifetime: to find her calling, to fix her company, and, if she doesn't screw it up—to capture a heart...

A fight for her rights. A job she can't quit. And a man who makes her burn...

It's not Shannon Calhoun's first rodeo. She's supposed to be running the show. But since her father's will landed her in a wretched cubicle, typing out press releases for her own family's company, she's been trapped in a job with no prospects, no control—and barely any cash.

When her old flame Billy Pagan turns up with a hundred rude questions and a thousand-dollar suit, Shannon isn't sure if the heat she feels is from humiliation, fury, or desire. But whatever else has happened, the chemistry between them has only intensified.

Long before he became Houston's best defense attorney, Billy had a thing for the spoiled rich girl who got away. But now that Shannon is hustling to save the family business, she's more irresistible than ever. Too bad about the murder investigation and the fraud that's going to bring the company crashing down around her.

Unless, of course, his Texas princess actually pulls off the save of a lifetime. With Billy's negotiating skills and Shannon's determination, the hardest part might be keeping the business away from the pleasure...